THE WORLD'S CLASSICS

THE TIME MACHINE
AND
THE ISLAND OF DOCTOR MOREAU

PATRICK PARRINDER, General Editor of H. G. Wells in World's Classics, is Professor of English at the University of Reading. He is the author and editor of several critical studies of H. G. Wells and science fiction, the most recent of which is *Shadows of the Future* (1995). He has also written books on literary criticism, on James Joyce, and on contemporary fiction and literary theory. He is a vice-president of the H. G. Wells Society.

THE WORLD'S CLASSICS

H. G. WELLS

The Time Machine
and
The Island of Doctor Moreau

Edited with an Introduction by
PATRICK PARRINDER

New York
OXFORD UNIVERSITY PRESS
1996

...iversity Press, Walton Street, Oxford OX2 6DP

Oxford New York

Athens Auckland Bangkok Bombay
...cutta Cape Town Dar es Salaam Delhi
...lorence Hong Kong Istanbul Karachi
...la Lumpur Madras Madrid Melbourne
...Mexico City Nairobi Paris Singapore
Taipei Tokyo Toronto

and associated companies in
Berlin Ibadan

...l is a trade mark of Oxford University Press

Editorial matter © Patrick Parrinder 1996

First published in the USA as a World's Classics paperback 1996

Library of Congress Cataloging in Publication Data
Wells, H. G. (Herbert George), 1866–1946.
[Time machine]
The time machine, and, The island of Doctor Moreau / H. G. Wells;
edited with an introduction by Patrick Parrinder.
1. Science fiction, English.   2. Animal experimentation—Fiction.
3. Time travel—Fiction.   I. Parrinder, Patrick.   II. Wells, H. G.
(Herbert George), 1866–1946. Island of Doctor Moreau.   III. Title.
IV. Title: Island of Doctor Moreau.
PR5774.T5 1996   823'.912—dc20   95–13712
ISBN 0–19–282825–8

1 3 5 7 9 10 8 6 4 2

Typeset by Graphicraft Typesetters Ltd., Hong Kong
Printed in Great Britain by
BPC Paperbacks Ltd.
Aylesbury, Bucks

CONTENTS

Acknowledgements   vi

Biographical Preface   vii

Introduction   xiii

Note on the Texts   xxxii

Select Bibliography   xxxix

A Chronology of H. G. Wells   xli

THE TIME MACHINE   1

THE ISLAND OF DOCTOR MOREAU   93

Appendix: The Introduction to the first edition of
The Island of Doctor Moreau   222

Explanatory Notes   224

ACKNOWLEDGEMENTS

This edition is greatly indebted to the labours of a small group of scholars concerned with Wells's published texts: notably David Lake, who has been generous with advice and encouragement, and Robert M. Philmus, who prepared the *Variorum Text* of *The Island of Doctor Moreau*. Where I have disagreed with their editorial judgements, I hope I have done so with due trepidation and care. I am also grateful to David Y. Hughes, especially for his identification of 'Pallinghurst Barrow'; to David Ketterer; to Toby Bainton, the Librarian at the University of Reading, whom I persuaded to buy a set of the Atlantic edition when it came on the market some years ago; and to my colleagues for sabbatical leave and other forms of support.

P.P.

BIOGRAPHICAL PREFACE

Herbert George Wells's early life was a struggle against social and physical disadvantages. He was born on 21 September 1866 in Bromley, Kent, where his father was an unsuccessful small shopkeeper. Joseph Wells was originally a gardener by trade, and it was while he was working at Uppark, a large country mansion on the Sussex Downs, that he met and courted Sarah Neal, a lady's maid. Joe Wells's one claim to fame lay in his brief career as a professional cricketer; in 1862, bowling for Kent against Sussex, he took four wickets in four balls, a feat that still stands in the record books.

Much of Wells's childhood was spent in the basement kitchen at Atlas House, as the shop was called. At the age of 7, he was laid up for several weeks with a broken leg and became an avid reader. A photograph taken in 1876 shows the smart, well-groomed 10-year-old sitting at a table with a book laid open in front of him. However, the family fortunes declined towards insolvency, and soon his school fees remained unpaid. When he was barely into his teens his mother left home to return to Uppark as resident housekeeper. The young 'Bertie' also left home to become a draper's apprentice, working a thirteen-hour day and sleeping in a dormitory with the other apprentices. Like his heroes Kipps and Mr Polly, he felt he was bound to the drapery trade for the rest of his life.

After two years at Hyde's Drapery Emporium in Southsea, Wells left his situation, using the threat of suicide to force his mother to release him from his apprenticeship. His talents had made an impression on Horace Byatt, the headmaster of Midhurst Grammar School near Uppark, who took him on as a student assistant, and encouraged him to take a series of examinations in elementary science. There was a new scheme for training science teachers, and, thanks to his examination successes, in 1884 Wells was awarded a government scholarship to study biology at the Normal School of Science (now Imperial College) in London. Here, in what was perhaps the most decisive encounter of his life, he became a pupil of T. H. Huxley, the friend of Charles Darwin and champion of Darwin's evolutionary theory.

When he became a science student, Wells had already undergone a strenuous process of self-education. At Uppark, on his infrequent visits, he would steal away from the servants' quarters to the library of the great country house. Arriving in London from the English provinces steeped in the writings of Plato, Swift, Voltaire, and Gibbon, Wells found in post-Darwinian science a continuation of the subversive rationalism of the Enlightenment. The settled Victorian age was cracking up: scientific and technological developments, and the doctrines of socialism to which he soon became committed, would surely determine the future.

Wells took a prominent part in student life, entertaining his contemporaries at the Debating Society and editing the college magazine (where the earliest version of *The Time Machine* was published). His experiences in the biology lab under Huxley fired his imagination for the rest of his life. But Huxley soon fell ill, and Wells chafed at the limitations of the other professors. Moving on to study physics and geology, he became discontented with the utilitarian, teacher-training ethos of the Normal School, and failed his final examination in 1887. Physically he was in bad shape; his grant of one guinea a week was barely enough to live on. After leaving college he spent a few weeks in his first teaching post before suffering an accident on the football field which left him with a lung haemorrhage and a crushed kidney. Thin, undernourished, and suspected of being tubercular, Wells was now fighting for his life.

The next dozen years were punctuated with a series of dangerous relapses. He returned to London as a science teacher, took his B.Sc., and worked as a tutor for the

University Correspondence College. His first book, the *Text-Book of Biology*, is a product of this period. In 1893, when chronic ill-health forced him to give up teaching, he found he could make a living as a journalist, reviewing fiction and drama, writing scientific and educational essays, and—most importantly—producing short stories and comic sketches for the London evening papers. The 1890s, as he later recalled, were a golden age for the writer of short fiction. The magazines which bought his short stories also serialized the longer 'scientific romances'—*The Time Machine, The Island of Doctor Moreau, The Invisible Man, The War of the Worlds*, and *The First Men in the Moon*—which soon flowed from his pen. The impact of these books was immediate. Hailed as a 'man of genius' on the strength of *The Time Machine* in 1895, by the end of the century his books were already being translated into several languages. Soon he was moving in literary circles and making intimate friendships with such fellow-writers as Arnold Bennett, Joseph Conrad, George Gissing, Henry James, and Bernard Shaw.

In 1898, after a final bout of ill-health, Wells moved to Sandgate, where he had a house built suitable for an invalid and overlooking the English Channel. Conrad, James, and Stephen Crane were among his neighbours on the Kent coast. He finished the first of his autobiographical novels, *Love and Mr Lewisham*, and as his health improved his thoughts turned to the social and political themes pursued in a long series of books beginning with *Anticipations, The Discovery of the Future*, and *A Modern Utopia*. To the imaginative depiction of the future in his scientific romances he now added a reputation for serious social prophecy. He first joined and then spectacularly quarrelled with the Fabian Society of Shaw and the Webbs, becoming a leading figure of the intellectual Left. By the end of the Edwardian decade he had written his comic masterpieces *Kipps* and *The History of Mr Polly*, as well as *Tono-Bungay* with its combination of fictive autobiography and a scathing, panoramic view of English society.

Wells was coming to rival Hardy and Kipling as one of the most famous and prestigious writers of the English-speaking world. Yet he remained restless and troubled, and his career was soon to take another decisive turn.

After a brief first marriage he had settled down with Amy Catherine Robbins ('Jane'), with whom he had two sons. His marriage remained stable although he soon embarked on the long series of sexual relationships he was to describe in *H. G. Wells in Love*, the posthumous third volume of his autobiography. His brief liaison with a young Fabian led both to his suffrage novel *Ann Veronica* and to the birth of a daughter, Anna Jane. In 1912 Rebecca West, then a young journalist, scoffed at him as the 'old maid among novelists' in a review of his novel *Marriage*; Wells and West became lovers shortly afterwards and, all too soon, Rebecca gave birth to a son. These events not only caused an atmosphere of scandal but— together with his quarrel with the Fabians—suggested an outlet for his crusading instincts. After 1910 his main fictional vehicle was the 'discussion novel' or novel of ideas, a mixture of semi-autobiographical narrative with a series of treatises or dialogues about the state of the world and the changing conditions of male–female relationships.

The New Machiavelli was his first and best novel of this type. Among its successors the most notable was the best-selling *Mr Britling Sees It Through*, published at the height of the First World War. Wells had invented the slogan 'The War That Will End War', and he became increasingly concerned with peace-making and the setting up of a supranational authority to avoid future conflicts. He now returned quite explicitly to the role of an educator, writing a series of encyclopaedic textbooks beginning with *The Outline of History*. His concern with promoting world citizenship and the idea of a World State were reflected in the *Outline* and in campaigning manuals such as *The Open Conspiracy*. Characteristically, *The Outline of History* ends with a review of humanity's prospects in the twentieth century which includes one of Wells's most memorable sayings: 'Human history becomes more and more a race between education and catastrophe.'

With *The Outline of History* Wells reached the height of his fame. He met Lenin in 1920, and in 1934 he revisited Washington and Moscow for well-publicized conversations with Roosevelt and Stalin. His *Experiment in Autobiography*, which ends with an account of these meetings, sums up his political outlook under the heading 'The Idea of a Planned World'. But, as he entered his seventies, he found in the rise of Fascism a cruel and reactionary parody of his ideal of a new and rational world order. Wells reacted to the age of the dictators by committing himself more explicitly than he had done earlier to the values of liberal democracy and human rights. He became the leading spirit behind the Sankey Declaration of the Rights of Man, which influenced the setting up of the United Nations.

As the Second World War approached, he once again suspected that civilization was on the verge of destroying itself. In some of his later imaginative fables he returned to the haunting pessimism of his early scientific romances. (Following the coinage of the American magazine editor Hugo Gernsback, the romances were now becoming known as 'science fiction'.) In *The Shape of Things to Come*, which was filmed by Wells and Alexander Korda as *Things to Come*, Wells returned to the mode of the future history, portraying humanity's recovery from a devastating mid-twentieth-century war, which he had pioneered twenty years earlier in *The World Set Free* with its forecast of nuclear weapons.

Wells spent the Second World War in London, staying on throughout the bombing in his house overlooking Regent's Park. He compiled and published a D.Sc. thesis for London University, but failed in his lifelong ambition to become a Fellow of the Royal Society. His last book, *Mind at the End of its Tether*, was black and despairing, though shortly before this he had expressed a far more resilient mood in *The Happy*

Turning. In *Mind at the End of its Tether*, he sums up the 'habitual interest' of his life as 'critical anticipation': 'Of everything he asks: "To what will this lead?"' Here the author of over 120 books and pamphlets was reaffirming the prophetic, speculative outlook that had been most strikingly expressed in his early science fiction, beginning with *The Time Machine* with its journey of thirty million years into the future.

Should Wells be summed up as an artist or a teacher, a journalist or a prophet? He was the first to admit that much of his writing had been careless, hurried and repetitive, and that all of it had designs upon the reader. He has at least three different literary personalities, as a scientific romancer in the tradition of Swift, Mary Shelley, and Poe, a comic novelist who may be seen as a successor of Dickens, and an educator and social critic like Carlyle, William Morris, and Bernard Shaw. Whatever his weaknesses he was a great intellectual liberator, the prophet of an open rather than a closed society, and one of the most dazzling literary figures of a period when the agency of mass communication was still the printed word (though in later years Wells eagerly turned on occasion to cinema and radio). Describing himself as a 'conscious common man', he wrote tirelessly for ordinary people, and is one of the great exemplars of the democratic man of letters.

INTRODUCTION

Eighteen ninety-five was Wells's *annus mirabilis*. So unknown was he at the beginning of the year that in May, when the first American edition of *The Time Machine* appeared, his name was printed as 'H. S. Wells' on the title-page and no one noticed the error. By the end of 1895 he had two fictional romances to his credit—*The Time Machine* and *The Wonderful Visit*—together with a collection of humorous essays and a volume of short stories. He had finished *The Island of Doctor Moreau*, to be published the following spring, and was about to sign a contract for the as-yet uncompleted *War of the Worlds*. The insecure former schoolteacher had metamorphosed into a story-teller of genius, confident of further successes, his imagination in full flood. If we only had Wells's productions of 1895 to go by, he would still be a remarkable writer, and would still be among the founding fathers of modern science fiction.

In *The Time Machine* and *The Island of Doctor Moreau* Wells's innovation was to set challenging scientific ideas in the context of a brief, fast-paced adventure narrative. *The Time Machine*, his most influential book, is little more than a novella. Within this small compass he evokes the vast perspectives appropriate to a vision of time, evolution, and human ecology—what the nineteenth century grandly referred to as 'man's place in nature'. To achieve this concentration of action and thought, each 'scientific romance' had to begin, as the Time Traveller begins, by controverting 'one or two ideas that are almost universally accepted' (p. 3). In Wellsian fiction travel along the time-dimension is possible, and wild animals can be shaped into human beings on the operating table. Invisibility, anti-gravity, Martians, and moon-men are all waiting to be discovered. Scientifically, these 'opposite ideas' might be in advance of their time or pure hocus-pocus.

Most of them were modern transpositions of folk-tale motifs such as the dragon, the beast-man, the magic wand, and the flying carpet. But where Wells differs from earlier writers of scientific fantasies is in his rigour in working out the logical consequences of each departure from conventional notions. The improbable invention becomes the basis of a controlled thought-experiment, estranging us from the familiar world and revealing it from a new angle. Edward Prendick, the narrator of *The Island of Doctor Moreau*, sums up the Wellsian fictional ideal when, imprisoned on Dr Moreau's island, he finds himself contemplating 'the whole balance of human life in miniature' (p. 184).

Like other great writers who have won instant popularity, Wells in his scientific romances was responding at a profound level to the opportunities of his age. One of these, in the 1890s, was an unprecedented demand for striking short fiction. The Victorian three-volume novel was dead and buried, and the New Journalism appealed to a public transformed by the spread of literacy and the growth of urban commuting and white-collar employment. The press was the dominant entertainment medium, and narrative flair and literary personality were marketable as never before. Forty years earlier the great pioneer of the modern short story, Edgar Allan Poe, had died in poverty and obscurity. Now Rudyard Kipling and Robert Louis Stevenson were the 'tellers of tales' whose successes inspired every struggling writer of fiction for the newspapers and magazines.

The most newsworthy literary personality of the day was Oscar Wilde; and Wilde's disgrace and imprisonment for homosexuality were the most shocking public events of 1895 in England. Looking back on *The Island of Doctor Moreau* after a quarter of a century, Wells would declare that the 'scandalous trial and graceless and pitiless downfall of a man of genius' had influenced its conception,[1] though the first

---

[1] *Atlantic Edition of the Works of H. G. Wells* (London, 1924), vol. ii, p. ix.

drafts of the novel were already written when Wilde's ordeal began. The two men never met, but Wells and Wilde had a mutual friend in W. E. Henley, the indefatigable editor who commissioned *The Time Machine*. Kipling and Stevenson, too, were significant influences on the young Wells. Stevenson had died in 1894, the year in which Kipling published *The Jungle Book*, which is parodied by the 'Sayers of the Law' on Moreau's island. Wells's fiction parallels and surpasses Stevenson's *Strange Case of Dr Jekyll and Mr Hyde* (1886) in its portrayal of the dark side of the psyche and the precariousness of the cultural structures and moral restraints that were held to separate the 'human' from the 'animal' elements in our nature.

In *Dr Jekyll and Mr Hyde*, the respectable doctor uses drugs to create a second, criminal self in the laboratory. Stevenson, who had no scientific training, is not concerned with chemical or biological plausibility. The cognitive disciplines that figure in his story are those of criminal psychology and detective-work. In the early Wells, whether we think of the Time Traveller theorizing about the Eloi and Morlocks or of Prendick sheltering with the Beast Folk in a hut in the forest, the sciences that count are evolutionary biology and anthropology. Moreover, he was deeply schooled in the tradition of utopian and anti-utopian thought, from Plato and Swift to Edward Bellamy and William Morris. Wells was, from the beginning, a political writer where Stevenson and Poe were not.

One thing that Stevenson and Wells had in common was an upbringing tinged with Protestant fundamentalism. The split personality of Jekyll and Hyde and the bifurcation of humanity into *The Time Machine*'s Eloi and Morlocks echo the Calvinistic division of humanity into the Elect and the Damned. Wells's father, a happy-go-lucky games-player, and his devout, repressed mother embody the traditional English cultural divide between Cavalier and Puritan types. The word 'Eloi', Hebrew for 'God', is spoken by Jesus in St Mark's

Gospel, while 'Morlock' resembles 'Moloch', the name of an Old Testament idol and one of Milton's fallen angels. Dr Moreau, the ruthless, authoritarian and white-haired creator of souls, is to some extent a parody of the Old Testament God, and no sooner is he dead than Prendick instinctively tries to subjugate the Beast Folk by threatening them with the prospect of Moreau's resurrection. Science may provide the subject-matter of these stories, but they are full of satirical side-glances at the Christian account of the Creation, the Fall, and the Last Judgement.

In *The Time Machine*, the Newspaper Editor responds to the Time Traveller's dishevelled and haggard reappearance by wondering if he has 'Nebuchadnezzar phases' (p. 15)—an allusion to the Book of Daniel which may be lost on most modern readers. Following a prophetic dream, Nebuchadnezzar lost his kingdom and was driven from among men to make his dwelling with the beasts of the field. The narrator of *The War of the Worlds* speaks of his 'sense of dethronement' and of being reduced to an 'animal among the animals' by the Martian invasion. Like an animal, he is forced to 'lurk and watch, to run and hide; the fear and empire of man had passed away'.[2] The Time Traveller and Prendick suffer a similar fate. Prendick at his lowest point differs from Moreau's Beast-Men only in his superior ability to cheat and mislead them: 'An animal may be ferocious and cunning enough, but it takes a real man to tell a lie', he reflects (p. 209).

What was it in Wells's outlook and experience that led to these haunting visions of human beings reduced to animal status? *The Time Machine* and *The Island of Doctor Moreau* reveal the intensity of his imaginative response to the Darwinian theory, which he encountered as a student of T. H. Huxley's in 1884. Huxley, 'Darwin's bulldog', had trounced Bishop Wilberforce in a famous debate on the evolutionary

---

[2] *The War of the Worlds*, World's Classics edn. (New York, 1995), 147.

theory at the British Association for the Advancement of Science in 1861. The question at issue between Huxley and the bishop was, were humans more closely allied to the apes or the angels? Huxley convinced his hearers that the biological view of the 'descent of man' was not incompatible with human dignity. Writing a generation later when the fact of evolution was almost universally accepted (though its mechanism remained controversial), Wells went much further than Darwin or Huxley in questioning the grounds of human superiority and self-satisfaction.

Although the theory of evolution is indissolubly connected with the name of Charles Darwin, the idea had begun to take root well before the publication of *The Origin of Species* in 1859. Geologists and palaeontologists had revealed the vast age of the earth and the presence of extinct animals throughout the fossil record. The discovery of the dinosaurs (the word 'dinosaur', meaning a fearsome lizard, dates from 1841) lent a new meaning to the biblical legends of the Flood and of a vanished race of giants. Dinosaur bones took a hold on the popular imagination that they have never relinquished. Wells appeals to these sentiments in the Epilogue to *The Time Machine*, where his narrator speculates that the Time Traveller might have visited the Jurassic past. Darwin's theory of natural selection set out to explain the processes of development that could have led without divine intervention from the Jurassic and earlier phases to the present state of the animal kingdom. Wells remained faithful to the theory of natural selection at a time when many biologists were still sceptical. (The significance of Mendel's work on genetics, which gave powerful support to the Darwinian hypothesis, was not recognized until the twentieth century.)

The creation of new species and genera by the dying out of some genetic strains and the gradual modification of others is an immensely slow process. Moreover, the new species that establish themselves are little more than the survivors on a corpse-strewn evolutionary battlefield. Darwin conceived of natural selection as the mechanism of evolution as a result of studying Thomas Robert Malthus's *Essay on the Principle of Population* (1798). Malthus had demonstrated (in Darwin's words) that 'many more individuals of each species are born than can possibly survive'.[3] (By 'survival' Darwin means survival to the age of reproduction.) Since each individual member of a species is to some extent unique, Darwin concluded that the constant variation within each species gave some individuals a better chance of surviving and reproducing themselves; these individuals, the harbingers of a new evolutionary trait, were said to be 'naturally selected'. Darwin's account of evolution through natural selection is resolutely optimistic—but his readers tended to see things differently. Writing a generation after *The Origin of Species*, the young Wells seemed almost to revel in the bleakness of the evolutionary narrative. 'Natural selection', he declared in his early science journalism, 'is selection by Death.' 'The long roll of palaeontology is half filled with the records of extermination.'[4]

This epic of death and extermination had been turned into a great popular spectacle by the natural-history museums of the later nineteenth century. The new museums, with their temple-like construction, dinosaur galleries, and ubiquitous skeletons, rivalled the railroad stations, boulevards, exhibition halls, and parliament buildings in their contribution to the civic architecture of the major industrialized nations. Wells as a child was taken to see the life-size plaster reproductions of the dinosaurs at the Crystal Palace in Sydenham. His student days were spent across the road from the Natural History Museum in South Kensington, which opened in 1881. Both buildings are among the models for the Palace of Green Porcelain in *The Time Machine*.

Wells's vision of humanity and the natural world reflects

[3] Charles Darwin, *The Origin of Species*, 6th edn. (London, 1910), 3.
[4] Wells, *Early Writings in Science and Science Fiction*, ed. R. M. Philmus and D. Y. Hughes (Berkeley, 1975), 211, 170.

not only the course of evolutionary history but the practical realities of biological instruction in the classroom. As every teenager knows, beyond a certain point the decision whether to study biology is influenced by the student's attitude to dissection. Wells's own *Text-Book of Biology*, published in 1893 and several times reprinted, is not a book for those who are squeamish about cutting up frogs and rabbits. At a higher level, first-year medical students proceed from animal dissections to their first human corpse. Though he never studied medicine, the anatomy and physiology of human beings is a topic of speculation throughout Wells's scientific romances. On the fly-leaf of the copy of his biology textbook that he presented to Amy Catherine Robbins, his pupil and future wife, he drew a rough pen-and-ink sketch, one of the numerous 'picshuas' with which he liked to amuse his family and friends. The subject of the 'picshua' is a rabbit dissecting a man.[5]

In the spring of 1893 Wells suffered a recurrence of the lung haemorrhages that had begun after his footballing accident several years earlier. It was this relapse that ended his career as a science teacher and forced him to earn a living from writing. He was diagnosed (erroneously) as a consumptive, and the damage to his lung and kidney must have given him a frightening sense of mortality. (The short humorous essay that he wrote about this experience is entitled 'How I Died'.[6]) These brushes with physical debility and death underlie both the prophetic urge of *The Time Machine* and what his contemporaries saw as the morbidity of *The Island of Doctor Moreau*. *The Time Machine* envisages a future of 'zoological retrogression',[7] together with the coming heat-death of the solar system. (Had Wells been writing in the early twentieth century when the implications of radioactivity

---

[5] Copy of *Text-Book of Biology* in Wells Collection, University of Illinois at Urbana-Champaign.

[6] Reprinted in *Certain Personal Matters* (London, 1897).

[7] Wells, 'Zoological Retrogression', in *Early Writings*, 158–68.

were better understood, he would have had to extend the Time Traveller's journey by a billion years or more.) In *The Island of Doctor Moreau*, the comfortable assumption that progress from the bestial to the civilized state and vice versa ought to take many millennia suffers a rude shock. In Dr Moreau's laboratory animals can acquire human characteristics within a few days, and once they are set free to roam his island the process of reversion takes only a few months. The time-scale of Prendick's narrative suggests less the stateliness of evolutionary change than the spread of disease and degeneration throughout the human body.

Wells's apprenticeship as a science-fiction author began in the student magazine that he founded in the 1880s, the *Science Schools Journal*. It was here that a primitive serial version of *The Time Machine* was published with the title 'The Chronic Argonauts'. Wells's inventor, Dr Nebogipfel, expounds the principles of time-travelling before disappearing and then reappearing on his machine; but the story breaks off before we can hear of his journey, which has taken him and his unwilling passenger to the year 17,901. Shortly after the final instalment had been published in 1888, Wells wrote to his friend Elizabeth Healey that 'The Chronic Argonauts is no joke. There is a sequel—It is the latest Delphic voice but the Tripod is not yet broken.'[8] There were further intermediate stages in the writing of *The Time Machine*, including the serial stories that Wells contributed to W. E. Henley's papers the *National Observer* and the *New Review*. Nevertheless, the prophetic 'sequel' promised in his letter to Healey is, in effect, the narrative that we now have before us.

It begins, fittingly enough, with a paradox. The Time Traveller is expounding a 'recondite matter', but he is doing so not to a learned audience sitting uncomfortably in a lecture-hall,

---

[8] Quoted in B. Loing, *H. G. Wells à l'œuvre: Les débuts d'un écrivain (1894–1900)* (Paris, 1984), 406.

but to a miscellaneous group of friends after dinner at his house. It is an atmosphere in which 'thought runs gracefully free of the trammels of precision' (p. 3). The word 'recondite', from the Latin *recondere* meaning to put away or hide, was perhaps more common in the nineteenth century than it is now; and it was most frequently used in scientific contexts. The *Oxford Dictionary* cites Herbert Spencer as speaking of the 'most recondite and abstract inquiries of Science'. The Traveller's guests sip their champagne around a brightly burning fire in chairs that, 'being his patents, embraced and caressed us rather than submitted to be sat upon' (p. 3). The setting for his demonstration of a time machine is carefully staged, and no hypnotist or spiritualist could do more to establish his ascendancy and dull the critical faculties of his hearers.

The Time Traveller's friends know him as an inventor and illusionist who is not above playing practical jokes on them. The Medical Man recalls the ghost he showed them last Christmas. At times in the opening section Wells's narrative resembles the contemporary proceedings of the Society for Psychical Research, which sent its observers to spiritualist séances with the aim of detecting instances of fraud. When the Traveller comes to demonstrate the miniature time machine, he makes sure that his guests all have a clear view of it, and then asks the Psychologist to press the lever to start it on its voyage. The breath of wind that blows out the candle, the ghostly vision of the vanishing machine, and the narrator's assertions that there was no trickery are all reminiscent of the anxious depositions of psychic investigators. But the Traveller is a scientist, and what he shows his guests is not the appearance of a ghost but the disappearance of a piece of solid machinery. Then, as if to clinch the question of experimental verification, he travels into the future himself. The narrative undergoes a profound change, from the tale of a suburban conjuring-trick to one of sublime vision and prophetic import—the riddle of the future being symbolized by the Sphinx that the Traveller confronts at the end of an exhilarating, terrifying journey. He has reached the year 802,701.

Why 802,701? The downward curve of the future revealed by *The Time Machine* broadly mirrors the upward curve of prehistory. The rate of human biological evolution—or in this case devolution—by natural selection is a function of the interval between generations and the slow reproduction rate of human beings. This means that the immense distance of time crossed by the Traveller roughly matches the development of *homo sapiens* as revealed by the archaeological record. (Today, however, the length of human prehistory has been greatly extended and the most primitive 'missing link' ancestor of humanity is dated at 4.4 million years old.) In addition, the figure 802,701 may be taken to imply a process of cyclic descent and degeneration; but there are other considerations which may have led Wells to this curious number. In 'The Chronic Argonauts' the two voyagers reached the year 17,901, that is, 1901 plus 16,000 years. If we locate the invention of the time machine early in the twentieth century (like the Martian invasion in *The War of the Worlds*), then 802,701 also implies 1901 as baseline: it is 1901 plus 800,800 years. Four-fifths of a million years might account for biological evolution, but why the additional 800 years? A likely answer is that the apparently seamless future depicted in the age of the Eloi and Morlocks conceals two different time-scales, one for biological evolution, the other more appropriate to the social, cultural, and architectural features of Wells's future society.

The inhabitants of the future live among the ruins of a monumental civilization which had evidently been knowledgeable about, and culturally continuous with, our own. The two unmistakable signs of this are the future museum—the Palace of Green Porcelain—and the antiquarian and revivalist architecture first seen in the statue of the White Sphinx. Thanks to a hidden double time-scale, Wells is able both to exhibit a future humanity reduced to bestial status and to offer a series of satirical reflections on modern civilization and its prospects. At first the Traveller thinks he has entered a communist utopia. What he has in mind is evidently the pastoral communism envisaged in William Morris's *News from Nowhere* (1890), rather than the high-tech future metropolis of Edward Bellamy's *Looking Backward* (1887), to which Morris was responding.[9] Later Wells's protagonist tries out a Marxist or quasi-Marxist interpretation of the two degenerate races, with the Eloi standing for a decadent aristocracy and the Morlocks as the vengeful, dispossessed workers. Finally he comes to see them in biological terms as predator and prey. His dislike and dread of the Morlocks is so strong that he never really accepts that they remain civilized to some extent, despite the evidence that they 'farm' the Eloi, feeding and clothing them until it is time to butcher them in underground abattoirs. The world of the Eloi and Morlocks is, in truth, more alien than the Traveller—carried away by his understandable predilections for beautiful people and splendid architecture—can fully acknowledge.

Though the Eloi welcome his arrival and teach him their language, the Traveller is soon disillusioned by their failure to live up to his intellectual expectations. At one point he complains of having 'no convenient cicerone' (after the Italian for tourist guide) 'in the pattern of the Utopian books' (p. 50). Instead, he has to make do with the dumb devotion of Weena, whom he has saved from drowning. Most readers find his mixture of condescension and callousness towards Weena hard to take, perhaps because Wells's underlying premiss is equivocal here. Mentally and physically, she is in some ways more like a pet animal than a human companion; in this respect she might be compared with the Dog Man in

---

[9] See Patrick Parrinder, 'News from Nowhere, The Time Machine, and the Break-Up of Classical Realism', *Science-Fiction Studies*, 3 (1976), 265–74.

The Island of Doctor Moreau. Yet Wells's (possibly misguided) narrator alludes to Weena in the final sentence of the story, finding in her existence a token that 'even when mind and strength had gone, gratitude and a mutual tenderness still lived on in the heart of man' (p. 91). On Weena's slender shoulders rests the whole burden of human survival.

The Traveller's first impressions of the Eloi and Morlocks mark a telling contrast. In his trance-like state before the Sphinx, he foresees that in this future society he may be reduced to a 'foul creature', an animal among the animals; but a moment later, when the first of the Eloi appears, he quickly regains confidence. They seem to meet on terms of equality: 'He came straight up to me and laughed into my eyes' (p. 23). (In retrospect, such mutual recognition as this implies is entirely superficial.) Now consider the Traveller's first encounter with a Morlock at close quarters:

A pair of eyes, luminous by reflection against the daylight without, was watching me out of the darkness.

The old instinctive dread of wild beasts came upon me. I clenched my hands and steadfastly looked into the glaring eyeballs. I was afraid to turn . . . Overcoming my fear to some extent, I advanced a step and spoke. I will admit that my voice was harsh and ill-controlled. I put out my hand and touched something soft. At once the eyes darted sideways, and something white ran past me. (p. 46)

Earlier, as he looked into the sightless eyes of the Sphinx, it was the Traveller who turned away in panic. Now his confrontation with the Morlock results in instant enmity and ill-controlled aggression. Even before his meeting with the Morlocks we have witnessed the Time Traveller's emotional instability; the rest of his time in 802,701 will be divided between rational ethnological observation and outbursts of compulsive brutality. The more that he learns of his antagonists' mental operations and way of life, the more he must hate them and regard them as irretrievably bestial. His (well-founded) fear of being trapped by the Morlocks is an effective satire on the utopian romances of the near future which are among the principal precursors of *The Time Machine*. The visitors who bring back news of the socialist utopias of Bellamy and Morris are only too anxious to be allowed to reside there permanently. The Time Traveller, by contrast, would have left the world of the Eloi and Morlocks sooner had he been able to. When he finally makes his melodramatic escape, it is only to face a further ordeal in the age of giant crabs, followed by the sunset world in which life has apparently returned into the sea. This 'remote and awful twilight' (p. 85) is set 30 million years ahead.

Wells's Traveller is a somewhat flawed individual—at times violent, self-pitying, and vain—who shows immense daring and claims to have solved the greatest mystery facing mankind, the riddle of human destiny. Brief though the story is, it offers an image of modern heroism with both classical and Romantic overtones. To the Eloi and Morlocks he must seem an almost supernatural being, behaving cruelly and erratically like one of the Greek gods. He arrives in the middle of a thunderstorm, and the Morlocks especially come to associate him with blinding light and heat. Like Prometheus stealing fire from heaven, he takes camphor and a box of matches from the Palace of Green Porcelain. In human eyes, his legendary status is assured by the fact that no sooner has he come back and told his story than he disappears on a second journey. The loyal narrator (presumably identifiable with 'Hillyer' whom the Traveller sees momentarily just before his return in section 12) tells us that even before the time machine was made, its inventor had no illusions about the future: he 'saw in the growing pile of civilisation only a foolish heaping that must inevitably fall back upon and destroy its makers in the end' (p. 91). Undaunted, he refuses to remain in ignorance of what Wells in one of his later prophetic novels called the Shape of Things to Come. It is the Time Traveller's second journey that finally marks the distance between him and ordinary complacent humanity.

He remains in thrall to the time-dimension, just as Morris's and Bellamy's narrators were in thrall to utopia.

In *The Island of Doctor Moreau* the scientist as hero is succeeded by the scientist as villain. Both the Traveller and Moreau are modern counterparts of the legendary wizard or alchemist working in secret and in his own household. Like Mary Shelley's Frankenstein, Dr Moreau and his assistant are in exile from the wider scientific community symbolized by the modern university. Moreau had to move his laboratory from England to an uninhabited Pacific island when his experiments on live animals were exposed by a journalist. Montgomery was forced to abandon his medical studies at University College, London, after some unspecified lapse (presumably involving sexual deviancy). Moreau's disgrace reflects the controversy over vivisection, which was more than a quarter-of-a-century old when Wells was writing. The Vivisection Act limiting the practice of dissection in England had come into effect in 1876. Edward Prendick, an amateur biologist, obscurely remembers the journalist's pamphlet detailing the 'Moreau horrors'. Once he is on the island, Prendick becomes convinced that Moreau's grisly experiments are conducted not on animals but on human beings, and that he is a predestined victim. At this point, the horrors that reverberate through the novel address not just nineteenth-century anxieties but the most nightmarish of twentieth-century abuses of science, such as the medical experiments on human subjects carried out in the Nazi death-camps.

Since Moreau is both a Frankenstein figure and a precursor of the scientist as war criminal, it would be easy to assume that he has little in common with more respectable, orthodox researchers. But this is not wholly the case. He published his earlier results in learned journals and engaged— with 'brutal directness' (p. 123), admittedly—in public discussion. Prendick feels that, at the time of his disgrace, he should have had more widespread support from the scientific community. Central to Moreau's creed is the belief that 'The study of Nature makes a man at last as ruthless as Nature' (p. 163). Without such ruthlessness, as the great twentieth-century physiologist J. B. S. Haldane has testified, few of the advances in surgery and biotechnology that we now take for granted would have been possible. Haldane, a champion of modern scientific materialism, could have had Moreau in mind when he wrote that 'if every physical and chemical invention is a blasphemy, every biological invention is a perversion'.[10]

The Time Traveller outlines his invention right at the beginning of *The Time Machine*, but Dr Moreau's explanation has to be forced out of him. By the time that it comes, two-thirds of the way through the narrative, Prendick has undergone a degree of emotional disturbance from which he will never fully recover. (Wells here shows an early understanding of the effects of psychological trauma, or 'shell-shock' as it would be called after the First World War.) Prendick's excitable narrative makes this a more lurid and sensational novel than *The Time Machine*, though many of its underlying themes are similar.

Apart from its concluding paragraphs *The Island of Doctor Moreau* is set entirely in the Pacific, a favourite locale for English adventure fiction from Defoe to Stevenson and R. M. Ballantyne, but one which Wells knew only from his reading. The extensive nautical vocabulary of the opening chapters is found nowhere else in his writings, and must have been mugged up for the occasion; for all that, Wells's prose is at its most vivid and least literary in this short novel. Where Moreau's retreat differs from the South Sea islands of earlier writers is in the absence of native inhabitants. Nor are there any indigenous animals. Virtually everything has been imported into the fantastic artificial safari park that Moreau

[10] J. B. S. Haldane, *Daedalus: Or Science and the Future* (London, 1923), 44.

has dreamed up. (This aspect of Wells's novel in turn has inspired its many modern admirers, down to Michael Crichton's *Jurassic Park*.) The brief introduction to the first edition—suppressed in most later editions during Wells's lifetime, but reprinted in this volume as an Appendix—identifies Moreau's island with a small volcanic outcrop, Noble's Isle, visited by a naval party four years after the events that Prendick recounts. The only living things that the sailors found were hogs, rabbits, white moths, and 'some rather peculiar rats' (p. 222). The hogs and rabbits were doubtless brought in by Moreau and Montgomery, while the rats might have come from Moreau's laboratory; the likelihood is, however, that all of his experimental fauna has become extinct.

Prendick's story begins melodramatically with a shipwreck, a narrow escape from being eaten by his fellow-castaways, and salvation by the timely arrival of the *Ipecacuanha*, which soon appears to be a ship out of hell. The drink he is given to revive him resembles iced blood. Montgomery, his rescuer, and the ship's drunken captain are at loggerheads over the cargo of animals for which Montgomery is responsible. Meanwhile, Prendick has become aware of the peculiar gaze of Montgomery's assistant, M'ling.

M'ling is dressed in blue overalls, but his appearance and behaviour are stamped inescapably with what the nineteenth century called the Mark of the Beast—though Prendick does not recognize this at first. As he was carried on board the *Ipecacuanha* he registered a 'dark face with extraordinary eyes' (p. 99). Later, looking into M'ling's eyes, he is reminded of the 'forgotten horrors of childhood' (p. 110) and feels an instinctive dread; but it is M'ling, not he, who turns away first. Prendick's encounters with M'ling foreshadow his many later moments of eye-contact with the Beast People on the island, notably his psychological duel with the Leopard Man in Chapter 9. These episodes of inter-species power-struggle expressed through the gaze do much to intensify the fear and horror in the story. To meet an animal face to face and to look it in the eyes is an unusual experience for most people, both because of physical differences and because of our preconceptions which prevent us from encountering animals on terms of equality. In Wells's novels such mutual probings reveal the uneasy threshold between humanity and non-humanity.

In *The Island of Doctor Moreau*, the master-vivisectionist subjugates the Beast Folk to his will, torturing them in the laboratory, changing their shapes, and then making them observe the Law prohibiting any return to their instinctual behaviour. Once Moreau is dead, Prendick soon abandons his half-hearted attempt to take over his authority, preferring instead to compromise with the Beast Folk and (for a time) to share their huts in the forest. If Moreau is guilty of criminal ruthlessness, many of Prendick's actions are muddled and inglorious. His terror of Moreau is manifestly exaggerated. Had he been less stand-offish towards Montgomery, he might have averted or at least postponed the latter's self-destruction. Moreover—a practical rather than a psychological blunder—it is Prendick who, without pausing to investigate, kicks over the lamp which eventually sets fire to the compound and Moreau's laboratory. Prendick's loss of human status and his reduction to an animal existence is partly the consequence of his own mistakes.

At the same time, it is these very mistakes which invite our sympathy. Prendick is a castaway whose haunted and terrorized imagination is—unlike Moreau's diabolical imagination—an all-too-human weakness. As he introduces Prendick to the island, Moreau self-consciously describes his laboratory as a 'kind of Bluebeard's chamber', adding that it is 'Nothing very dreadful really—to a sane man' (p. 121). Moreau's self-assurance about the criteria for sanity takes us to the heart of the debate over vivisection and other morally questionable scientific procedures. On Moreau's island torture and pain are inescapable because he alone wills these things and believes he can justify them. (Wells was clearly aware of the theological parallel with the human suffering permitted by an omnipotent God.) As Prendick listens to the crying of the puma, he reflects that 'It was as if all the pain in the world had found a voice' (p. 127). Today we are more familiar with representations of torture, both in the news media and in fiction, than Wells's contemporaries were. We may have become a little desensitized to those aspects of *The Island of Doctor Moreau* that made one of its early reviewers accuse its author of having tasted blood.[11] Yet the raw suffering in this novel is only momentarily present in *The Time Machine*, and it is hardly ever found in Wells's later fiction. What may be more typically Wellsian is Prendick's loss of faith in 'the sanity of the world' (p. 185)—his generalized sense of universal insanity.

When its author commented on *The Island of Doctor Moreau* in retrospect, he seemed to find it an awkward text that he had to explain away. 'Now and then, though I rarely admit it, the universe projects itself towards me in a hideous grimace', he confided in introducing the novel in 1933.[12] After his early scientific romances, Wells's books would often take the form of programmatic statements about the meaning of life; but occasionally he would become exasperated with the political failures of the twentieth century and ask once again, as he had asked in *The Time Machine* and *The Island of Doctor Moreau*, whether life had any meaning at all. (Above all, he was to do so in his distressing last book *Mind at the End of its Tether*.) What redeems Prendick's narrative from total despair is an artistic complexity which, by the end of his life, Wells could no longer command. That complexity guarantees the novel's status as (so to speak) the black classic among Wells's writings.

In 1933 he described *The Time Machine* and *The Island of*

[11] *H. G. Wells: The Critical Heritage*, ed. P. Parrinder (London, 1972), 44. The reviewer was P. Chalmers Mitchell.

[12] *H. G. Wells's Literary Criticism*, ed. P. Parrinder and R. M. Philmus (Sussex, 1980), 243.

Doctor Moreau as 'consciously grim under the influence of Swift's tradition'.[13] The grotesque parade of the Beast Folk and the marvellously vivid account of their semi-humanity and subsequent reversion are, perhaps, the nearest that any modern writer has come to the demented lucidity of Book Four of *Gulliver's Travels*. Prendick at the end, back in London but still convinced that he is an animal living among Beast Folk, is very consciously modelled on Gulliver after his return to England. But there are moments, too, of a different sort of comedy, gentler and less self-lacerating than Swift's— for Wells, ruthlessly rationalistic though he could be, is not a paranoid author. Prendick's relationship with the St Bernard Dog Man, and his instinctive humbugging of this loyal beast, show that he remains agreeably human even at the lowest point in his fortunes. Moreover, the last note of the book is one of qualified hope. Both the narrator of *The Time Machine* and Prendick manage to salvage something—which may or may not be illusory—from the wreckage of zoological retrogression and human dethronement. Hillyer resolutely, perhaps foolhardily, observes in response to the Time Traveller's pessimism that: 'If that is so, it remains for us to live as though it were not so' (p. 91). Prendick finds solace in the 'vast and eternal laws of matter', and declares that 'I hope, or I could not live' (p. 221). Through and beyond the time of his early science fiction Wells, too, went on hoping that something would come of the human experiment.

[13] Ibid.

xxxi

NOTE ON THE TEXTS

The Time Machine, subtitled 'An Invention', was first produced in book form by the London publisher William Heinemann at the end of May 1895; *The Island of Doctor Moreau* followed from the same publisher in April 1896. *The Time Machine* was dedicated to the poet William Ernest Henley, under whose editorship parts of the story had previously appeared in the *National Observer* and *New Review* in 1894–5. Wells later acknowledged that Henley's encouragement, and the tight format needed for a serial story in the monthly *New Review*, were largely responsible for the final shape of *The Time Machine*.

The compositional process leading from Wells's 1888 story 'The Chronic Argonauts' through the extant manuscript drafts and the 1894–5 serial versions has been studied by a number of scholars (see Select Bibliography). The subsequent publishing history of *The Time Machine* remained unclear until very recently. The Heinemann text stayed in print in various editions throughout Wells's lifetime and beyond; but so did two other quite different versions of Wells's text. The first of these, the American edition published by Henry Holt in 1895, pre-dates Heinemann and is closer to the *New Review* serial version. It includes a brief 'kangaroo and centipede' episode (in what would be section 11 of the present text) which Wells later deleted, and excludes the Epilogue. The second version of *The Time Machine* diverging from the Heinemann is the slightly revised text that Wells prepared for the Atlantic edition of his collected works in 1924. It is on this that—despite the continuing availability of the Heinemann and Holt texts and their derivatives—most modern editions, including the present one, are based.

In his preface to Volume I of the Atlantic edition, Wells introduced the revised text of *The Time Machine* as follows:

[the writer] has found a copy of the book in which, somewhen about 1898 or 1899, he marked out a few modifications in arrangement and improvements in expression. Almost all these suggested changes he has accepted, so that what the reader gets here is a revised definitive version a quarter of a century old. (London, 1924, xxii)

The new text is readily identifiable by its deletion of chapter-titles, reducing Heinemann's sixteen named chapters to twelve numbered sections. The Atlantic edition was carefully proof-read, but it cannot be accepted as wholly definitive since a few small errors remained to be corrected in subsequent editions of *The Time Machine*—notably the version included in Wells's *Complete Short Stories*, published in 1927 by Ernest Benn, and the 1931 Random House edition, which has illustrations by W. A. Dwiggins and a new preface specially written by Wells.

The Atlantic edition was limited to 1,670 numbered sets, and was never reprinted. The later editions improve upon the Atlantic at certain points, but introduce a host of new typographical errors. The present edition, therefore, uses the Atlantic as copy-text, corrected against Benn and Random House where appropriate. In one instance, following David Lake's published recommendation, a reading found only in Holt and in Wells's manuscript has been adopted. This and all other substantive emendations to the Atlantic are listed below. The original Heinemann chapter-titles are listed under 'Selected Variant Readings'. One of these, 'The Further Vision', now provides the commonly accepted name for the episode (section 11) to which it refers.

The published texts of *The Island of Doctor Moreau* have a broadly similar history. Once again the book has continued to exist in competing versions; but on this occasion Wells made a much larger number of stylistic changes in preparing the Atlantic edition. The most obvious change, however—the deletion of the Introduction to the story by the narrator's nephew, Charles Edward Prendick—first appears in the new edition of *Moreau* published as one of Heinemann's Sevenpenny Novels in 1913. The Introduction by his nephew claims to corroborate Edward Prendick's story by identifying Moreau's island with Noble's Isle, an uninhabited volcanic outcrop supposedly visited by sailors from the Royal Navy ship *Scorpion* in 1891, four years after the events of the main narrative. (The only other appearance of Charles Edward Prendick, or 'C.E.P.', is as the author of a footnote to Chapter XV of the first Heinemann edition, confirming that his uncle's description corresponds in every respect with Noble's Isle.) The deleted Introduction has continued to figure in versions of the earlier Heinemann text produced under other imprints, both during Wells's lifetime and since. It survives as a curiosity even though Wells rightly judged it to be an unnecessary embellishment to the main story. In the present edition it appears as an Appendix.

The evolution of *The Island of Doctor Moreau* through the manuscript versions and the first American edition (published by Stone and Kimball in 1896) has been fully studied by Robert M. Philmus and others. Unlike *The Time Machine, Moreau* has no extensive prehistory, nor—most unusually for a Wellsian scientific romance—was the story serialized. The substance of Dr Moreau's explanation in Chapter XIV did, however, appear in Wells's essay 'The Limits of Individual Plasticity', published in the *Saturday Review* in January 1895. Wells acknowledged this in a prefatory note to the first edition, adding that: 'Strange as it may seem to the unscientific reader, there can be no denying that, whatever amount of credibility attaches to the detail of this story, the manufacture of monsters—and perhaps even of *quasi*-human monsters—is within the possibilities of vivisection.'

Wells's revisions for the Atlantic edition of *Moreau* have a more complex history than appears at first sight. Very recently it has been established beyond doubt that the Stone and Kimball edition, like the Holt edition of *The Time Machine*, represents an earlier version of the text even though it was published four months after the British edition. (The main reason for this would have been the slowness of communication, in the days before air transport, between the British author or his agent and the American publishers and printers.) According to Robert M. Philmus, the Atlantic revisions emerged out of a more extensive set of proposed changes made by Wells in preparing a text for the French translator of *Moreau*, Henry-D. Davray. (Davray's translation was published by Mercure de France in 1901.) Once again, the Atlantic text thus incorporated changes envisaged but not executed by Wells a quarter of a century earlier.

Unfortunately, the Atlantic edition also reproduces a number of errors—or apparent errors—inherited from the 1913 Heinemann reprint. For the present edition, I have taken the Atlantic as copy-text on the grounds that its stylistic changes are nearly all palpable improvements, pruning the text of a good deal of youthful over-writing. I have corrected the Atlantic against earlier editions where necessary, but have taken no account of any edition later than 1924. There are, however, a few minor instances in which the text included in *The Scientific Romances of H. G. Wells* (1933; published in the USA as *Seven Famous Novels by H. G. Wells*, 1934) reverts to that of the Heinemann editions.

All the substantive emendations to the Atlantic texts of *The Time Machine* and *Moreau* to be found in the present edition are listed in the first table below. In three instances, I have preferred a reading occurring only in the Stone and Kimball edition of *Moreau* and in MS. Another emendation calling for comment is the change from longitude '105°E.' to '105°W.' in the final paragraph of the Appendix. '105°E.', printed in all editions that contain the Introduction, is manifestly at variance with the co-ordinates given in the preceding paragraphs, and makes Prendick's wanderings geographically nonsensical. '105°W.', however, places him in the vicinity of the Galapagos Islands, an amateur biologist following (accidentally or not) in Darwin's footsteps.

Note on the Texts

Key to editions cited:
(i) *The Time Machine*: A = Atlantic, B = Benn 1927, H = Heinemann 1895, Ho = Holt 1895, R = Random House 1931.
(ii) *The Island of Doctor Moreau*: A = Atlantic, H = Heinemann 1896, H2 = Heinemann 1913, S = Stone and Kimball.

EMENDATIONS IN SUBSTANTIVE READINGS

The Time Machine

page/line	Reading adopted, and texts which contain it	Atlantic reading rejected, and texts which contain it
(22.28)	hawk wings above R	hawk wins above A B H
(51.17–18)	of the human inheritance B R	of human inheritance A [of her human inheritance H]
(54.25, 78.3)	Upper-world people R	Over-world people A B H
(73.6)	it spit and flared up Ho	it split and flared up A B H R

The Island of Doctor Moreau

page/line		
(97.26–7)	breaker of water H S	beaker of water A H2
(131.4)	raising and stamping H S	rising and stamping A H2
(133.13)	in a level place among H S	in a level among A H2
(147.35)	Flesh or Fish H2	Flesh of Fish A [Flesh nor Fish H]
(149.26)	grey creature H S	great creature A H2
(149.34)	Flesh or Fish S	Flesh nor Fish A H H2
(159.8)	modifications of the passions H H2 S	modification of the passions A
(167.2)	stares out at me H S	stares at me A H2
(168.16)	he had left me H S	he left me A H2
(185.20–1)	end to their natural animosities H S	end of their natural animosities A H2
(191.6–7)	hot stillness of the tropical afternoon H S	hot stillness of the hot tropical afternoon A H2

(205.23)	in the opposite H S	in an opposite A H2
(205.25)	of the huts H S	of the hut A H2
(206.30)	specked and half-decayed fruit S	specked and half-decayed branches A H H2
(214.23)	it is as well I H2	it is well I A [it is as well that I H S]
(216.21)	upon these untravelled seas H H2 S	upon untravelled seas A
(218.25)	all that had happened S	all that happened A H H2

Appendix

| (222.30) | 105°W. | 105°E. |

SELECTED VARIANT READINGS

The Time Machine

The 16 chapters of H are titled as follows: I Introduction; II The Machine; III The Time Traveller Returns; IV Time Travelling; V In the Golden Age; VI The Sunset of Mankind; VII A Sudden Shock; VIII Explanation; IX The Morlocks; X When the Night Came; XI The Palace of Green Porcelain; XII In the Darkness; XIII The Trap of the White Sphinx; XIV The Further Vision; XV The Time Traveller Returns; XVI After the Story. Chapter XVI is followed by the Epilogue. Most chapter-divisions correspond to the section-divisions in A, with the following exceptions: I and II comprise §1; V and VI comprise §4; VII and VIII comprise §5; XV and XVI comprise §12.

page	A reading	H reading
(27)	the exquisite little sounds of their language caused an immense amount of amusement.	their exquisite little sounds of the language caused an immense amount of genuine, if uncivil, amusement.
(37)	weeping with absolute wretchedness.	weeping with absolute wretchedness, even anger at the folly of leaving the

		machine having leaked away with my strength.
(91)	the lonely saline lakes	the lonely saline seas

The Island of Doctor Moreau

(102)	'I'm ready,' I said. He led the way out of the cabin.	I had the discretion to ask no more.
(106)	an ugly temper	one of those slow pertinacious tempers that will warm day after day to a white heat and never again cool to forgiveness
(110)	a silent black figure, staring at the waves.	a silent black figure, staring at the stars.
(145)	went a drifting smoke, pungent in whiffs to nose and eyes.	a drifting smoke, pungent in whiffs to nose and eyes, went drifting.
(149)	'It is well. Many are troubled with big nails.'	'It is well.'
(188)	'It's just possible you may need it.'	'To tell you the truth, I feel anxious somehow.'
(198)	I saw something out of the tail of my eye, a red flicker, and turned sharply.	I saw something out of the tail of my eye, a red figure, and turned sharply.

SELECT BIBLIOGRAPHY

The most engaging and informative account of H. G. Wells's life and work is still his own *Experiment in Autobiography* (2 vols., London and New York, 1934). This may be supplemented by two excellent modern scholarly biographies, *The Time Traveller: The Life of H. G. Wells* by Norman and Jeanne Mackenzie (New York, 1973; revised edn., London, 1987), and *H. G. Wells: Desperately Mortal* by David C. Smith (New Haven, Conn., and London, 1986). For a general guide to Wells's fiction see *An H. G. Wells Companion* by J. R. Hammond (London and New York, 1979). *H. G. Wells* by Michael Draper (Basingstoke and London, 1987) is a general critical study.

For a collection of critical responses to Wells's writings during his lifetime see *H. G. Wells: The Critical Heritage*, ed. Patrick Parrinder (London and Boston, 1972). There are selections of more recent criticism in *H. G. Wells: A Collection of Critical Essays*, ed. Bernard Bergonzi (Englewood Cliffs, NJ, 1976), and *Critical Essays on H. G. Wells*, ed. John Huntington (Boston, 1991). The H. G. Wells Society publishes an annual journal, *The Wellsian*, as well as a *Comprehensive Bibliography* of Wells's writings (4th edn., London, 1986).

The Time Machine is easily the most widely discussed of Wells's works, with an extensive critical literature. The following studies are particularly recommended for their coverage of *The Time Machine* and *The Island of Doctor Moreau*: Bernard Bergonzi, *The Early H. G. Wells* (Manchester and Toronto, 1961); Roslynn D. Haynes, *H. G. Wells: Discoverer of the Future* (London, 1980); John Huntington, *The Logic of Fantasy: H. G. Wells and Science Fiction* (New York, 1982); and Frank McConnell, *The Science Fiction of H. G. Wells* (New York, 1981). The collection of Wells's *Early Writings in Science and Science Fiction*, ed. Robert M. Philmus and David Y. Hughes (Berkeley and Los Angeles, 1975) includes the *National Observer* and *New Review* texts of *The Time Machine*, together with much other relevant material; see also *The Definitive Time Machine*, ed. Harry M. Geduld (Bloomington and Indianapolis, 1987). For the textual evolution of *The Island of Doctor Moreau*, see the *Variorum Text*, ed. Robert M. Philmus (Athens, Ga. and

London, 1993). Wells's manuscript revision of both novels is considered in great detail by Bernard Loing, *H. G. Wells à l'œuvre* (Paris, 1984).

For Wells's relation to his precursors in science fiction and for the influence of *The Time Machine* and *The Island of Doctor Moreau* on his successors see especially Brian W. Aldiss and David Wingrove, *Trillion Year Spree: The History of Science Fiction* (London, 1986); Robert M. Philmus, *Into the Unknown: The Evolution of Science Fiction from Francis Godwin to H. G. Wells* (Berkeley and Los Angeles, 1970); Brian Stableford, *Scientific Romance in Britain 1890–1950* (London, 1985); and Darko Suvin, *Metamorphoses of Science Fiction* (New Haven, Conn., and London, 1979).

A CHRONOLOGY OF H. G. WELLS

1866   21 Sept.: Herbert George Wells born at Bromley, Kent, England, the third son of a small shopkeeper.

1874–80 Attends Morley's Commercial Academy, Bromley.

1880   Wells's mother becomes housekeeper at Uppark. He works as a draper at Messrs Rodgers and Denyer, Windsor, but is dismissed after two months.

1880–1 Temporary posts in a school at Wookey, Somerset, and in a chemist's shop at Midhurst, Sussex.

1881   Feb.–Mar.: pupil at Midhurst Grammar School. May: starts work at Hyde's Drapery Emporium, Southsea, where he signs articles of apprenticeship in June.

1883   July: leaves his post in the drapery. Sept.: becomes student assistant at Midhurst Grammar School.

1884   Sept.: enters the Normal School of Science, South Kensington, to study biology under T. H. Huxley on a government scholarship.

1885   Success in first-year exams leads to renewal of scholarship. Sept.: studies physics under Professor Guthrie. Active in Debating Society.

1886   Studies geology under Professor Judd. Dec.: becomes founding editor of *Science Schools Journal*.

1887   June: leaves South Kensington without a degree. July: assistant at Holt Academy, Wrexham, North Wales. 30 Aug.: footballing accident leads to a crushed kidney and a lung haemorrhage. Nov.: returns to Uppark.

1888   Apr.–June: 'The Chronic Argonauts' serialized in *Science Schools Journal*.

1889   Jan.: assistant at Henley House School, Kilburn.

1890   B.Sc., University of London. Tutor at University Correspondence College, London.

1891   31 Oct.: marries his cousin, Isabel Mary Wells.

1893   17 May: recurrence of illness forces him to give up teaching. *Text-Book of Biology* published. Dec.: leaves Isabel to live with his student Amy Catherine Robbins.

1895   Publishes *Select Conversations with an Uncle*, *The Time Machine*, *The Wonderful Visit*, and *The Stolen Bacillus* (short stories). Jan.–May: drama critic for *Pall Mall Gazette*. May: moves to Woking, Surrey. 27 Oct.: marries Amy Catherine ('Jane').

1895–7 Chief fiction reviewer for *Saturday Review*.

1896   *The Island of Doctor Moreau* and *The Wheels of Chance* published. Moves to Worcester Park, Surrey.

1897   *The Invisible Man* published.

1898   Jan.: *The War of the Worlds* published. Mar.–Apr.: visits Rome in the company of George Gissing. Aug.: taken ill on holiday at Seaford. Advised not to return to Worcester Park. Sept.: moves to Sandgate, Kent.

1899   *When the Sleeper Wakes* published.

1900   *Love and Mr Lewisham* published. Dec.: moves into Spade House, Sandgate, designed by C. F. A. Voysey.

1901   Son, George Philip ('Gip'), born. Publishes *The First Men in the Moon* and *Anticipations*.

1902   Jan.: lectures on *The Discovery of the Future* at the Royal Institution.

1903   *Mankind in the Making* published. Son, Frank Richard, born. Joins Fabian Society.

1904   *The Food of the Gods* published.

1905   *A Modern Utopia* and *Kipps* published.

1906   Jan.: launches campaign to change Fabian Society constitution. Mar.–May: first visit to United States. *In the Days of the Comet* and *The Future in America* published.

1908   *New Worlds for Old*, *The War in the Air*, and *First and Last Things* published. Sept.: resigns from Fabian Society.

1909   *Tono-Bungay* and *Ann Veronica* published. Moves to Church Row, Hampstead. Dec.: daughter, Anna Jane, born to Amber Reeves after her marriage to G. R. Blanco-White.

1910   *The History of Mr Polly* published.

1911   *The New Machiavelli* and *The Country of The Blind, and Other Stories* published. Moves to Easton Glebe, Dunmow, Essex.

1912   *Marriage* published.

1913   *The Passionate Friends* published.

1914   Aug.: son, Anthony, born to Rebecca West. *The World Set Free, The Wife of Sir Isaac Harman,* and *The War That Will End War* published.

1915   *Boon, Bealby,* and *The Research Magnificent* published.

1916   *Mr Britling Sees It Through* published.

1917   *God the Invisible King* and *The Soul of a Bishop* published.

1918   *Joan and Peter* published.

1919   *The Undying Fire* published.

1920   Oct.: visits Russia and meets Lenin. *The Outline of History* and *Russia in the Shadows* published.

1922   *The Secret Places of the Heart* and *A Short History of the World* published.

1923   *Men Like Gods* published. Sept.: sets up house at Grasse, Alpes-Maritimes, with Odette Keun. Ends relationship with Rebecca West.

1924   *The Dream* published.

1924–7   *The Atlantic Edition of the Works of H. G. Wells* (28 volumes with prefaces by Wells) published.

1925   *Christina Alberta's Father* published.

1926   *The World of William Clissold* published.

1927   *Complete Short Stories* published. 6 Oct.: death of 'Jane' Wells.

1928   *The Open Conspiracy* and *Mr Blettsworthy on Rampole Island* published.

1930   *The Autocracy of Mr Parham* and *The Science of Life* published. Moves to London from Easton Glebe.

1931   *The Work, Wealth and Happiness of Mankind* published.

Chronology

1932   *After Democracy* and *The Bulpington of Blup* published.

1933   Ends relationship with Odette Keun and abandons house at Grasse. *The Shape of Things to Come* published.

1934   Interviews Stalin and Roosevelt. *Experiment in Autobiography* published.

1935   Moves to his last home at Hanover Terrace, London.

1936   Feb.: film, *Things to Come*, premiered in London. *The Croquet Player* published.

1937   *Star Begotten* and *Brynhild* published.

1938   *World Brain* and *Apropos of Dolores* published. Dec.: visits Australia.

1939   *The Holy Terror* and *The New World Order* published.

1940   *The Rights of Man* and *Babes in the Darkling Wood* published.

1941   *You Can't Be Too Careful* published.

1942   *Phoenix* and *The Conquest of Time* published. D.Sc., University of London.

1943   *Crux Ansata* published.

1945   *The Happy Turning* and *Mind at the End of its Tether* published.

1946   13 Aug.: dies in his house at Hanover Terrace.

THE TIME MACHINE

THE Time Traveller (for so it will be convenient to speak of him) was expounding a recondite matter to us. His grey eyes shone and twinkled, and his usually pale face was flushed and animated. The fire burned brightly, and the soft radiance of the incandescent lights in the lilies of silver caught the bubbles that flashed and passed in our glasses. Our chairs, being his patents, embraced and caressed us rather than submitted to be sat upon, and there was that luxurious after-dinner atmosphere when thought runs gracefully free of the trammels of precision. And he put it to us in this way—marking the points with a lean forefinger—as we sat and lazily admired his earnestness over this new paradox (as we thought it) and his fecundity.

'You must follow me carefully. I shall have to controvert one or two ideas that are almost universally accepted. The geometry, for instance, they taught you at school is founded on a misconception.'

'Is not that rather a large thing to expect us to begin upon?' said Filby, an argumentative person with red hair.

'I do not mean to ask you to accept anything without reasonable ground for it. You will soon admit as much as I need from you. You know of course that a mathematical line, a line of thickness *nil*, has no real existence. They taught you that? Neither has a mathematical plane. These things are mere abstractions.'

'That is all right,' said the Psychologist.

'Nor, having only length, breadth, and thickness, can a cube have a real existence.'

'There I object,' said Filby. 'Of course a solid body may exist. All real things——'

'So most people think. But wait a moment. Can an *instantaneous* cube exist?'

'Don't follow you,' said Filby.

'Can a cube that does not last for any time at all, have a real existence?'

Filby became pensive. 'Clearly,' the Time Traveller proceeded, 'any real body must have extension in *four* directions: it must have Length, Breadth, Thickness, and—Duration. But through a natural infirmity of the flesh, which I will explain to you in a moment, we incline to overlook this fact. There are really four dimensions, three which we call the three planes of Space, and a fourth, Time. There is, however, a tendency to draw an unreal distinction between the former three dimensions and the latter, because it happens that our consciousness moves intermittently in one direction along the latter from the beginning to the end of our lives.'

'That,' said a very young man, making spasmodic efforts to relight his cigar over the lamp; 'that . . . very clear indeed.'

'Now, it is very remarkable that this is so extensively overlooked,' continued the Time Traveller, with a slight accession of cheerfulness. 'Really this is what is meant by the Fourth Dimension, though some people who talk about the Fourth Dimension do not know they mean it. It is only another way of looking at Time. *There is no difference between Time and any of the three dimensions of Space except that our consciousness moves along it*. But some foolish people have got hold of the wrong side of that idea. You have all heard what they have to say about this Fourth Dimension?'

'*I* have not,' said the Provincial Mayor.

'It is simply this. That Space, as our mathematicians have it, is spoken of as having three dimensions, which one may call Length, Breadth, and Thickness, and is always definable by reference to three planes, each at right angles to the others. But some philosophical people have been asking why *three* dimensions particularly—why not another direction at right angles to the other three?—and have even tried to construct a Four-Dimensional geometry. Professor Simon

Newcomb was expounding this to the New York Mathematical Society only a month or so ago.* You know how on a flat surface, which has only two dimensions, we can represent a figure of a three-dimensional solid, and similarly they think that by models of three dimensions they could represent one of four—if they could master the perspective of the thing. See?'

'I think so,' murmured the Provincial Mayor; and, knitting his brows, he lapsed into an introspective state, his lips moving as one who repeats mystic words. 'Yes, I think I see it now,' he said after some time, brightening in a quite transitory manner.

'Well, I do not mind telling you I have been at work upon this geometry of Four Dimensions for some time. Some of my results are curious. For instance, here is a portrait of a man at eight years old, another at fifteen, another at seventeen, another at twenty-three, and so on. All these are evidently sections, as it were, Three-Dimensional representations of his Four-Dimensioned being, which is a fixed and unalterable thing.

'Scientific people,' proceeded the Time Traveller, after the pause required for the proper assimilation of this, 'know very well that Time is only a kind of Space. Here is a popular scientific diagram, a weather record. This line I trace with my finger shows the movement of the barometer. Yesterday it was so high, yesterday night it fell, then this morning it rose again, and so gently upward to here. Surely the mercury did not trace this line in any of the dimensions of Space generally recognised? But certainly it traced such a line, and that line, therefore, we must conclude was along the Time-Dimension.'

'But,' said the Medical Man, staring hard at a coal in the fire, 'if Time is really only a fourth dimension of Space, why is it, and why has it always been, regarded as something different? And why cannot we move about in Time as we move about in the other dimensions of Space?'

The Time Traveller smiled. 'Are you so sure we can move freely in Space? Right and left we can go, backward and forward freely enough, and men always have done so. I admit we move freely in two dimensions. But how about up and down? Gravitation limits us there.'

'Not exactly,' said the Medical Man. 'There are balloons.'

'But before the balloons, save for spasmodic jumping and the inequalities of the surface, man had no freedom of vertical movement.'

'Still they could move a little up and down,' said the Medical Man.

'Easier, far easier down than up.'

'And you cannot move at all in Time, you cannot get away from the present moment.'

'My dear sir, that is just where you are wrong. That is just where the whole world has gone wrong. We are always getting away from the present moment. Our mental existences, which are immaterial and have no dimensions, are passing along the Time-Dimension with a uniform velocity from the cradle to the grave. Just as we should travel *down* if we began our existence fifty miles above the earth's surface.'

'But the great difficulty is this,' interrupted the Psychologist. 'You *can* move about in all directions of Space, but you cannot move about in Time.'

'That is the germ of my great discovery. But you are wrong to say that we cannot move about in Time. For instance, if I am recalling an incident very vividly I go back to the instant of its occurrence: I become absent-minded, as you say. I jump back for a moment. Of course we have no means of staying back for any length of time, any more than a savage or an animal has of staying six feet above the ground. But a civilised man is better off than the savage in this respect. He can go up against gravitation in a balloon, and why should he not hope that ultimately he may be able to stop or accelerate his drift along the Time-Dimension, or even turn about and travel the other way?'

6

'Oh, *this*,' began Filby, 'is all——'

'Why not?' said the Time Traveller.

'It's against reason,' said Filby.

'What reason?' said the Time Traveller.

'You can show black is white by argument,' said Filby, 'but you will never convince me.'

'Possibly not,' said the Time Traveller. 'But now you begin to see the object of my investigations into the geometry of Four Dimensions. Long ago I had a vague inkling of a machine——'

'To travel through Time!' exclaimed the Very Young Man.

'That shall travel indifferently in any direction of Space and Time, as the driver determines.'

Filby contented himself with laughter.

'But I have experimental verification,' said the Time Traveller.

'It would be remarkably convenient for the historian,' the Psychologist suggested. 'One might travel back and verify the accepted account of the Battle of Hastings, for instance!'

'Don't you think you would attract attention?' said the Medical Man. 'Our ancestors had no great tolerance for anachronisms.'

'One might get one's Greek from the very lips of Homer and Plato,' the Very Young Man thought.

'In which case they would certainly plough you for the Little-go.* The German scholars have improved Greek so much.'

'Then there is the future,' said the Very Young Man. 'Just think! One might invest all one's money, leave it to accumulate at interest, and hurry on ahead!'

'To discover a society,' said I, 'erected on a strictly communistic basis.'

'Of all the wild extravagant theories!' began the Psychologist.

'Yes, so it seemed to me, and so I never talked of it until——'

'Experimental verification!' cried I. 'You are going to verify *that*?'

'The experiment!' cried Filby, who was getting brain-weary.

'Let's see your experiment anyhow,' said the Psychologist, 'though it's all humbug, you know.'

The Time Traveller smiled round at us. Then, still smiling faintly, and with his hands deep in his trousers pockets, he walked slowly out of the room, and we heard his slippers shuffling down the long passage to his laboratory.

The Psychologist looked at us. 'I wonder what he's got?'

'Some sleight-of-hand trick or other,' said the Medical Man, and Filby tried to tell us about a conjurer he had seen at Burslem; but before he had finished his preface the Time Traveller came back, and Filby's anecdote collapsed.

The thing the Time Traveller held in his hand was a glittering metallic framework, scarcely larger than a small clock, and very delicately made. There was ivory in it, and some transparent crystalline substance. And now I must be explicit, for this that follows—unless his explanation is to be accepted—is an absolutely unaccountable thing. He took one of the small octagonal tables that were scattered about the room, and set it in front of the fire, with two legs on the hearth rug. On this table he placed the mechanism. Then he drew up a chair, and sat down. The only other object on the table was a small shaded lamp, the bright light of which fell full upon the model. There were also perhaps a dozen candles about, two in brass candlesticks upon the mantel and several in sconces, so that the room was brilliantly illuminated. I sat in a low armchair nearest the fire, and I drew this forward so as to be almost between the Time Traveller and the fireplace. Filby sat behind him, looking over his shoulder. The Medical Man and the Provincial Mayor watched him in profile from the right, the Psychologist from the left. The Very Young Man stood behind the Psychologist. We were all on the alert. It appears incredible to me that any kind of trick, however subtly conceived and however

8

adroitly done, could have been played upon us under these conditions.

The Time Traveller looked at us, and then at the mechanism. 'Well?' said the Psychologist.

'This little affair,' said the Time Traveller, resting his elbows upon the table and pressing his hands together above the apparatus, 'is only a model. It is my plan for a machine to travel through time. You will notice that it looks singularly askew, and that there is an odd twinkling appearance about this bar, as though it was in some way unreal.' He pointed to the part with his finger. 'Also, here is one little white lever, and here is another.'

The Medical Man got up out of his chair and peered into the thing. 'It's beautifully made,' he said.

'It took two years to make,' retorted the Time Traveller. Then, when we had all imitated the action of the Medical Man, he said: 'Now I want you clearly to understand that this lever, being pressed over, sends the machine gliding into the future, and this other reverses the motion. This saddle represents the seat of a time traveller. Presently I am going to press the lever, and off the machine will go. It will vanish, pass into future Time, and disappear. Have a good look at the thing. Look at the table too, and satisfy yourselves there is no trickery. I don't want to waste this model, and then be told I'm a quack.'

There was a minute's pause perhaps. The Psychologist seemed about to speak to me, but changed his mind. Then the Time Traveller put forth his finger towards the lever. 'No,' he said suddenly. 'Lend me your hand.' And turning to the Psychologist, he took that individual's hand in his own and told him to put out his forefinger. So that it was the Psychologist himself who sent forth the model Time Machine on its interminable voyage. We all saw the lever turn. I am absolutely certain there was no trickery. There was a breath of wind, and the lamp flame jumped. One of the candles on the mantel was blown out, and the little machine suddenly swung round, became indistinct, was seen as a ghost for a second perhaps, as an eddy of faintly glittering brass and ivory; and it was gone—vanished! Save for the lamp the table was bare.

Every one was silent for a minute. Then Filby said he was damned.

The Psychologist recovered from his stupor, and suddenly looked under the table. At that the Time Traveller laughed cheerfully. 'Well?' he said, with a reminiscence of the Psychologist. Then, getting up, he went to the tobacco jar on the mantel, and with his back to us began to fill his pipe.

We stared at each other. 'Look here,' said the Medical Man, 'are you in earnest about this? Do you seriously believe that that machine has travelled into time?'

'Certainly,' said the Time Traveller, stooping to light a spill at the fire. Then he turned, lighting his pipe, to look at the Psychologist's face. (The Psychologist, to show that he was not unhinged, helped himself to a cigar and tried to light it uncut.) 'What is more, I have a big machine nearly finished in there'—he indicated the laboratory—'and when that is put together I mean to have a journey on my own account.'

'You mean to say that that machine has travelled into the future?' said Filby.

'Into the future or the past—I don't, for certain, know which.'

After an interval the Psychologist had an inspiration. 'It must have gone into the past if it has gone anywhere,' he said.

'Why?' said the Time Traveller.

'Because I presume that it has not moved in space, and if it travelled into the future it would still be here all this time, since it must have travelled through this time.'

'But,' said I, 'if it travelled into the past it would have been visible when we came first into this room; and last Thursday when we were here; and the Thursday before that; and so forth!'

'Serious objections,' remarked the Provincial Mayor, with an air of impartiality, turning towards the Time Traveller.

'Not a bit,' said the Time Traveller, and, to the Psychologist: 'You think. *You* can explain that. It's presentation below the threshold, you know, diluted presentation.'

'Of course,' said the Psychologist, and reassured us. 'That's a simple point of psychology. I should have thought of it. It's plain enough, and helps the paradox delightfully. We cannot see it, nor can we appreciate this machine, any more than we can the spoke of a wheel spinning, or a bullet flying through the air. If it is travelling through time fifty times or a hundred times faster than we are, if it gets through a minute while we get through a second, the impression it creates will of course be only one-fiftieth or one-hundredth of what it would make if it were not travelling in time. That's plain enough.' He passed his hand through the space in which the machine had been. 'You see?' he said, laughing.

We sat and stared at the vacant table for a minute or so. Then the Time Traveller asked us what we thought of it all.

'It sounds plausible enough to-night,' said the Medical Man; 'but wait until to-morrow. Wait for the common sense of the morning.'

'Would you like to see the Time Machine itself?' asked the Time Traveller. And therewith, taking the lamp in his hand, he led the way down the long, draughty corridor to his laboratory. I remember vividly the flickering light, his queer, broad head in silhouette, the dance of the shadows, how we all followed him, puzzled but incredulous, and how there in the laboratory we beheld a larger edition of the little mechanism which we had seen vanish from before our eyes. Parts were of nickel, parts of ivory, parts had certainly been filed or sawn out of rock crystal. The thing was generally complete, but the twisted crystalline bars lay unfinished upon the bench beside some sheets of drawings, and I took one up for a better look at it. Quartz it seemed to be.

'Look here,' said the Medical Man, 'are you perfectly

serious? Or is this a trick—like that ghost you showed us last Christmas?'

'Upon that machine,' said the Time Traveller, holding the lamp aloft, 'I intend to explore time. Is that plain? I was never more serious in my life.'

None of us quite knew how to take it.

I caught Filby's eye over the shoulder of the Medical Man, and he winked at me solemnly.

2

I THINK that at that time none of us quite believed in the Time Machine. The fact is, the Time Traveller was one of those men who are too clever to be believed: you never felt that you saw all round him; you always suspected some subtle reserve, some ingenuity in ambush, behind his lucid frankness. Had Filby shown the model and explained the matter in the Time Traveller's words, we should have shown *him* far less scepticism. For we should have perceived his motives: a pork butcher could understand Filby. But the Time Traveller had more than a touch of whim among his elements, and we distrusted him. Things that would have made the fame of a less clever man seemed tricks in his hands. It is a mistake to do things too easily. The serious people who took him seriously never felt quite sure of his deportment: they were somehow aware that trusting their reputations for judgment with him was like furnishing a nursery with egg-shell china. So I don't think any of us said very much about time travelling in the interval between that Thursday and the next, though its odd potentialities ran, no doubt, in most of our minds: its plausibility, that is, its practical incredibleness, the curious possibilities of anachronism and of utter confusion it suggested. For my own part, I was particularly preoccupied with the trick of the model. That I remember discussing with the Medical Man, whom I met on Friday at the Linnæan.* He said he had seen a similar thing at Tübingen, and laid considerable stress on the blowing out of the candle. But how the trick was done he could not explain.

The next Thursday I went again to Richmond*—I suppose I was one of the Time Traveller's most constant guests—and, arriving late, found four or five men already assembled in his drawing-room. The Medical Man was standing before the fire with a sheet of paper in one hand and his watch in the other. I looked round for the Time Traveller, and—'It's half past seven now,' said the Medical Man. 'I suppose we'd better have dinner?'

'Where's——?' said I, naming our host.

'You've just come? It's rather odd. He's unavoidably detained. He asks me in this note to lead off with dinner at seven if he's not back. Says he'll explain when he comes.'

'It seems a pity to let the dinner spoil,' said the Editor of a well-known daily paper; and thereupon the Doctor rang the bell.

The Psychologist was the only person besides the Doctor and myself who had attended the previous dinner. The other men were Blank, the Editor aforementioned, a certain journalist, and another—a quiet, shy man with a beard—whom I didn't know, and who, as far as my observation went, never opened his mouth all the evening. There was some speculation at the dinner table about the Time Traveller's absence, and I suggested time travelling, in a half jocular spirit. The Editor wanted that explained to him, and the Psychologist volunteered a wooden account of the 'ingenious paradox and trick' we had witnessed that day week. He was in the midst of his exposition when the door from the corridor opened slowly and without noise. I was facing the door, and saw it first. 'Hallo!' I said. 'At last!' And the door opened wider, and the Time Traveller stood before us. I gave a cry of surprise. 'Good heavens! man, what's the matter?' cried the Medical Man, who saw him next. And the whole tableful turned towards the door.

He was in an amazing plight. His coat was dusty and dirty, and smeared with green down the sleeves; his hair disordered, and as it seemed to me greyer—either with dust and dirt or because its colour had actually faded. His face was ghastly pale; his chin had a brown cut on it—a cut half healed; his expression was haggard and drawn, as by intense suffering. For a moment he hesitated in the doorway, as if he had been dazzled by the light. Then he came into the room. He walked with just such a limp as I have seen in footsore tramps. We stared at him in silence, expecting him to speak.

He said not a word, but came painfully to the table, and made a motion towards the wine. The Editor filled a glass of champagne, and pushed it towards him. He drained it, and it seemed to do him good: for he looked round the table, and the ghost of his old smile flickered across his face. 'What on earth have you been up to, man?' said the Doctor. The Time Traveller did not seem to hear. 'Don't let me disturb you,' he said, with a certain faltering articulation. 'I'm all right.' He stopped, held out his glass for more, and took it off at a draught. 'That's good,' he said. His eyes grew brighter, and a faint colour came into his cheeks. His glance flickered over our faces with a certain dull approval, and then went round the warm and comfortable room. Then he spoke again, still as it were feeling his way among his words. 'I'm going to wash and dress, and then I'll come down and explain things. . . . Save me some of that mutton. I'm starving for a bit of meat.'

He looked across at the Editor, who was a rare visitor, and hoped he was all right. The Editor began a question. 'Tell you presently,' said the Time Traveller. 'I'm—funny! Be all right in a minute.'

He put down his glass, and walked towards the staircase door. Again I remarked his lameness and the soft padding sound of his footfall, and standing up in my place, I saw his feet as he went out. He had nothing on them but a pair of tattered, blood-stained socks. Then the door closed upon him.

I had half a mind to follow, till I remembered how he detested any fuss about himself. For a minute, perhaps, my mind was wool gathering. Then, 'Remarkable Behaviour of an Eminent Scientist,' I heard the Editor say, thinking (after his wont) in headlines. And this brought my attention back to the bright dinner table.

'What's the game?' said the Journalist. 'Has he been doing the Amateur Cadger?* I don't follow.' I met the eye of the Psychologist, and read my own interpretation in his face. I thought of the Time Traveller limping painfully upstairs. I don't think any one else had noticed his lameness.

The first to recover completely from this surprise was the Medical Man, who rang the bell—the Time Traveller hated to have servants waiting at dinner—for a hot plate. At that the Editor turned to his knife and fork with a grunt, and the Silent Man followed suit. The dinner was resumed. Conversation was exclamatory for a little while, with gaps of wonderment; and then the Editor got fervent in his curiosity. 'Does our friend eke out his modest income with a crossing? or has he his Nebuchadnezzar phases?'* he inquired. 'I feel assured it's this business of the Time Machine,' I said, and took up the Psychologist's account of our previous meeting. The new guests were frankly incredulous. The Editor raised objections. 'What *was* this time travelling? A man couldn't cover himself with dust by rolling in a paradox, could he?' And then, as the idea came home to him, he resorted to caricature. Hadn't they any clothes-brushes in the Future? The Journalist, too, would not believe at any price, and joined the Editor in the easy work of heaping ridicule on the whole thing. They were both the new kind of journalist—very joyous, irreverent young men. 'Our Special Correspondent in the Day after To-morrow reports,' the Journalist was saying— or rather shouting—when the Time Traveller came back. He was dressed in ordinary evening clothes, and nothing save his haggard look remained of the change that had startled me.

'I say,' said the Editor hilariously, 'these chaps here say you have been travelling into the middle of next week!! Tell us all about little Rosebery,* will you? What will you take for the lot?'

The Time Traveller came to the place reserved for him without a word. He smiled quietly, in his old way. 'Where's my mutton?' he said. 'What a treat it is to stick a fork into meat again!'

'Story!' cried the Editor.

'Story be damned!' said the Time Traveller. 'I want something to eat. I won't say a word until I get some peptone* into my arteries. Thanks. And the salt.'

'One word,' said I. 'Have you been time travelling?'

'Yes,' said the Time Traveller, with his mouth full, nodding his head.

'I'd give a shilling a line for a verbatim note,'* said the Editor. The Time Traveller pushed his glass towards the Silent Man and rang it with his finger nail; at which the Silent Man, who had been staring at his face, started convulsively, and poured him wine. The rest of the dinner was uncomfortable. For my own part, sudden questions kept on rising to my lips, and I dare say it was the same with the others. The Journalist tried to relieve the tension by telling anecdotes of Hettie Potter.* The Time Traveller devoted his attention to his dinner, and displayed the appetite of a tramp. The Medical Man smoked a cigarette, and watched the Time Traveller through his eyelashes. The Silent Man seemed even more clumsy than usual, and drank champagne with regularity and determination out of sheer nervousness. At last the Time Traveller pushed his plate away, and looked round us. 'I suppose I must apologise,' he said. 'I was simply starving. I've had a most amazing time.' He reached out his hand for a cigar, and cut the end. 'But come into the smoking-room. It's too long a story to tell over greasy plates.' And ringing the bell in passing, he led the way into the adjoining room.

'You have told Blank, and Dash, and Chose about the

machine?' he said to me, leaning back in his easy chair and naming the three new guests.

'But the thing's a mere paradox,' said the Editor.

'I can't argue to-night. I don't mind telling you the story, but I can't argue. I will,' he went on, 'tell you the story of what has happened to me, if you like, but you must refrain from interruptions. I want to tell it. Badly. Most of it will sound like lying. So be it! It's true—every word of it, all the same. I was in my laboratory at four o'clock, and since then . . . I've lived eight days . . . such days as no human being ever lived before! I'm nearly worn out, but I shan't sleep till I've told this thing over to you. Then I shall go to bed. But no interruptions! Is it agreed?'

'Agreed,' said the Editor, and the rest of us echoed 'Agreed.' And with that the Time Traveller began his story as I have set it forth. He sat back in his chair at first, and spoke like a weary man. Afterwards he got more animated. In writing it down I feel with only too much keenness the inadequacy of pen and ink—and, above all, my own inadequacy—to express its quality. You read, I will suppose, attentively enough; but you cannot see the speaker's white, sincere face in the bright circle of the little lamp, nor hear the intonation of his voice. You cannot know how his expression followed the turns of his story! Most of us hearers were in shadow, for the candles in the smoking-room had not been lighted, and only the face of the Journalist and the legs of the Silent Man from the knees downward were illuminated. At first we glanced now and again at each other. After a time we ceased to do that, and looked only at the Time Traveller's face.

3

'I TOLD some of you last Thursday of the principles of the Time Machine, and showed you the actual thing itself, incomplete in the workshop. There it is now, a little travel-worn, truly; and one of the ivory bars is cracked, and a brass rail bent; but the rest of it's sound enough. I expected to finish it on Friday; but on Friday, when the putting together was nearly done, I found that one of the nickel bars was exactly one inch too short, and this I had to get remade; so that the thing was not complete until this morning. It was at ten o'clock to-day that the first of all Time Machines began its career. I gave it a last tap, tried all the screws again, put one more drop of oil on the quartz rod, and sat myself in the saddle. I suppose a suicide who holds a pistol to his skull feels much the same wonder at what will come next as I felt then. I took the starting lever in one hand and the stopping one in the other, pressed the first, and almost immediately the second. I seemed to reel; I felt a nightmare sensation of falling; and, looking round, I saw the laboratory exactly as before. Had anything happened? For a moment I suspected that my intellect had tricked me. Then I noted the clock. A moment before, as it seemed, it had stood at a minute or so past ten; now it was nearly half past three!

'I drew a breath, set my teeth, gripped the starting lever with both hands, and went off with a thud. The laboratory got hazy and went dark. Mrs Watchett came in and walked, apparently without seeing me, towards the garden door. I suppose it took her a minute or so to traverse the place, but to me she seemed to shoot across the room like a rocket. I pressed the lever over to its extreme position. The night came like the turning out of a lamp, and in another moment came to-morrow. The laboratory grew faint and hazy, then fainter and ever fainter. To-morrow night came black, then day again, night again, day again, faster and faster still. An eddying murmur filled my ears, and a strange, dumb confusedness descended on my mind.

'I am afraid I cannot convey the peculiar sensations of time travelling. They are excessively unpleasant. There is a feeling exactly like that one has upon a switchback—of a helpless headlong motion! I felt the same horrible anticipation, too, of an imminent smash. As I put on pace, night followed day like the flapping of a black wing. The dim suggestion of the laboratory seemed presently to fall away from me, and I saw the sun hopping swiftly across the sky, leaping it every minute, and every minute marking a day. I supposed the laboratory had been destroyed and I had come into the open air. I had a dim impression of scaffolding, but I was already going too fast to be conscious of any moving things. The slowest snail that ever crawled dashed by too fast for me. The twinkling succession of darkness and light was excessively painful to the eye. Then, in the intermittent darknesses, I saw the moon spinning swiftly through her quarters from new to full, and had a faint glimpse of the circling stars. Presently, as I went on, still gaining velocity, the palpitation of night and day merged into one continuous greyness; the sky took on a wonderful deepness of blue, a splendid luminous colour like that of early twilight; the jerking sun became a streak of fire, a brilliant arch, in space; the moon a fainter fluctuating band; and I could see nothing of the stars, save now and then a brighter circle flickering in the blue.

'The landscape was misty and vague. I was still on the hillside upon which this house now stands, and the shoulder rose above me grey and dim. I saw trees growing and changing like puffs of vapour, now brown, now green; they grew, spread, shivered, and passed away. I saw huge buildings rise up faint and fair, and pass like dreams. The whole surface of the earth seemed changed—melting and flowing under my eyes. The little hands upon the dials that registered my speed raced round faster and faster. Presently I noted that the sun belt swayed up and down, from solstice to solstice, in a minute or less, and that consequently my pace was over a year a minute; and minute by minute the white snow flashed across the world, and vanished, and was followed by the bright, brief green of spring.

'The unpleasant sensations of the start were less poignant now. They merged at last into a kind of hysterical exhilaration.

I remarked indeed a clumsy swaying of the machine, for which I was unable to account. But my mind was too confused to attend to it, so with a kind of madness growing upon me, I flung myself into futurity. At first I scarce thought of stopping, scarce thought of anything but these new sensations. But presently a fresh series of impressions grew up in my mind—a certain curiosity and therewith a certain dread—until at last they took complete possession of me. What strange developments of humanity, what wonderful advances upon our rudimentary civilisation, I thought, might not appear when I came to look nearly into the dim elusive world that raced and fluctuated before my eyes! I saw great and splendid architecture rising about me, more massive than any buildings of our own time, and yet, as it seemed, built of glimmer and mist. I saw a richer green flow up the hillside, and remain there without any wintry intermission. Even through the veil of my confusion the earth seemed very fair. And so my mind came round to the business of stopping.

'The peculiar risk lay in the possibility of my finding some substance in the space which I, or the machine, occupied. So long as I travelled at a high velocity through time, this scarcely mattered; I was, so to speak, attenuated—was slipping like a vapour through the interstices of intervening substances! But to come to a stop involved the jamming of myself, molecule by molecule, into whatever lay in my way; meant bringing my atoms into such intimate contact with those of the obstacle that a profound chemical reaction—possibly a far-reaching explosion—would result, and blow myself and my apparatus out of all possible dimensions—into the Unknown. This possibility had occurred to me again and again while I was making the machine; but then I had cheerfully accepted it as an unavoidable risk—one of the risks a man has got to take! Now the risk was inevitable, I no longer saw it in the same cheerful light. The fact is that, insensibly, the absolute strangeness of everything, the sickly jarring and swaying of the machine, above all, the feeling of prolonged falling, had absolutely upset my nerve. I told myself that I could never stop, and with a gust of petulance I resolved to stop forthwith. Like an impatient fool, I lugged over the lever, and incontinently the thing went reeling over, and I was flung headlong through the air.

'There was the sound of a clap of thunder in my ears. I may have been stunned for a moment. A pitiless hail was hissing round me, and I was sitting on soft turf in front of the overset machine. Everything still seemed grey, but presently I remarked that the confusion in my ears was gone. I looked round me. I was on what seemed to be a little lawn in a garden, surrounded by rhododendron bushes, and I noticed that their mauve and purple blossoms were dropping in a shower under the beating of the hail-stones. The rebounding, dancing hail hung in a cloud over the machine, and drove along the ground like smoke. In a moment I was wet to the skin. "Fine hospitality," said I, "to a man who has travelled innumerable years to see you."

'Presently I thought what a fool I was to get wet. I stood up and looked round me. A colossal figure, carved apparently in some white stone, loomed indistinctly beyond the rhododendrons through the hazy downpour. But all else of the world was invisible.

'My sensations would be hard to describe. As the columns of hail grew thinner, I saw the white figure more distinctly. It was very large, for a silver birch-tree touched its shoulder. It was of white marble, in shape something like a winged sphinx, but the wings, instead of being carried vertically at the sides, were spread so that it seemed to hover. The pedestal, it appeared to me, was of bronze, and was thick with verdigris. It chanced that the face was towards me; the sightless eyes seemed to watch me; there was the faint shadow of a smile on the lips. It was greatly weather-worn, and that imparted an unpleasant suggestion of disease. I stood looking at it for a little space—half a minute, perhaps, or half an hour. It seemed to advance and to recede as the hail drove before it denser or thinner. At last I tore my eyes from it for a moment, and saw that the hail curtain had worn threadbare, and that the sky was lightening with the promise of the sun.

'I looked up again at the crouching white shape, and the full temerity of my voyage came suddenly upon me. What might appear when that hazy curtain was altogether withdrawn? What might not have happened to men? What if cruelty had grown into a common passion? What if in this interval the race had lost its manliness, and had developed into something inhuman, unsympathetic, and overwhelmingly powerful? I might seem some old-world savage animal, only the more dreadful and disgusting for our common likeness— a foul creature to be incontinently slain.

'Already I saw other vast shapes—huge buildings with intricate parapets and tall columns, with a wooded hillside dimly creeping in upon me through the lessening storm. I was seized with a panic fear. I turned frantically to the Time Machine, and strove hard to readjust it. As I did so the shafts of the sun smote through the thunderstorm. The grey downpour was swept aside and vanished like the trailing garments of a ghost. Above me, in the intense blue of the summer sky, some faint brown shreds of cloud whirled into nothingness. The great buildings about me stood out clear and distinct, shining with the wet of the thunderstorm, and picked out in white by the unmelted hailstones piled along their courses. I felt naked in a strange world. I felt as perhaps a bird may feel in the clear air, knowing the hawk wings above and will swoop. My fear grew to frenzy. I took a breathing space, set my teeth, and again grappled fiercely, wrist and knee, with the machine. It gave under my desperate onset and turned over. It struck my chin violently. One hand on the saddle, the other on the lever, I stood panting heavily in attitude to mount again.

'But with this recovery of a prompt retreat my courage recovered. I looked more curiously and less fearfully at this world of the remote future. In a circular opening, high up in the wall of the nearer house, I saw a group of figures clad in rich soft robes. They had seen me, and their faces were directed towards me.

'Then I heard voices approaching me. Coming through the bushes by the White Sphinx were the heads and shoulders of men running. One of these emerged in a pathway leading straight to the little lawn upon which I stood with my machine. He was a slight creature—perhaps four feet high— clad in a purple tunic, girdled at the waist with a leather belt. Sandals or buskins—I could not clearly distinguish which— were on his feet; his legs were bare to the knees, and his head was bare. Noticing that, I noticed for the first time how warm the air was.

'He struck me as being a very beautiful and graceful creature, but indescribably frail. His flushed face reminded me of the more beautiful kind of consumptive—that hectic beauty of which we used to hear so much. At the sight of him I suddenly regained confidence. I took my hands from the machine.

4

'IN another moment we were standing face to face, I and this fragile thing out of futurity. He came straight up to me and laughed into my eyes. The absence from his bearing of any sign of fear struck me at once. Then he turned to the two others who were following him and spoke to them in a strange and very sweet and liquid tongue.

'There were others coming, and presently a little group of perhaps eight or ten of these exquisite creatures were about me. One of them addressed me. It came into my head, oddly enough, that my voice was too harsh and deep for them. So I shook my head, and, pointing to my ears, shook it again. He came a step forward, hesitated, and then touched my hand.

Then I felt other soft little tentacles upon my back and shoulders. They wanted to make sure I was real. There was nothing in this at all alarming. Indeed, there was something in these pretty little people that inspired confidence—a graceful gentleness, a certain childlike ease. And besides, they looked so frail that I could fancy myself flinging the whole dozen of them about like nine-pins. But I made a sudden motion to warn them when I saw their little pink hands feeling at the Time Machine. Happily then, when it was not too late, I thought of a danger I had hitherto forgotten, and reaching over the bars of the machine I unscrewed the little levers that would set it in motion, and put these in my pocket. Then I turned again to see what I could do in the way of communication.

'And then, looking more nearly into their features, I saw some further peculiarities in their Dresden-china type of prettiness. Their hair, which was uniformly curly, came to a sharp end at the neck and cheek; there was not the faintest suggestion of it on the face, and their ears were singularly minute. The mouths were small, with bright red, rather thin lips, and the little chins ran to a point. The eyes were large and mild; and—this may seem egotism on my part—I fancied even then that there was a certain lack of the interest I might have expected in them.

'As they made no effort to communicate with me, but simply stood round me smiling and speaking in soft cooing notes to each other, I began the conversation. I pointed to the Time Machine and to myself. Then, hesitating for a moment how to express time, I pointed to the sun. At once a quaintly pretty little figure in chequered purple and white followed my gesture, and then astonished me by imitating the sound of thunder.

'For a moment I was staggered, though the import of his gesture was plain enough. The question had come into my mind abruptly: were these creatures fools? You may hardly understand how it took me. You see I had always anticipated that the people of the year Eight Hundred and Two Thousand odd would be incredibly in front of us in knowledge, art, everything. Then one of them suddenly asked me a question that showed him to be on the intellectual level of one of our five-year-old children—asked me, in fact, if I had come from the sun in a thunderstorm! It let loose the judgment I had suspended upon their clothes, their frail light limbs, and fragile features. A flow of disappointment rushed across my mind. For a moment I felt that I had built the Time Machine in vain.

'I nodded, pointed to the sun, and gave them such a vivid rendering of a thunderclap as startled them. They all withdrew a pace or so and bowed. Then came one laughing towards me, carrying a chain of beautiful flowers altogether new to me, and put it about my neck. The idea was received with melodious applause; and presently they were all running to and fro for flowers, and laughingly flinging them upon me until I was almost smothered with blossom. You who have never seen the like can scarcely imagine what delicate and wonderful flowers countless years of culture had created. Then some one suggested that their plaything should be exhibited in the nearest building, and so I was led past the sphinx of white marble, which had seemed to watch me all the while with a smile at my astonishment, towards a vast grey edifice of fretted stone. As I went with them the memory of my confident anticipations of a profoundly grave and intellectual posterity came, with irresistible merriment, to my mind.

'The building had a huge entry, and was altogether of colossal dimensions. I was naturally most occupied with the growing crowd of little people, and with the big open portals that yawned before me shadowy and mysterious. My general impression of the world I saw over their heads was of a tangled waste of beautiful bushes and flowers, a long-neglected and yet weedless garden. I saw a number of tall spikes of strange white flowers, measuring a foot perhaps across the spread of the waxen petals. They grew scattered, as if wild, among the variegated shrubs, but, as I say, I did not examine them closely at this time. The Time Machine was left deserted on the turf among the rhododendrons.

'The arch of the doorway was richly carved, but naturally I did not observe the carving very narrowly, though I fancied I saw suggestions of old Phœnician decorations* as I passed through, and it struck me that they were very badly broken and weather-worn. Several more brightly clad people met me in the doorway, and so we entered, I, dressed in dingy nineteenth-century garments, looking grotesque enough, garlanded with flowers, and surrounded by an eddying mass of bright, soft-coloured robes and shining white limbs, in a melodious whirl of laughter and laughing speech.

'The big doorway opened into a proportionately great hall hung with brown. The roof was in shadow, and the windows, partially glazed with coloured glass and partially unglazed, admitted a tempered light. The floor was made up of huge blocks of some very hard white metal, not plates nor slabs, blocks, and it was so much worn, as I judged by the going to and fro of past generations, as to be deeply channelled along the more frequented ways. Transverse to the length were innumerable tables made of slabs of polished stone, raised perhaps a foot from the floor, and upon these were heaps of fruits. Some I recognised as a kind of hypertrophied raspberry and orange, but for the most part they were strange.

'Between the tables was scattered a great number of cushions. Upon these my conductors seated themselves, signing for me to do likewise. With a pretty absence of ceremony they began to eat the fruit with their hands, flinging peel and stalks and so forth, into the round openings in the sides of the tables. I was not loth to follow their example, for I felt thirsty and hungry. As I did so I surveyed the hall at my leisure.

'And perhaps the thing that struck me most was its dilapidated look. The stained-glass windows, which displayed only

26

a geometrical pattern, were broken in many places, and the curtains that hung across the lower end were thick with dust. And it caught my eye that the corner of the marble table near me was fractured. Nevertheless, the general effect was extremely rich and picturesque. There were, perhaps, a couple of hundred people dining in the hall, and most of them, seated as near to me as they could come, were watching me with interest, their little eyes shining over the fruit they were eating. All were clad in the same soft, and yet strong, silky material.

'Fruit, by the bye, was all their diet. These people of the remote future were strict vegetarians, and while I was with them, in spite of some carnal cravings, I had to be frugivorous also. Indeed, I found afterwards that horses, cattle, sheep, dogs, had followed the Ichthyosaurus into extinction. But the fruits were very delightful; one, in particular, that seemed to be in season all the time I was there—a floury thing in a three-sided husk—was especially good, and I made it my staple. At first I was puzzled by all these strange fruits, and by the strange flowers I saw, but later I began to perceive their import.

'However, I am telling you of my fruit dinner in the distant future now. So soon as my appetite was a little checked, I determined to make a resolute attempt to learn the speech of these new men of mine. Clearly that was the next thing to do. The fruits seemed a convenient thing to begin upon, and holding one of these up I began a series of interrogative sounds and gestures. I had some considerable difficulty in conveying my meaning. At first my efforts met with a stare of surprise or inextinguishable laughter,* but presently a fair-haired little creature seemed to grasp my intention and repeated a name. They had to chatter and explain the business at great length to each other, and my first attempts to make the exquisite little sounds of their language caused an immense amount of amusement. However, I felt like a schoolmaster amidst children, and persisted, and presently I had a score of noun substantives at least at my command; and then I got to demonstrative pronouns, and even the verb "to eat." But it was slow work, and the little people soon tired and wanted to get away from my interrogations, so I determined, rather of necessity, to let them give their lessons in little doses when they felt inclined. And very little doses I found they were before long, for I never met people more indolent or more easily fatigued.

'A queer thing I soon discovered about my little hosts, and that was their lack of interest. They would come to me with eager cries of astonishment, like children, but like children they would soon stop examining me and wander away after some other toy. The dinner and my conversational beginnings ended, I noted for the first time that almost all those who had surrounded me at first were gone. It is odd, too, how speedily I came to disregard these little people. I went out through the portal into the sunlit world again so soon as my hunger was satisfied. I was continually meeting more of these men of the future, who would follow me a little distance, chatter and laugh about me, and, having smiled and gesticulated in a friendly way, leave me again to my own devices.

'The calm of evening was upon the world as I emerged from the great hall, and the scene was lit by the warm glow of the setting sun. At first things were very confusing. Everything was so entirely different from the world I had known—even the flowers. The big building I had left was situate on the slope of a broad river valley, but the Thames had shifted, perhaps, a mile from its present position. I resolved to mount to the summit of a crest, perhaps a mile and a half away, from which I could get a wider view of this our planet in the year Eight Hundred and Two Thousand Seven Hundred and One A. D. For that, I should explain, was the date the little dials of my machine recorded.

'As I walked I was watchful for every impression that could possibly help to explain the condition of ruinous splendour in which I found the world—for ruinous it was. A little way up the hill, for instance, was a great heap of granite, bound together by masses of aluminium, a vast labyrinth of precipitous walls and crumbled heaps, amidst which were thick heaps of very beautiful pagoda-like plants—nettles possibly—but wonderfully tinted with brown about the leaves, and incapable of stinging. It was evidently the derelict remains of some vast structure, to what end built I could not determine. It was here that I was destined, at a later date, to have a very strange experience—the first intimation of a still stranger discovery—but of that I will speak in its proper place.

'Looking round with a sudden thought, from a terrace on which I rested for a while, I realised that there were no small houses to be seen. Apparently the single house, and possibly even the household, had vanished. Here and there among the greenery were palace-like buildings, but the house and the cottage, which form such characteristic features of our own English landscape, had disappeared.

'"Communism," said I to myself.

'And on the heels of that came another thought. I looked at the half dozen little figures that were following me. Then, in a flash, I perceived that all had the same form of costume, the same soft hairless visage, and the same girlish rotundity of limb. It may seem strange, perhaps, that I had not noticed this before. But everything was so strange. Now, I saw the fact plainly enough. In costume, and in all the differences of texture and bearing that now mark off the sexes from each other, these people of the future were alike. And the children seemed to my eyes to be but the miniatures of their parents. I judged, then, that the children of that time were extremely precocious, physically at least, and I found afterwards abundant verification of my opinion.

'Seeing the ease and security in which these people were living, I felt that this close resemblance of the sexes was after all what one would expect; for the strength of a man and the softness of a woman, the institution of the family, and the differentiation of occupations are mere militant necessities of an age of physical force. Where population is balanced and abundant, much child-bearing becomes an evil rather than a blessing to the State; where violence comes but rarely and offspring are secure, there is less necessity—indeed there is no necessity—for an efficient family, and the specialisation of the sexes with reference to their children's needs disappears. We see some beginnings of this even in our own time, and in this future age it was complete. This, I must remind you, was my speculation at the time. Later, I was to appreciate how far it fell short of the reality.

'While I was musing upon these things, my attention was attracted by a pretty little structure, like a well under a cupola. I thought in a transitory way of the oddness of wells still existing, and then resumed the thread of my speculations. There were no large buildings towards the top of the hill, and as my walking powers were evidently miraculous, I was presently left alone for the first time. With a strange sense of freedom and adventure I pushed on up to the crest.

'There I found a seat of some yellow metal that I did not recognise, corroded in places with a kind of pinkish rust and half smothered in soft moss, the arm rests cast and filed into the resemblance of griffins' heads. I sat down on it, and I surveyed the broad view of our old world under the sunset of that long day. It was as sweet and fair a view as I have ever seen. The sun had already gone below the horizon and the west was flaming gold, touched with some horizontal bars of purple and crimson. Below was the valley of the Thames, in which the river lay like a band of burnished steel. I have already spoken of the great palaces dotted about among the variegated greenery, some in ruins and some still occupied. Here and there rose a white or silvery figure in the waste garden of the earth, here and there came the sharp vertical line of some cupola or obelisk. There were no hedges, no signs of proprietary rights, no evidences of agriculture; the whole earth had become a garden.

'So watching, I began to put my interpretation upon the things I had seen, and as it shaped itself to me that evening, my interpretation was something in this way. (Afterwards I found I had got only a half-truth—or only a glimpse of one facet of the truth.)

'It seemed to me that I had happened upon humanity upon the wane. The ruddy sunset set me thinking of the sunset of mankind. For the first time I began to realise an odd consequence of the social effort in which we are at present engaged. And yet, come to think, it is a logical consequence enough. Strength is the outcome of need; security sets a premium on feebleness. The work of ameliorating the conditions of life—the true civilising process that makes life more and more secure—had gone steadily on to a climax. One triumph of a united humanity over Nature had followed another. Things that are now mere dreams had become projects deliberately put in hand and carried forward. And the harvest was what I saw!

'After all, the sanitation and the agriculture of to-day are still in the rudimentary stage. The science of our time has attacked but a little department of the field of human disease, but, even so, it spreads its operations very steadily and persistently. Our agriculture and horticulture destroy a weed just here and there and cultivate perhaps a score or so of wholesome plants, leaving the greater number to fight out a balance as they can. We improve our favourite plants and animals—and how few they are—gradually by selective breeding; now a new and better peach, now a seedless grape, now a sweeter and larger flower, now a more convenient breed of cattle. We improve them gradually, because our ideals are vague and tentative, and our knowledge is very limited; because Nature, too, is shy and slow in our clumsy hands. Some day all this will be better organised, and still better. That is the drift of the current in spite of the eddies. The whole world will be intelligent, educated, and cooperating; things will move faster and faster towards the subjugation of Nature.

In the end, wisely and carefully we shall readjust the balance of animal and vegetable life to suit our human needs.

'This adjustment, I say, must have been done, and done well; done indeed for all time, in the space of Time across which my machine had leaped. The air was free from gnats, the earth from weeds or fungi; everywhere were fruits and sweet and delightful flowers; brilliant butterflies flew hither and thither. The ideal of preventive medicine was attained. Diseases had been stamped out. I saw no evidence of any contagious diseases during all my stay. And I shall have to tell you later that even the processes of putrefaction and decay had been profoundly affected by these changes.

'Social triumphs, too, had been effected. I saw mankind housed in splendid shelters, gloriously clothed, and as yet I had found them engaged in no toil. There were no signs of struggle, neither social nor economical struggle. The shop, the advertisement, traffic, all that commerce which constitutes the body of our world, was gone. It was natural on that golden evening that I should jump at the idea of a social paradise. The difficulty of increasing population had been met, I guessed, and population had ceased to increase.

'But with this change in condition comes inevitably adaptations to the change. What, unless biological science is a mass of errors, is the cause of human intelligence and vigour? Hardship and freedom: conditions under which the active, strong, and subtle survive and the weaker go to the wall; conditions that put a premium upon the loyal alliance of capable men, upon self-restraint, patience, and decision. And the institution of the family, and the emotions that arise therein, the fierce jealousy, the tenderness for offspring, parental self-devotion, all found their justification and support in the imminent dangers of the young. *Now*, where are these imminent dangers? There is a sentiment arising, and it will grow, against connubial jealousy, against fierce maternity, against passion of all sorts; unnecessary things now, and things that make us uncomfortable, savage survivals, discords in a refined and pleasant life.

'I thought of the physical slightness of the people, their lack of intelligence, and those big abundant ruins, and it strengthened my belief in a perfect conquest of Nature. For after the battle comes Quiet. Humanity had been strong, energetic, and intelligent, and had used all its abundant vitality to alter the conditions under which it lived. And now came the reaction of the altered conditions.

'Under the new conditions of perfect comfort and security, that restless energy, that with us is strength, would become weakness. Even in our own time certain tendencies and desires, once necessary to survival, are a constant source of failure. Physical courage and the love of battle, for instance, are no great help—may even be hindrances—to a civilised man. And in a state of physical balance and security, power, intellectual as well as physical, would be out of place. For countless years I judged there had been no danger of war or solitary violence, no danger from wild beasts, no wasting disease to require strength of constitution, no need of toil. For such a life, what we should call the weak are as well equipped as the strong, are indeed no longer weak. Better equipped indeed they are, for the strong would be fretted by an energy for which there was no outlet. No doubt the exquisite beauty of the buildings I saw was the outcome of the last surgings of the now purposeless energy of mankind before it settled down into perfect harmony with the conditions under which it lived—the flourish of that triumph which began the last great peace. This has ever been the fate of energy in security; it takes to art and to eroticism, and then come languor and decay.

'Even this artistic impetus would at last die away—had almost died in the Time I saw. To adorn themselves with flowers, to dance, to sing in the sunlight; so much was left of the artistic spirit, and no more. Even that would fade in the end into a contented inactivity. We are kept keen on the grindstone of pain and necessity, and, it seemed to me, that here was that hateful grindstone broken at last!

'As I stood there in the gathering dark I thought that in this simple explanation I had mastered the problem of the world—mastered the whole secret of these delicious people. Possibly the checks they had devised for the increase of population had succeeded too well, and their numbers had rather diminished than kept stationary. That would account for the abandoned ruins. Very simple was my explanation, and plausible enough—as most wrong theories are!

5

'As I stood there musing over this too perfect triumph of man, the full moon, yellow and gibbous,* came up out of an overflow of silver light in the north-east. The bright little figures ceased to move about below, a noiseless owl flitted by, and I shivered with the chill of the night. I determined to descend and find where I could sleep.

'I looked for the building I knew. Then my eye travelled along to the figure of the White Sphinx upon the pedestal of bronze, growing distinct as the light of the rising moon grew brighter. I could see the silver birch against it. There was the tangle of rhododendron bushes, black in the pale light, and there was the little lawn. I looked at the lawn again. A queer doubt chilled my complacency. "No," said I stoutly to myself, "that was not the lawn."

'But it *was* the lawn. For the white leprous face of the sphinx was towards it. Can you imagine what I felt as this conviction came home to me? But you cannot. The Time Machine was gone!

'At once, like a lash across the face, came the possibility of losing my own age, of being left helpless in this strange new world. The bare thought of it was an actual physical sensation.

34

I could feel it grip me at the throat and stop my breathing. In another moment I was in a passion of fear and running with great leaping strides down the slope. Once I fell head-long and cut my face; I lost no time in stanching the blood, but jumped up and ran on, with a warm trickle down my cheek and chin. All the time I ran I was saying to myself, "They have moved it a little, pushed it under the bushes out of the way." Nevertheless, I ran with all my might. All the time, with the certainty that sometimes comes with excessive dread, I knew that such assurance was folly, knew instinctively that the machine was removed out of my reach. My breath came with pain. I suppose I covered the whole distance from the hill crest to the little lawn, two miles, perhaps, in ten minutes. And I am not a young man. I cursed aloud, as I ran, at my confident folly in leaving the machine, wasting good breath thereby. I cried aloud, and none answered. Not a creature seemed to be stirring in that moonlit world.

'When I reached the lawn my worst fears were realised. Not a trace of the thing was to be seen. I felt faint and cold when I faced the empty space among the black tangle of bushes. I ran round it furiously, as if the thing might be hidden in a corner, and then stopped abruptly, with my hands clutching my hair. Above me towered the sphinx, upon the bronze pedestal, white, shining, leprous, in the light of the rising moon. It seemed to smile in mockery of my dismay.

'I might have consoled myself by imagining the little people had put the mechanism in some shelter for me, had I not felt assured of their physical and intellectual inadequacy. That is what dismayed me: the sense of some hitherto unsuspected power, through whose intervention my invention had vanished. Yet, of one thing I felt assured: unless some other age had produced its exact duplicate, the machine could not have moved in time. The attachment of the levers—I will show you the method later—prevented any one from tampering with it in that way when they were removed. It had moved, and was hid, only in space. But then, where could it be?

'I think I must have had a kind of frenzy. I remember running violently in and out among the moonlit bushes all round the sphinx, and startling some white animal that, in the dim light, I took for a small deer. I remember, too, late that night, beating the bushes with my clenched fists until my knuckles were gashed and bleeding from the broken twigs. Then, sobbing and raving in my anguish of mind, I went down to the great building of stone. The big hall was dark, silent, and deserted. I slipped on the uneven floor, and fell over one of the malachite tables, almost breaking my shin. I lit a match and went on past the dusty curtains, of which I have told you.

'There I found a second great hall covered with cushions, upon which, perhaps, a score or so of the little people were sleeping. I have no doubt they found my second appearance strange enough, coming suddenly out of the quiet darkness with inarticulate noises and the splutter and flare of a match. For they had forgotten about matches. "Where is my Time Machine?" I began, bawling like an angry child, laying hands upon them and shaking them up together. It must have been very queer to them. Some laughed, most of them looked sorely frightened. When I saw them standing round me, it came into my head that I was doing as foolish a thing as it was possible for me to do under the circumstances, in trying to revive the sensation of fear. For, reasoning from their daylight behaviour, I thought that fear must be forgotten.

'Abruptly, I dashed down the match, and, knocking one of the people over in my course, went blundering across the big dining-hall again, out under the moonlight. I heard cries of terror and their little feet running and stumbling this way and that. I do not remember all I did as the moon crept up the sky. I suppose it was the unexpected nature of my loss that maddened me. I felt hopelessly cut off from my own kind—a strange animal in an unknown world. I must have raved to and fro, screaming and crying upon God and Fate. I have a memory of horrible fatigue, as the long night of despair wore away; of looking in this impossible place and that; of groping among moonlit ruins and touching strange creatures in the black shadows; at last, of lying on the ground near the sphinx and weeping with absolute wretchedness. I had nothing left but misery. Then I slept, and when I woke again it was full day, and a couple of sparrows were hopping round me on the turf within reach of my arm.

'I sat up in the freshness of the morning, trying to remember how I had got there, and why I had such a profound sense of desertion and despair. Then things came clear in my mind. With the plain, reasonable daylight, I could look my circumstances fairly in the face. I saw the wild folly of my frenzy overnight, and I could reason with myself. Suppose the worst? I said. Suppose the machine altogether lost—perhaps destroyed? It behoves me to be calm and patient, to learn the way of the people, to get a clear idea of the method of my loss, and the means of getting materials and tools; so that in the end, perhaps, I may make another. That would be my only hope, a poor hope perhaps, but better than despair. And, after all, it was a beautiful and curious world.

'But probably the machine had only been taken away. Still, I must be calm and patient, find its hiding-place, and recover it by force or cunning. And with that I scrambled to my feet and looked about me, wondering where I could bathe. I felt weary, stiff, and travel-soiled. The freshness of the morning made me desire an equal freshness. I had exhausted my emotion. Indeed, as I went about my business, I found myself wondering at my intense excitement overnight. I made a careful examination of the ground about the little lawn. I wasted some time in futile questionings, conveyed, as well as I was able, to such of the little people as came by. They all failed to understand my gestures; some were simply stolid, some thought it was a jest and laughed at me. I had the hardest task in the world to keep my hands off their pretty laughing faces. It was a foolish impulse, but the devil begotten of fear and blind anger was ill curbed and still eager to take advantage of my perplexity. The turf gave better counsel. I found a groove ripped in it, about midway between the pedestal of the sphinx and the marks of my feet where, on arrival, I had struggled with the overturned machine. There were other signs of removal about, with queer narrow footprints like those I could imagine made by a sloth. This directed my closer attention to the pedestal. It was, as I think I have said, of bronze. It was not a mere block, but highly decorated with deep framed panels on either side. I went and rapped at these. The pedestal was hollow. Examining the panels with care I found them discontinuous with the frames. There were no handles or keyholes, but possibly the panels, if they were doors, as I supposed, opened from within. One thing was clear enough to my mind. It took no very great mental effort to infer that my Time Machine was inside that pedestal. But how it got there was a different problem.

'I saw the heads of two orange-clad people coming through the bushes and under some blossom-covered apple-trees towards me. I turned smiling to them and beckoned them to me. They came, and then, pointing to the bronze pedestal, I tried to intimate my wish to open it. But at my first gesture towards this they behaved very oddly. I don't know how to convey their expression to you. Suppose you were to use a grossly improper gesture to a delicate-minded woman—it is how she would look. They went off as if they had received the last possible insult. I tried a sweet-looking little chap in white next, with exactly the same result. Somehow, his manner made me feel ashamed of myself. But, as you know, I wanted the Time Machine, and I tried him once more. As he turned off, like the others, my temper got the better of me. In three strides I was after him, had him by the loose part of his robe round the neck, and began dragging him towards the sphinx. Then I saw the horror and repugnance of his face, and all of a sudden I let him go.

'But I was not beaten yet. I banged with my fist at the bronze panels. I thought I heard something stir inside—to be explicit, I thought I heard a sound like a chuckle—but I must have been mistaken. Then I got a big pebble from the river, and came and hammered till I had flattened a coil in the decorations, and the verdigris came off in powdery flakes. The delicate little people must have heard me hammering in gusty outbreaks a mile away on either hand, but nothing came of it. I saw a crowd of them upon the slopes, looking furtively at me. At last, hot and tired, I sat down to watch the place. But I was too restless to watch long; I am too Occidental for a long vigil. I could work at a problem for years, but to wait inactive for twenty-four hours—that is another matter.

'I got up after a time, and began walking aimlessly through the bushes towards the hill again. "Patience," said I to myself. "If you want your machine again you must leave that sphinx alone. If they mean to take your machine away, it's little good your wrecking their bronze panels, and if they don't, you will get it back as soon as you can ask for it. To sit among all those unknown things before a puzzle like that is hopeless. That way lies monomania. Face this world. Learn its ways, watch it, be careful of too hasty guesses at its meaning. In the end you will find clues to it all." Then suddenly the humour of the situation came into my mind: the thought of the years I had spent in study and toil to get into the future age, and now my passion of anxiety to get out of it. I had made myself the most complicated and the most hopeless trap that ever a man devised. Although it was at my own expense, I could not help myself. I laughed aloud.

'Going through the big palace, it seemed to me that the little people avoided me. It may have been my fancy, or it may have had something to do with my hammering at the gates of bronze. Yet I felt tolerably sure of the avoidance. I was careful, however, to show no concern and to abstain from any pursuit of them, and in the course of a day or two things got back to the old footing. I made what progress I could in the language, and in addition I pushed my explorations here and there. Either I missed some subtle point, or their language was excessively simple—almost exclusively composed of concrete substantives and verbs. There seemed to be few, if any, abstract terms, or little use of figurative language. Their sentences were usually simple and of two words, and I failed to convey or understand any but the simplest propositions. I determined to put the thought of my Time Machine and the mystery of the bronze doors under the sphinx as much as possible in a corner of memory, until my growing knowledge would lead me back to them in a natural way. Yet a certain feeling, you may understand, tethered me in a circle of a few miles round the point of my arrival.

'So far as I could see, all the world displayed the same exuberant richness as the Thames valley. From every hill I climbed I saw the same abundance of splendid buildings, endlessly varied in material and style, the same clustering thickets of evergreens, the same blossom-laden trees and tree-ferns. Here and there water shone like silver, and beyond, the land rose into blue undulating hills, and so faded into the serenity of the sky. A peculiar feature, which presently attracted my attention, was the presence of certain circular wells, several, as it seemed to me, of a very great depth. One lay by the path up the hill, which I had followed during my first walk. Like the others, it was rimmed with bronze, curiously wrought, and protected by a little cupola from the rain. Sitting by the side of these wells, and peering down into the shafted darkness, I could see no gleam of water, nor could I start any reflection with a lighted match. But in all of them I heard a certain sound: a thud—thud—thud, like the beating of some big engine; and I discovered, from the flaring of my matches, that a steady current of air set down the shafts. Further, I threw a scrap of paper into the throat of one, and, instead of fluttering slowly down, it was at once sucked swiftly out of sight.

'After a time, too, I came to connect these wells with tall towers standing here and there upon the slopes; for above them there was often just such a flicker in the air as one sees on a hot day above a sun-scorched beach. Putting things together, I reached a strong suggestion of an extensive system of subterranean ventilation, whose true import it was difficult to imagine. I was at first inclined to associate it with the sanitary apparatus of these people. It was an obvious conclusion, but it was absolutely wrong.

'And here I must admit that I learned very little of drains and bells and modes of conveyance, and the like conveniences, during my time in this real future. In some of these visions of Utopias and coming times which I have read, there is a vast amount of detail about building, and social arrangements, and so forth. But while such details are easy enough to obtain when the whole world is contained in one's imagination, they are altogether inaccessible to a real traveller amid such realities as I found here. Conceive the tale of London which a negro, fresh from Central Africa, would take back to his tribe! What would he know of railway companies, of social movements, of telephone and telegraph wires, of the Parcels Delivery Company, and postal orders and the like? Yet we, at least, should be willing enough to explain these things to him! And even of what he knew, how much could he make his untravelled friend either apprehend or believe? Then, think how narrow the gap between a negro and a white man of our own times, and how wide the interval between myself and these of the Golden Age! I was sensible of much which was unseen, and which contributed to my comfort; but save for a general impression of automatic organisation, I fear I can convey very little of the difference to your mind.

'In the matter of sepulture, for instance, I could see no signs of crematoria nor anything suggestive of tombs. But it occurred to me that, possibly, there might be cemeteries (or crematoria) somewhere beyond the range of my explorings. This, again, was a question I deliberately put to myself, and my curiosity was at first entirely defeated upon the point. The thing puzzled me, and I was led to make a further remark, which puzzled me still more: that aged and infirm among this people there were none.

'I must confess that my satisfaction with my first theories of an automatic civilisation and a decadent humanity did not long endure. Yet I could think of no other. Let me put my difficulties. The several big palaces I had explored were mere living places, great dining-halls and sleeping apartments. I could find no machinery, no appliances of any kind. Yet these people were clothed in pleasant fabrics that must at times need renewal, and their sandals, though undecorated, were fairly complex specimens of metal-work. Somehow such things must be made. And the little people displayed no vestige of a creative tendency. There were no shops, no workshops, no sign of importations among them. They spent all their time in playing gently, in bathing in the river, in making love in a half-playful fashion, in eating fruit and sleeping. I could not see how things were kept going.

'Then, again, about the Time Machine: something, I knew not what, had taken it into the hollow pedestal of the White Sphinx. *Why?* For the life of me I could not imagine. Those waterless wells, too, those flickering pillars. I felt I lacked a clue. I felt—how shall I put it? Suppose you found an inscription, with sentences here and there in excellent plain English, and, interpolated therewith, others made up of words, of letters even, absolutely unknown to you? Well, on the third day of my visit, that was how the world of Eight Hundred and Two Thousand Seven Hundred and One presented itself to me!

'That day, too, I made a friend—of a sort. It happened that, as I was watching some of the little people bathing in a shallow, one of them was seized with cramp and began drifting downstream. The main current ran rather swiftly, but not too strongly for even a moderate swimmer. It will give you an idea, therefore, of the strange deficiency in these creatures, when I tell you that none made the slightest attempt to rescue the weakly crying little thing which was drowning before their eyes. When I realised this, I hurriedly slipped off my clothes, and, wading in at a point lower down, I caught the poor mite and drew her safe to land. A little rubbing of the limbs soon brought her round, and I had the satisfaction of seeing she was all right before I left her. I had got to such a low estimate of her kind that I did not expect any gratitude from her. In that, however, I was wrong.

'This happened in the morning. In the afternoon I met my little woman, as I believe it was, as I was returning towards my centre from an exploration, and she received me with cries of delight and presented me with a big garland of flowers —evidently made for me and me alone. The thing took my imagination. Very possibly I had been feeling desolate. At any rate I did my best to display my appreciation of the gift. We were soon seated together in a little stone arbour, engaged in conversation, chiefly of smiles. The creature's friendliness affected me exactly as a child's might have done. We passed each other flowers, and she kissed my hands. I did the same to hers. Then I tried talk, and found that her name was Weena, which, though I don't know what it meant, somehow seemed appropriate enough. That was the beginning of a queer friendship which lasted a week, and ended—as I will tell you!

'She was exactly like a child. She wanted to be with me always. She tried to follow me everywhere, and on my next journey out and about it went to my heart to tire her down, and leave her at last, exhausted and calling after me rather plaintively. But the problems of the world had to be mastered. I had not, I said to myself, come into the future to carry on a miniature flirtation. Yet her distress when I left her was very great, her expostulations at the parting were sometimes frantic, and I think, altogether, I had as much trouble as comfort from her devotion. Nevertheless she was, somehow, a very great comfort. I thought it was mere childish affection that made her cling to me. Until it was too late, I did not clearly know what I had inflicted upon her when I left her. Nor until it was too late did I clearly understand what she was to me. For, by merely seeming fond of me, and showing in her weak, futile way that she cared for me, the little doll of a creature presently gave my return to the neighbourhood of the White Sphinx almost the feeling of coming home; and I would watch for her tiny figure of white and gold so soon as I came over the hill.

'It was from her, too, that I learned that fear had not yet left the world. She was fearless enough in the daylight, and she had the oddest confidence in me; for once, in a foolish moment, I made threatening grimaces at her, and she simply laughed at them. But she dreaded the dark, dreaded shadows, dreaded black things. Darkness to her was the one thing dreadful. It was a singularly passionate emotion, and it set me thinking and observing. I discovered then, among other things, that these little people gathered into the great houses after dark, and slept in droves. To enter upon them without a light was to put them into a tumult of apprehension. I never found one out of doors, or one sleeping alone within doors, after dark. Yet I was still such a blockhead that I missed the lesson of that fear, and in spite of Weena's distress, I insisted upon sleeping away from these slumbering multitudes.

'It troubled her greatly, but in the end her odd affection for me triumphed, and for five of the nights of our acquaintance, including the last night of all, she slept with her head pillowed on my arm. But my story slips away from me as I speak of her. It must have been the night before her rescue that I was awakened about dawn. I had been restless, dreaming most disagreeably that I was drowned, and that seaanemones were feeling over my face with their soft palps. I woke with a start, and with an odd fancy that some greyish animal had just rushed out of the chamber. I tried to get to sleep again, but I felt restless and uncomfortable. It was that dim grey hour when things are just creeping out of darkness, when everything is colourless and clear cut, and yet unreal.

I got up, and went down into the great hall, and so out upon the flagstones in front of the palace. I thought I would make a virtue of necessity, and see the sunrise.

'The moon was setting, and the dying moonlight and the first pallor of dawn were mingled in a ghastly half-light. The bushes were inky black, the ground a sombre grey, the sky colourless and cheerless. And up the hill I thought I could see ghosts. Three several times, as I scanned the slope, I saw white figures. Twice I fancied I saw a solitary white, ape-like creature running rather quickly up the hill, and once near the ruins I saw a leash of them carrying some dark body. They moved hastily. I did not see what became of them. It seemed that they vanished among the bushes. The dawn was still indistinct, you must understand. I was feeling that chill, uncertain, early-morning feeling you may have known. I doubted my eyes.

'As the eastern sky grew brighter, and the light of the day came on and its vivid colouring returned upon the world once more, I scanned the view keenly. But I saw no vestige of my white figures. They were mere creatures of the half-light. "They must have been ghosts," I said; "I wonder whence they dated." For a queer notion of Grant Allen's* came into my head, and amused me. If each generation die and leave ghosts, he argued, the world at last will get overcrowded with them. On that theory they would have grown innumerable some Eight Hundred Thousand Years hence, and it was no great wonder to see four at once. But the jest was unsatisfying, and I was thinking of these figures all the morning, until Weena's rescue drove them out of my head. I associated them in some indefinite way with the white animal I had startled in my first passionate search for the Time Machine. But Weena was a pleasant substitute. Yet all the same, they were soon destined to take far deadlier possession of my mind.

'I think I have said how much hotter than our own was the weather of this Golden Age. I cannot account for it. It may be that the sun was hotter, or the earth nearer the sun. It is usual to assume that the sun will go on cooling steadily in the future. But people, unfamiliar with such speculations as those of the younger Darwin, forget that the planets must ultimately fall back one by one into the parent body.* As these catastrophes occur, the sun will blaze with renewed energy; and it may be that some inner planet had suffered this fate. Whatever the reason, the fact remains that the sun was very much hotter than we know it.

'Well, one very hot morning—my fourth, I think—as I was seeking shelter from the heat and glare in a colossal ruin near the great house where I slept and fed, there happened this strange thing: Clambering among these heaps of masonry, I found a narrow gallery, whose end and side windows were blocked by fallen masses of stone. By contrast with the brilliancy outside, it seemed at first impenetrably dark to me. I entered it groping, for the change from light to blackness made spots of colour swim before me. Suddenly I halted spellbound. A pair of eyes, luminous by reflection against the daylight without, was watching me out of the darkness.

'The old instinctive dread of wild beasts came upon me. I clenched my hands and steadfastly looked into the glaring eyeballs. I was afraid to turn. Then the thought of the absolute security in which humanity appeared to be living came to my mind. And then I remembered that strange terror of the dark. Overcoming my fear to some extent, I advanced a step and spoke. I will admit that my voice was harsh and ill-controlled. I put out my hand and touched something soft. At once the eyes darted sideways, and something white ran past me. I turned with my heart in my mouth, and saw a queer little ape-like figure, its head held down in a peculiar manner, running across the sunlit space behind me. It blundered against a block of granite, staggered aside, and in a moment was hidden in a black shadow beneath another pile of ruined masonry.

'My impression of it is, of course, imperfect; but I know it was a dull white, and had strange large greyish-red eyes; also that there was flaxen hair on its head and down its back. But, as I say, it went too fast for me to see distinctly. I cannot even say whether it ran on all-fours, or only with its forearms held very low. After an instant's pause I followed it into the second heap of ruins. I could not find it at first; but, after a time in the profound obscurity, I came upon one of those round well-like openings of which I have told you, half closed by a fallen pillar. A sudden thought came to me. Could this Thing have vanished down the shaft? I lit a match, and, looking down, I saw a small, white, moving creature, with large bright eyes which regarded me steadfastly as it retreated. It made me shudder. It was so like a human spider! It was clambering down the wall, and now I saw for the first time a number of metal foot and hand rests forming a kind of ladder down the shaft. Then the light burned my fingers and fell out of my hand, going out as it dropped, and when I had lit another the little monster had disappeared.

'I do not know how long I sat peering down that well. It was not for some time that I could succeed in persuading myself that the thing I had seen was human. But, gradually, the truth dawned on me: that Man had not remained one species, but had differentiated into two distinct animals: that my graceful children of the Upper World were not the sole descendants of our generation, but that this bleached, obscene, nocturnal Thing, which had flashed before me, was also heir to all the ages.

'I thought of the flickering pillars and of my theory of an underground ventilation. I began to suspect their true import. And what, I wondered, was this Lemur* doing in my scheme of a perfectly balanced organisation? How was it related to the indolent serenity of the beautiful Upper-worlders? And what was hidden down there, at the foot of that shaft? I sat upon the edge of the well telling myself that, at any rate, there was nothing to fear, and that there I must descend for the solution of my difficulties. And withal I was absolutely afraid to go! As I hesitated, two of the beautiful Upper-world people came running in their amorous sport across the daylight into the shadow. The male pursued the female, flinging flowers at her as he ran.

'They seemed distressed to find me, my arm against the overturned pillar, peering down the well. Apparently it was considered bad form to remark these apertures; for when I pointed to this one, and tried to frame a question about it in their tongue, they were still more visibly distressed and turned away. But they were interested by my matches, and I struck some to amuse them. I tried them again about the well, and again I failed. So presently I left them, meaning to go back to Weena, and see what I could get from her. But my mind was already in revolution; my guesses and impressions were slipping and sliding to a new adjustment. I had now a clue to the import of these wells, to the ventilating towers, to the mystery of the ghosts; to say nothing of a hint at the meaning of the bronze gates and the fate of the Time Machine! And very vaguely there came a suggestion towards the solution of the economic problem that had puzzled me.

'Here was the new view. Plainly, this second species of Man was subterranean. There were three circumstances in particular which made me think that its rare emergence above ground was the outcome of a long-continued underground habit. In the first place, there was the bleached look common in most animals that live largely in the dark—the white fish of the Kentucky caves, for instance. Then, those large eyes, with that capacity for reflecting light, are common features of nocturnal things—witness the owl and the cat. And last of all, that evident confusion in the sunshine, that hasty yet fumbling and awkward flight towards dark shadow, and that peculiar carriage of the head while in the light—all reinforced the theory of an extreme sensitiveness of the retina.

'Beneath my feet, then, the earth must be tunnelled enormously, and these tunnellings were the habitat of the new race. The presence of ventilating-shafts and wells along the hill

slopes—everywhere, in fact, except along the river valley—
showed how universal were its ramifications. What so natural, then, as to assume that it was in this artificial Underworld that such work as was necessary to the comfort of the
daylight race was done? The notion was so plausible that I
at once accepted it, and went on to assume the *how* of this
splitting of the human species. I dare say you will anticipate
the shape of my theory; though, for myself, I very soon felt
that it fell far short of the truth.

'At first, proceeding from the problems of our own age, it
seemed clear as daylight to me that the gradual widening of
the present merely temporary and social difference between
the Capitalist and the Labourer, was the key to the whole
position. No doubt it will seem grotesque enough to you—
and wildly incredible!—and yet even now there are existing
circumstances to point that way. There is a tendency to util-
ise underground space for the less ornamental purposes of
civilisation; there is the Metropolitan Railway in London, for
instance, there are new electric railways, there are subways,
there are underground workrooms and restaurants, and they
increase and multiply. Evidently, I thought, this tendency
had increased till industry had gradually lost its birthright in
the sky. I mean that it had gone deeper and deeper into
larger and ever larger underground factories, spending a still-
increasing amount of its time therein, till, in the end—! Even
now, does not an East-end worker live in such artificial conditions as practically to be cut off from the natural surface of
the earth?

'Again, the exclusive tendency of richer people—due, no
doubt, to the increasing refinement of their education, and
the widening gulf between them and the rude violence of the
poor—is already leading to the closing, in their interest, of
considerable portions of the surface of the land. About London, for instance, perhaps half the prettier country is shut in
against intrusion. And this same widening gulf—which is due
to the length and expense of the higher educational process

and the increased facilities for and temptations towards refined habits on the part of the rich—will make that exchange
between class and class, that promotion by intermarriage
which at present retards the splitting of our species along
lines of social stratification, less and less frequent. So, in the
end, above ground you must have the Haves, pursuing pleasure and comfort, and beauty, and below ground the Have-
nots, the Workers getting continually adapted to the conditions
of their labour. Once they were there, they would no doubt
have to pay rent, and not a little of it, for the ventilation of
their caverns; and if they refused, they would starve or be
suffocated for arrears. Such of them as were so constituted
as to be miserable and rebellious would die; and, in the end,
the balance being permanent, the survivors would become as
well adapted to the conditions of underground life, and as
happy in their way, as the Upper-world people were to theirs.
As it seemed to me, the refined beauty and the etiolated
pallor followed naturally enough.

'The great triumph of Humanity I had dreamed of took a
different shape in my mind. It had been no such triumph of
moral education and general cooperation as I had imagined.
Instead, I saw a real aristocracy, armed with a perfected
science and working to a logical conclusion the industrial
system of to-day. Its triumph had not been simply a triumph
over Nature, but a triumph over Nature and the fellow man.
This, I must warn you, was my theory at the time. I had no
convenient cicerone in the pattern of the Utopian books.*
My explanation may be absolutely wrong. I still think it is the
most plausible one. But even on this supposition the balanced civilisation that was at last attained must have long
since passed its zenith, and was now far fallen into decay.
The too-perfect security of the Upper-worlders had led them
to a slow movement of degeneration, to a general dwindling
in size, strength, and intelligence. That I could see clearly
enough already. What had happened to the Undergrounders
I did not yet suspect; but, from what I had seen of the

Morlocks—that, by the bye, was the name by which these creatures were called—I could imagine that the modification of the human type was even far more profound than among the "Eloi," the beautiful race that I already knew.

'Then came troublesome doubts. Why had the Morlocks taken my Time Machine? For I felt sure it was they who had taken it. Why, too, if the Eloi were masters, could they not restore the machine to me? And why were they so terribly afraid of the dark? I proceeded, as I have said, to question Weena about this Underworld, but here again I was disappointed. At first she would not understand my questions, and presently she refused to answer them. She shivered as though the topic was unendurable. And when I pressed her, perhaps a little harshly, she burst into tears. They were the only tears, except my own, I ever saw in that Golden Age. When I saw them I ceased abruptly to trouble about the Morlocks, and was only concerned in banishing these signs of the human inheritance from Weena's eyes. And very soon she was smiling and clapping her hands while I solemnly burned a match.

6

'It may seem odd to you, but it was two days before I could follow up the new-found clue in what was manifestly the proper way. I felt a peculiar shrinking from those pallid bodies. They were just the half-bleached colour of the worms and things one sees preserved in spirit in a zoological museum. And they were filthily cold to the touch. Probably my shrinking was largely due to the sympathetic influence of the Eloi, whose disgust of the Morlocks I now began to appreciate.

'The next night I did not sleep well. Probably my health was a little disordered. I was oppressed with perplexity and doubt. Once or twice I had a feeling of intense fear for which I could perceive no definite reason. I remember creeping noiselessly into the great hall where the little people were sleeping in the moonlight—that night Weena was among them—and feeling reassured by their presence. It occurred to me, even then, that in the course of a few days the moon must pass through its last quarter, and the nights grow dark, when the appearances of these unpleasant creatures from below, these whitened Lemurs, this new vermin that had replaced the old, might be more abundant. And on both these days I had the restless feeling of one who shirks an inevitable duty. I felt assured that the Time Machine was only to be recovered by boldly penetrating these underground mysteries. Yet I could not face the mystery. If only I had had a companion it would have been different. But I was so horribly alone, and even to clamber down into the darkness of the well appalled me. I don't know if you will understand my feeling, but I never felt quite safe at my back.

'It was this restlessness, this insecurity, perhaps, that drove me further and further afield in my exploring expeditions. Going to the south-westward towards the rising country that is now called Combe Wood, I observed far off, in the direction of nineteenth-century Banstead, a vast green structure, different in character from any I had hitherto seen. It was larger than the largest of the palaces or ruins I knew, and the façade had an Oriental look: the face of it having the lustre, as well as the pale-green tint, a kind of bluish-green, of a certain type of Chinese porcelain. This difference in aspect suggested a difference in use, and I was minded to push on and explore. But the day was growing late, and I had come upon the sight of the place after a long and tiring circuit; so I resolved to hold over the adventure for the following day, and I returned to the welcome and the caresses of little Weena. But next morning I perceived clearly enough that my curiosity regarding the Palace of Green Porcelain was a piece of self-deception, to enable me to shirk, by another day, an experience I dreaded. I resolved I would make the descent without further waste of time, and started out in the early morning towards a well near the ruins of granite and aluminium.

'Little Weena ran with me. She danced beside me to the well, but when she saw me lean over the mouth and look downward, she seemed strangely disconcerted. "Good-bye, little Weena," I said, kissing her; and then, putting her down, I began to feel over the parapet for the climbing hooks. Rather hastily, I may as well confess, for I feared my courage might leak away! At first she watched me in amazement. Then she gave a most piteous cry, and, running to me, she began to pull at me with her little hands. I think her opposition nerved me rather to proceed. I shook her off, perhaps a little roughly, and in another moment I was in the throat of the well. I saw her agonised face over the parapet, and smiled to reassure her. Then I had to look down at the unstable hooks to which I clung.

'I had to clamber down a shaft of perhaps two hundred yards. The descent was effected by means of metallic bars projecting from the sides of the well, and these being adapted to the needs of a creature much smaller and lighter than myself, I was speedily cramped and fatigued by the descent. And not simply fatigued! One of the bars bent suddenly under my weight, and almost swung me off into the blackness beneath. For a moment I hung by one hand, and after that experience I did not dare to rest again. Though my arms and back were presently acutely painful, I went on clambering down the sheer descent with as quick a motion as possible. Glancing upward, I saw the aperture, a small blue disk, in which a star was visible, while little Weena's head showed as a round black projection. The thudding sound of a machine below grew louder and more oppressive. Everything save that little disk above was profoundly dark, and when I looked up again Weena had disappeared.

'I was in an agony of discomfort. I had some thought of trying to go up the shaft again, and leave the Underworld alone. But even while I turned this over in my mind I continued to descend. At last, with intense relief, I saw dimly coming up, a foot to the right of me, a slender loophole in the wall. Swinging myself in, I found it was the aperture of a narrow horizontal tunnel in which I could lie down and rest. It was not too soon. My arms ached, my back was cramped, and I was trembling with the prolonged terror of a fall. Besides this, the unbroken darkness had had a distressing effect upon my eyes. The air was full of the throb and hum of machinery pumping air down the shaft.

'I do not know how long I lay. I was roused by a soft hand touching my face. Starting up in the darkness I snatched at my matches and, hastily striking one, I saw three stooping white creatures similar to the one I had seen above ground in the ruin, hastily retreating before the light. Living, as they did, in what appeared to me impenetrable darkness, their eyes were abnormally large and sensitive, just as are the pupils of the abysmal fishes, and they reflected the light in the same way. I have no doubt they could see me in that rayless obscurity, and they did not seem to have any fear of me apart from the light. But, so soon as I struck a match in order to see them, they fled incontinently, vanishing into dark gutters and tunnels, from which their eyes glared at me in the strangest fashion.

'I tried to call to them, but the language they had was apparently different from that of the Upper-world people; so that I was needs left to my own unaided efforts, and the thought of flight before exploration was even then in my mind. But I said to myself, "You are in for it now," and, feeling my way along the tunnel, I found the noise of machinery grow louder. Presently the walls fell away from me, and I came to a large open space, and, striking another match, saw that I had entered a vast arched cavern, which stretched into utter darkness beyond the range of my light. The view I had of it was as much as one could see in the burning of a match.

'Necessarily my memory is vague. Great shapes like big

machines rose out of the dimness, and cast grotesque black shadows, in which dim spectral Morlocks sheltered from the glare. The place, by the bye, was very stuffy and oppressive, and the faint halitus* of freshly shed blood was in the air. Some way down the central vista was a little table of white metal, laid with what seemed a meal. The Morlocks at any rate were carnivorous! Even at the time, I remember wondering what large animal could have survived to furnish the red joint I saw. It was all very indistinct: the heavy smell, the big unmeaning shapes, the obscene figures lurking in the shadows, and only waiting for the darkness to come at me again! Then the match burned down, and stung my fingers, and fell, a wriggling red spot in the blackness.

'I have thought since how particularly ill equipped I was for such an experience. When I had started with the Time Machine, I had started with the absurd assumption that the men of the Future would certainly be infinitely ahead of ourselves in all their appliances. I had come without arms, without medicine, without anything to smoke—at times I missed tobacco frightfully!—even without enough matches. If only I had thought of a Kodak!* I could have flashed that glimpse of the Underworld in a second, and examined it at leisure. But, as it was, I stood there with only the weapons and the powers that Nature had endowed me with—hands, feet, and teeth; these, and four safety-matches that still remained to me.

'I was afraid to push my way in among all this machinery in the dark, and it was only with my last glimpse of light I discovered that my store of matches had run low. It had never occurred to me until that moment that there was any need to economise them, and I had wasted almost half the box in astonishing the Upper-worlders, to whom fire was a novelty. Now, as I say, I had four left, and while I stood in the dark, a hand touched mine, lank fingers came feeling over my face, and I was sensible of a peculiar unpleasant odour. I fancied I heard the breathing of a crowd of those dreadful little beings about me. I felt the box of matches in my hand being gently disengaged, and other hands behind me plucking at my clothing. The sense of these unseen creatures examining me was indescribably unpleasant. The sudden realisation of my ignorance of their ways of thinking and doing came home to me very vividly in the darkness. I shouted at them as loudly as I could. They started away, and then I could feel them approaching me again. They clutched at me more boldly, whispering odd sounds to each other. I shivered violently, and shouted again—rather discordantly. This time they were not so seriously alarmed, and they made a queer laughing noise as they came back at me. I will confess I was horribly frightened. I determined to strike another match and escape under the protection of its glare. I did so, and eking out the flicker with a scrap of paper from my pocket, I made good my retreat to the narrow tunnel. But I had scarce entered this when my light was blown out, and in the blackness I could hear the Morlocks rustling like wind among leaves, and pattering like the rain, as they hurried after me.

'In a moment I was clutched by several hands, and there was no mistaking that they were trying to haul me back. I struck another light, and waved it in their dazzled faces. You can scarce imagine how nauseatingly inhuman they looked—those pale, chinless faces and great, lidless, pinkish-grey eyes!—as they stared in their blindness and bewilderment. But I did not stay to look, I promise you: I retreated again, and when my second match had ended, I struck my third. It had almost burned through when I reached the opening into the shaft. I lay down on the edge, for the throb of the great pump below made me giddy. Then I felt sideways for the projecting hooks, and, as I did so, my feet were grasped from behind, and I was violently tugged backward. I lit my last match . . . and it incontinently went out. But I had my hand on the climbing bars now, and, kicking violently, I disengaged myself from the clutches of the Morlocks, and was speedily clambering up the shaft, while they stayed peering and blinking up at me: all but one little wretch who followed me for some way, and well-nigh secured my boot as a trophy.

'That climb seemed interminable to me. With the last twenty or thirty feet of it a deadly nausea came upon me. I had the greatest difficulty in keeping my hold. The last few yards was a frightful struggle against this faintness. Several times my head swam, and I felt all the sensations of falling. At last, however, I got over the well-mouth somehow, and staggered out of the ruin into the blinding sunlight. I fell upon my face. Even the soil smelt sweet and clean. Then I remember Weena kissing my hands and ears, and the voices of others among the Eloi. Then, for a time, I was insensible.

7

'Now, indeed, I seemed in a worse case than before. Hitherto, except during my night's anguish at the loss of the Time Machine, I had felt a sustaining hope of ultimate escape, but that hope was staggered by these new discoveries. Hitherto I had merely thought myself impeded by the childish simplicity of the little people, and by some unknown forces which I had only to understand to overcome; but there was an altogether new element in the sickening quality of the Morlocks—a something inhuman and malign. Instinctively I loathed them. Before, I had felt as a man might feel who had fallen into a pit: my concern was with the pit and how to get out of it. Now I felt like a beast in a trap, whose enemy would come upon him soon.

'The enemy I dreaded may surprise you. It was the darkness of the new moon. Weena had put this into my head by some at first incomprehensible remarks about the Dark Nights. It was not now such a very difficult problem to guess what the coming Dark Nights might mean. The moon was on the wane: each night there was a longer interval of darkness. And I now understood to some slight degree at least the reason of the fear of the little Upper-world people for the dark. I wondered vaguely what foul villainy it might be that the Morlocks did under the new moon. I felt pretty sure now that my second hypothesis was all wrong. The Upper-world people might once have been the favoured aristocracy, and the Morlocks their mechanical servants; but that had long since passed away. The two species that had resulted from the evolution of man were sliding down towards, or had already arrived at, an altogether new relationship. The Eloi, like the Carlovingian kings,* had decayed to a mere beautiful futility. They still possessed the earth on sufferance: since the Morlocks, subterranean for innumerable generations, had come at last to find the daylit surface intolerable. And the Morlocks made their garments, I inferred, and maintained them in their habitual needs, perhaps through the survival of an old habit of service. They did it as a standing horse paws with his foot, or as a man enjoys killing animals in sport: because ancient and departed necessities had impressed it on the organism. But, clearly, the old order was already in part reversed. The Nemesis of the delicate ones was creeping on apace. Ages ago, thousands of generations ago, man had thrust his brother man out of the ease and the sunshine. And now that brother was coming back—changed! Already the Eloi had begun to learn one old lesson anew. They were becoming reacquainted with Fear. And suddenly there came into my head the memory of the meat I had seen in the Underworld. It seemed odd how it floated into my mind: not stirred up as it were by the current of my meditations, but coming in almost like a question from outside. I tried to recall the form of it. I had a vague sense of something familiar, but I could not tell what it was at the time.

'Still, however helpless the little people in the presence of their mysterious Fear, I was differently constituted. I came out of this age of ours, this ripe prime of the human race, when Fear does not paralyse and mystery has lost its terrors. I at least would defend myself. Without further delay I determined to make myself arms and a fastness where I might sleep. With that refuge as a base, I could face this strange world with some of that confidence I had lost in realising to what creatures night by night I lay exposed. I felt I could never sleep again until my bed was secure from them. I shuddered with horror to think how they must already have examined me.

'I wandered during the afternoon along the valley of the Thames, but found nothing that commended itself to my mind as inaccessible. All the buildings and trees seemed easily practicable to such dexterous climbers as the Morlocks, to judge by their wells, must be. Then the tall pinnacles of the Palace of Green Porcelain and the polished gleam of its walls came back to my memory; and in the evening, taking Weena like a child upon my shoulder, I went up the hills towards the south-west. The distance, I had reckoned, was seven or eight miles, but it must have been nearer eighteen. I had first seen the place on a moist afternoon when distances are deceptively diminished. In addition, the heel of one of my shoes was loose, and a nail was working through the sole—they were comfortable old shoes I wore about indoors—so that I was lame. And it was already long past sunset when I came in sight of the palace, silhouetted black against the pale yellow of the sky.

'Weena had been hugely delighted when I began to carry her, but after a time she desired me to let her down, and ran along by the side of me, occasionally darting off on either hand to pick flowers to stick in my pockets. My pockets had always puzzled Weena, but at the last she had concluded that they were an eccentric kind of vase for floral decoration. At least she utilised them for that purpose. And that reminds me! In changing my jacket I found . . .'

The Time Traveller paused, put his hand into his pocket, and silently placed two withered flowers, not unlike very large white mallows, upon the little table. Then he resumed his narrative.

'As the hush of evening crept over the world and we proceeded over the hill crest towards Wimbledon, Weena grew tired and wanted to return to the house of grey stone. But I pointed out the distant pinnacles of the Palace of Green Porcelain to her, and contrived to make her understand that we were seeking a refuge there from her Fear. You know that great pause that comes upon things before the dusk? Even the breeze stops in the trees. To me there is always an air of expectation about that evening stillness. The sky was clear, remote, and empty save for a few horizontal bars far down in the sunset. Well, that night the expectation took the colour of my fears. In that darkling calm my senses seemed preternaturally sharpened. I fancied I could even feel the hollowness of the ground beneath my feet: could, indeed, almost see through it the Morlocks in their ant-hill going hither and thither and waiting for the dark. In my excitement I fancied that they would receive my invasion of their burrows as a declaration of war. And why had they taken my Time Machine?

'So we went on in the quiet, and the twilight deepened into night. The clear blue of the distance faded, and one star after another came out. The ground grew dim and the trees black. Weena's fears and her fatigue grew upon her. I took her in my arms and talked to her and caressed her. Then, as the darkness grew deeper, she put her arms round my neck, and, closing her eyes, tightly pressed her face against my shoulder. So we went down a long slope into a valley, and there in the dimness I almost walked into a little river. This I waded, and went up the opposite side of the valley, past a number of sleeping houses, and by a statue—a Faun, or some such figure, *minus* the head. Here too were acacias. So far I had seen nothing of the Morlocks, but it was yet early in the night, and the darker hours before the old moon rose were still to come.

'From the brow of the next hill I saw a thick wood spreading wide and black before me. I hesitated at this. I could see no end to it, either to the right or the left. Feeling tired—my feet in particular, were very sore—I carefully lowered Weena from my shoulder as I halted, and sat down upon the turf. I could no longer see the Palace of Green Porcelain, and I was in doubt of my direction. I looked into the thickness of the wood and thought of what it might hide. Under that dense tangle of branches one would be out of sight of the stars. Even were there no other lurking danger—a danger I did not care to let my imagination loose upon—there would still be all the roots to stumble over and the tree-boles to strike against. I was very tired, too, after the excitements of the day; so I decided that I would not face it, but would pass the night upon the open hill.

'Weena, I was glad to find, was fast asleep. I carefully wrapped her in my jacket, and sat down beside her to wait for the moonrise. The hillside was quiet and deserted, but from the black of the wood there came now and then a stir of living things. Above me shone the stars, for the night was very clear. I felt a certain sense of friendly comfort in their twinkling. All the old constellations had gone from the sky, however: that slow movement which is imperceptible in a hundred human lifetimes, had long since rearranged them in unfamiliar groupings. But the Milky Way, it seemed to me, was still the same tattered streamer of star-dust as of yore. Southward (as I judged it) was a very bright red star that was new to me; it was even more splendid than our own green Sirius. And amid all these scintillating points of light one bright planet shone kindly and steadily like the face of an old friend.

'Looking at these stars suddenly dwarfed my own troubles and all the gravities of terrestrial life. I thought of their unfathomable distance, and the slow inevitable drift of their movements out of the unknown past into the unknown future. I thought of the great precessional cycle that the pole of the earth describes. Only forty times* had that silent revolution occurred during all the years that I had traversed. And during these few revolutions all the activity, all the traditions, the complex organisations, the nations, languages, literatures, aspirations, even the mere memory of Man as I knew him, had been swept out of existence. Instead were these frail creatures who had forgotten their high ancestry, and the white Things of which I went in terror. Then I thought of the Great Fear that was between the two species, and for the first time, with a sudden shiver, came the clear knowledge of what the meat I had seen might be. Yet it was too horrible! I looked at little Weena sleeping beside me, her face white and starlike under the stars, and forthwith dismissed the thought.

'Through that long night I held my mind off the Morlocks as well as I could, and whiled away the time by trying to fancy I could find signs of the old constellations in the new confusion. The sky kept very clear, except for a hazy cloud or so. No doubt I dozed at times. Then, as my vigil wore on, came a faintness in the eastward sky, like the reflection of some colourless fire, and the old moon rose, thin and peaked and white. And close behind, and overtaking it, and overflowing it, the dawn came, pale at first, and then growing pink and warm. No Morlocks had approached us. Indeed, I had seen none upon the hill that night. And in the confidence of renewed day it almost seemed to me that my fear had been unreasonable. I stood up and found my foot with the loose heel swollen at the ankle and painful under the heel; so I sat down again, took off my shoes, and flung them away.

'I awakened Weena, and we went down into the wood, now green and pleasant instead of black and forbidding. We found some fruit wherewith to break our fast. We soon met others of the dainty ones, laughing and dancing in the sunlight as though there was no such thing in nature as the night. And then I thought once more of the meat that I had seen. I felt assured now of what it was, and from the bottom of my heart I pitied this last feeble rill from the great flood

of humanity. Clearly, at some time in the Long-Ago of human decay the Morlocks' food had run short. Possibly they
had lived on rats and suchlike vermin. Even now man is far
less discriminating and exclusive in his food than he was—
far less than any monkey. His prejudice against human flesh
is no deep-seated instinct. And so these inhuman sons of
men—! I tried to look at the thing in a scientific spirit. After
all, they were less human and more remote than our cannibal
ancestors of three or four thousand years ago. And the intelligence that would have made this state of things a torment
had gone. Why should I trouble myself? These Eloi were
mere fatted cattle, which the ant-like Morlocks preserved
and preyed upon—probably saw to the breeding of. And
there was Weena dancing at my side!

'Then I tried to preserve myself from the horror that was
coming upon me, by regarding it as a rigorous punishment of
human selfishness. Man had been content to live in ease and
delight upon the labours of his fellow man, had taken Necessity as his watchword and excuse, and in the fulness of time
Necessity had come home to him. I even tried a Carlyle-like
scorn of this wretched aristocracy in decay.* But this attitude
of mind was impossible. However great their intellectual
degradation, the Eloi had kept too much of the human form
not to claim my sympathy, and to make me perforce a sharer
in their degradation and their Fear.

'I had at that time very vague ideas as to the course I
should pursue. My first was to secure some safe place of
refuge, and to make myself such arms of metal or stone as I
could contrive. That necessity was immediate. In the next
place, I hoped to procure some means of fire, so that I should
have the weapon of a torch at hand, for nothing, I knew,
would be more efficient against these Morlocks. Then I
wanted to arrange some contrivance to break open the doors
of bronze under the White Sphinx. I had in mind a battering-
ram. I had a persuasion that if I could enter those doors and
carry a blaze of light before me I should discover the Time

Machine and escape. I could not imagine the Morlocks were strong enough to move it far away. Weena I had resolved to bring with me to our own time. And turning such schemes over in my mind I pursued our way towards the building which my fancy had chosen as our dwelling.

8

'I FOUND the Palace of Green Porcelain, when we approached it about noon, deserted and falling into ruin. Only ragged vestiges of glass remained in its windows, and great sheets of the green facing had fallen away from the corroded metallic framework. It lay very high upon a turfy down, and looking north-eastward before I entered it, I was surprised to see a large estuary, or even creek, where I judged Wandsworth and Battersea must once have been. I thought then—though I never followed up the thought—of what might have happened, or might be happening, to the living things in the sea.

'The material of the Palace proved on examination to be indeed porcelain, and along the face of it I saw an inscription in some unknown character. I thought, rather foolishly, that Weena might help me to interpret this, but I only learned that the bare idea of writing had never entered her head. She always seemed to me, I fancy, more human than she was, perhaps because her affection was so human.

'Within the big valves of the door—which were open and broken—we found, instead of the customary hall, a long gallery lit by many side windows. At the first glance I was reminded of a museum. The tiled floor was thick with dust, and a remarkable array of miscellaneous objects was shrouded in the same grey covering. Then I perceived, standing strange and gaunt in the centre of the hall, what was clearly the lower part of a huge skeleton. I recognised by the oblique feet that it was some extinct creature after the fashion of the Megatherium.* The skull and the upper bones lay beside it in the thick dust, and in one place, where rain-water had dropped through a leak in the roof, the thing itself had been worn away. Further in the gallery was the huge skeleton barrel of a Brontosaurus. My museum hypothesis was confirmed. Going towards the side I found what appeared to be sloping shelves, and, clearing away the thick dust, I found the old familiar glass cases of our own time. But they must have been air-tight to judge from the fair preservation of some of their contents.

'Clearly we stood among the ruins of some latter-day South Kensington!* Here, apparently, was the Palæontological Section, and a very splendid array of fossils it must have been, though the inevitable process of decay that had been staved off for a time, and had, through the extinction of bacteria and fungi, lost ninety-nine hundredths of its force, was, nevertheless, with extreme sureness if with extreme slowness at work again upon all its treasures. Here and there I found traces of the little people in the shape of rare fossils broken to pieces or threaded in strings upon reeds. And the cases had in some instances been bodily removed—by the Morlocks as I judged. The place was very silent. The thick dust deadened our footsteps. Weena, who had been rolling a sea-urchin down the sloping glass of a case, presently came, as I stared about me, and very quietly took my hand and stood beside me.

'And at first I was so much surprised by this ancient monument of an intellectual age, that I gave no thought to the possibilities it presented. Even my preoccupation about the Time Machine receded a little from my mind.

'To judge from the size of the place, this Palace of Green Porcelain had a great deal more in it than a Gallery of Palæontology; possibly historical galleries; it might be, even a library! To me, at least in my present circumstances, these would be vastly more interesting than this spectacle of old-time geology in decay. Exploring, I found another short gallery running transversely to the first. This appeared to be devoted to minerals, and the sight of a block of sulphur set my mind running on gunpowder. But I could find no saltpetre; indeed, no nitrates of any kind. Doubtless they had deliquesced ages ago. Yet the sulphur hung in my mind, and set up a train of thinking. As for the rest of the contents of that gallery, though on the whole they were the best preserved of all I saw, I had little interest. I am no specialist in mineralogy, and I went on down a very ruinous aisle running parallel to the first hall I had entered. Apparently this section had been devoted to natural history, but everything had long since passed out of recognition. A few shrivelled and blackened vestiges of what had once been stuffed animals, desiccated mummies in jars that had once held spirit, a brown dust of departed plants; that was all! I was sorry for that, because I should have been glad to trace the patient readjustments by which the conquest of animated nature had been attained. Then we came to a gallery of simply colossal proportions, but singularly ill-lit, the floor of it running downward at a slight angle from the end at which I entered. At intervals white globes hung from the ceiling—many of them cracked and smashed—which suggested that originally the place had been artificially lit. Here I was more in my element, for rising on either side of me were the huge bulks of big machines, all greatly corroded and many broken down, but some still fairly complete. You know I have a certain weakness for mechanism, and I was inclined to linger among these; the more so as for the most part they had the interest of puzzles, and I could make only the vaguest guesses at what they were for. I fancied that if I could solve their puzzles I should find myself in possession of powers that might be of use against the Morlocks.

'Suddenly Weena came very close to my side. So suddenly that she startled me. Had it not been for her I do not think I should have noticed that the floor of the gallery sloped at all.[1]

---

[1] It may be, of course, that the floor did not slope, but that the museum was built into the side of a hill.—ED.

The end I had come in at was quite above ground, and was lit by rare slit-like windows. As you went down the length, the ground came up against these windows, until at last there was a pit like the "area" of a London house before each, and only a narrow line of daylight at the top. I went slowly along, puzzling about the machines, and had been too intent upon them to notice the gradual diminution of the light, until Weena's increasing apprehensions drew my attention. Then I saw that the gallery ran down at last into a thick darkness. I hesitated, and then, as I looked round me, I saw that the dust was less abundant and its surface less even. Further away towards the dimness, it appeared to be broken by a number of small narrow footprints. My sense of the immediate presence of the Morlocks revived at that. I felt that I was wasting my time in this academic examination of machinery. I called to mind that it was already far advanced in the afternoon, and that I had still no weapon, no refuge, and no means of making a fire. And then down in the remote blackness of the gallery I heard a peculiar pattering, and the same odd noises I had heard down the well.

'I took Weena's hand. Then, struck with a sudden idea, I left her and turned to a machine from which projected a lever not unlike those in a signal-box. Clambering upon the stand, and grasping this lever in my hands, I put all my weight upon it sideways. Suddenly Weena, deserted in the central aisle, began to whimper. I had judged the strength of the lever pretty correctly, for it snapped after a minute's strain, and I rejoined her with a mace in my hand more than sufficient, I judged, for any Morlock skull I might encounter. And I longed very much to kill a Morlock or so. Very inhuman, you may think, to want to go killing one's own descendants! But it was impossible, somehow, to feel any humanity in the things. Only my disinclination to leave Weena, and a persuasion that if I began to slake my thirst for murder my Time Machine might suffer, restrained me from going straight down the gallery and killing the brutes I heard.

'Well, mace in one hand and Weena in the other, I went out of that gallery and into another and still larger one, which at the first glance reminded me of a military chapel hung with tattered flags. The brown and charred rags that hung from the sides of it, I presently recognised as the decaying vestiges of books. They had long since dropped to pieces, and every semblance of print had left them. But here and there were warped boards and cracked metallic clasps that told the tale well enough. Had I been a literary man I might, perhaps, have moralised upon the futility of all ambition. But as it was, the thing that struck me with keenest force was the enormous waste of labour to which this sombre wilderness of rotting paper testified. At the time I will confess that I thought chiefly of the *Philosophical Transactions* and my own seventeen papers upon physical optics.

'Then, going up a broad staircase, we came to what may once have been a gallery of technical chemistry. And here I had not a little hope of useful discoveries. Except at one end where the roof had collapsed, this gallery was well preserved. I went eagerly to every unbroken case. And at last, in one of the really air-tight cases, I found a box of matches. Very eagerly I tried them. They were perfectly good. They were not even damp. I turned to Weena. "Dance," I cried to her in her own tongue. For now I had a weapon indeed against the horrible creatures we feared. And so, in that derelict museum, upon the thick soft carpeting of dust, to Weena's huge delight, I solemnly performed a kind of composite dance, whistling *The Land of the Leal** as cheerfully as I could. In part it was a modest *cancan*, in part a step-dance, in part a skirt-dance (so far as my tail-coat permitted), and in part original. For I am naturally inventive, as you know.

'Now, I still think that for this box of matches to have escaped the wear of time for immemorial years was a most strange, as for me it was a most fortunate thing. Yet, oddly enough, I found a far unlikelier substance, and that was camphor. I found it in a sealed jar, that by chance, I suppose, had been really hermetically sealed. I fancied at first that it was paraffin wax, and smashed the glass accordingly. But the odour of camphor was unmistakable. In the universal decay this volatile substance had chanced to survive, perhaps through many thousands of centuries. It reminded me of a sepia painting I had once seen done from the ink of a fossil Belemnite* that must have perished and become fossilised millions of years ago. I was about to throw it away, but I remembered that it was inflammable and burned with a good bright flame—was, in fact, an excellent candle—and I put it in my pocket. I found no explosives, however, nor any means of breaking down the bronze doors. As yet my iron crowbar was the most helpful thing I had chanced upon. Nevertheless I left that gallery greatly elated.

'I cannot tell you all the story of that long afternoon. It would require a great effort of memory to recall my explorations in at all the proper order. I remember a long gallery of rusting stands of arms, and how I hesitated between my crowbar and a hatchet or a sword. I could not carry both, however, and my bar of iron promised best against the bronze gates. There were numbers of guns, pistols, and rifles. The most were masses of rust, but many were of some new metal, and still fairly sound. But any cartridges or powder there may once have been had rotted into dust. One corner I saw was charred and shattered; perhaps, I thought, by an explosion among the specimens. In another place was a vast array of idols—Polynesian, Mexican, Grecian, Phœnician, every country on earth I should think. And here, yielding to an irresistible impulse, I wrote my name upon the nose of a steatite monster from South America* that particularly took my fancy.

'As the evening drew on, my interest waned. I went through gallery after gallery, dusty, silent, often ruinous, the exhibits sometimes mere heaps of rust and lignite, sometimes fresher. In one place I suddenly found myself near the model of a tin-mine, and then by the merest accident I discovered, in an air-tight case, two dynamite cartridges! I shouted "Eureka," and smashed the case with joy. Then came a doubt. I hesitated. Then, selecting a little side gallery, I made my essay. I never felt such a disappointment as I did in waiting five, ten, fifteen minutes for an explosion that never came. Of course the things were dummies, as I might have guessed from their presence. I really believe that, had they not been so, I should have rushed off incontinently and blown sphinx, bronze doors, and (as it proved) my chances of finding the Time Machine, all together into non-existence.

'It was after that, I think, that we came to a little open court within the palace. It was turfed, and had three fruit-trees. So we rested and refreshed ourselves. Towards sunset I began to consider our position. Night was creeping upon us, and my inaccessible hiding-place had still to be found. But that troubled me very little now. I had in my possession a thing that was, perhaps, the best of all defences against the Morlocks—I had matches! I had the camphor in my pocket, too, if a blaze were needed. It seemed to me that the best thing we could do would be to pass the night in the open, protected by a fire. In the morning there was the getting of the Time Machine. Towards that, as yet, I had only my iron mace. But now, with my growing knowledge, I felt very differently towards those bronze doors. Up to this, I had refrained from forcing them, largely because of the mystery on the other side. They had never impressed me as being very strong, and I hoped to find my bar of iron not altogether inadequate for the work.

9

'WE emerged from the palace while the sun was still in part above the horizon. I was determined to reach the White Sphinx early the next morning, and ere the dusk I purposed pushing through the woods that had stopped me on the previous journey. My plan was to go as far as possible that night, and then, building a fire, to sleep in the protection of its glare. Accordingly, as we went along I gathered any sticks or dried grass I saw, and presently had my arms full of such litter. Thus loaded, our progress was slower than I had anticipated, and besides Weena was tired. And I began to suffer from sleepiness too; so that it was full night before we reached the wood. Upon the shrubby hill of its edge Weena would have stopped, fearing the darkness before us; but a singular sense of impending calamity, that should indeed have served me as a warning, drove me onward. I had been without sleep for a night and two days, and I was feverish and irritable. I felt sleep coming upon me, and the Morlocks with it.

'While we hesitated, among the black bushes behind us, and dim against their blackness, I saw three crouching figures. There was scrub and long grass all about us, and I did not feel safe from their insidious approach. The forest, I calculated, was rather less than a mile across. If we could get through it to the bare hillside, there, as it seemed to me, was an altogether safer resting-place; I thought that with my matches and my camphor I could contrive to keep my path illuminated through the woods. Yet it was evident that if I was to flourish matches with my hands I should have to abandon my firewood; so, rather reluctantly, I put it down. And then it came into my head that I would amaze our friends behind by lighting it. I was to discover the atrocious folly of this proceeding, but it came to my mind as an ingenious move for covering our retreat.

'I don't know if you have ever thought what a rare thing flame must be in the absence of man and in a temperate climate. The sun's heat is rarely strong enough to burn, even when it is focussed by dewdrops, as is sometimes the case in more tropical districts. Lightning may blast and blacken, but it rarely gives rise to widespread fire. Decaying vegetation may occasionally smoulder with the heat of its fermentation, but this rarely results in flame. In this decadence, too, the art of fire-making had been forgotten on the earth. The red tongues that went licking up my heap of wood were an altogether new and strange thing to Weena.

'She wanted to run to it and play with it. I believe she would have cast herself into it had I not restrained her. But I caught her up, and, in spite of her struggles, plunged boldly before me into the wood. For a little way the glare of my fire lit the path. Looking back presently, I could see, through the crowded stems, that from my heap of sticks the blaze had spread to some bushes adjacent, and a curved line of fire was creeping up the grass of the hill. I laughed at that, and turned again to the dark trees before me. It was very black, and Weena clung to me convulsively, but there was still, as my eyes grew accustomed to the darkness, sufficient light for me to avoid the stems. Overhead it was simply black, except where a gap of remote blue sky shone down upon us here and there. I struck none of my matches because I had no hand free. Upon my left arm I carried my little one, in my right hand I had my iron bar.

'For some way I heard nothing but the crackling twigs under my feet, the faint rustle of the breeze above, and my own breathing and the throb of the blood-vessels in my ears. Then I seemed to know of a pattering about me. I pushed on grimly. The pattering grew more distinct, and then I caught the same queer sounds and voices I had heard in the Underworld. There were evidently several of the Morlocks, and they were closing in upon me. Indeed, in another minute I felt a tug at my coat, then something at my arm. And Weena shivered violently, and became quite still.

'It was time for a match. But to get one I must put her down. I did so, and, as I fumbled with my pocket, a struggle began in the darkness about my knees, perfectly silent on her part and with the same peculiar cooing sounds from the Morlocks. Soft little hands, too, were creeping over my coat and back, touching even my neck. Then the match scratched and fizzed. I held it flaring, and saw the white backs of the Morlocks in flight amid the trees. I hastily took a lump of camphor from my pocket, and prepared to light it as soon as the match should wane. Then I looked at Weena. She was lying clutching my feet and quite motionless, with her face to the ground. With a sudden fright I stooped to her. She seemed scarcely to breathe. I lit the block of camphor and flung it to the ground, and as it spit and flared up and drove back the Morlocks and the shadows, I knelt down and lifted her. The wood behind seemed full of the stir and murmur of a great company!

'She seemed to have fainted. I put her carefully upon my shoulder and rose to push on, and then there came a horrible realisation. In manœuvring with my matches and Weena, I had turned myself about several times, and now I had not the faintest idea in what direction lay my path. For all I knew, I might be facing back towards the Palace of Green Porcelain. I found myself in a cold sweat. I had to think rapidly what to do. I determined to build a fire and encamp where we were. I put Weena, still motionless, down upon a turfy bole, and very hastily, as my first lump of camphor waned, I began collecting sticks and leaves. Here and there out of the darkness round me the Morlocks' eyes shone like carbuncles.*

'The camphor flickered and went out. I lit a match, and as I did so, two white forms that had been approaching Weena dashed hastily away. One was so blinded by the light that he came straight for me and I felt his bones grind under the blow of my fist. He gave a whoop of dismay, staggered a little way, and fell down. I lit another piece of camphor, and went on gathering my bonfire. Presently I noticed how dry was some of the foliage above me, for since my arrival on the Time Machine, a matter of a week, no rain had fallen. So, instead of casting about among the trees for fallen twigs, I began leaping up and dragging down branches. Very soon I had a choking smoky fire of green wood and dry sticks, and could economise my camphor. Then I turned to where Weena lay beside my iron mace. I tried what I could to revive her, but she lay like one dead. I could not even satisfy myself whether or not she breathed.

'Now, the smoke of the fire beat over towards me, and it must have made me heavy of a sudden. Moreover, the vapour of camphor was in the air. My fire would not need replenishing for an hour or so. I felt very weary after my exertion, and sat down. The wood, too, was full of a slumbrous murmur that I did not understand. I seemed just to nod and open my eyes. But all was dark, and the Morlocks had their hands upon me. Flinging off their clinging fingers I hastily felt in my pocket for the match-box, and—it had gone! Then they gripped and closed with me again. In a moment I knew what had happened. I had slept, and my fire had gone out, and the bitterness of death came over my soul. The forest seemed full of the smell of burning wood. I was caught by the neck, by the hair, by the arms, and pulled down. It was indescribably horrible in the darkness to feel all these soft creatures heaped upon me. I felt as if I was in a monstrous spider's web. I was overpowered, and went down. I felt little teeth nipping at my neck. I rolled over, and as I did so my hand came against my iron lever. It gave me strength. I struggled up, shaking the human rats from me, and, holding the bar short, I thrust where I judged their faces might be. I could feel the succulent giving of flesh and bone under my blows, and for a moment I was free.

'The strange exultation that so often seems to accompany hard fighting came upon me. I knew that both I and Weena were lost, but I determined to make the Morlocks pay for their meat. I stood with my back to a tree, swinging the iron bar before me. The whole wood was full of the stir and cries of them. A minute passed. Their voices seemed to rise to a higher pitch of excitement, and their movements grew faster. Yet none came within reach. I stood glaring at the blackness. Then suddenly came hope. What if the Morlocks were afraid? And close on the heels of that came a strange thing. The darkness seemed to grow luminous. Very dimly I began to see the Morlocks about me—three battered at my feet—and then I recognised, with incredulous surprise, that the others were running, in an incessant stream, as it seemed, from behind me, and away through the wood in front. And their backs seemed no longer white, but reddish. As I stood agape, I saw a little red spark go drifting across a gap of starlight between the branches, and vanish. And at that I understood the smell of burning wood, the slumbrous murmur that was growing now into a gusty roar, the red glow, and the Morlocks' flight.

'Stepping out from behind my tree and looking back, I saw, through the black pillars of the nearer trees, the flames of the burning forest. It was my first fire coming after me. With that I looked for Weena, but she was gone. The hissing and crackling behind me, the explosive thud as each fresh tree burst into flame, left little time for reflection. My iron bar still gripped, I followed in the Morlocks' path. It was a close race. Once the flames crept forward so swiftly on my right as I ran that I was outflanked and had to strike off to the left. But at last I emerged upon a small open space, and as I did so, a Morlock came blundering towards me, and past me, and went on straight into the fire!

'And now I was to see the most weird and horrible thing, I think, of all that I beheld in that future age. This whole space was as bright as day with the reflection of the fire. In the centre was a hillock or tumulus, surmounted by a scorched hawthorn. Beyond this was another arm of the burning forest, with yellow tongues already writhing from it, completely encircling the space with a fence of fire. Upon the hillside were some thirty or forty Morlocks, dazzled by the light and heat, and blundering hither and thither against each other in their bewilderment. At first I did not realise their blindness, and struck furiously at them with my bar, in a frenzy of fear, as they approached me, killing one and crippling several more. But when I had watched the gestures of one of them groping under the hawthorn against the red sky, and heard their moans, I was assured of their absolute helplessness and misery in the glare, and I struck no more of them.

'Yet every now and then one would come straight towards me, setting loose a quivering horror that made me quick to elude him. At one time the flames died down somewhat, and I feared the foul creatures would presently be able to see me. I was even thinking of beginning the fight by killing some of them before this should happen; but the fire burst out again brightly, and I stayed my hand. I walked about the hill among them and avoided them, looking for some trace of Weena. But Weena was gone.

'At last I sat down on the summit of the hillock, and watched this strange incredible company of blind things groping to and fro, and making uncanny noises to each other, as the glare of the fire beat on them. The coiling uprush of smoke streamed across the sky, and through the rare tatters of that red canopy, remote as though they belonged to another universe, shone the little stars. Two or three Morlocks came blundering into me, and I drove them off with blows of my fists, trembling as I did so.

'For the most part of that night I was persuaded it was a nightmare. I bit myself and screamed in a passionate desire to awake. I beat the ground with my hands, and got up and sat down again, and wandered here and there, and again sat down. Then I would fall to rubbing my eyes and calling upon God to let me awake. Thrice I saw Morlocks put their heads down in a kind of agony and rush into the flames. But, at last, above the subsiding red of the fire, above the streaming masses of black smoke and the whitening and blackening tree stumps, and the diminishing numbers of these dim creatures, came the white light of the day.

'I searched again for traces of Weena, but there were none. It was plain that they had left her poor little body in the forest. I cannot describe how it relieved me to think that it had escaped the awful fate to which it seemed destined. As I thought of that, I was almost moved to begin a massacre of the helpless abominations about me, but I contained myself. The hillock, as I have said, was a kind of island in the forest. From its summit I could now make out through a haze of smoke the Palace of Green Porcelain, and from that I could get my bearings for the White Sphinx. And so, leaving the remnant of these damned souls still going hither and thither and moaning, as the day grew clearer, I tied some grass about my feet and limped on across smoking ashes and among black stems, that still pulsated internally with fire, towards the hiding-place of the Time Machine. I walked slowly, for I was almost exhausted, as well as lame, and I felt the intensest wretchedness for the horrible death of little Weena. It seemed an overwhelming calamity. Now, in this old familiar room, it is more like the sorrow of a dream than an actual loss. But that morning it left me absolutely lonely again—terribly alone. I began to think of this house of mine, of this fireside, of some of you, and with such thoughts came a longing that was pain.

'But, as I walked over the smoking ashes under the bright morning sky, I made a discovery. In my trouser pocket were still some loose matches. The box must have leaked before it was lost.

10

'ABOUT eight or nine in the morning I came to the same seat of yellow metal from which I had viewed the world upon the evening of my arrival. I thought of my hasty conclusions upon that evening and could not refrain from laughing bitterly at my confidence. Here was the same beautiful scene, the same abundant foliage, the same splendid palaces and magnificent ruins, the same silver river running between its fertile banks. The gay robes of the beautiful people moved hither and thither among the trees. Some were bathing in exactly the place where I had saved Weena, and that suddenly gave me a keen stab of pain. And like blots upon the landscape rose the cupolas above the ways to the Underworld. I understood now what all the beauty of the Upper-world people covered. Very pleasant was their day, as pleasant as the day of the cattle in the field. Like the cattle, they knew of no enemies and provided against no needs. And their end was the same.

'I grieved to think how brief the dream of the human intellect had been. It had committed suicide. It had set itself steadfastly towards comfort and ease, a balanced society with security and permanency as its watchword, it had attained its hopes—to come to this at last. Once, life and property must have reached almost absolute safety. The rich had been assured of his wealth and comfort, the toiler assured of his life and work. No doubt in that perfect world there had been no unemployed problem, no social question left unsolved. And a great quiet had followed.

'It is a law of nature we overlook, that intellectual versatility is the compensation for change, danger, and trouble. An animal perfectly in harmony with its environment is a perfect mechanism. Nature never appeals to intelligence until habit and instinct are useless. There is no intelligence where there is no change and no need of change. Only those animals partake of intelligence that have to meet a huge variety of needs and dangers.

'So, as I see it, the Upper-world man had drifted towards his feeble prettiness, and the Underworld to mere mechanical industry. But that perfect state had lacked one thing even for mechanical perfection—absolute permanency. Apparently as time went on, the feeding of the Underworld, however it was effected, had become disjointed. Mother Necessity, who had been staved off for a few thousand years, came back again, and she began below. The Underworld being in contact with machinery, which, however perfect, still needs some little thought outside habit, had probably retained perforce rather more initiative, if less of every other human character, than the upper. And when other meat failed them, they turned to what old habit had hitherto forbidden. So I say I saw it in my last view of the world of Eight Hundred and Two Thousand Seven Hundred and One. It may be as wrong an explanation as mortal wit could invent. It is how the thing shaped itself to me, and as that I give it to you.

'After the fatigues, excitements, and terrors of the past days, and in spite of my grief, this seat and the tranquil view and the warm sunlight were very pleasant. I was very tired and sleepy, and soon my theorising passed into dozing. Catching myself at that, I took my own hint, and spreading myself out upon the turf I had a long and refreshing sleep.

'I awoke a little before sunsetting. I now felt safe against being caught napping by the Morlocks, and, stretching myself, I came on down the hill towards the White Sphinx. I had my crowbar in one hand, and the other hand played with the matches in my pocket.

'And now came a most unexpected thing. As I approached the pedestal of the sphinx I found the bronze valves were open. They had slid down into grooves.

'At that I stopped short before them, hesitating to enter.

'Within was a small apartment, and on a raised place in the corner of this was the Time Machine. I had the small levers in my pocket. So here, after all my elaborate preparations for the siege of the White Sphinx, was a meek surrender. I threw my iron bar away, almost sorry not to use it.

'A sudden thought came into my head as I stooped towards the portal. For once, at least, I grasped the mental operations of the Morlocks. Suppressing a strong inclination to laugh, I stepped through the bronze frame and up to the Time Machine. I was surprised to find it had been carefully oiled and cleaned. I have suspected since that the Morlocks had even partially taken it to pieces while trying in their dim way to grasp its purpose.

'Now as I stood and examined it, finding a pleasure in the mere touch of the contrivance, the thing I had expected happened. The bronze panels suddenly slid up and struck the frame with a clang. I was in the dark—trapped. So the Morlocks thought. At that I chuckled gleefully.

'I could already hear their murmuring laughter as they came towards me. Very calmly I tried to strike the match. I had only to fix on the levers and depart then like a ghost. But I had overlooked one little thing. The matches were of that abominable kind that light only on the box.

'You may imagine how all my calm vanished. The little brutes were close upon me. One touched me. I made a sweeping blow in the dark at them with the levers, and began to scramble into the saddle of the machine. Then came one hand upon me and then another. Then I had simply to fight against their persistent fingers for my levers, and at the same time feel for the studs over which these fitted. One, indeed, they almost got away from me. As it slipped from my hand, I had to butt in the dark with my head—I could hear the Morlock's skull ring—to recover it. It was a nearer thing than the fight in the forest, I think, this last scramble.

'But at last the lever was fixed and pulled over. The clinging hands slipped from me. The darkness presently fell from my eyes. I found myself in the same grey light and tumult I have already described.

11

'I HAVE already told you of the sickness and confusion that comes with time travelling. And this time I was not seated properly in the saddle, but sideways and in an unstable fashion. For an indefinite time I clung to the machine as it swayed and vibrated, quite unheeding how I went, and when I brought myself to look at the dials again I was amazed to find where I had arrived. One dial records days, another thousands of days, another millions of days, and another thousands of millions. Now, instead of reversing the levers I had pulled them over so as to go forward with them, and when

I came to look at these indicators I found that the thousands hand was sweeping round as fast as the seconds hand of a watch—into futurity.

'As I drove on, a peculiar change crept over the appearance of things. The palpitating greyness grew darker; then—though I was still travelling with prodigious velocity—the blinking succession of day and night, which was usually indicative of a slower pace, returned, and grew more and more marked. This puzzled me very much at first. The alternations of night and day grew slower and slower, and so did the passage of the sun across the sky, until they seemed to stretch through centuries. At last a steady twilight brooded over the earth, a twilight only broken now and then when a comet glared across the darkling sky. The band of light that had indicated the sun had long since disappeared; for the sun had ceased to set—it simply rose and fell in the west, and grew ever broader and more red. All trace of the moon had vanished. The circling of the stars, growing slower and slower, had given place to creeping points of light. At last, some time before I stopped, the sun, red and very large, halted motionless upon the horizon, a vast dome glowing with a dull heat, and now and then suffering a momentary extinction. At one time it had for a little while glowed more brilliantly again, but it speedily reverted to its sullen red heat. I perceived by this slowing down of its rising and setting that the work of the tidal drag was done.* The earth had come to rest with one face to the sun, even as in our own time the moon faces the earth. Very cautiously, for I remembered my former headlong fall, I began to reverse my motion. Slower and slower went the circling hands until the thousands one seemed motionless and the daily one was no longer a mere mist upon its scale. Still slower, until the dim outlines of a desolate beach grew visible.

'I stopped very gently and sat upon the Time Machine, looking round. The sky was no longer blue. North-eastward it was inky black, and out of the blackness shone brightly and steadily the pale white stars. Overhead it was a deep Indian red and starless, and south-eastward it grew brighter to a glowing scarlet where, cut by the horizon, lay the huge hull of the sun, red and motionless. The rocks about me were of a harsh reddish colour, and all the trace of life that I could see at first was the intensely green vegetation that covered every projecting point on their south-eastern face. It was the same rich green that one sees on forest moss or on the lichen in caves: plants which like these grow in a perpetual twilight.

'The machine was standing on a sloping beach. The sea stretched away to the south-west, to rise into a sharp bright horizon against the wan sky. There were no breakers and no waves, for not a breath of wind was stirring. Only a slight oily swell rose and fell like a gentle breathing, and showed that the eternal sea was still moving and living. And along the margin where the water sometimes broke was a thick incrustation of salt—pink under the lurid sky. There was a sense of oppression in my head, and I noticed that I was breathing very fast. The sensation reminded me of my only experience of mountaineering, and from that I judged the air to be more rarefied than it is now.

'Far away up the desolate slope I heard a harsh scream, and saw a thing like a huge white butterfly go slanting and fluttering up into the sky and, circling, disappear over some low hillocks beyond. The sound of its voice was so dismal that I shivered and seated myself more firmly upon the machine. Looking round me again, I saw that, quite near, what I had taken to be a reddish mass of rock was moving slowly towards me. Then I saw the thing was really a monstrous crab-like creature. Can you imagine a crab as large as yonder table, with its many legs moving slowly and uncertainly, its big claws swaying, its long antennæ, like carters' whips, waving and feeling, and its stalked eyes gleaming at you on either side of its metallic front? Its back was corrugated and ornamented with ungainly bosses, and a greenish incrustation blotched it here and there. I could see the many palps of its complicated mouth flickering and feeling as it moved.

'As I stared at this sinister apparition crawling towards me, I felt a tickling on my cheek as though a fly had lighted there. I tried to brush it away with my hand, but in a moment it returned, and almost immediately came another by my ear. I struck at this, and caught something threadlike. It was drawn swiftly out of my hand. With a frightful qualm, I turned, and saw that I had grasped the antenna of another monster crab that stood just behind me. Its evil eyes were wriggling on their stalks, its mouth was all alive with appetite, and its vast ungainly claws, smeared with an algal slime, were descending upon me. In a moment my hand was on the lever, and I had placed a month between myself and these monsters. But I was still on the same beach, and I saw them distinctly now as soon as I stopped. Dozens of them seemed to be crawling here and there, in the sombre light, among the foliated sheets of intense green.

'I cannot convey the sense of abominable desolation that hung over the world. The red eastern sky, the northward blackness, the salt Dead Sea, the stony beach crawling with these foul, slow-stirring monsters, the uniform poisonous-looking green of the lichenous plants, the thin air that hurts one's lungs; all contributed to an appalling effect. I moved on a hundred years, and there was the same red sun—a little larger, a little duller—the same dying sea, the same chill air, and the same crowd of earthy crustacea creeping in and out among the green weed and the red rocks. And in the westward sky I saw a curved pale line like a vast new moon.

'So I travelled, stopping ever and again, in great strides of a thousand years or more, drawn on by the mystery of the earth's fate, watching with a strange fascination the sun grow larger and duller in the westward sky, and the life of the old earth ebb away. At last, more than thirty million years hence, the huge red-hot dome of the sun had come to obscure nearly a tenth part of the darkling heavens. Then I stopped once more, for the crawling multitude of crabs had disappeared, and the red beach, save for its livid green liverworts and lichens, seemed lifeless. And now it was flecked with white. A bitter cold assailed me. Rare white flakes ever and again came eddying down. To the north-eastward, the glare of snow lay under the starlight of the sable sky, and I could see an undulating crest of hillocks pinkish white. There were fringes of ice along the sea margin, with drifting masses further out; but the main expanse of that salt ocean, all bloody under the eternal sunset, was still unfrozen.

'I looked about me to see if any traces of animal life remained. A certain indefinable apprehension still kept me in the saddle of the machine. But I saw nothing moving, in earth or sky or sea. The green slime on the rocks alone testified that life was not extinct. A shallow sand-bank had appeared in the sea and the water had receded from the beach. I fancied I saw some black object flopping about upon this bank, but it became motionless as I looked at it, and I judged that my eye had been deceived, and that the black object was merely a rock. The stars in the sky were intensely bright and seemed to me to twinkle very little.

'Suddenly I noticed that the circular westward outline of the sun had changed; that a concavity, a bay, had appeared in the curve. I saw this grow larger. For a minute perhaps I stared aghast at this blackness that was creeping over the day, and then I realised that an eclipse was beginning. Either the moon or the planet Mercury was passing across the sun's disk. Naturally, at first I took it to be the moon, but there is much to incline me to believe that what I really saw was the transit of an inner planet passing very near to the earth.

'The darkness grew apace; a cold wind began to blow in freshening gusts from the east, and the showering white flakes in the air increased in number. From the edge of the sea came a ripple and whisper. Beyond these lifeless sounds the world was silent. Silent? It would be hard to convey the stillness of it. All the sounds of man, the bleating of sheep, the cries of birds, the hum of insects, the stir that makes the background of our lives—all that was over. As the darkness thickened, the eddying flakes grew more abundant, dancing before my eyes; and the cold of the air more intense. At last, one by one, swiftly, one after the other, the white peaks of the distant hills vanished into blackness. The breeze rose to a moaning wind. I saw the black central shadow of the eclipse sweeping towards me. In another moment the pale stars alone were visible. All else was rayless obscurity. The sky was absolutely black.

'A horror of this great darkness came on me. The cold, that smote to my marrow, and the pain I felt in breathing, overcame me. I shivered, and a deadly nausea seized me. Then like a red-hot bow in the sky appeared the edge of the sun. I got off the machine to recover myself. I felt giddy and incapable of facing the return journey. As I stood sick and confused I saw again the moving thing upon the shoal—there was no mistake now that it was a moving thing—against the red water of the sea. It was a round thing, the size of a football perhaps, or, it may be, bigger, and tentacles trailed down from it; it seemed black against the weltering blood-red water, and it was hopping fitfully about. Then I felt I was fainting. But a terrible dread of lying helpless in that remote and awful twilight sustained me while I clambered upon the saddle.

12

'So I came back. For a long time I must have been insensible upon the machine. The blinking succession of the days and nights was resumed, the sun got golden again, the sky blue. I breathed with greater freedom. The fluctuating contours of the land ebbed and flowed. The hands spun backward upon the dials. At last I saw again the dim shadows of houses, the evidences of decadent humanity. These, too, changed and passed, and others came. Presently, when the million dial was at zero, I slackened speed. I began to recognise our own petty and familiar architecture, the thousands hand ran back to the starting-point, the night and day flapped slower and slower. Then the old walls of the laboratory came round me. Very gently, now, I slowed the mechanism down.

'I saw one little thing that seemed odd to me. I think I have told you that when I set out, before my velocity became very high, Mrs Watchett had walked across the room, travelling, as it seemed to me, like a rocket. As I returned, I passed again across that minute when she traversed the laboratory. But now her every motion appeared to be the exact inversion of her previous ones. The door at the lower end opened, and she glided quietly up the laboratory, back foremost, and disappeared behind the door by which she had previously entered. Just before that I seemed to see Hillyer for a moment; but he passed like a flash.

'Then I stopped the machine, and saw about me again the old familiar laboratory, my tools, my appliances just as I had left them. I got off the thing very shakily, and sat down upon my bench. For several minutes I trembled violently. Then I became calmer. Around me was my old workshop again, exactly as it had been. I might have slept there, and the whole thing have been a dream.

'And yet, not exactly! The thing had started from the south-east corner of the laboratory. It had come to rest again in the north-west, against the wall where you saw it. That gives you the exact distance from my little lawn to the pedestal of the White Sphinx, into which the Morlocks had carried my machine.

'For a time my brain went stagnant. Presently I got up and came through the passage here, limping, because my heel was still painful, and feeling sorely begrimed. I saw the *Pall Mall Gazette** on the table by the door. I found the date was indeed to-day, and looking at the timepiece, saw the hour was almost eight o'clock. I heard your voices and the clatter of plates. I hesitated—I felt so sick and weak. Then I sniffed good wholesome meat, and opened the door on you. You know the rest. I washed, and dined, and now I am telling you the story.'

'I know,' he said, after a pause, 'that all this will be absolutely incredible to you. To me the one incredible thing is that I am here to-night in this old familiar room, looking into your friendly faces and telling you these strange adventures.'

He looked at the Medical Man. 'No. I cannot expect you to believe it. Take it as a lie—or a prophecy. Say I dreamed it in the workshop. Consider I have been speculating upon the destinies of our race until I have hatched this fiction. Treat my assertion of its truth as a mere stroke of art to enhance its interest. And taking it as a story, what do you think of it?'

He took up his pipe, and began, in his old accustomed manner, to tap with it nervously upon the bars of the grate. There was a momentary stillness. Then chairs began to creak and shoes to scrape upon the carpet. I took my eyes off the Time Traveller's face, and looked round at his audience. They were in the dark, and little spots of colour swam before them. The Medical Man seemed absorbed in the contemplation of our host. The Editor was looking hard at the end of his cigar—the sixth. The Journalist fumbled for his watch. The others, as far as I remember, were motionless.

The Editor stood up with a sigh. 'What a pity it is you're not a writer of stories!' he said, putting his hand on the Time Traveller's shoulder.

'You don't believe it?'

'Well——'

'I thought not.'

The Time Traveller turned to us. 'Where are the matches?' he said. He lit one and spoke over his pipe, puffing. 'To tell you the truth . . . I hardly believe it myself. . . . And yet . . .'

His eye fell with a mute inquiry upon the withered white flowers upon the little table. Then he turned over the hand holding his pipe, and I saw he was looking at some half-healed scars on his knuckles.

The Medical Man rose, came to the lamp, and examined the flowers. 'The gynæceum's odd,'* he said. The Psychologist leant forward to see, holding out his hand for a specimen.

'I'm hanged if it isn't a quarter to one,' said the Journalist. 'How shall we get home?'

'Plenty of cabs at the station,' said the Psychologist.

'It's a curious thing,' said the Medical Man; 'but I certainly don't know the natural order of these flowers. May I have them?'

The Time Traveller hesitated. Then suddenly: 'Certainly not.'

'Where did you really get them?' said the Medical Man.

The Time Traveller put his hand to his head. He spoke like one who was trying to keep hold of an idea that eluded him. 'They were put into my pocket by Weena, when I travelled into Time.' He stared round the room. 'I'm damned if it isn't all going. This room and you and the atmosphere of every day is too much for my memory. Did I ever make a Time Machine, or a model of a Time Machine? Or is it all only a dream? They say life is a dream, a precious poor dream at times—but I can't stand another that won't fit. It's madness. And where did the dream come from? . . . I must look at that machine. If there *is* one!'

He caught up the lamp swiftly, and carried it, flaring red, through the door into the corridor. We followed him. There in the flickering light of the lamp was the machine sure enough, squat, ugly, and askew; a thing of brass, ebony, ivory, and translucent glimmering quartz. Solid to the touch—for I put out my hand and felt the rail of it—and with brown spots and smears upon the ivory, and bits of grass and moss upon the lower parts, and one rail bent awry.

The Time Traveller put the lamp down on the bench, and ran his hand along the damaged rail. 'It's all right now,' he said. 'The story I told you was true. I'm sorry to have brought you out here in the cold.' He took up the lamp, and, in an absolute silence, we returned to the smoking-room.

He came into the hall with us and helped the Editor on with his coat. The Medical Man looked into his face and, with a certain hesitation, told him he was suffering from overwork, at which he laughed hugely. I remember him standing in the open doorway, bawling good night.

I shared a cab with the Editor. He thought the tale a 'gaudy lie.' For my own part I was unable to come to a conclusion. The story was so fantastic and incredible, the telling so credible and sober. I lay awake most of the night thinking about it. I determined to go next day and see the Time Traveller again. I was told he was in the laboratory, and being on easy terms in the house, I went up to him. The laboratory, however, was empty. I stared for a minute at the Time Machine and put out my hand and touched the lever. At that the squat substantial-looking mass swayed like a bough shaken by the wind. Its instability startled me extremely, and I had a queer reminiscence of the childish days when I used to be forbidden to meddle. I came back through the corridor. The Time Traveller met me in the smoking-room. He was coming from the house. He had a small camera under one arm and a knapsack under the other. He laughed when he saw me, and gave me an elbow to shake. 'I'm frightfully busy,' said he, 'with that thing in there.'

'But is it not some hoax?' I said. 'Do you really travel through time?'

'Really and truly I do.' And he looked frankly into my eyes. He hesitated. His eye wandered about the room. 'I only want half an hour,' he said. 'I know why you came, and it's awfully good of you. There's some magazines here. If you'll stop to lunch I'll prove you this time travelling up to the hilt, specimens and all. If you'll forgive my leaving you now?'

I consented, hardly comprehending then the full import of his words, and he nodded and went on down the corridor. I heard the door of the laboratory slam, seated myself in a chair, and took up a daily paper. What was he going to do before lunch-time? Then suddenly I was reminded by an advertisement that I had promised to meet Richardson, the publisher, at two. I looked at my watch, and saw that I could barely save that engagement. I got up and went down the passage to tell the Time Traveller.

As I took hold of the handle of the door I heard an exclamation, oddly truncated at the end, and a click and a thud. A gust of air whirled round me as I opened the door, and from within came the sound of broken glass falling on the floor. The Time Traveller was not there. I seemed to see a ghostly, indistinct figure sitting in a whirling mass of black and brass for a moment—a figure so transparent that the bench behind with its sheets of drawings was absolutely distinct; but this phantasm vanished as I rubbed my eyes. The Time Machine had gone. Save for a subsiding stir of dust, the further end of the laboratory was empty. A pane of the skylight had, apparently, just been blown in.

I felt an unreasonable amazement. I knew that something strange had happened, and for the moment could not distinguish what the strange thing might be. As I stood staring, the door into the garden opened, and the man-servant appeared.

We looked at each other. Then ideas began to come. 'Has Mr —— gone out that way?' said I.

'No, sir. No one has come out this way. I was expecting to find him here.'

At that I understood. At the risk of disappointing Richardson I stayed on, waiting for the Time Traveller; waiting for the second, perhaps still stranger story, and the specimens and photographs he would bring with him. But I am beginning now to fear that I must wait a lifetime. The Time Traveller vanished three years ago. And, as everybody knows now, he has never returned.

EPILOGUE

ONE cannot choose but wonder. Will he ever return? It may be that he swept back into the past, and fell among the blood-drinking, hairy savages of the Age of Unpolished Stone; into the abysses of the Cretaceous Sea; or among the grotesque saurians, the huge reptilian brutes of the Jurassic times. He may even now—if I may use the phrase—be wandering on some plesiosaurus-haunted Oolitic coral reef,* or beside the lonely saline lakes of the Triassic Age. Or did he go forward, into one of the nearer ages, in which men are still men, but with the riddles of our own time answered and its wearisome problems solved? Into the manhood of the race: for I, for my own part, cannot think that these latter days of weak experiment, fragmentary theory, and mutual discord are indeed man's culminating time! I say, for my own part. He, I know—for the question had been discussed among us long before the Time Machine was made—thought but cheerlessly of the Advancement of Mankind, and saw in the growing pile of civilisation only a foolish heaping that must inevitably fall back upon and destroy its makers in the end. If that is so, it remains for us to live as though it were not so. But to me the future is still black and blank—is a vast ignorance, lit at a few casual places by the memory of his story. And I have by me, for my comfort, two strange white flowers—shrivelled now, and brown and flat and brittle—to witness that even when mind and strength had gone, gratitude and a mutual tenderness still lived on in the heart of man.

THE ISLAND OF
DOCTOR MOREAU

CONTENTS

I.	In the Dingey of the 'Lady Vain'	97
II.	The Man Who Was Going Nowhere	100
III.	The Strange Face	103
IV.	At the Schooner's Rail	108
V.	The Landing on the Island	111
VI.	The Evil-Looking Boatmen	115
VII.	The Locked Door	120
VIII.	The Crying of the Puma	124
IX.	The Thing in the Forest	127
X.	The Crying of the Man	137
XI.	The Hunting of the Man	140
XII.	The Sayers of the Law	145
XIII.	A Parley	153
XIV.	Doctor Moreau Explains	158
XV.	Concerning the Beast Folk	168
XVI.	How the Beast Folk Tasted Blood	173
XVII.	A Catastrophe	186
XVIII.	The Finding of Moreau	190
XIX.	Montgomery's 'Bank Holiday'	194
XX.	Alone with the Beast Folk	202
XXI.	The Reversion of the Beast Folk	207
XXII.	The Man Alone	218

I

IN THE DINGEY* OF THE 'LADY VAIN'

I DO not propose to add anything to what has already been written concerning the loss of the *Lady Vain*. As everyone knows, she collided with a derelict when ten days out from Callao.* The long-boat with seven of the crew was picked up eighteen days after by HM gun-boat *Myrtle*, and the story of their privations has become almost as well known as the far more terrible *Medusa* case.* I have now, however, to add to the published story of the *Lady Vain* another as horrible, and certainly far stranger. It has hitherto been supposed that the four men who were in the dingey perished, but this is incorrect. I have the best of evidence for this assertion—I am one of the four men.

But, in the first place, I must state that there never were four men in the dingey; the number was three. Constans, who was 'seen by the captain to jump into the gig'* (*Daily News*, March 17, 1887), luckily for us, and unluckily for himself, did not reach us. He came down out of the tangle of ropes under the stays of the smashed bowsprit; some small rope caught his heel as he let go and he hung for a moment head downward, and then fell and struck a block or spar floating in the water. We pulled towards him, but he never came up.

I say luckily for us he did not reach us, and I might also add luckily for himself, for there were only a small breaker of water* and some soddened ship's biscuits with us—so sudden had been the alarm, so unprepared the ship for any disaster. We thought the people on the launch would be better provisioned (though it seems they were not), and we tried to hail them. They could not have heard us, and the next morning when the drizzle cleared—which was not until past midday—we could see nothing of them. We could not

97

stand up to look about us because of the pitching of the boat. The sea ran in great rollers, and we had much ado to keep the boat's head to them. The two other men who had escaped so far with me were a man named Helmar, a passenger like myself, and a seaman whose name I don't know, a short sturdy man with a stammer.

We drifted famishing, and, after our water had come to an end, tormented by an intolerable thirst, for eight days altogether. After the second day the sea subsided slowly to a glassy calm. It is quite impossible for the ordinary reader to imagine those eight days. He has not—luckily for himself—anything in his memory to imagine with. After the first day we said little to one another, and lay in our places in the boat and stared at the horizon, or watched, with eyes that grew larger and more haggard every day, the misery and weakness gaining upon our companions. The sun became pitiless. The water ended on the fourth day, and we were already thinking strange things and saying them with our eyes; but it was, I think, the sixth before Helmar gave voice to the thing we all had in mind. I remember our voices dry and thin, so that we bent towards one another and spared our words. I stood out against it with all my might, was rather for scuttling the boat and perishing together among the sharks that followed us; but when Helmar said that if his proposal was accepted we should have drink, the sailor came round to him.

I would not draw lots, however, and in the night the sailor whispered to Helmar again and again, and I sat in the bows with my clasp-knife in my hand—though I doubt if I had the stuff in me to fight. And in the morning I agreed to Helmar's proposal, and we handed halfpence to find the odd man.

The lot fell upon the sailor, but he was the strongest of us and would not abide by it, and attacked Helmar with his hands. They grappled together and almost stood up. I crawled along the boat to them, intending to help Helmar by grasping the sailor's leg, but the sailor stumbled with the swaying of the boat, and the two fell upon the gunwale and rolled overboard together. They sank like stones. I remember laughing at that and wondering why I laughed. The laugh caught me suddenly like a thing from without.

I lay across one of the thwarts* for I know not how long, thinking that if I had the strength I would drink sea water and madden myself to die quickly. And even as I lay there I saw, with no more interest than if it had been a picture, a sail come up towards me over the sky-line. My mind must have been wandering, and yet I remember all that happened quite distinctly. I remember how my head swayed with the seas, and the horizon with the sail above it danced up and down. But I also remember as distinctly that I had a persuasion that I was dead, and that I thought what a jest it was they should come too late by such a little to catch me in my body.

For an endless period, as it seemed to me, I lay with my head on the thwart watching the dancing schooner—she was a little ship, schooner-rigged fore and aft—come up out of the sea. She kept tacking to and fro in a widening compass, for she was sailing dead into the wind. It never entered my head to attempt to attract attention, and I do not remember anything distinctly after the sight of her side, until I found myself in a little cabin aft. There is a dim half memory of being lifted up to the gangway and of a big round countenance, covered with freckles and surrounded with red hair, staring at me over the bulwarks. I also had a disconnected impression of a dark face with extraordinary eyes close to mine, but that I thought was a nightmare until I met it again. I fancy I recollect some stuff being poured in between my teeth. And that is all.

II

THE MAN WHO WAS GOING NOWHERE

THE cabin in which I found myself was small and rather untidy. A youngish man with flaxen hair, a bristly straw-coloured moustache, and a dropping nether lip was sitting and holding my wrist. For a minute we stared at one another without speaking. He had watery grey expressionless eyes.

Then just overhead came a sound like an iron bedstead being knocked about and the low angry growling of some large animal. At the same time the man spoke again.

He repeated his question: 'How do you feel now?'

I think I said I felt all right. I could not recollect how I had got there. He must have seen the question in my face, for my voice was inaccessible to me.

'You were picked up in a boat—starving. The name on the boat was the *Lady Vain*, and there were queer marks on the gunwale.'* At the same time my eye caught my hand, so thin that it looked like a dirty skin purse full of loose bones, and all the business of the boat came back to me.

'Have some of this,' said he, and gave me a dose of some scarlet stuff, iced.

It tasted like blood, and made me feel stronger.

'You were in luck,' said he, 'to get picked up by a ship with a medical man aboard.' He spoke with a slobbering articulation, with the ghost of a lisp.

'What ship is this?' I said slowly, hoarse from my long silence.

'It's a little trader from Arica* and Callao. I never asked where she came from in the beginning. Out of the land of born fools, I guess. I'm a passenger myself from Arica. The silly ass who owns her—he's captain too, named Davis—he's lost his certificate or something. You know the kind of man—calls the thing the *Ipecacuanha*—of all silly infernal names, though when there's much of a sea without any wind she certainly acts according.'*

Then the noise overhead began again, a snarling growl and the voice of a human being together. Then another voice telling some 'Heaven-forsaken idiot' to desist.

'You were nearly dead,' said my interlocutor. 'It was a very near thing indeed. But I've put some stuff into you now. Notice your arms sore? Injections. You've been insensible for nearly thirty hours.'

I thought slowly. I was distracted now by the yelping of a number of dogs. 'May I have solid food?' I asked.

'Thanks to me,' he said. 'Even now the mutton is boiling.'

'Yes,' I said, with assurance; 'I could eat some mutton.'

'But,' said he, with a momentary hesitation, 'you know I'm dying to hear how you came to be alone in the boat.' I thought I detected a certain suspicion in his eyes.

'Damn that howling!'

He suddenly left the cabin, and I heard him in violent controversy with some one who seemed to me to talk gibberish in response to him. The matter sounded as though it ended in blows, but in that I thought my ears were mistaken. Then he shouted at the dogs and returned to the cabin.

'Well?' said he, in the doorway. 'You were just beginning to tell me.'

I told him my name, Edward Prendick, and how I had taken to natural history as a relief from the dulness of my comfortable independence. He seemed interested in this. 'I've done some science myself—I did my Biology at University College,—getting out the ovary of the earthworm and the radula of the snail* and all that. Lord! it's ten years ago. But go on, go on—tell me about the boat.'

He was evidently satisfied with the frankness of my story, which I told in concise sentences enough,—for I felt horribly weak,—and when it was finished he reverted presently to the topic of natural history and his own biological studies. He began to question me closely about Tottenham Court Road and Gower Street. 'Is Caplatzi still flourishing? What a shop that was!'* He had evidently been a very ordinary medical student, and drifted incontinently to the topic of the music-halls. He told me some anecdotes. 'Left it all,' he said, 'ten years ago. How jolly it used to be! But I made a young ass of myself. . . . Played myself out before I was twenty-one. I dare say it's all different now. . . . But I must look up that ass of a cook and see what he's doing to your mutton.'

The growling overhead was renewed, so suddenly and with so much savage anger that it startled me. 'What's that?' I called after him, but the door had closed. He came back again with the boiled mutton, and I was so excited by the appetising smell of it, that I forgot the noise of the beast forthwith.

After a day of alternate sleep and feeding I was so far recovered as to be able to get from my bunk to the scuttle* and see the green seas trying to keep pace with us. I judged the schooner was running before the wind. Montgomery—that was the name of the flaxen-haired man—came in again as I stood there, and I asked him for some clothes. He lent me some duck things* of his own, for those I had worn in the boat, he said, had been thrown overboard. They were rather loose for me, for he was large and long in his limbs.

He told me casually that the captain was three parts drunk in his own cabin. As I assumed the clothes I began asking him some questions about the destination of the ship. He said the ship was bound to Hawaii, but that it had to land him first.

'Where?' said I.

'It's an island. . . . Where I live. So far as I know, it hasn't got a name.'

He stared at me with his nether lip dropping, and looked so wilfully stupid of a sudden that it came into my head that he desired to avoid my questions. 'I'm ready,' I said. He led the way out of the cabin.

III

THE STRANGE FACE

AT the companion* was a man obstructing our way. He was standing on the ladder with his back to us, peering over the combing of the hatchway.* He was, I could see, a misshapen man, short, broad, and clumsy, with a crooked back, a hairy neck, and a head sunk between his shoulders. He was dressed in dark blue serge, and had peculiarly thick coarse black hair. I heard the unseen dogs growl furiously, and forthwith he ducked back, coming into contact with the hand I put out to fend him off from myself. He turned with animal swiftness.

The black face thus flashed upon me startled me profoundly. The facial part projected, forming something dimly suggestive of a muzzle, and the huge half-open mouth showed as big white teeth as I had ever seen in a human mouth. His eyes were bloodshot at the edges, with scarcely a rim of white round the hazel pupils. There was a curious glow of excitement in his face.

'Confound you!' said Montgomery. 'Why the devil don't you get out of the way?' The black-faced man started aside without a word.

I went on up the companion, still staring at him almost against my will as I did so. Montgomery stayed at the foot for a moment. 'You have no business here, you know,' he said in a deliberate tone. 'Your place is forward.'

The black-faced man cowered. 'They . . . won't have me forward.' He spoke slowly, with a hoarse quality in his voice.

'Won't have you forward!' said Montgomery in a menacing voice. 'But I tell you to go.' He was on the brink of saying something further, then looked up at me suddenly and followed me up the ladder. I had paused half-way through the hatchway, looking back, still astonished beyond measure at the grotesque ugliness of this black-faced creature. I had never beheld such a repulsive and extraordinary face before, and yet—if the contradiction is credible—I experienced at the same time an odd feeling that in some way I *had* already encountered exactly the features and gestures that now amazed me. Afterwards it occurred to me that probably I had seen him as I was lifted aboard, and yet that scarcely satisfied my suspicion of a previous acquaintance. Yet how one could have set eyes on so singular a face and have forgotten the precise occasion passed my imagination.

Montgomery's movement to follow me released my attention, and I turned and looked about me at the flush deck of the little schooner. I was already half prepared by the sounds I had heard for what I saw. Certainly I never beheld a deck so dirty. It was littered with scraps of carrot, shreds of green stuff, and indescribable filth. Fastened by chains to the mainmast were a number of grisly staghounds, who now began leaping and barking at me, and by the mizzen a huge puma was cramped in a little iron cage, far too small even to give it turning-room. Further under the starboard bulwark were some big hutches containing a number of rabbits, and a solitary llama was squeezed in a mere box of a cage forward. The dogs were muzzled by leather straps. The only human being on deck was a gaunt and silent sailor at the wheel.

The patched and dirty spankers* were tense before the wind, and up aloft the little ship seemed carrying every sail she had. The sky was clear, the sun midway down the western sky; long waves, capped by the breeze with froth, were running with us. We went past the steersman to the taffrail* and stared side by side for a space at the water foaming under the stern and the bubbles dancing and vanishing in her wake. I turned and surveyed the unsavoury length of the ship.

'Is this an ocean menagerie?' said I.

'Looks like it,' said Montgomery.

'What are these beasts for? Merchandise, curios? Does the captain think he is going to sell them somewhere in the South Seas?'

'It looks like it, doesn't it?' said Montgomery, and turned towards the wake again.

Suddenly we heard a yelp and a volley of furious blasphemy coming from the companion hatchway, and the deformed man with the black face clambered up hurriedly. He was immediately followed by a heavy red-haired man in a white cap. At the sight of the former the staghounds, who had all tired of barking at me by this time, became furiously excited, howling and leaping against their chains. The black hesitated before them, and this gave the red-haired man time to come up with him and deliver a tremendous blow between the shoulder-blades with his fist. The poor devil went down like a felled ox, and rolled in the dirt among the furiously excited dogs. It was lucky for him they were muzzled. The red-haired man gave a yawp of exultation and stood staggering and, as it seemed to me, in serious danger of either going backward down the companion hatchway, or forward upon his victim.

So soon as the second man had appeared, Montgomery had started violently. 'Steady on there!' he cried, in a tone of remonstrance. A couple of sailors appeared on the forecastle.

The black-faced man, howling in a singular voice, rolled about under the feet of the dogs. No one attempted to help him. The brutes did their best to worry him, butting their muzzles at him. There was a quick dance of their lithe grey bodies over the clumsy prostrate figure. The sailors forward shouted to them as though it was admirable sport. Montgomery gave an angry exclamation, and went striding down the deck. I followed him.

In another second the black-faced man had scrambled up and was staggering forward. He stumbled up against the bulwark by the main shrouds, where he remained panting and glaring over his shoulder at the dogs. The red-haired man laughed a satisfied laugh.

'Look here, captain,' said Montgomery, with his lisp a little accentuated, gripping the elbows of the red-haired man; 'this won't do.'

I stood behind Montgomery. The captain came half round and regarded him with the dull and solemn eyes of a drunken man. 'Wha' won't do?' he said; and added, after looking sleepily into Montgomery's face for a minute, 'Blasted Sawbones!'

With a sudden movement he shook his arms free, and after two ineffectual attempts stuck his freckled fists into his side-pockets.

'That man's a passenger,' said Montgomery. 'I'd advise you to keep your hands off him.'

'Go to hell!' said the captain loudly. He suddenly turned and staggered towards the side. 'Do what I like on my own ship,' he said.

I think Montgomery might have left him then—seeing the brute was drunk. But he only turned a shade paler, and followed the captain to the bulwarks.

'Look here, captain,' he said. 'That man of mine is not to be ill-treated. He has been hazed* ever since he came aboard.'

For a minute alcoholic fumes kept the captain speechless. 'Blasted Sawbones!' was all he considered necessary.

I could see that Montgomery had an ugly temper, and I saw too that this quarrel had been some time growing. 'The man's drunk,' said I, perhaps officiously; 'you'll do no good.'

Montgomery gave an ugly twist to his dropping lip. 'He's always drunk. Do you think that excuses his assaulting his passengers?'

'My ship,' began the captain, waving his hand unsteadily towards the cages, 'was a clean ship. Look at it now.' It was certainly anything but clean. 'Crew,' continued the captain, 'clean respectable crew.'

'You agreed to take the beasts.'

'I wish I'd never set eyes on your infernal island. What the devil . . . want beasts for on an island like that? Then that man of yours . . . Understood he was a man. He's a lunatic. And he hadn't no business aft. Do you think the whole damned ship belongs to you?'

'Your sailors began to haze the poor devil as soon as he came aboard.'

'That's just what he is—he's a devil, an ugly devil. My men can't stand him. *I* can't stand him. None of us can't stand him. Nor *you* either.'

Montgomery turned away. '*You* leave that man alone, anyhow,' he said, nodding his head as he spoke.

But the captain meant to quarrel now. He raised his voice: 'If he comes this end of the ship again I'll cut his insides out, I tell you. Cut out his blasted insides! Who are *you* to tell *me* what *I'm* to do. I tell you I'm captain of the ship—Captain and Owner. I'm the law here, I tell you—the law and the prophets.* I bargained to take a man and his attendant to and from Arica and bring back some animals. I never bargained to carry a mad devil and a silly Sawbones, a ——'

Well, never mind what he called Montgomery. I saw the latter take a step forward, and interposed. 'He's drunk,' said I. The captain began some abuse even fouler than the last. 'Shut up,' I said, turning on him sharply, for I had seen danger in Montgomery's white face. With that I brought the downpour on myself.

However, I was glad to avert what was uncommonly near a scuffle, even at the price of the captain's drunken ill-will. I do not think I have ever heard quite so much vile language come in a continuous stream from any man's lips before, though I have frequented eccentric company enough. I found some of it hard to endure—though I am a mild-tempered man. But certainly when I told the captain to shut up I had forgotten I was merely a bit of human flotsam, cut off from my resources and with my fare unpaid, a mere casual dependant on the bounty—or speculative enterprise—of the ship. He reminded me of it with considerable vigour. But at any rate I prevented a fight.

IV

AT THE SCHOONER'S RAIL

THAT night land was sighted after sundown, and the schooner hove to. Montgomery intimated that was his destination. It was too far to see any details; it seemed to me then simply a low-lying patch of dim blue in the uncertain blue-grey sea. An almost vertical streak of smoke went up from it into the sky.

The captain was not on deck when it was sighted. After he had vented his wrath on me he had staggered below, and I understand he went to sleep on the floor of his own cabin. The mate practically assumed the command. He was the gaunt, taciturn individual we had seen at the wheel. Apparently he too was in an evil temper with Montgomery. He took not the slightest notice of either of us. We dined with him in a sulky silence, after a few ineffectual efforts on my part to talk. It struck me, too, that the men regarded my companion and his animals in a singularly unfriendly manner. I found Montgomery very reticent about his purpose with these creatures and about his destination, and though I was sensible of a growing curiosity I did not press him.

We remained talking on the quarter-deck until the sky was thick with stars. Except for an occasional sound in the yellow-lit forecastle, and a movement of the animals now and then, the night was very still. The puma lay crouched together, watching us with shining eyes, a black heap in the corner of its cage. The dogs seemed to be asleep. Montgomery produced some cigars.

He talked to me of London in a tone of half-painful reminiscence, asking all kinds of questions about changes that had taken place. He spoke like a man who had loved his life there, and had been suddenly and irrevocably cut off from it. I gossiped as well as I could of this and that. All the time the strangeness of him was shaping itself in my mind, and as I talked I peered at his odd pallid face in the dim light of the binnacle lantern behind me. Then I looked out at the darkling sea, where in the dimness his little island was hidden.

This man, it seemed to me, had come out of Immensity merely to save my life. To-morrow he would drop over the side and vanish again out of my existence. Even had it been under commonplace circumstances it would have made me a trifle thoughtful. But in the first place was the singularity of an educated man living on this unknown little island, and coupled with that, the extraordinary nature of his luggage. I found myself repeating the captain's question: What did he want with the beasts? Why, too, had he pretended they were not his when I had remarked about them at first? Then again, in his personal attendant there was a bizarre quality that had impressed me profoundly. These circumstances threw a haze of mystery round the man. They laid hold of my imagination and hampered my tongue.

Towards midnight our talk of London died away, and we stood side by side leaning over the bulwarks, and staring dreamily over the silent starlit sea, each pursuing his own thoughts. It was the atmosphere for sentiment, and I began upon my gratitude.

'If I may say it,' said I, after a time, 'you have saved my life.'

'Chance,' he answered; 'just chance.'

'I prefer to make my thanks to the accessible agent.'

'Thank no one. You had the need, and I the knowledge, and I injected and fed you much as I might have collected a specimen. I was bored, and wanted something to do. If I'd been jaded that day, or hadn't liked your face, well—it's a curious question where you would have been now.'

This damped my mood a little. 'At any rate—' I began.

'It's a chance, I tell you,' he interrupted, 'as everything is in a man's life. Only the asses won't see it. Why am I here now—an outcast from civilisation—instead of being a happy man enjoying all the pleasures of London? Simply because—

eleven years ago—I lost my head for ten minutes on a foggy night.'

He stopped. 'Yes?' said I.

'That's all.'

We relapsed into silence. Presently he laughed. 'There's something in this starlight that loosens one's tongue. I'm an ass, and yet somehow I would like to tell you.'

'Whatever you tell me, you may rely upon my keeping to myself. . . . If that's it.'

He was on the point of beginning, and then shook his head doubtfully. 'Don't,' said I. 'It is all the same to me. After all, it is better to keep your secret. There's nothing gained but a little relief, if I respect your confidence. If I don't . . . well?'

He grunted undecidedly. I felt I had him at a disadvantage, had caught him in the mood of indiscretion; and, to tell the truth, I was not curious to learn what might have driven a young medical student out of London. I have an imagination. I shrugged my shoulders, and turned away. Over the taffrail leaned a silent black figure, staring at the waves. It was Montgomery's strange attendant. It looked over its shoulder quickly with my movement, then looked away again.

It may seem a little thing to you, perhaps, but it came like a sudden blow to me. The only light near us was a lantern at the wheel. The creature's face was turned for one brief instant out of the dimness of the stern towards this illumination, and I saw that the eyes that glanced at me shone with a pale-green light.

I did not know then that a reddish luminosity, at least, is not uncommon in human eyes. The thing came to me as a stark inhumanity. That black figure, with its eyes of fire, struck down through all my adult thoughts and feelings, and for a moment the forgotten horrors of childhood came back to my mind. Then the effect passed as it had come. An uncouth black figure of a man, a figure of no particular import, hung over the taffrail, against the starlight, and I found Montgomery was speaking to me.

'I'm thinking of turning in, then,' said he; 'if you've had enough of this.'

I answered him incongruously. We went below, and he wished me good night at the door of my cabin.

That night I had some very unpleasant dreams. The waning moon rose late. Its light struck a ghostly faint white beam across my cabin, and made an ominous shape on the planking by my bunk. Then the staghounds woke and began howling and baying, so that I dreamed fitfully and scarcely slept until the approach of dawn.

V

THE LANDING ON THE ISLAND

IN the early morning—it was the second morning after my recovery, and I believe the fourth after I was picked up—I awoke through an avenue of tumultuous dreams, dreams of guns and howling mobs, and became sensible of a hoarse shouting above me. I rubbed my eyes, and lay listening to the noise, doubtful for a little while of my whereabouts. Then came a sudden pattering of bare feet, the sound of heavy objects being thrown about, a violent creaking and rattling of chains. I heard the swish of the water as the ship was suddenly brought round, and a foamy yellow-green wave flew across the little round window and left it streaming. I jumped into my clothes and went on deck.

As I came up the ladder I saw against the flushed sky—for the sun was just rising—the broad back and red hair of the captain, and over his shoulder the puma spinning from a tackle rigged on to the mizzen spanker-boom. The poor brute seemed horribly scared, and crouched in the bottom of its little cage. 'Overboard with 'em!' bawled the captain. 'Overboard with 'em! We'll have a clean ship soon of the whole bilin' of 'em.'*

He stood in my way, so that I had perforce to tap his shoulder to come on deck. He came round with a start, and staggered back a few paces to stare at me. It needed no expert eye to tell that the man was still drunk. 'Hullo!' said he stupidly, and then with a light coming into his eyes, 'Why, it's Mister—Mister——?'

'Prendick,' said I.

'Prendick be damned!' said he. 'Shut Up—that's your name. Mister Shut Up.'

It was no good answering the brute. But I certainly did not expect his next move. He held out his hand to the gangway by which Montgomery stood talking to a massive white-haired man in dirty blue flannels, who had apparently just come aboard. 'That way, Mister Blasted Shut Up. That way,' roared the captain.

Montgomery and his companion turned as he spoke.

'What do you mean?' said I.

'That way, Mister Blasted Shut Up—that's what I mean. Overboard, Mister Shut Up—and sharp. We're clearing the ship out, cleaning the whole blessed ship out. And overboard you go.'

I stared at him dumbfounded. Then it occurred to me it was exactly the thing I wanted. The lost prospect of a journey as sole passenger with this quarrelsome sot was not one to mourn over. I turned towards Montgomery.

'Can't have you,' said Montgomery's companion concisely.

'You can't have me!' said I, aghast. He had the squarest and most resolute face I ever set eyes upon.

'Look here,' I began, turning to the captain.

'Overboard,' said the captain. 'This ship ain't for beasts and worse than beasts, any more. Overboard you go . . . Mister Shut Up. If they can't have you, you goes adrift. But anyhow you go! With your Friends. I've done with this blessed island forevermore amen! I've had enough of it.'

'But, Montgomery,' I appealed.

He distorted his lower lip, and nodded his head hopelessly

at the grey-haired man beside him, to indicate his powerless-ness to help me.

'I'll see to *you* presently,' said the captain.

Then began a curious three-cornered altercation. Alternately I appealed to one and another of the three men, first to the grey-haired man to let me land, and then to the drunken captain to keep me aboard. I even bawled entreaties to the sailors. Montgomery said never a word; only shook his head. 'You're going overboard, I tell you,' was the captain's refrain. . . . 'Law be damned! I'm king here.'

At last, I must confess, my voice suddenly broke in the middle of a vigorous threat. I felt a gust of hysterical petulance, and went aft, and stared dismally at nothing.

Meanwhile the sailors progressed rapidly with the task of unshipping the packages and caged animals. A large launch with two standing lugs* lay under the lee of the schooner, and into this the assortment of goods was swung. I did not then see the hands from the island that were receiving the packages, for the hull of the launch was hidden from me by the side of the schooner.

Neither Montgomery nor his companion took the slightest notice of me, but busied themselves in assisting and directing the four or five sailors who were unloading the goods. The captain went forward, interfering rather than assisting. I was alternately despairful and desperate. Once or twice, as I stood waiting there for things to accomplish themselves, I could not resist an impulse to laugh at my miserable quandary. I felt all the wretcheder for the lack of a breakfast. Hunger and a shortage of blood-corpuscles take all the manhood from a man. I perceived pretty clearly that I had not the stamina either to resist what the captain chose to do to expel me, or to force myself upon Montgomery and his companion. So I waited passively upon fate, and the work of transferring Montgomery's possessions to the launch went on as if I did not exist.

Presently that work was finished, and then came a struggle;

I was hauled, resisting weakly enough, to the gangway. Even then I noticed the oddness of the brown faces of the men who were with Montgomery in the launch. But the launch was now fully laden, and was shoved off hastily. A broadening gap of green water appeared under me, and I pushed back with all my strength to avoid falling headlong.

The hands in the launch shouted derisively, and I heard Montgomery curse at them. And then the captain, the mate and one of the seamen helping him, ran me aft towards the stern. The dingey of the *Lady Vain* had been towing behind; it was half full of water, had no oars, and was quite unvictualled. I refused to go aboard her, and flung myself full-length on the deck. In the end they swung me into her by a rope—for they had no stern ladder—and cut me adrift.

I drifted slowly from the schooner. In a kind of stupor I watched all hands take to the rigging and slowly but surely she came round to the wind. The sails fluttered, and then bellied out as the wind came into them. I stared at her weather-beaten side heeling steeply towards me. And then she passed out of my range of view.

I did not turn my head to follow her. At first I could scarcely believe what had happened. I crouched in the bottom of the dingey, stunned, and staring blankly at the vacant oily sea. Then I realised I was in that little hell of mine again, now half-swamped. Looking back over the gunwale I saw the schooner standing away from me, with the red-haired captain mocking at me over the taffrail; and, turning towards the island, saw the launch growing smaller as she approached the beach.

Abruptly the cruelty of this desertion became clear to me. I had no means of reaching the land unless I should chance to drift there. I was still weak, you must remember, from my exposure in the boat; I was empty and very faint, or I should have had more heart. But as it was I suddenly began to sob and weep as I had never done since I was a little child. The tears ran down my face. In a passion of despair I struck with my fists at the water in the bottom of the boat, and kicked savagely at the gunwale. I prayed aloud to God that he would let me die.

VI

THE EVIL-LOOKING BOATMEN

BUT the islanders, seeing I was really adrift, took pity on me. I drifted very slowly to the eastward, approaching the island slantingly, and presently I saw with hysterical relief the launch come round and return towards me. She was heavily laden, and as she drew near I could make out Montgomery's white-haired broad-shouldered companion sitting cramped up with the dogs and several packing-cases in the stern-sheets. This individual stared fixedly at me without moving or speaking. The black-faced cripple was glaring at me as fixedly in the bows near the puma. There were three other men besides, strange brutish-looking fellows, at whom the staghounds were snarling savagely. Montgomery, who was steering, brought the boat by me and, rising, caught and fastened my painter to the tiller* to tow me—for there was no room aboard.

I had recovered from my hysterical phase by this time, and answered his hail as he approached bravely enough. I told him the dingey was nearly swamped, and he reached me a piggin.* I was jerked back as the rope tightened between the boats. For some time I was busy baling.

It was not until I had got the water under—for the water in the dingey had been shipped, the boat was perfectly sound—that I had leisure to look at the people in the launch again.

The white-haired man, I found, was still regarding me steadfastly, but with an expression, as I now fancied, of some perplexity. When my eyes met his he looked down at the staghounds that sat between his knees. He was a powerfully

115

built man, as I have said, with a fine forehead and rather heavy features; but his eyes had that odd drooping of the skin above the lids that often comes with advancing years, and the fall of his heavy mouth at the corners gave him an expression of pugnacious resolution. He talked to Montgomery in a tone too low for me to hear. From him my eyes travelled to his three men, and a strange crew they were. I saw only their faces, yet there was something in their faces—I knew not what—that gave me a spasm of disgust. I looked steadily at them, and the impression did not pass though I failed to see what had occasioned it. They seemed to me then to be brown men, but their limbs were oddly swathed in some thin dirty white stuff down even to the fingers and feet. I have never seen men so wrapped up before, and women so only in the East. They wore turbans, too, and thereunder peered out their elfin faces at me, faces with protruding lower jaws and bright eyes. They had lank black hair almost like horse-hair, and seemed, as they sat, to exceed in stature any race of men I have seen. The white-haired man, who I knew was a good six feet in height, sat a head below any one of the three. I found afterwards that really none were taller than myself, but their bodies were abnormally long and the thigh part of the leg short and curiously twisted. At any rate they were an amazingly ugly gang, and over the heads of them, under the forward lug, peered the black face of the man whose eyes were luminous in the dark.

As I stared at them they met my gaze, and then first one and then another turned away from my direct stare and looked at me in an odd furtive manner. It occurred to me that I was perhaps annoying them, and I turned my attention to the island we were approaching.

It was low, and covered with thick vegetation, chiefly of the inevitable palm-trees. From one point a thin white thread of vapour rose slantingly to an immense height, and then frayed out like a down feather. We were now within the embrace of a broad bay flanked on either hand by a low promontory. The beach was of a dull grey sand, and sloped steeply up to a ridge, perhaps sixty or seventy feet above the sea-level, and irregularly set with trees and undergrowth. Half-way up was a square stone enclosure that I found subsequently was built partly of coral and partly of pumiceous lava. Two thatched roofs peeped from within this enclosure.

A man stood awaiting us at the water's edge. I fancied, while we were still far off, that I saw some other and very grotesque-looking creatures scuttle into the bushes upon the slope, but I saw nothing of these as we drew nearer. This man was of a moderate size, and with a black negroid face. He had a large, almost lipless mouth, extraordinary, lank arms, long thin feet and bow legs, and stood with his heavy face thrust forward staring at us. He was dressed like Montgomery and his white-haired companion, in jacket and trousers of blue serge.

As we came still nearer, this individual began to run to and fro on the beach, making the most grotesque movements. At a word of command from Montgomery the four men in the launch sprang up with singular awkward gestures and struck the lugs. Montgomery steered us round and into a narrow little dock excavated in the beach. Then the man on the beach hastened towards us. This dock, as I call it, was really a mere ditch just long enough at this phase of the tide to take the long-boat.

I heard the bows ground in the sand, staved the dingey off the rudder of the big boat with my piggin, and, freeing the painter, landed. The three muffled men, with the clumsiest movements, scrambled out upon the sand, and forthwith set to landing the cargo, assisted by the man on the beach. I was struck especially with the curious movements of the legs of the three swathed and bandaged boatmen—not stiff they were, but distorted in some odd way, almost as if they were jointed in the wrong place. The dogs were still snarling, and strained at their chains after these men, as the white-haired man landed with them.

The three big fellows spoke to one another in odd guttural tones, and the man who had waited for us on the beach began chattering to them excitedly—a foreign language, as I fancied—as they laid hands on some bales piled near the stern. Somewhere I had heard such a voice before, and I could not think where. The white-haired man stood holding in a tumult of six dogs and bawling orders over their din. Montgomery, having unshipped the rudder, landed likewise, and all set to work at unloading. I was too faint, what with my long fast and the sun beating down on my bare head, to offer any assistance.

Presently the white-haired man seemed to recollect my presence, and came up to me. 'You look,' said he, 'as though you had not breakfasted.'

His little eyes were a brilliant black under his heavy brows. 'I must apologise for that. Now you are our guest, we must make you comfortable—though you are uninvited, you know.'

He looked keenly into my face. 'Montgomery says you are an educated man, Mr Prendick—says you know something of science. May I ask what that signifies?'

I told him I had spent some years at the Royal College of Science, and had done some research in biology under Huxley.* He raised his eyebrows slightly at that.

'That alters the case a little, Mr Prendick,' he said with a trifle more respect in his manner. 'As it happens, we are biologists here. This is a biological station—of a sort.' His eye rested on the men in white, who were busily hauling the puma, on rollers, towards the walled yard. 'I and Montgomery, at least,' he added.

Then, 'When you will be able to get away, I can't say. We're off the track to anywhere. We see a ship once in a twelvemonth or so.'

He left me abruptly and went up the beach past this group, and, I think, entered the enclosure. The other two men were with Montgomery erecting a pile of smaller packages on a low-wheeled truck. The llama was still on the launch with the rabbit-hutches; the staghounds still lashed to the thwarts. The pile of things completed, all three men laid hold of the truck, and began shoving the ton-weight or so upon it after the puma. Presently Montgomery left them, and, coming back to me, held out his hand.

'I'm glad,' said he, 'for my own part. That captain was a silly ass. He'd have made things lively for you.'

'It was you,' said I, 'that saved me again.'

'That depends. You'll find this island an infernally rum place, I promise you. I'd watch my goings carefully if I were you. He—' He hesitated, and seemed to alter his mind about what was on his lips. 'I wish you'd help me with these rabbits,' he said.

His procedure with the rabbits was singular. I waded in with him and helped him lug one of the hutches ashore. No sooner was that done than he opened the door of it, and tilting the thing on one end, turned its living contents out on the ground. They fell in a struggling heap one on the top of the other. He clapped his hands, and forthwith they went off with that hopping run of theirs, fifteen or twenty of them, I should think, up the beach. 'Increase and multiply, my friends,' said Montgomery. 'Replenish the island. Hitherto we've had a certain lack of meat here.'

As I watched them disappearing, the white-haired man returned with a brandy flask and some biscuits.

'Something to go on with, Prendick,' said he in a far more familiar tone than before.

I made no ado, but set to work on the biscuits at once, while the white-haired man helped Montgomery to release about a score more of the rabbits. Three big hutches, however, went up to the house with the puma. The brandy I did not touch, for I have been an abstainer from my birth.

VII

THE LOCKED DOOR

THE reader will perhaps understand that at first everything was so strange about me, and my position was the outcome of such unexpected adventures, that I had no discernment of the relative strangeness of this or that thing about me. I followed the llama up the beach, and was overtaken by Montgomery who asked me not to enter the stone enclosure. I noticed then that the puma in its cage and the pile of packages had been placed outside the entrance to this quadrangle.

I turned and saw that the launch had now been unloaded, run out again, and beached, and the white-haired man was walking towards us. He addressed Montgomery.

'And now comes the problem of this uninvited guest. What are we to do with him?'

'He knows something of science,' said Montgomery.

'I'm itching to get to work again—with this new stuff,' said the grey-haired man, nodding towards the enclosure. His eyes grew brighter.

'I dare say you are,' said Montgomery in anything but a cordial tone.

'We can't send him over there, and we can't spare the time to build him a new shanty. And we certainly can't take him into our confidence just yet.'

'I'm in your hands,' said I. I had no idea of what he meant by 'over there.'

'I've been thinking of the same things,' Montgomery answered. 'There's my room with the outer door——'

'That's it,' said the elder man promptly, looking at Montgomery, and all three of us went towards the enclosure. 'I'm sorry to make a mystery, Mr Prendick—but you'll remember you're uninvited. Our little establishment here contains a secret or so, is a kind of Bluebeard's Chamber, in fact. Nothing very dreadful really—to a sane man. But just now—as we don't know you——'

'Decidedly,' said I; 'I should be a fool to take offence at any want of confidence.'

He twisted his heavy mouth into a faint smile—he was one of those saturnine people who smile with the corners of the mouth down—and bowed his acknowledgment of my complaisance. The main entrance to the enclosure we passed; it was a heavy wooden gate, framed in iron and locked, with the cargo of the launch piled outside it; and at the corner we came to a small doorway I had not previously observed. The grey-haired man produced a bundle of keys from the pocket of his greasy blue jacket, opened this door, and entered. His keys and the elaborate locking up of the place, even while it was still under his eye, struck me as peculiar.

I followed him, and found myself in a small apartment, plainly but not uncomfortably furnished, and with its inner door, which was slightly ajar, opening into a paved courtyard. This inner door Montgomery at once closed. A hammock was slung across the darker corner of the room, and a small unglazed window, defended by an iron bar, looked out towards the sea.

This, the grey-haired man told me, was to be my apartment, and the inner door, which, 'for fear of accidents,' he said, he would lock on the other side, was my limit inward. He called my attention to a convenient deck chair before the window, and to an array of old books, chiefly, I found, surgical works and editions of the Latin and Greek classics—languages I cannot read with any comfort—on a shelf near the hammock. He left the room by the outer door, as if to avoid opening the inner one again.

'We usually have our meals in here,' said Montgomery, and then, as if in doubt, went out after the other. 'Moreau,' I heard him call, and for the moment I do not think I noticed.

Then as I handled the books on the shelf it came up in consciousness: where had I heard the name of Moreau before?

I sat down before the window, took out the biscuits that still remained to me, and ate them with an excellent appetite. 'Moreau?'

Through the window I saw one of those unaccountable men in white lugging a packing-case along the beach. Presently the window-frame hid him. Then I heard a key inserted and turned in the lock behind me. After a little while I heard, through the locked door, the noise of the staghounds, which had now been brought up from the beach. They were not barking, but sniffing and growling in a curious fashion. I could hear the rapid patter of their feet and Montgomery's voice soothing them.

I was very much impressed by the elaborate secrecy of these two men regarding the contents of the place, and for some time I was thinking of that, and of the unaccountable familiarity of the name of Moreau. But so odd is the human memory, that I could not then recall that well-known name in its proper connection. From that my thoughts went to the indefinable queerness of the deformed and white-swathed man on the beach. I never saw such a gait, such odd motions, as he pulled at the box. I recalled that none of these men had spoken to me, though most of them I had found looking at me at one time or another in a peculiar furtive manner, quite unlike the frank stare of your unsophisticated savage. I wondered what language they spoke. They had all seemed remarkably taciturn, and when they did speak, endowed with very uncanny voices. What was wrong with them? Then I recalled the eyes of Montgomery's ungainly attendant.

Just as I was thinking of him, he came in. He was now dressed in white, and carried a little tray with some coffee and boiled vegetables thereon. I could hardly repress a shuddering recoil as he came, bending amiably, and placed the tray before me on the table.

Then astonishment paralysed me. Under his stringy black

locks I saw his ear! It jumped upon me suddenly, close to my face. The man had pointed ears, covered with a fine fur!

'Your breakfast, sair,' he said. I stared at his face without attempting to answer him. He turned and went towards the door, regarding me oddly over his shoulder.

I followed him out with my eyes, and as I did so, by some trick of unconscious cerebration, there came surging into my head the phrase; 'The Moreau—Hollows' was it? 'The Moreau—?' Ah! it sent my memory back ten years. 'The Moreau Horrors.' The phrase drifted loose in my mind for a moment, and then I saw it in red lettering on a little buff-coloured pamphlet, that to read made one shiver and creep. Then I remembered distinctly all about it. That long-forgotten pamphlet came back with startling vividness to my mind. I had been a mere lad then, and Moreau was, I suppose, about fifty; a prominent and masterful physiologist, well known in scientific circles for his extraordinary imagination and his brutal directness in discussion. Was this the same Moreau? He had published some very astonishing facts in connection with the transfusion of blood, and, in addition, was known to be doing valuable work on morbid growths. Then suddenly his career was closed. He had to leave England. A journalist obtained access to his laboratory in the capacity of laboratory assistant, with the deliberate intention of making sensational exposures; and by the help of a shocking accident—if it was an accident—his gruesome pamphlet became notorious. On the day of its publication a wretched dog, flayed and other-wise mutilated, escaped from Moreau's house.

It was in the silly season,* and a prominent editor, a cousin of the temporary laboratory assistant, appealed to the con-science of the nation. It was not the first time that con-science has turned against the methods of research. The doctor was simply howled out of the country. It may be he deserved to be, but I still think the tepid support of his fellow investigators and his desertion by the great body of scientific workers, was a shameful thing. Yet some of his experiments, by the journalist's account, were wantonly cruel. He might perhaps have purchased his social peace by abandoning his investigations, but he apparently preferred the latter, as most men would who have once fallen under the overmastering spell of research. He was unmarried, and had indeed nothing but his own interests to consider. . . .

I felt convinced that this must be the same man. Everything pointed to it. It dawned upon me to what end the puma and the other animals, which had now been brought with other luggage into the enclosure behind the house, were destined; and a curious faint odour, the halitus* of something familiar, an odour that had been in the background of my consciousness hitherto, suddenly came forward into the forefront of my thoughts. It was the antiseptic odour of the operating-room. I heard the puma growling through the wall, and one of the dogs yelped as though it had been struck.

Yet surely, and especially to another scientific man, there was nothing so horrible in vivisection as to account for this secrecy. And by some odd leap in my thoughts the pointed ears and luminous eyes of Montgomery's attendant came back again before me with the sharpest definition. I stared out at the green sea, frothing under a freshening breeze, and let these and other strange memories of the last few days chase each other through my mind.

What could it mean? A locked enclosure on a lonely island, a notorious vivisector, and these crippled and distorted men? . . .

VIII

THE CRYING OF THE PUMA

MONTGOMERY interrupted my tangle of mystification and suspicion about one, and his grotesque attendant followed him with a tray bearing bread, some herbs, and other eatables, a flask of whisky, a jug of water, and three glasses and knives. I glanced askance at this strange creature, and found him watching me with his queer restless eyes. Montgomery said he would lunch with me, but that Moreau was too preoccupied with some work to come.

'Moreau!' said I; 'I know that name.'

'The devil you do!' said he. 'What an ass I was to mention it to you. I might have thought. Anyhow, it will give you an inkling of our—mysteries. Whisky?'

'No thanks—I'm an abstainer.'

'I wish I'd been. But it's no use locking the door after the steed is stolen. It was that infernal stuff led to my coming here. That and a foggy night. I thought myself in luck at the time when Moreau offered to get me off. It's queer. . . .'

'Montgomery,' said I suddenly, as the outer door closed; 'why has your man pointed ears?'

'Damn!' he said, over his first mouthful of food. He stared at me for a moment, and then repeated, 'Pointed ears?'

'Little points to them,' said I as calmly as possible, with a catch in my breath; 'and a fine brown fur at the edges.'

He helped himself to whisky and water with great deliberation. 'I was under the impression . . . that his hair covered his ears.'

'I saw them as he stooped by me to put that coffee you sent to me on the table. And his eyes shine in the dark.'

By this time Montgomery had recovered from the surprise of my question. 'I always thought,' he said deliberately, with a certain accentuation of his flavouring of lisp; 'that there *was* something the matter with his ears. From the way he covered them. . . . What were they like?'

I was persuaded from his manner that this ignorance was a pretence. Still I could hardly tell the man I thought him a liar. 'Pointed,' I said; 'rather small and furry—distinctly furry. But the whole man is one of the strangest beings I ever set eyes on.'

A sharp, hoarse cry of animal pain came from the enclosure

behind us. Its depth and volume testified to the puma. I saw Montgomery wince.

'Yes!' he said.

'Where did you pick the creature up?'

'Er—San Francisco. . . . He's an ugly brute, I admit. Half-witted, you know. Can't remember where he came from. But I'm used to him, you know. We both are. How does he strike you?'

'He's unnatural,' I said. 'There's something about him. . . . Don't think me fanciful, but it gives me a nasty little sensation, a tightening of my muscles, when he comes near me. It's a touch . . . of the diabolical, in fact.'

Montgomery had stopped eating while I told him this. 'Rum,' he said. '*I* can't see it.'

He resumed his meal. 'I had no idea of it,' he said, and masticated. 'The crew of the schooner . . . must have felt it the same. . . . Made a dead set at the poor devil. . . . You saw the captain?'

Suddenly the puma howled again, this time more painfully. Montgomery swore under his breath. I had half a mind to attack him about the men on the beach. Then the poor brute within gave vent to a series of short, sharp screams.

'Your men on the beach,' said I; 'what race are they?'

'Excellent fellows, aren't they?' said he absent-mindedly, knitting his brows as the animal yelled. I said no more. There was another outcry worse than the former. He looked at me with his dull grey eyes, and then took some more whisky. He tried to draw me into a discussion about alcohol, professing to have saved my life with it. He seemed anxious to lay stress on the fact that I owed my life to him. I answered him distractedly. Presently our meal came to an end, the mis-shapen monster with the pointed ears cleared away, and Montgomery left me alone in the room again. All the time he was in a state of ill-concealed irritation at the noise of the vivisected puma. He spoke of his odd want of nerve, and left me to the obvious application.

I found myself that the cries were singularly irritating, and they grew in depth and intensity as the afternoon wore on. They were painful at first, but their constant resurgence at last altogether upset my balance. I flung aside a crib of Horace* I had been reading, and began to clench my fists, to bite my lips, and pace the room.

Presently I got to stopping my ears with my fingers.

The emotional appeal of these yells grew upon me steadily, grew at last to such an exquisite expression of suffering that I could stand it in that confined room no longer. I stepped out of the door into the slumberous heat of the late afternoon, and walking past the main entrance—locked again I noticed—turned the corner of the wall.

The crying sounded even louder out of doors. It was as if all the pain in the world had found a voice. Yet had I known such pain was in the next room, and had it been dumb, I believe—I have thought since—I could have stood it well enough. It is when suffering finds a voice and sets our nerves quivering that this pity comes troubling us. But in spite of the brilliant sunlight and the green fans of the trees waving in the soothing sea-breeze, the world was a confusion, blurred with drifting black and red phantasms, until I was out of earshot of the house in the stone wall.

IX

THE THING IN THE FOREST

I STRODE through the undergrowth that clothed the ridge behind the house, scarcely heeding whither I went, passed on through the shadow of a thick cluster of straight-stemmed trees beyond it, and so presently found myself some way on the other side of the ridge, and descending towards a streamlet that ran through a narrow valley. I paused and listened. The distance I had come, or the intervening masses of thicket, deadened any sound that might be coming from the enclosure. The air was still. Then with a rustle a rabbit emerged, and went scampering up the slope before me. I hesitated, and sat down in the edge of the shade.

The place was a pleasant one. The rivulet was hidden by the luxuriant vegetation of the banks, save at one point, where I caught a triangular patch of its glittering water. On the further side I saw through a bluish haze a tangle of trees and creepers, and above these again the luminous blue of the sky. Here and there a splash of white or crimson marked the blooming of some trailing epiphyte.* I let my eyes wander over this scene for a while, and then began to turn over in my mind again the strange peculiarities of Montgomery's man. But it was too hot to think elaborately, and presently I fell into a tranquil state midway between dozing and waking.

From this I was aroused, after I know not how long, by a rustling amidst the greenery on the other side of the stream. For a moment I could see nothing but the waving summits of the ferns and reeds. Then suddenly upon the bank of the stream appeared something—at first I could not distinguish what it was. It bowed its head to the water and began to drink. Then I saw it was a man, going on all fours like a beast!

He was clothed in bluish cloth, and was of a copper-coloured hue, with black hair. It seemed that grotesque ugliness was an invariable character of these islanders. I could hear the suck of the water at his lips as he drank.

I leaned forward to see him better, and a piece of lava, detached by my hand, went pattering down the slope. He looked up guiltily, and his eyes met mine. Forthwith he scrambled to his feet and stood wiping his clumsy hand across his mouth and regarding me. His legs were scarcely half the length of his body. So, staring one another out of countenance, we remained for perhaps the space of a minute. Then, stopping to look back once or twice, he slunk off among the bushes to the right of me, and I heard the swish of the fronds grow faint in the distance and die away. Every now and then he regarded me with a steadfast stare. Long after he had disappeared I remained sitting up staring in the direction of his retreat. My drowsy tranquillity had gone.

I was startled by a noise behind me, and, turning suddenly, saw the flapping white tail of a rabbit vanishing up the slope. I jumped to my feet.

The apparition of this grotesque half-bestial creature had suddenly populated the stillness of the afternoon for me. I looked around me rather nervously, and regretted that I was unarmed. Then I thought that the man I had just seen had been clothed in bluish cloth, had not been naked as a savage would have been, and I tried to persuade myself from that fact that he was after all probably a peaceful character, that the dull ferocity of his countenance belied him.

Yet I was greatly disturbed at the apparition. I walked to the left along the slope, turning my head about and peering this way and that among the straight stems of the trees. Why should a man go on all fours and drink with his lips? Presently I heard an animal wailing again, and taking it to be the puma, I turned about and walked in a direction diametrically opposite to the sound. This led me down to the stream, across which I stepped and pushed my way up through the undergrowth beyond.

I was startled by a great patch of vivid scarlet on the ground, and going up to it found it to be a peculiar fungus branched and corrugated like a foliaceous lichen, but deliquescing into slime at the touch. And then in the shadow of some luxuriant ferns I came upon an unpleasant thing, the dead body of a rabbit, covered with shining flies but still warm, and with its head torn off. I stopped aghast at the sight of the scattered blood. Here at least was one visitor to the island disposed of!

There were no traces of other violence about it. It looked as though it had been suddenly snatched up and killed. And as I stared at the little furry body came the difficulty of how the thing had been done. The vague dread that had been in my mind since I had seen the inhuman face of the man at the stream grew distincter as I stood there. I began to realise the hardihood of my expedition among these unknown people. The thicket about me became altered to my imagination. Every shadow became something more than a shadow, became an ambush, every rustle became a threat. Invisible things seemed watching me.

I resolved to go back to the enclosure on the beach. I suddenly turned away and thrust myself violently—possibly even frantically—through the bushes, anxious to get a clear space about me again.

I stopped just in time to prevent myself emerging upon an open space. It was a kind of glade in the forest made by a fall; seedlings were already starting up to struggle for the vacant space, and beyond, the dense growth of stems and twining vines and splashes of fungus and flowers closed in again. Before me, squatting together upon the fungoid ruins of a huge fallen tree, and still unaware of my approach, were three grotesque human figures.

One was evidently a female. The other two were men. They were naked, save for swathings of scarlet cloth about their middles, and their skins were of a dull pinkish drab colour, such as I had seen in no savages before. They had fat heavy chinless faces, retreating foreheads, and a scant bristly hair upon their heads. Never before had I seen such bestial-looking creatures.

They were talking, or at least one of the men was talking to the other two, and all three had been too closely interested to heed the rustling of my approach. They swayed their heads and shoulders from side to side. The speaker's words came thick and sloppy, and though I could hear them distinctly I could not distinguish what he said. He seemed to me to be reciting some complicated gibberish. Presently his articulation became shriller, and spreading his hands he rose to his feet.

At that time the others began to gibber in unison, also

rising to their feet, spreading their hands, and swaying their bodies in rhythm with their chant. I noticed then the abnormal shortness of their legs and their lank clumsy feet. All three began slowly to circle round, raising and stamping their feet and waving their arms; a kind of tune crept into their rhythmic recitation, and a refrain—'Aloola' or 'Baloola' it sounded like. Their eyes began to sparkle and their ugly faces to brighten with an expression of strange pleasure. Saliva dropped from their lipless mouths.

Suddenly, as I watched their grotesque and unaccountable gestures, I perceived clearly for the first time what it was that had offended me, what had given me the two inconsistent and conflicting impressions of utter strangeness and yet of the strangest familiarity. The three creatures engaged in this mysterious rite were human in shape, and yet human beings with the strangest air about them of some familiar animal. Each of these creatures, despite its human form, its rag of clothing, and the rough humanity of its bodily form, had woven into it, into its movements, into the expression of its countenance, into its whole presence, some now irresistible suggestion of a hog, a swinish taint, the unmistakable mark of the beast.

I stood overcome by this realisation, and then the most horrible questionings came rushing into my mind. They began leaping into the air, first one and then the other, whooping and grunting. Then one slipped, and for a moment was on all fours, to recover indeed forthwith. But that transitory gleam of the true animalism of these monsters was enough.

I turned as noiselessly as possible, and becoming every now and then rigid with the fear of being discovered as a branch cracked or leaf rustled, I pushed back into the bushes. It was long before I grew bolder and dared to move freely.

My one idea for the moment was to get away from these foul beings, and I scarcely noticed that I had emerged upon a faint pathway amidst the trees. Then, suddenly traversing a little glade, I saw with an unpleasant start two clumsy legs among the trees, walking with noiseless footsteps parallel with my course, and perhaps thirty yards away from me. The head and upper part of the body were hidden by a tangle of creeper. I stopped abruptly, hoping the creature did not see me. The feet stopped as I did. So nervous was I that I controlled an impulse to headlong flight with the utmost difficulty.

Then, looking hard, I distinguished through the interlacing network the head and body of the brute I had seen drinking. He moved his head. There was an emerald flash in his eyes as he glanced at me from the shadow of the trees, a half-luminous colour, that vanished as he turned his head again. He was motionless for a moment, and then with noiseless tread began running through the green confusion. In another moment he had vanished behind some bushes. I could not see him, but I felt that he had stopped and was watching me again.

What on earth was he—man or animal? What did he want with me? I had no weapon, not even a stick. Flight would be madness. At any rate the Thing, whatever it was, lacked the courage to attack me. Setting my teeth hard I walked straight towards him. I was anxious not to show the fear that seemed chilling my backbone. I pushed through a tangle of tall white-flowered bushes, and saw him twenty yards beyond, looking over his shoulder at me and hesitating. I advanced a step or two looking steadfastly into his eyes.

'Who are you?' said I. He tried to meet my gaze.

'No!' he said suddenly, and, turning, went bounding away from me through the undergrowth. Then he turned and stared at me again. His eyes shone brightly out of the dusk under the trees.

My heart was in my mouth, but I felt my only chance was to face the danger, and walked steadily towards him. He turned again and vanished into the dusk. Once more I thought I caught the glint of his eyes, and that was all.

For the first time I realised how the lateness of the hour might affect me. The sun had set some minutes since, the swift dusk of the tropics was already fading out of the eastern sky, and a pioneer moth fluttered silently by my head. Unless I would spend the night among the unknown dangers of the mysterious forest, I must hasten back to the enclosure.

The thought of a return to that pain-haunted refuge was extremely disagreeable, but still more so was the idea of being overtaken in the open by darkness, and all that darkness might conceal. I gave one more look into the blue shadows that had swallowed up this odd creature, and then retraced my way down the slope towards the stream, going as I judged in the direction from which I had come.

I walked eagerly, perplexed by all these things, and presently found myself in a level place among scattered trees. The colourless clearness that comes after the sunset flush was darkling. The blue sky above grew momentarily deeper, and the little stars one by one pierced the attenuated light; the interspaces of the trees, the gaps in the further vegetation that had been hazy blue in the daylight, grew black and mysterious.

I pushed on. Colour vanished from the world, the tree tops rose against the luminous blue sky in inky silhouette, and all below that outline melted into formless blackness. Presently the trees grew thinner, and the shrubby undergrowth more abundant. Then there was a desolate space covered with white sand, and then another expanse of tangled bushes.

I was tormented by a faint rustling upon my right hand. I thought at first it was fancy, for whenever I stopped there was silence save for the evening breeze in the tree tops. Then when I went on again there was an echo to my footsteps.

I moved away from the thickets, keeping to the more open ground, and endeavouring by sudden turns now and then to surprise this thing, if it existed, in the act of creeping upon me. I saw nothing, and nevertheless my sense of another presence grew steadily. I increased my pace, and after some time came to a slight ridge, crossed it and turned sharply, regarding it steadfastly from the further side. It came out black and clear-cut against the darkling sky.

And presently a shapeless lump heaved up momentarily against the skyline and vanished again. I felt assured now that my tawny-faced antagonist was stalking me again. And coupled with that was another unpleasant realisation, that I had lost my way.

For a time I hurried on hopelessly perplexed, pursued by that stealthy approach. Whatever it was, the thing either lacked the courage to attack me, or it was waiting to take me at some disadvantage. I kept studiously to the open. At times I would turn and listen, and presently I half-persuaded myself that my pursuer had abandoned the chase, or was a mere creation of my disordered imagination. Then I heard the sound of the sea. I quickened my footsteps almost to a run, and immediately there was a stumble in my rear.

I turned suddenly and stared at the uncertain trees behind me. One black shadow seemed to leap into another. I listened rigid, and heard nothing but the whisper of the blood in my ears. I thought that my nerves were unstrung and that my imagination was tricking me, and turned resolutely towards the sound of the sea again.

In a minute or so the trees grew thinner, and I emerged upon a bare low headland running out into the sombre water. The night was calm and clear, and the reflection of the growing multitude of the stars shivered in the tranquil heaving of the sea. Some way out, the wash upon an irregular band of reef shone with a pallid light of its own. Westward I saw the zodiacal light mingling with the yellow brilliance of the evening star. The coast fell away from me to the east, and westward it was hidden by the shoulder of the cape. Then I recalled the fact that Moreau's beach lay to the west.

A twig snapped behind me and there was a rustle. I turned, and stood facing the dark trees. I could see nothing—or else I could see too much. Every dark form in the dimness had its ominous quality, its peculiar suggestion of alert watchfulness. So I stood for perhaps a minute, and then, with an eye to the trees still, turned westward to cross the headland. And as I moved, one among the lurking shadows moved to follow me.

My heart beat quickly. Presently the broad sweep of a bay to the westward became visible, and I halted again. The noiseless shadow halted a dozen yards from me. A little point of light shone on the further bend of the curve, and the grey sweep of the sandy beach lay faint under the starlight. Perhaps two miles away was that little point of light. To get to the beach I should have to go through the trees where the shadows lurked, and down a bushy slope.

I could see the thing rather more distinctly now. It was no animal, for it stood erect. At that I opened my mouth to speak, and found a hoarse phlegm choked my voice. I tried again, and shouted, 'Who is there?' There was no answer. I advanced a step. The thing did not move; only gathered itself together. My foot struck a stone.

That gave me an idea. Without taking my eyes off the black form before me I stooped and picked up this lump of rock. But at my motion the thing turned abruptly as a dog might have done, and slunk obliquely into the further darkness. Then I recalled a schoolboy expedient against big dogs, twisted the rock into my handkerchief, and gave this a turn round my wrist. I heard a movement further off among the shadows as if the thing was in retreat. Then suddenly my tense excitement gave way; I broke into a profuse perspiration and fell a-trembling, with my adversary routed and this weapon in my hand.

It was some time before I could summon resolution to go down through the trees and bushes upon the flank of the headland to the beach. At last I did it at a run, and as I emerged from the thicket upon the sand I heard some other body come crashing after me.

At that I completely lost my head with fear, and began running along the sand. Forthwith there came the swift patter of soft feet in pursuit. I gave a wild cry and redoubled my pace. Some dim black things about three or four times the size of rabbits went running or hopping up from the beach towards the bushes as I passed. So long as I live I shall remember the terror of that chase. I ran near the water's edge, and heard every now and then the splash of the feet that gained upon me. Far away, hopelessly far, was the yellow light. All the night about us was black and still. Splash, splash came the pursuing feet nearer and nearer. I felt my breath going, for I was quite out of training; it whooped as I drew it, and I felt a pain like a knife in my side. I perceived the thing would come up with me long before I reached the enclosure, and, desperate and sobbing for breath, I wheeled round upon it and struck at it as it came up to me—struck with all my strength. The stone came out of the sling of the handkerchief as I did so.

As I turned, the thing, which had been running on all fours, rose to its feet, and the missile fell fair on its left temple. The skull rang loud and the animal-man blundered into me, thrust me back with his hands, and went staggering past me to fall headlong upon the sand with its face in the water. And there it lay still.

I could not bring myself to approach that black heap. I left it there with the water rippling round it under the still stars, and, giving it a wide berth, pursued my way towards the yellow glow of the house. And presently, with a positive effect of relief, came the pitiful moaning of the puma, the sound that had originally driven me out to explore this mysterious island. At that, though I was faint and horribly fatigued, I gathered together all my strength and began running again towards the light. It seemed to me a voice was calling me.

X

THE CRYING OF THE MAN

As I drew near the house I saw that the light shone from the open door of my room; and then I heard, coming from out the darkness at the side of that orange oblong, the voice of Montgomery shouting 'Prendick.'

I continued running. Presently I heard him again. I replied by a feeble 'Hullo!' and in another moment had staggered up to him.

'Where have you been?' said he, holding me at arm's length, so that the light from the door fell on my face. 'We have both been so busy that we forgot about you until about half an hour ago.'

He led me into the room and sat me down in the deck chair. For a while I was blinded by the light. 'We did not think you would start to explore this island of ours without telling us,' he said. And then, 'I was afraid! But . . . what . . . . Hullo!'

For my last remaining strength slipped from me, and my head fell forward on my chest. I think he found a certain satisfaction in giving me brandy. 'For God's sake,' said I, 'fasten that door.'

'You've been meeting some of our curiosities, eh?' said he. He locked the door and turned to me again. He asked me no questions, but gave me some more brandy and water, and pressed me to eat. I was in a state of collapse. He said something vague about his forgetting to warn me, and asked me briefly when I left the house and what I had seen. I answered him as briefly in fragmentary sentences. 'Tell me what it all means,' said I, in a state bordering on hysterics.

'It's nothing so very dreadful,' said he. 'But I think you have been about enough for one day.' The puma suddenly gave a sharp yell of pain. At that he swore under his breath.

'I'm damned,' said he, 'if this place is not as bad as Gower Street—with its cats.'

'Montgomery,' said I, 'what was that thing that came after me. Was it a beast, or was it a man?'

'If you don't sleep to-night,' he said, 'you'll be off your head to-morrow.'

I stood up in front of him. 'What was that thing that came after me?' I asked.

He looked me squarely in the eyes and twisted his mouth askew. His eyes, which had seemed animated a minute before, went dull. 'From your account,' said he, 'I'm thinking it was a bogle.'*

I felt a gust of intense irritation that passed as quickly as it came. I flung myself into the chair again and pressed my hands on my forehead. The puma began again.

Montgomery came round behind me and put his hand on my shoulder. 'Look here, Prendick,' he said; 'I had no business to let you drift out into this silly island of ours. But it's not so bad as you think, man. Your nerves are worked to rags. Let me give you something that will make you sleep. *That* . . . will keep on for hours yet. You simply must get to sleep, or I won't answer for it.'

I did not reply. I bowed forward and covered my face with my hands. Presently he returned with a small measure containing a dark liquid. This he gave me. I took it unresistingly, and he helped me into the hammock.

When I awoke it was broad day. For a little while I lay flat, staring at the roof above me. The rafters, I observed, were made out of the timbers of a ship. Then I turned my head and saw a meal prepared for me on the table. I perceived that I was hungry, and prepared to clamber out of the hammock which, very politely anticipating my intention, twisted round and deposited me upon all-fours on the floor.

I got up and sat down before the food. I had a heavy feeling in my head, and only the vaguest memory at first of the things that had happened overnight. The morning breeze blew very pleasantly through the unglazed window, and that and the food contributed to the sense of animal comfort I experienced. Presently the door behind me, the door inward towards the yard of the enclosure, opened. I turned and saw Montgomery's face. 'All right?' said he. 'I'm frightfully busy.' And he shut the door. Afterwards I discovered that he forgot to re-lock it.

Then I recalled the expression of his face the previous night, and with that the memory of all I had experienced reconstructed itself before me. Even as that fear returned to me came a cry from within. But this time it was not the cry of the puma.

I put down the mouthful that hesitated upon my lips, and listened. Silence, save for the whisper of the morning breeze. I began to think my ears had deceived me.

After a long pause I resumed my meal, but with my ears still vigilant. Presently I heard something else very faint and low. I sat as if frozen in my attitude. Though it was faint and low, it moved me more profoundly than all that I had hitherto heard of the abominations behind the wall. There was no mistake this time in the quality of the dim broken sounds, no doubt at all of their source; for it was groaning, broken by sobs and gasps of anguish. It was no brute this time. It was a human being in torment!

And as I realised this I rose, and in three steps had crossed the room, seized the handle of the door into the yard, and flung it open before me.

'Prendick, man! Stop!' cried Montgomery, intervening. A startled deerhound yelped and snarled. There was blood, I saw, in the sink, brown and some scarlet, and I smelled the peculiar smell of carbolic acid. Then through an open doorway beyond in the dim light of the shadow, I saw something bound painfully upon a framework, scarred, red, and bandaged. And then blotting this out appeared the face of old Moreau, white and terrible.

In a moment he had gripped me by the shoulder with a

hand that was smeared red, had twisted me off my feet, and flung me headlong back into my own room. He lifted me as though I was a little child. I fell at full length upon the floor, and the door slammed and shut out the passionate intensity of his face. Then I heard the key turn in the lock, and Montgomery's voice in expostulation.

'Ruin the work of a lifetime!' I heard Moreau say.

'He does not understand,' said Montgomery, and other things that were inaudible.

'I can't spare the time yet,' said Moreau.

The rest I did not hear. I picked myself up and stood trembling, my mind a chaos of the most horrible misgivings. Could the vivisection of men be possible? The question shot like lightning across a tumultuous sky. And suddenly the clouded horror of my mind condensed into a vivid realisation of my danger.

XI

THE HUNTING OF THE MAN

IT came before my mind with an unreasonable hope of escape, that the outer door of my room was still open to me. I was convinced now, absolutely assured, that Moreau had been vivisecting a human being. All the time since I had heard his name I had been trying to link in my mind in some way the grotesque animalism of the islanders with his abominations; and now I thought I saw it all. That memory of his works in the transfusion of blood recurred to me. These creatures I had seen were the victims of some hideous experiment!

These sickening scoundrels had merely intended to keep me back, to fool me with their display of confidence, and presently to fall upon me with a fate more horrible than death, with torture, and after torture the most hideous degradation it was possible to conceive—to send me off, a lost soul, a beast, to the rest of their Comus rout.* I looked round for some weapon. Nothing. Then, with an inspiration, I turned over the deck chair, put my foot on the side of it, and tore away the side rail. It happened that a nail came away with the wood, and, projecting, gave a touch of danger to an otherwise petty weapon. I heard a step outside, incontinently flung open the door, and found Montgomery within a yard of it. He meant to lock the outer door.

I raised this nailed stick of mine and cut at his face, but he sprang back. I hesitated a moment, then turned and fled round the corner of the house. 'Prendick!' I heard his astonished cry. 'Don't be a silly ass, man!'

Another minute, thought I, and he would have had me locked in, and as ready as a hospital rabbit for my fate. He emerged behind the corner, for I heard him shout, 'Prendick!' Then he began to run after me, shouting things as he ran.

This time, running blindly, I went northeastward, in a direction at right angles to my previous expedition. Once, as I went running headlong up the beach, I glanced over my shoulder and saw his attendant with him. I ran furiously up the slope, over it, then turned eastward along a rocky valley, fringed on either side with jungle. I ran perhaps a mile altogether, my chest straining, my heart beating in my ears, and then, hearing nothing of Montgomery or his man and feeling upon the verge of exhaustion, I doubled sharply back towards the beach, as I judged, and lay down in the shelter of a canebrake.

There I remained for a long time, too fearful to move, and indeed too fearful even to plan a course of action. The wild scene about me lay sleeping silently under the sun, and the only sound near me was the thin hum of some small gnats that had discovered me. Presently I became aware of a drowsy breathing sound—the soughing of the sea upon the beach.

After about an hour I heard Montgomery shouting my name far away to the north. That set me thinking of my plan of action. As I interpreted it then, this island was inhabited only by these two vivisectors and their animalised victims. Some of these, no doubt, they could press into their service against me, if need arose. I knew both Moreau and Montgomery carried revolvers; and, save for a feeble bar of deal spiked with a small nail, the merest mockery of a mace, I was unarmed.

So I lay still where I was until I began to think of food and drink. And at that moment the real hopelessness of my position came home to me. I knew no way of getting anything to eat; I was too ignorant of botany to discover any resort of root or fruit that might lie about me; I had no means of trapping the few rabbits upon the island. It grew blanker the more I turned the prospect over. At last, in the desperation of my position, my mind turned to the animal-men I had encountered. I tried to find some hope in what I remembered of them. In turn I recalled each one I had seen, and tried to draw some augury of assistance from my memory.

Then suddenly I heard a staghound bay, and at that realised a new danger. I took little time to think, or they would have caught me then, but snatching up my nailed stick rushed headlong from my hiding place towards the sound of the sea. I remember a growth of thorny plants with spines that stabbed like penknives. I emerged, bleeding and with torn clothes, upon the lip of a long creek opening northward. I went straight into the waves without a minute's hesitation, wading up the creek, and presently finding myself knee-deep in a little stream. I scrambled out at last on the westward bank, and, with my heart beating loudly in my ears, crept into a tangle of ferns to await the issue. I heard the dog—it was only one—draw nearer, and yelp when it came to the thorns. Then I heard no more, and presently began to think I had escaped.

The minutes passed, the silence lengthened out, and at last, after an hour of security, my courage began to return to me.

142

By this time I was no longer very terrified or very miserable. For I had, as it were, passed the limit of terror and despair. I felt now that my life was practically lost, and that persuasion made me capable of daring anything. I had even a certain wish to encounter Moreau face to face. And as I had waded into the water, I remembered that if I were too hard pressed at least one path of escape from torment still lay open to me—they could not very well prevent my drowning myself. I had half a mind to drown myself then, but an odd wish to see the whole adventure out, a queer impersonal spectacular interest in myself, restrained me. I stretched my limbs, sore and painful from the pricks of the spiny plants, and stared around me at the trees; and, so suddenly that it seemed to jump out of the green tracery about it, my eyes lit upon a black face watching me.

I saw that it was the simian creature who had met the launch upon the beach. He was clinging to the oblique stem of a palm-tree. I gripped my stick, and stood up facing him. He began chattering. 'You, you, you,' was all I could distinguish at first. Suddenly he dropped from the tree, and in another moment was holding the fronds apart, and staring curiously at me.

I did not feel the same repugnance towards this creature that I had experienced in my encounters with the other Beast Men. 'You,' he said, 'in the boat.' He was a man then—at least, as much of a man as Montgomery's attendant—for he could talk.

'Yes,' I said, 'I came in the boat. From the ship.'

'Oh!' he said, and his bright restless eyes travelled over me, to my hands, to the stick I carried, to my feet, to the tattered places in my coat and the cuts and scratches I had received from the thorns. He seemed puzzled at something. His eyes came back to my hands. He held his own hand out, and counted his digits slowly, 'One, Two, Three, Four, Five—eh?'

I did not grasp his meaning then. Afterwards I was to find

that a great proportion of these Beast People had malformed hands, lacking sometimes even three digits. But guessing this was in some way a greeting, I did the same thing by way of reply. He grinned with immense satisfaction. Then his quick roving glance went round again. He made a swift movement, and vanished. The fern fronds he had stood between came swishing together.

I pushed out of the brake after him, and was astonished to find him swinging cheerfully by one lank arm from a rope of creepers that looped down from the foliage overhead. His back was to me.

'Hullo!' said I.

He came down with a twisting jump, and stood facing me. 'I say,' said I, 'where can I get something to eat?'

'Eat!' he said. 'Eat man's food now.' And his eyes went back to the swing of ropes. 'At the huts.'

'But where are the huts?'

'Oh!'

'I'm new, you know.'

At that he swung round, and set off at a quick walk. All his motions were curiously rapid. 'Come along,' said he. I went with him to see the adventure out. I guessed the huts were some rough shelter, where he and some more of these Beast People lived. I might perhaps find them friendly, find some handle in their minds to take hold of. I did not know yet how far they were from the human heritage I ascribed to them.

My ape-like companion trotted along by my side, with his hands hanging down and his jaw thrust forward. I wondered what memory he might have in him. 'How long have you been on this island?' said I.

'How long?' he asked. And, after having the question repeated, he held up three fingers. The creature was little better than an idiot. I tried to make out what he meant by that, and it seems I bored him. After another question or two, he suddenly left my side and sprang at some fruit that hung from a tree. He pulled down a handful of prickly husks, and went on eating the contents. I noted this with satisfaction, for here, at least, was a hint for feeding. I tried him with some other questions, but his chattering prompt responses were, as often as not, at cross-purposes with my question. Some few were appropriate, others quite parrot-like.

I was so intent upon these peculiarities that I scarcely noted the path we followed. Presently we came to trees, all charred and brown, and so to a bare place covered with a yellow-white incrustation, across which went a drifting smoke, pungent in whiffs to nose and eyes. On our right, over a shoulder of bare rock, I saw the level blue of the sea. The path coiled down abruptly into a narrow ravine between two tumbled and knotty masses of blackish scoriæ.* Into this we plunged.

It was extremely dark, this passage, after the blinding sunlight reflected from the sulphurous ground. Its walls grew steep, and approached one another. Blotches of green and crimson drifted across my eyes. My conductor stopped suddenly. 'Home,' said he, and I stood on the floor of a chasm that was at first absolutely dark to me. I heard some strange noises, and thrust the knuckles of my left hand into my eyes. I became aware of a disagreeable odour like that of a monkey's cage ill-cleaned. Beyond, the rock opened again upon a gradual slope of sunlit greenery, and on either hand the light smote down through a narrow channel into the central gloom.

XII

THE SAYERS OF THE LAW

THEN something cold touched my hand. I started violently, and saw close to me a dim pinkish thing, looking more like a flayed child than anything else in the world. The creature had exactly the mild but repulsive features of a sloth, the same low forehead and slow gestures. As the first shock of the change of light passed, I saw about me more distinctly. The little sloth-like creature was standing and staring at me. My conductor had vanished.

This place was a narrow passage between high walls of lava, a crack in its knotted flow; and on either side interwoven heaps of sea-mat, palm fans and reeds leaning against the rock, formed rough and impenetrably dark dens. The winding way up the ravine between these was scarcely three yards wide, and was disfigured by lumps of decaying fruit pulp and other refuse which accounted for the disagreeable stench of the place.

The little pink sloth creature was still blinking at me when my Ape Man reappeared at the aperture of the nearest of these dens, and beckoned me in. As he did so a slouching monster wriggled out of one of the places further up this strange street, and stood up in featureless silhouette against the bright green beyond, staring at me. I hesitated—had half a mind to bolt the way I had come—and then, determined to go through with the adventure, gripped my nailed stick about the middle, and crawled into the little evil-smelling lean-to after my conductor.

It was a semicircular space, shaped like the half of a beehive, and against the rocky wall that formed the inner side of it was a pile of variegated fruits, cocoanuts and others. Some rough vessels of lava and wood stood about the floor, and one on a rough stool. There was no fire. In the darkest corner of the hut sat a shapeless mass of darkness that grunted 'Hey!' as I came in, and my Ape Man stood in the dim light of the doorway and held out a split cocoanut to me as I crawled into the other corner and squatted down. I took it and began gnawing it, as serenely as possible in spite of my tense trepidation and the nearly intolerable closeness of the den. The little pink sloth creature stood in the aperture of the hut, and something else with a drab face and bright eyes came staring over its shoulder.

'Hey,' came out of the lump of mystery opposite. 'It is a

man! It is a man!' gabbled my conductor—'a man, a man, a live man, like me.'

'Shut up!' said the voice from the dark, and grunted. I gnawed my cocoanut amid an impressive silence. I peered hard into the blackness, but could distinguish nothing. 'It is a man,' the voice repeated. 'He comes to live with us?' It was a thick voice with something in it, a kind of whistling overtone, that struck me as peculiar, but the English accent was strangely good.

The Ape Man looked at me as though he expected something. I perceived the pause was interrogative. 'He comes to live with you,' I said.

'It is a man. He must learn the Law.'

I began to distinguish now a deeper blackness in the black, a vague outline of a hunched-up figure. Then I noticed the opening of the place was darkened by two more heads. My hand tightened on my stick. The thing in the dark repeated in a louder tone, 'Say the words.' I had missed its last remark. 'Not to go on all-Fours; that is the Law'—it repeated in a kind of singsong.

I was puzzled. 'Say the words,' said the Ape Man, repeating, and the figures in the doorway echoed this with a threat in the tone of their voices. I realised I had to repeat this idiotic formula. And then began the insanest ceremony. The voice in the dark began intoning a mad litany, line by line, and I and the rest to repeat it. As they did so, they swayed from side to side, and beat their hands upon their knees, and I followed their example. I could have imagined I was already dead and in another world. The dark hut, these grotesque dim figures, just flecked here and there by a glimmer of light, and all of them swaying in unison and chanting:—

'Not to go on all-Fours; *that* is the Law. Are we not Men?
'Not to suck up Drink; *that* is the Law. Are we not Men?
'Not to eat Flesh or Fish; *that* is the Law. Are we not Men?
'Not to claw Bark of Trees; *that* is the Law. Are we not Men?

'Not to chase other Men; *that* is the Law. Are we not Men?'

And so from the prohibition of these acts of folly, on to the prohibition of what I thought then were the maddest, most impossible, and most indecent things one could well imagine. A kind of rhythmic fervour fell on all of us; we gabbled and swayed faster and faster, repeating this amazing law. Superficially the contagion of these brute men was upon me, but deep down within me laughter and disgust struggled together. We ran through a long list of prohibitions, and then the chant swung round to a new formula:

'*His* is the House of Pain.

'*His* is the Hand that makes.

'*His* is the Hand that wounds.

'*His* is the Hand that heals.'

And so on for another long series, mostly quite incomprehensible gibberish to me, about *Him*, whoever he might be. I could have fancied it was a dream, but never before have I heard chanting in a dream.

'*His* is the lightning-flash,' we sang. '*His* is the deep salt sea.'

A horrible fancy came into my head that Moreau, after animalising these men, had infected their dwarfed brains with a kind of deification of himself. However, I was too keenly aware of white teeth and strong claws about me to stop my chanting on that account. '*His* are the stars in the sky.'

At last that song ended. I saw the Ape Man's face shining with perspiration, and my eyes being now accustomed to the darkness, I saw more distinctly the figure in the corner from which the voice came. It was the size of a man, but it seemed covered with a dull grey hair almost like a Skye terrier. What was it? What were they all? Imagine yourself surrounded by the most horrible cripples and maniacs it is possible to conceive, and you may understand a little of my feelings with these grotesque caricatures of humanity about me.

'He is a five-man, a five-man, a five-man . . . like me,' said the Ape Man.

I held out my hands. The grey creature in the corner leaned forward. 'Not to run on all-Fours; that is the Law. Are we not Men?' he said. He put out a strangely distorted talon, and gripped my fingers. The thing was almost like the hoof of a deer produced into claws. I could have yelled with surprise and pain. His face came forward and peered at my nails, came forward into the light of the opening of the hut, and I saw with a quivering disgust that it was like the face of neither man nor beast, but a mere shock of grey hair, with three shadowy overarchings to mark the eyes and mouth.

'He has little nails,' said this grisly creature in his hairy beard. 'It is well. Many are troubled with big nails.'

He threw my hand down, and instinctively I gripped my stick. 'Eat roots and herbs—it is His will,' said the Ape Man.

'I am the Sayer of the Law,' said the grey figure. 'Here come all that be new, to learn the Law. I sit in the darkness and say the Law.'

'It is even so,' said one of the beasts in the doorway.

'Evil are the punishments of those who break the Law. None escape.'

'None escape,' said the Beast Folk, glancing furtively at each other.

'None, none,' said the Ape Man. 'None escape. See! I did a little thing, a wrong thing, once. I jabbered, jabbered, stopped talking. None could understand. I am burned, branded in the hand. He is great, he is good!'

'None escape,' said the grey creature in the corner.

'None escape,' said the Beast People, looking askance at one another.

'For every one the want that is bad,' said the grey Sayer of the Law. 'What you will want, we do not know. We shall know. Some want to follow things that move, to watch and slink and wait and spring, to kill and bite, bite deep and rich, sucking the blood. . . . It is bad. "Not to chase other Men; that is the Law. *Are we not Men?* Not to eat Flesh or Fish; that is the Law. *Are we not Men?*"'

'None escape,' said a dappled brute standing in the doorway.

'For every one the want that is bad,' said the grey Sayer of the Law. 'Some want to go tearing with teeth and hands into the roots of things, snuffing into the earth. . . . It is bad.'

'None escape,' said the men in the door.

. 'Some go clawing trees, some go scratching at the graves of the dead; some go fighting with foreheads or feet or claws; some bite suddenly, none giving occasion; some love uncleanness.'

'None escape,' said the Ape Man, scratching his calf.

'None escape,' said the little pink sloth creature.

'Punishment is sharp and sure. Therefore learn the Law. Say the words,' and incontinently he began again the strange litany of the Law, and again I and all these creatures began singing and swaying. My head reeled with this jabbering and the close stench of the place, but I kept on, trusting to find presently some chance of a new development. 'Not to go on all-Fours; that is the Law. *Are we not Men?*'

We were making such a noise that I noticed nothing of a tumult outside until some one, who, I think, was one of the two Swine Men I had seen, thrust his head over the little pink sloth creature and shouted something excitedly, something that I did not catch. Incontinently those at the opening of the hut vanished, my Ape Man rushed out, the thing that had sat in the dark followed him—I only observed it was big and clumsy, and covered with silvery hair—and I was left alone.

Then before I reached the aperture I heard the yelp of a staghound.

In another moment I was standing outside the hovel, my chair-rail in my hand, every muscle of me quivering. Before me were the clumsy backs of perhaps a score of these Beast People, their misshapen heads half hidden by their shoulder-blades. They were gesticulating excitedly. Other half-animal faces glared interrogation out of the hovels. Looking in the direction in which they faced I saw coming through the haze under the trees beyond the end of the passage of dens the dark figure and awful white face of Moreau. He was holding the leaping staghound back, and close behind him came Montgomery, revolver in hand.

For a moment I stood horror-struck.

I turned and saw the passages behind me blocked by another heavy brute with a huge grey face and twinkling little eyes, advancing towards me. I looked round and saw to the right of me, and half a dozen yards in front of me, a narrow gap in the wall of rock through which a ray of light slanted into the shadows. 'Stop!' cried Moreau, as I strode towards this, and then, 'Hold him!' At that, first one face turned towards me, and then others. Their bestial minds were happily slow.

I dashed my shoulder into a clumsy monster who was turning to see what Moreau meant, and flung him forward into another. I felt his hands fly round, clutching at me and missing me. The little pink sloth creature dashed at me and I cut it over, gashed down its ugly face with the nail in my stick, and in another minute I was scrambling up a steep side pathway, a kind of sloping chimney out of the ravine. I heard a howl behind me, and cries of 'Catch him!' 'Hold him!' and the grey-faced creature appeared behind me and jammed his huge bulk into the cleft. 'Go on, go on!' they howled. I clambered up the narrow cleft in the rock, and came out upon the sulphur on the westward side of the village of the Beast Men.

I ran over the white space and down a steep slope through a scattered growth of trees, and came to a low-lying stretch of tall reeds. Through this I pushed into a dark thick undergrowth that was black and succulent under foot. That gap was altogether fortunate for me, for the narrow way slanting obliquely upward must have impeded the nearer pursuers. As I plunged into the reeds the foremost had only just emerged from the gap. I broke my way through this undergrowth for some minutes. The air behind me and about me was soon full of threatening cries. I heard the tumult of my pursuers in the gap up the slope, then the crashing of the reeds, and every now and then the crackling of a branch. Some of the creatures roared like excited beasts of prey. The staghound yelped to the left. I heard Moreau and Montgomery shouting in the same direction. I turned sharply to the right. It seemed to me even then that I heard Montgomery shouting for me to run for my life.

Presently the ground gave, rich and oozy, under my feet; but I was desperate, and went headlong into it, struggled through knee-deep, and so came to a winding path among tall canes. The noise of my pursuers passed away to my left. In one place three strange pink hopping animals, about the size of cats, bolted before my footsteps. This pathway ran uphill, across another open space covered with white incrustation, and plunged into a cane-brake again.

Then suddenly it turned parallel with the edge of a steep walled gap which came without warning like the haha of an English park*—turned with unexpected abruptness. I was still running with all my might, and I never saw this drop until I was flying headlong through the air.

I fell on my forearms and head, among thorns, and rose with a torn ear and bleeding face. I had fallen into a precipitous ravine, rocky and thorny, full of a hazy mist that drifted about me in wisps, and with a narrow streamlet, from which this mist came, meandering down the centre. I was astonished at this thin fog in the full blaze of daylight, but I had no time to stand wondering then. I turned to my right down-stream, hoping to come to the sea in that direction, and so have my way open to drown myself. It was only later I found that I had dropped my nailed stick in my fall.

Presently the ravine grew narrower for a space, and carelessly I stepped into the stream. I jumped out again pretty quickly, for the water was almost boiling. I noticed, too, there was a thin sulphurous scum drifting upon its coiling water. Almost immediately came a turn in the ravine and the indistinct blue horizon. The nearer sea was flashing the sun from a myriad facets. I saw my death before me.

But I was hot and panting. I felt more than a touch of exultation, too, at having distanced my pursuers. It was not in me then to go out and drown myself. My blood was too warm.

I stared back the way I had come. I listened. Save for the hum of the gnats and the chirp of some small insects that hopped among the thorns, the air was absolutely still.

Then came the yelp of a dog, very faint, and a chattering and gibbering, the snap of a whip and voices. They grew louder, then fainter again. The noise receded up the stream and faded away. For a while the chase was over.

But I knew now how much hope of help for me lay in the Beast People.

XIII

A PARLEY

I TURNED again and went on down towards the sea. I found the hot stream broadened out to a shallow weedy sand, in which an abundance of crabs, and long-bodied, many-legged creatures started from my footfall. I walked to the very edge of the salt water, and then I felt I was safe. I turned and stared—arms akimbo—at the thick green behind me, into which the steamy ravine cut like a smoking gash. But as I say, I was too full of excitement, and—a true saying, though those who have never known danger may doubt it—too desperate to die.

Then it came into my head that there was one chance before me yet. While Moreau and Montgomery and their bestial rabble chased me through the island, might I not go round the beach until I came to their enclosure?—make a flank march upon them, in fact, and then with a rock lugged out of their loosely built wall perhaps smash in the lock of the smaller door and see what I could find—knife, pistol, or what-not—to fight them with when they returned? It was at any rate a chance of getting a price for my life.

So I turned to the westward and walked along by the water's edge. The setting sun flashed his blinding heat into my eyes. The slight Pacific tide was running in with a gentle ripple.

Presently the shore fell away southward and the sun came round upon my right hand. Then suddenly, far in front of me, I saw first one and then several figures emerging from the bushes—Moreau with his grey staghound, then Montgomery, and two others. At that I stopped.

They saw me and began gesticulating and advancing. I stood watching them approach. The two Beast Men came running forward to cut me off from the undergrowth inland. Montgomery came running also, but straight towards me. Moreau followed slower with the dog.

At last I roused myself from inaction, and turning seaward walked straight into the water. The water was very shallow at first. I was thirty yards out before the waves reached to my waist. Dimly I could see the intertidal creatures darting away from my feet.

'What are you doing, man?' cried Montgomery.

I turned, standing waist-deep, and stared at them.

Montgomery stood panting at the margin of the water. His face was bright red with exertion, his long flaxen hair blown about his head, and his dropping nether lip showed his irregular teeth. Moreau was just coming up, his face pale and firm, and the dog at his hand barked at me. Both men had heavy whips. Further up the beach stared the Beast Men.

'What am I doing?—I am going to drown myself,' said I.

Montgomery and Moreau looked at one another. 'Why?' asked Moreau.

'Because that is better than being tortured by you.'

'I told you so,' said Montgomery, and Moreau said something in a low tone.

'What makes you think I shall torture you?' asked Moreau.

'What I saw,' I said. 'And those—yonder.'

'Hush!' said Moreau, and held up his hand.

'I will not,' said I; 'they were men: what are they now? I at least will not be like them.' I looked past my interlocutors. Up the beach were M'ling, Montgomery's attendant, and one of the white swathed brutes from the boat. Further up, in the shadow of the trees, I saw my little Ape Man, and behind him some other dim figures.

'Who are these creatures?' said I, pointing to them, and raising my voice more and more that it might reach them. 'They were men—men like yourselves, whom you have infected with some bestial taint, men whom you have enslaved, and whom you still fear.—You who listen,' I cried, pointing now to Moreau, and shouting past him to the Beast Men, 'You who listen! Do you not see these men still fear you, go in dread of you? Why then do you fear them? You are many——'

'For God's sake,' cried Montgomery, 'stop that, Prendick!'

'Prendick!' cried Moreau.

They both shouted together as if to drown my voice. And behind them lowered the staring faces of the Beast Men, wondering, their deformed hands hanging down, their shoulders hunched up. They seemed, as I fancied then, to be trying to understand me, to remember something of their human past.

I went on shouting, I scarcely remember what. That Moreau and Montgomery could be killed; that they were not to be feared: that was the burthen of what I put into the heads of the Beast People to my own ultimate undoing. I saw the green-eyed man in the dark rags, who had met me on the evening of my arrival, come out from among the trees, and others followed him to hear me better.

At last for want of breath I paused.

'Listen to me for a moment,' said the steady voice of Moreau, 'and then say what you will.'

'Well?' said I.

He coughed, thought, then shouted: 'Latin, Prendick! Bad Latin! Schoolboy Latin! But try and understand. *Hi non sunt homines, sunt animalia qui nos habemus . . .* vivisected.* A humanising process. I will explain. Come ashore.'

I laughed. 'A pretty story,' said I. 'They talk, build houses, cook. They were men. It's likely I'll come ashore.'

'The water just beyond where you stand is deep . . . and full of sharks.'

'That's my way,' said I. 'Short and sharp. Presently.'

'Wait a minute.' He took something out of his pocket that flashed back the sun, and dropped the object at his feet. 'That's a loaded revolver,' said he. 'Montgomery here will do the same. Now we are going up the beach until you are satisfied the distance is safe. Then come and take the revolvers.'

'Not I. You have a third between you.'

'I want you to think over things, Prendick. In the first place, I never asked you to come upon this island. In the next, we had you drugged last night, had we wanted to work you any mischief; and in the next, now your first panic is over, and you can think a little—is Montgomery here quite up to the character you give him? We have chased you for your good. Because this island is full of . . . inimical phenomena. Why should we want to shoot you when you have just offered to drown yourself?'

'Why did you set . . . your people on to me when I was in the hut?'

'We felt sure of catching you and bringing you out of danger. Afterwards we drew away from the scent—for your good.'

I mused. It seemed just possible. Then I remembered something again.

'But I saw,' said I, 'in the enclosure——'

'That was the puma.'

'Look here, Prendick,' said Montgomery. 'You're a silly

156

ass. Come out of the water and take these revolvers, and talk. We can't do anything more then than we could do now.'

I will confess that then, and indeed always, I distrusted and dreaded Moreau. But Montgomery was a man I felt I understood.

'Go up the beach,' said I, after thinking, and added, 'holding your hands up.'

'Can't do that,' said Montgomery, with an explanatory nod over his shoulder. 'Undignified.'

'Go up to the trees, then,' said I, 'as you please.'

'It's a damned silly ceremony,' said Montgomery.

Both turned and faced the six or seven grotesque creatures, who stood there in the sunlight, solid, casting shadows, moving, and yet so incredibly unreal. Montgomery cracked his whip at them, and forthwith they all turned and fled helter-skelter into the trees. And when Montgomery and Moreau were at a distance I judged sufficient, I waded ashore, and picked up and examined the revolvers. To satisfy myself against the subtlest trickery I discharged one at a rounded lump of lava, and had the satisfaction of seeing the stone pulverised and the beach splashed with lead.

Still I hesitated for a moment.

'I'll take the risk,' said I, at last, and with a revolver in each hand I walked up the beach towards them.

'That's better,' said Moreau, without affectation. 'As it is, you have wasted the best part of my day with your confounded panic.'

And with a touch of contempt that humiliated me he and Montgomery turned and went on in silence before me.

The knot of Beast Men, still wondering, stood back among the trees. I passed them as serenely as possible. One started to follow me, but retreated again when Montgomery cracked his whip. The rest stood silent—watching. They may once have been animals. But never before did I see an animal trying to think.

XIV

DOCTOR MOREAU EXPLAINS

'AND now, Prendick, I will explain,' said Doctor Moreau, so soon as we had eaten and drunk. 'I must confess you are the most dictatorial guest I ever entertained. I warn you that this is the last I do to oblige you. The next thing you threaten to commit suicide about I shan't do—even at some personal inconvenience.'

He sat in my deck chair, a cigar half consumed in his white dexterous-looking fingers. The light of the swinging lamp fell on his white hair; he stared through the little window out at the starlight. I sat as far away from him as possible, the table between us and the revolvers to hand. Montgomery was not present. I did not yet care to be with the two of them in such a little room.

'You admit that vivisected human being, as you called it, is after all only the puma?' said Moreau. He had made me visit that horror in the inner room to assure myself of its inhumanity.

'It is the puma,' I said, 'still alive, but cut and mutilated as I pray I may never see living flesh again. Of all vile——'

'Never mind that,' said Moreau. 'At least spare me those youthful horrors. Montgomery used to be just the same. You admit it is the puma. Now be quiet while I reel off my physiological lecture to you.' And forthwith, beginning in the tone of a man supremely bored, but presently warming a little, he explained his work to me. He was very simple and convincing. Now and then there was a touch of sarcasm in his voice. Presently I found myself hot with shame at our mutual positions.

The creatures I had seen were not men, had never been men. They were animals—humanised animals—triumphs of vivisection.

'You forget all that a skilled vivisector can do with living things,' said Moreau. 'For my own part I'm puzzled why the things I have done here have not been done before. Small efforts of course have been made—amputation, tongue-cutting, excisions. Of course you know a squint may be induced or cured by surgery? Then in the case of excisions you have all kinds of secondary changes, pigmentary disturbances, modifications of the passions, alterations in the secretion of fatty tissue. I have no doubt you have heard of these things?'

'Of course,' said I. 'But these foul creatures of yours——'

'All in good time,' said he, waving his hand at me; 'I am only beginning. Those are trivial cases of alteration. Surgery can do better things than that. There is building up as well as breaking down and changing. You have heard, perhaps, of a common surgical operation resorted to in cases where the nose has been destroyed. A flap of skin is cut from the forehead, turned down on the nose, and heals in the new position. This is a kind of grafting in a new position of part of an animal upon itself. Grafting of freshly obtained material from another animal is also possible—the case of teeth, for example. The grafting of skin and bone is done to facilitate healing. The surgeon places in the middle of the wound pieces of skin snipped from another animal, or fragments of bone from a victim freshly killed. Hunter's cockspur—possibly you have heard of that—flourished on the bull's neck.* And the rhinoceros rats of the Algerian Zouaves* are also to be thought of—monsters manufactured by transferring a slip from the tail of an ordinary rat to its snout, and allowing it to heal in that position.'

'Monsters manufactured!' said I. 'Then you mean to tell me——'

'Yes. These creatures you have seen are animals carven and wrought into new shapes. To that—to the study of the plasticity of living forms—my life has been devoted. I have studied for years, gaining in knowledge as I go. I see you look horrified, yet I am telling you nothing new. It all lay on the surface of practical anatomy years ago, but no one had the temerity to touch it. It's not simply the outward form of an animal I can change. The physiology, the chemical rhythm of the creature may also be made to undergo an enduring modification, of which vaccination and other methods of inoculation with living or dead matter are examples that will no doubt be familiar to you. A similar operation is the transfusion of blood, with which subject indeed I began. These are all familiar cases. Less so, and probably far more extensive, were the operations of those mediæval practitioners who made dwarfs and beggar cripples and show-monsters; some vestiges of whose art still remain in the preliminary manipulation of the young mountebank or contortionist. Victor Hugo gives an account of them in "L'Homme qui Rit"*. . . . But perhaps my meaning grows plain now. You begin to see that it is a possible thing to transplant tissue from one part of an animal to another or from one animal to another, to alter its chemical reactions and methods of growth, to modify the articulation of its limbs, and indeed to change it in its most intimate structure?

'And yet this extraordinary branch of knowledge has never been sought as an end, and systematically, by modern investigators, until I took it up! Some such things have been hit upon in the last resort of surgery; most of the kindred evidence that will recur to your mind has been demonstrated, as it were, by accident—by tyrants, by criminals, by the breeders of horses and dogs, by all kinds of untrained clumsy-handed men working for their own immediate ends. I was the first man to take up this question armed with antiseptic surgery, and with a really scientific knowledge of the laws of growth.

'Yet one would imagine it must have been practised in secret before. Such creatures as the Siamese Twins. . . . And in the vaults of the Inquisition. No doubt their chief aim was artistic torture, but some at least of the inquisitors must have had a touch of scientific curiosity. . . .'

'But,' said I. 'These things—these animals *talk!*'

He said that was so, and proceeded to point out that the possibilities of vivisection do not stop at a mere physical metamorphosis. A pig may be educated. The mental structure is even less determinate than the bodily. In our growing science of hypnotism we find the promise of a possibility of replacing old inherent instincts by new suggestions, grafted upon or replacing the inherited fixed ideas. Very much indeed of what we call moral education is such an artificial modification and perversion of instinct; pugnacity is trained into courageous self-sacrifice, and suppressed sexuality into religious emotion. And the great difference between man and monkey is in the larynx, he said, in the incapacity to frame delicately different sound-symbols by which thought could be sustained. In this I failed to agree with him, but with a certain incivility he declined to notice my objection. He repeated that the thing was so, and continued his account of his work.

But I asked him why he had taken the human form as a model. There seemed to me then, and there still seems to me now, a strange wickedness in that choice.

He confessed that he had chosen that form by chance. 'I might just as well have worked to form sheep into llamas, and llamas into sheep. I suppose there is something in the human form that appeals to the artistic turn of mind more powerfully than any animal shape can. But I've not confined myself to man-making. Once or twice . . .' He was silent, for a minute perhaps. 'These years! How they have slipped by! And here I have wasted a day saving your life, and am now wasting an hour explaining myself!'

'But,' said I, 'I still do not understand. Where is your justification for inflicting all this pain? The only thing that could excuse vivisection to me would be some application——'

'Precisely,' said he. 'But you see I am differently constituted. We are on different platforms. You are a materialist.'

'I am *not* a materialist,' I began hotly.

'In my view—in my view. For it is just this question of pain that parts us. So long as visible or audible pain turns you sick, so long as your own pains drive you, so long as pain underlies your propositions about sin, so long, I tell you, you are an animal, thinking a little less obscurely what an animal feels. This pain——'

I gave an impatient shrug at such sophistry.

'Oh! but it is such a little thing. A mind truly opened to what science has to teach must see that it is a little thing. It may be that, save in this little planet, this speck of cosmic dust, invisible long before the nearest star could be attained— it may be, I say, that nowhere else does this thing called pain occur. But the laws we feel our way towards . . . Why, even on this earth, even among living things, what pain is there?'

He drew a little penknife, as he spoke, from his pocket, opened the smaller blade and moved his chair so that I could see his thigh. Then, choosing the place deliberately, he drove the blade into his leg and withdrew it.

'No doubt you have seen that before. It does not hurt a pin-prick. But what does it show? The capacity for pain is not needed in the muscle, and it is not placed there; it is but little needed in the skin, and only here and there over the thigh is a spot capable of feeling pain. Pain is simply our intrinsic medical adviser to warn us and stimulate us. All living flesh is not painful, nor is all nerve, nor even all sensory nerve. There's no taint of pain, real pain, in the sensations of the optic nerve. If you wound the optic nerve you merely see flashes of light, just as disease of the auditory nerve merely means a humming in our ears. Plants do not feel pain; the lower animals—it's possible that such animals as the starfish and crayfish do not feel pain. Then with men, the more intelligent they become the more intelligently they will see after their own welfare, and the less they will need the goad to keep them out of danger. I never yet heard of a useless thing that was not ground out of existence by evolution sooner or later. Did you? And pain gets needless.

'Then I am a religious man, Prendick, as every sane man must be. It may be I fancy I have seen more of the ways of this world's Maker than you—for I have sought his laws, in *my* way, all my life, while you, I understand, have been collecting butterflies. And I tell you, pleasure and pain have nothing to do with heaven and hell. Pleasure and pain—Bah! What is your theologian's ecstasy but Mahomet's houri in the dark?* This store men and women set on pleasure and pain, Prendick, is the mark of the beast upon them, the mark of the beast from which they came. Pain! Pain and pleasure— they are for us, only so long as we wriggle in the dust. . . .

'You see, I went on with this research just the way it led me. That is the only way I ever heard of research going. I asked a question, devised some method of getting an answer, and got—a fresh question. Was this possible, or that possible? You cannot imagine what this means to an investigator, what an intellectual passion grows upon him. You cannot imagine the strange colourless delight of these intellectual desires. The thing before you is no longer an animal, a fellow-creature, but a problem. Sympathetic pain—all I know of it I remember as a thing I used to suffer from years ago. I wanted—it was the only thing I wanted—to find out the extreme limit of plasticity in a living shape.'

'But,' said I, 'the thing is an abomination——'

'To this day I have never troubled about the ethics of the matter. The study of Nature makes a man at last as remorseless as Nature. I have gone on, not heeding anything but the question I was pursuing, and the material has . . . dripped into the huts yonder. . . . It is nearly eleven years since we came here, I and Montgomery and six Kanakas.* I remember the green stillness of the island and the empty ocean about us as though it was yesterday. The place seemed waiting for me.

'The stores were landed and the house was built. The Kanakas founded some huts near the ravine. I went to work here upon what I had brought with me. Some disagreeable things happened at first. I began with a sheep, and killed it after a day and a half by a slip of the scalpel; I took another sheep and made a thing of pain and fear, and left it bound up to heal. It looked quite human to me when I had finished it, but when I went to it I was discontented with it; it remembered me and was terrified beyond imagination, and it had no more than the wits of a sheep. The more I looked at it the clumsier it seemed, until at last I put the monster out of its misery. These animals without courage, these fear-haunted pain-driven things, without a spark of pugnacious energy to face torment—they are no good for man-making.

'Then I took a gorilla I had, and upon that, working with infinite care, and mastering difficulty after difficulty, I made my first man. All the week, night and day, I moulded him. With him it was chiefly the brain that needed moulding; much had to be added, much changed. I thought him a fair specimen of the negroid type when I had done him, and he lay, bandaged, bound, and motionless before me. It was only when his life was assured that I left him, and came into the room and found Montgomery much as you are. He had heard some of the cries as the thing grew human, cries like those that disturbed *you* so. I didn't take him completely into my confidence at first. And the Kanakas, too, had realised something of it. They were scared out of their wits by the sight of me. I got Montgomery over to me—in a way, but I and he had the hardest job to prevent the Kanakas deserting. Finally they did, and so we lost the yacht. I spent many days educating the brute—altogether I had him for three or four months. I taught him the rudiments of English, gave him ideas of counting, even made the thing read the alphabet. But at that he was slow—though I've met with idiots slower. He began with a clean sheet, mentally; had no memories left in his mind of what he had been. When his scars were quite healed, and he was no longer anything but painful and stiff, and able to converse a little, I took him yonder and introduced him to the Kanakas as an interesting stowaway.

'They were horribly afraid of him at first, somehow—which

offended me rather, for I was conceited about him—but his ways seemed so mild, and he was so abject, that after a time they received him and took his education in hand. He was quick to learn, very imitative and adaptive, and built himself a hovel rather better, it seemed to me, than their own shanties. There was one among the boys, a bit of a missionary, and he taught the thing to read, or at least to pick out letters, and gave him some rudimentary ideas of morality, but it seems the beast's habits were not all that is desirable.

'I rested from work for some days, and was in a mind to write an account of the whole affair to wake up English physiology. Then I came upon the creature squatting up in a tree gibbering at two of the Kanakas who had been teasing him. I threatened him, told him the inhumanity of such a proceeding, aroused his sense of shame, and came here resolved to do better before I took my work back to England. I have been doing better; but somehow the things drift back again, the stubborn beast flesh grows, day by day, back again. . . . I mean to do better things still. I mean to conquer that. This puma . . .

'But that's the story. All the Kanaka boys are dead now. One fell overboard the launch, and one died of a wounded heel that he poisoned in some way with plant-juice. Three went away in the yacht, and I suppose, and hope, were drowned. The other one . . . was killed. Well—I have replaced them. Montgomery went on much as you are disposed to do at first, and then . . .'

'What became of the other one?' said I sharply—'the other Kanaka who was killed?'

'The fact is, after I had made a number of human creatures I made a thing—' He hesitated.

'Yes?' said I.

'It was killed.'

'I don't understand,' said I; 'do you mean to say . . .'

'It killed the Kanaka—yes. It killed several other things that it caught. We chased it for a couple of days. It only got loose by accident—I never meant it to get away. It wasn't finished. It was purely an experiment. It was a limbless thing with a horrible face that writhed along the ground in a serpentine fashion. It was immensely strong and in infuriating pain, and it travelled rapidly in a rolling way like a porpoise swimming. It lurked in the woods for some days, doing mischief to all it came across, until we hunted it, and then it wriggled into the northern part of the island, and we divided the party to close in upon it. Montgomery insisted upon coming with me. The man had a rifle, and when his body was found one of the barrels was curved into the shape of an S, and very nearly bitten through. . . . Montgomery shot the thing. . . . After that I stuck to the ideal of humanity—except for little things.'

He became silent. I sat in silence watching his face.

'So for twenty years altogether—counting nine years in England—I have been going on, and there is still something in everything I do that defeats me, makes me dissatisfied, challenges me to further effort. Sometimes I rise above my level, sometimes I fall below it, but always I fall short of the things I dream. The human shape I can get now, almost with ease, so that it is lithe and graceful, or thick and strong; but often there is trouble with the hands and claws—painful things that I dare not shape too freely. But it is in the subtle grafting and reshaping one must needs do to the brain that my trouble lies. The intelligence is often oddly low, with unaccountable blank ends, unexpected gaps. And least satisfactory of all is something that I cannot touch, somewhere—I cannot determine where—in the seat of the emotions. Cravings, instincts, desires that harm humanity, a strange hidden reservoir to burst suddenly and inundate the whole being of the creature with anger, hate, or fear. These creatures of mine seemed strange and uncanny to you as soon as you began to observe them, but to me, just after I make them, they seem to be indisputable human beings. It's afterwards as I observe them that the persuasion fades. First one animal trait, then another, creeps to the surface and stares out at me. . . . But I will conquer yet. Each time I dip a living creature into the bath of burning pain I say: this time I will burn out all the animal, this time I will make a rational creature of my own. After all, what is ten years? Man has been a hundred thousand in the making.'

He thought darkly. 'But I am drawing near the fastness. This puma of mine . . .'

After a silence: 'And they revert. As soon as my hand is taken from them the beast begins to creep back, begins to assert itself again. . . .'

Another long silence.

'Then you take the things you make into those dens?' said I.

'They go. I turn them out when I begin to feel the beast in them, and presently they wander there. They all dread this house and me. There is a kind of travesty of humanity over there. Montgomery knows about it, for he interferes in their affairs. He has trained one or two of them to our service. He's ashamed of it, but I believe he half likes some of these beasts. It's his business, not mine. They only sicken me with a sense of failure. I take no interest in them. I fancy they follow in the lines the Kanaka missionary marked out, and have a kind of mockery of a rational life—poor beasts! There's something they call the Law. Sing hymns about "all thine." They build themselves their dens, gather fruit and pull herbs—marry even. But I can see through it all, see into their very souls, and see there nothing but the souls of beasts, beasts that perish—anger, and the lusts to live and gratify themselves. . . . Yet they're odd. Complex, like everything else alive. There is a kind of upward striving in them, part vanity, part waste sexual emotion, part waste curiosity. It only mocks me. . . . I have some hope of that puma; I have worked hard at her head and brain. . . .

'And now,' said he, standing up after a long gap of silence, during which we had each pursued our own thoughts; 'what do you think? Are you in fear of me still?'

I looked at him, and saw but a white-faced, white-haired man, with calm eyes. Save for his serenity, the touch almost of beauty that resulted from his set tranquillity and from his magnificent build, he might have passed muster among a hundred other comfortable old gentlemen. Then I shivered. By way of answer to his second question, I handed him a revolver with either hand.

'Keep them,' he said, and snatched at a yawn. He stood up, stared at me for a moment and smiled. 'You have had two eventful days,' said he. 'I should advise some sleep. I'm glad it's all clear. Good night.'

He thought me over for a moment, then went out by the inner door. I immediately turned the key in the outer one.

I sat down again, sat for a time in a kind of stagnant mood, so weary emotionally, mentally, and physically, that I could not think beyond the point at which he had left me. The black window stared at me like an eye. At last with an effort I put out the lamp, and got into the hammock. Very soon I was asleep.

XV

CONCERNING THE BEAST FOLK

I WOKE early. Moreau's explanation stood before my mind, clear and definite, from the moment of my awakening. I got out of the hammock and went to the door to assure myself that the key was turned. Then I tried the window bar, and found it firmly fixed. That these man-like creatures were in truth only bestial monsters, mere grotesque travesties of men, filled me with a vague uncertainty of their possibilities that was far worse than any definite fear. A tapping came at the door, and I heard the glutinous accents of M'ling speaking. I pocketed one of the revolvers (keeping one hand upon it) and opened to him.

'Good morning, sir,' he said, bringing in addition to the customary herb breakfast, an ill-cooked rabbit. Montgomery followed him. His roving eye caught the position of my arm, and he smiled askew.

The puma was resting to heal that day; but Moreau, who was singularly solitary in his habits, did not join us. I talked with Montgomery to clear my ideas of the way in which the Beast Folk lived. In particular, I was urgent to know how these inhuman monsters were kept from falling upon Moreau and Montgomery, and from rending one another.

He explained to me that the comparative safety of Moreau and himself was due to the limited mental scope of these monsters. In spite of their increased intelligence, and the tendency of their animal instincts to reawaken, they had certain Fixed Ideas implanted by Moreau in their minds which absolutely bounded their imaginations. They were really hypnotised, had been told certain things were impossible, and certain things were not to be done, and these prohibitions were woven into the texture of their minds beyond any possibility of disobedience or dispute. Certain matters, however, in which old instinct was at war with Moreau's convenience, were in a less stable condition. A series of prohibitions called the Law—I had already heard them recited—battled in their minds with the deep-seated, ever-rebellious cravings of their animal natures. This Law they were perpetually repeating, I found, and—perpetually breaking. Both Montgomery and Moreau displayed particular solicitude to keep them ignorant of the taste of blood. They feared the inevitable suggestions of that flavour.

Montgomery told me that the Law, especially among the feline Beast People, became oddly weakened about nightfall; that then the animal was at its strongest; a spirit of adventure sprang up in them at the dusk, they would dare things they never seemed to dream about by day. To that I owed my stalking by the Leopard Man on the night of my arrival. But during these earlier days of my stay they broke the Law only furtively, and after dark; in the daylight there was a general atmosphere of respect for its multifarious prohibitions.

And here perhaps I may give a few general facts about the island and the Beast People. The island, which was of irregular outline and lay low upon the wide sea, had a total area, I suppose, of seven or eight square miles. It was volcanic in origin, and was now fringed on three sides by coral reefs. Some fumaroles* to the northward, and a hot spring, were the only vestiges of the forces that had long since originated it. Now and then a faint quiver of earthquake would be sensible, and sometimes the ascent of the spire of smoke would be rendered tumultuous by gusts of steam. But that was all. The population of the island, Montgomery informed me, now numbered rather more than sixty of these strange creations of Moreau's art, not counting the smaller monstrosities which lived in the undergrowth and were without human form. Altogether he had made nearly a hundred and twenty, but many had died; and others, like the writhing Footless Thing of which he had told me, had come by violent ends. In answer to my question, Montgomery said that they actually bore offspring, but that these generally died. There was no evidence of the inheritance of the acquired human characteristics.* When they lived, Moreau took them and stamped the human form upon them. The females were less numerous than the males, and liable to much furtive persecution in spite of the monogamy the Law enjoined.

It would be impossible for me to describe these Beast People in detail—my eye has had no training in details—and unhappily I cannot sketch. Most striking perhaps in their general appearance was the disproportion between the legs of these creatures and the length of their bodies; and yet—so relative is our idea of grace—my eye became habituated to their forms, and at last I even fell in with their persuasion that my own long thighs were ungainly. Another point was the forward carriage of the head, and the clumsy and inhuman curvature of the spine. Even the Ape Man lacked that inward sinuous curve of the back that makes the human figure so graceful. Most had their shoulders hunched clumsily, and their short forearms hung weakly at their sides. Few of them were conspicuously hairy—at least, until the end of my time upon the island.

The next most obvious deformity was in their faces, almost all of which were prognathous,* malformed about the ears, with large and protuberant noses, very furry or very bristly hair, and often strangely coloured or strangely placed eyes. None could smile, though the Ape Man had a mirthless grin. Beyond these general characters their heads had little in common; each preserved the quality of its particular species: the human mark distorted but did not hide the leopard, the ox, or the sow, or other animal or animals from which the creature had been moulded. The voices too, varied exceedingly. The hands were always malformed; and though some surprised me by their unexpected humanity, almost all were deficient in the number of the digits, clumsy about the fingernails, and lacking any tactile sensibility.

The two most formidable animal-men were the Leopard Man and a creature made of hyæna and swine. Larger than these were the three bull creatures who pulled in the boat. Then came the Silvery Hairy Man, who was also the Sayer of the Law, M'ling, and a satyr-like creature of ape and goat. There were three Swine Men and a Swine Woman, a Horse-Rhinoceros creature, and several other females whose sources I did not ascertain. There were several Wolf creatures, a Bear-Bull, and a Saint Bernard Dog Man. I have already described the Ape Man, and there was a particularly hateful (and evil-smelling) old woman made of Vixen and Bear, whom I hated from the beginning. She was said to be a passionate votary of the Law. Smaller creatures were certain dappled youths and my little sloth creature.

At first I had a shivering horror of the brutes, felt all too keenly that they were still brutes, but insensibly I became a little habituated to the idea of them, and, moreover, I was affected by Montgomery's attitude towards them. He had been with them so long that he had come to regard them as almost normal human beings—his London days seemed a glorious impossible past to him. Only once in a year or so did he go to Arica to deal with Moreau's agent, a trader in animals there. He hardly met the finest type of mankind in that seafaring village of Spanish mongrels. The men aboard ship, he told me, seemed at first just as strange to him as the Beast Men seemed to me—unnaturally long in the leg, flat in the face, prominent in the forehead, suspicious, dangerous, and cold-hearted. In fact, he did not like men. His heart had warmed to me, he thought, because he had saved my life.

I fancied even then that he had a sneaking kindness for some of these metamorphosed brutes, a vicious sympathy with some of their ways, but that he attempted to veil from me at first.

M'ling, the black-faced man, his attendant, the first of the Beast Folk I had encountered, did not live with the others across the island, but in a small kennel at the back of the enclosure. The creature was scarcely so intelligent as the Ape Man, but far more docile, and the most human-looking of all the Beast Folk, and Montgomery had trained it to prepare food and indeed to discharge all the trivial domestic offices that were required. It was a complex trophy of Moreau's horrible skill, a bear tainted with dog and ox, and one of the most elaborately made of all the creatures. It treated Montgomery with a strange tenderness and devotion; sometimes he would notice it, pat it, call it half-mocking, half-jocular names, and so make it caper with extraordinary delight; sometimes he would ill-treat it, especially after he had been at the whisky, kicking it, beating it, pelting it with stones or lighted fusees.* But whether he treated it well or ill, it loved nothing so much as to be near him.

I say I became habituated to the Beast People, so that a thousand things that had seemed unnatural and repulsive speedily became natural and ordinary to me. I suppose everything in existence takes its colour from the average hue of our surroundings: Montgomery and Moreau were too peculiar and individual to keep my general impressions of humanity well defined. I would see one of the bovine creatures who worked the launch treading heavily through the undergrowth, and find myself trying hard to recall how he differed from some really human yokel trudging home from his mechanical labours; or I would meet the Fox-Bear Woman's vulpine shifty face, strangely human in its speculative cunning, and even imagine I had met it before in some city byway.

Yet every now and then the beast would flash out upon me beyond doubt or denial. An ugly-looking man, a hunchbacked human savage to all appearance, squatting in the aperture of one of the dens, would stretch his arms and yawn, showing with startling suddenness scissor-edged incisors and sabre-like canines, keen and brilliant as knives. Or in some narrow pathway, glancing with a transitory daring into the eyes of some lithe white-swathed female figure, I would suddenly see with a spasmodic revulsion that they had slit-like pupils, or, glancing down, note the curving nail with which she held her shapeless wrap about her. It is a curious thing, by-the-by, for which I am quite unable to account, that these weird creatures—the females I mean—had in the earlier days of my stay an instinctive sense of their own repulsive clumsiness, and displayed in consequence a more than human regard for the decencies and decorum of external costume.

XVI

HOW THE BEAST FOLK TASTED BLOOD

BUT my inexperience as a writer betrays me, and I wander from the thread of my story. After I had breakfasted with Montgomery he took me across the island to see the fumarole and the source of the hot spring, into whose scalding waters I had blundered on the previous day. Both of us carried whips and loaded revolvers. While going through a leafy jungle on our road thither we heard a rabbit squealing. We stopped and listened, but we heard no more; and presently we went on our way and the incident dropped out of our minds. Montgomery called my attention to certain little pink animals with long hind legs, that went leaping through the undergrowth. He told me they were creatures made of the offspring of the Beast People, that Moreau had invented. He had fancied they might serve for meat, but a rabbit-like habit of devouring their young had defeated this intention. I had already encountered some of these creatures, once during my moonlight flight from the Leopard Man, and once during my pursuit by Moreau on the previous day. By chance, one hopping to avoid us leaped into the hole caused by the up-rooting of a wind-blown tree. Before it could extricate itself we managed to catch it. It spat like a cat, scratched and kicked vigorously with its hind legs and made an attempt to bite, but its teeth were too feeble to inflict more than a painless pinch. It seemed to me rather a pretty little crea-ture, and as Montgomery stated that it never destroyed the turf by burrowing, and was very cleanly in its habits, I should imagine it might prove a convenient substitute for the com-mon rabbit in gentlemen's parks.

We also saw on our way the trunk of a tree barked in long strips and splintered deeply. Montgomery called my atten-tion to this. 'Not to claw Bark of Trees; *that* is the Law,' he said. 'Much some of them care for it!' It was after this, I think, that we met the Satyr and the Ape Man. The Satyr was a gleam of classical memory on the part of Moreau, his face ovine in expression—like the coarser Hebrew type—his voice a harsh bleat, his nether extremities Satanic.* He was gnaw-ing the husk of a pod-like fruit as he passed us. Both of them saluted Montgomery.

'Hail,' said they, 'to the Other with the whip!'

'There's a third with a whip now,' said Montgomery. 'So you'd better mind!'

'Was he not made?' said the Ape Man. 'He said—he said he was made.'

The Satyr Man looked curiously at me. 'The Third with the whip, he that walks weeping into the sea, has a thin white face.'

'He has a thin long whip,' said Montgomery.

'Yesterday he bled and wept,' said the Satyr. 'You never bleed nor weep. The Master does not bleed nor weep.'

'Ollendorffian beggar!'* said Montgomery. 'You'll bleed and weep if you don't look out.'

'He has five fingers; he is a five-man like me,' said the Ape Man.

'Come along, Prendick,' said Montgomery, taking my arm, and I went on with him.

The Satyr and the Ape Man stood watching us and making other remarks to each other.

'He says nothing,' said the Satyr. 'Men have voices.'

'Yesterday he asked me of things to eat,' said the Ape Man. 'He did not know.' Then they spoke inaudible things, and I heard the Satyr laughing.

It was on our way back that we came upon the dead rabbit. The red body of the wretched little beast was rent to pieces, many of the ribs stripped white, and the backbone indisputably gnawed.

At that Montgomery stopped. 'Good God!' said he, stooping down and picking up some of the crushed vertebræ to examine them more closely. 'Good God!' he repeated, 'what can this mean?'

'Some carnivore of yours has remembered its old habits,' I said, after a pause. 'This backbone has been bitten through.'

He stood staring, with his face white and his lip pulled askew. 'I don't like this,' he said slowly.

'I saw something of the same kind,' said I, 'the first day I came here.'

'The devil you did! What was it?'

'A rabbit with its head twisted off.'

'The day you came here?'

'The day I came here. In the undergrowth, at the back of the enclosure, when I came out in the evening. The head was completely wrung off.'

He gave a low whistle.

'And what is more, I have an idea which of your brutes did the thing. It's only a suspicion, you know. Before I came on the rabbit I saw one of your monsters drinking in the stream.'

'Sucking his drink?'

'Yes.'

'Not to suck your Drink; *that* is the Law. Much the brutes care for the Law, eh—when Moreau's not about?'

'It was the brute who chased me.'

'Of course,' said Montgomery; 'it's just the way with carnivores. After a kill they drink. It's the taste of blood, you know.

'What was the brute like?' he asked. 'Would you know him again?' He glanced about us, standing astride over the mess of dead rabbit, his eyes roving among the shadows and screens of greenery, the lurking-places and ambuscades of the forest, that bounded us in. 'The taste of blood,' he said again.

He took out his revolver, examined the cartridges in it, and replaced it. Then he began to pull at his dropping lip.

'I think I should know the brute again. I stunned him. He ought to have a handsome bruise on the forehead of him.'

'But then we have to *prove* he killed the rabbit,' said Montgomery. 'I wish I'd never brought the things here.'

I should have gone on, but he stayed there thinking over the mangled rabbit in a puzzle-headed way. As it was, I went to such a distance that the rabbit's remains were hidden.

'Come on!' I said.

Presently he woke up and came towards me. 'You see,' he said, almost in a whisper, 'they are all supposed to have a fixed idea against eating anything that runs on land. If some brute has by accident tasted blood . . .'

We went on some way in silence. 'I wonder what can have happened,' he said to himself. Then, after a pause, again: 'I did a foolish thing the other day. That servant of mine . . . I showed him how to skin and cook a rabbit. It's odd. . . . I saw him licking his hands. . . . It never occurred to me.'

Then: 'We must put a stop to this. I must tell Moreau.'

He could think of nothing else on our homeward journey.

Moreau took the matter even more seriously than Montgomery, and I need scarcely say I was infected by their evident consternation. 'We must make an example,' said Moreau. 'I've no doubt in my own mind that the Leopard Man was the sinner. But how can we prove it? I wish, Montgomery, you had kept your taste for meat in hand, and gone without these exciting novelties. We may find ourselves in a mess yet through it.'

'I was a silly ass,' said Montgomery. 'But the thing's done now. And you said I might have them, you know.'

'We must see to the thing at once,' said Moreau. 'I suppose, if anything should turn up, M'ling can take care of himself?'

'I'm not so sure of M'ling,' said Montgomery. 'I think I ought to know him.'

In the afternoon, Moreau, Montgomery, myself, and M'ling went across the island to the huts in the ravine. We three were armed. M'ling carried the little hatchet he used in chopping firewood, and some coils of wire. Moreau had a huge cowherd's horn slung over his shoulder. 'You will see a gathering of the Beast People,' said Montgomery. 'It's a pretty sight.' Moreau said not a word on the way, but his heavy white-fringed face was grim.

We crossed the ravine, down which smoked the stream of hot water, and followed the winding pathway through the cane-brakes until we reached a wide area covered over with a thick powdery yellow substance which I believe was sulphur.

Above the shoulder of a weedy bank the sea glittered. We came to a kind of shallow natural amphitheatre, and here the four of us halted. Then Moreau sounded the horn and broke the sleeping stillness of the tropical afternoon. He must have had strong lungs. The hooting note rose and rose amidst its echoes to at last an ear-penetrating intensity. 'Ah!' said Moreau, letting the curved instrument fall to his side again.

Immediately there was a crashing through the yellow canes, and a sound of voices from the dense green jungle that marked the morass through which I had run on the previous day. Then at three or four points on the edge of the sulphurous area appeared the grotesque forms of the Beast People, hurrying towards us. I could not help a creeping horror as I perceived first one and then another trot out from the trees or reeds, and come shambling along over the hot dust. But Moreau and Montgomery stood calmly enough, and, perforce, I stuck beside them. First to arrive was the Satyr, strangely unreal for all that he cast a shadow, and tossed the dust with his hoofs; after him from the brake came a monstrous lout, a thing of horse and rhinoceros, chewing a straw as it came; and then appeared the Swine Woman and two Wolf Women; then the Fox-Bear Witch with her red eyes in her peaked red face, and then others—all hurrying eagerly. As they came forward they began to cringe towards Moreau and chant, quite regardless of one another, fragments of the latter half of the litany of the Law: '*His* is the Hand that wounds, *His* is the Hand that heals,' and so forth.

As soon as they had approached within a distance of perhaps thirty yards they halted, and bowing on knees and elbows, began flinging the white dust upon their heads. Imagine the scene if you can. We three blue-clad men, with our misshapen black-faced attendant, standing in a wide expanse of sunlit yellow dust under the blazing blue sky, and surrounded by this circle of crouching and gesticulating monstrosities, some almost human save in their subtle expression and gestures, some like cripples, some so strangely distorted as to resemble nothing but the denizens of our wildest dreams. And beyond were the reedy lines of a cane-brake in one direction and a dense tangle of palm-trees on the other, separating us from the ravine with the huts, and to the north the hazy horizon of the Pacific Ocean.

'Sixty-two, sixty-three,' counted Moreau. 'There are four more.'

'I do not see the Leopard Man,' said I.

Presently Moreau sounded the great horn again, and at the sound of it all the Beast People writhed and grovelled in the dust. Then, slinking out of the cane-brake, stooping near the ground, and trying to join the dust-throwing circle behind Moreau's back, came the Leopard Man. And I saw that his forehead was bruised. The last of the Beast People to arrive was the little Ape Man. The earlier animals, hot and weary with their grovelling, shot vicious glances at him.

'Cease,' said Moreau, in his firm loud voice, and the Beast People sat back upon their hams and rested from their worshipping.

'Where is the Sayer of the Law?' said Moreau, and the hairy grey monster bowed his face in the dust.

'Say the words,' said Moreau, and forthwith all in the kneeling assembly, swaying from side to side and dashing up the sulphur with their hands, first the right hand and a puff of dust, and then the left, began once more to chant their strange litany.

When they reached 'Not to eat Flesh or Fish; *that* is the Law,' Moreau held up his lank white hand. '*Stop!*' he cried, and there fell absolute silence upon them all.

I think they all knew and dreaded what was coming. I looked round at their strange faces. When I saw their wincing attitudes and the furtive dread in their bright eyes, I wondered that I had ever believed them to be men.

'That Law has been broken,' said Moreau.

'None escape,' from the faceless creature with the Silvery

179

Hair. 'None escape,' repeated the kneeling circle of Beast People.

'Who is he?' cried Moreau, and looked round at their faces, cracking his whip. I fancied the Hyæna-Swine looked dejected, so, too, did the Leopard Man. Moreau stopped, facing this creature, who cringed towards him with the memory and dread of infinite torment. 'Who is he?' repeated Moreau, in a voice of thunder.

'Evil is he who breaks the Law,' chanted the Sayer of the Law.

Moreau looked into the eyes of the Leopard Man, and seemed to be dragging the very soul out of the creature.

'Who breaks the Law—' said Moreau, taking his eyes off his victim and turning towards us. It seemed to me there was a touch of exultation in his voice.

'—goes back to the House of Pain,' they all clamoured; 'goes back to the House of Pain, O Master!'

'Back to the House of Pain—back to the House of Pain,' gabbled the Ape Man, as though the idea was sweet to him.

'Do you hear?' said Moreau, turning back to the criminal, 'my friend . . . Hullo!'

For the Leopard Man, released from Moreau's eye, had risen straight from his knees, and now, with eyes aflame and his huge feline tusks flashing out from under his curling lips, leaped towards his tormentor. I am convinced that only the madness of unendurable fear could have prompted this attack. The whole circle of threescore monsters seemed to rise about us. I drew my revolver. The two figures collided. I saw Moreau reeling back from the Leopard Man's blow. There was wild yelling and howling all about us. Every one was moving rapidly. For a moment I thought it was a general revolt.

The furious face of the Leopard Man flashed by mine, with M'ling close in pursuit. I saw the yellow eyes of the Hyæna-Swine blazing with excitement, his attitude as if he were half resolved to attack me. The Satyr, too, glared at me

over the Hyæna-Swine's hunched shoulders. I heard the crack
of Moreau's pistol, and saw the pink flash dart across the
tumult. The whole crowd seemed to swing round in the
direction of the glint of fire, and I, too, was swung round by
the magnetism of the movement. In another second I was
running, one of a tumultuous shouting crowd, in pursuit of
the escaping Leopard Man.

That is all I can tell definitely. I saw the Leopard Man
strike Moreau, and then everything spun about me until I
was running headlong.

M'ling was ahead, close in pursuit of the fugitive. Behind,
their tongues already lolling out, ran the Wolf-Women in
great leaping strides. The Swine-Folk followed, squealing with
excitement, and the two Bull Men in their swathings of white.
Then came Moreau in a cluster of the Beast People, his
wide-brimmed straw hat blown off, his revolver in hand, and
his lank white hair streaming out. The Hyæna-Swine ran
beside me, keeping pace with me, and glancing furtively at
me out of his feline eyes, and the others came pattering and
shouting behind us.

The Leopard Man went bursting his way through the long
canes, which sprang back as he passed and rattled in M'ling's
face. We others in the rear found a trampled path for us
when we reached the brake. The chase lay through the brake
for perhaps a quarter of a mile, and then plunged into a
dense thicket that retarded our movements exceedingly,
though we went through it in a crowd together—fronds flick-
ing into our faces, ropy creepers catching us under the chin
or gripping our ankles, thorny plants hooking into and tearing cloth and flesh together.

'He has gone on all-fours through this,' panted Moreau,
now just ahead of me.

'None escape,' said the Wolf-Bear, laughing into my face
with the exultation of hunting.

We burst out again among rocks, and saw the quarry ahead,
running lightly on all-fours, and snarling at us over his

shoulder. At that the Wolf-Folk howled with delight. The thing was still clothed, and, at a distance, its face still seemed human, but the carriage of its four limbs was feline, and the furtive droop of its shoulder was distinctly that of a hunted animal. It leaped over some thorny yellow-flowering bushes and was hidden. M'ling was half-way across the space.

Most of us now had lost the first speed of the chase, and had fallen into a longer and steadier stride. I saw, as we traversed the open, that the pursuit was now spreading from a column into a line. The Hyæna-Swine still ran close to me, watching me as it ran, every now and then puckering its muzzle with a snarling laugh.

At the edge of the rocks the Leopard Man, realising he was making for the projecting cape upon which he had stalked me on the night of my arrival, had doubled in the undergrowth. But Montgomery had seen the manœuvre, and turned him again.

So, panting, tumbling against rocks, torn by brambles, impeded by ferns and reeds, I helped to pursue the Leopard Man who had broken the Law, and the Hyæna-Swine ran, laughing savagely, by my side. I staggered on, my head reeling, and my heart beating against my ribs, tired almost to death, and yet not daring to lose sight of the chase, lest I should be left alone with this horrible companion. I staggered on in spite of infinite fatigue and the dense heat of the tropical afternoon.

And at last the fury of the hunt slackened. We had pinned the wretched brute into a corner of the island. Moreau, whip in hand, marshalled us all into an irregular line, and we advanced now slowly, shouting to one another as we advanced, and tightening the cordon about our victim. He lurked, noiseless and invisible, in the bushes through which I had run from him during that midnight pursuit.

'Steady!' cried Moreau; 'steady!' as the ends of the line crept round the tangle of undergrowth, and hemmed the brute in.

''Ware a rush!' came the voice of Montgomery from beyond the thicket.

I was on the slope above the bushes. Montgomery and Moreau beat along the beach beneath. Slowly we pushed in among the fretted network of branches and leaves. The quarry was silent.

'Back to the House of Pain, the House of Pain, the House of Pain!' yelped the voice of the Ape Man, some twenty yards to the right.

When I heard that I forgave the poor wretch all the fear he had inspired in me.

I heard the twigs snap and the boughs swish aside before the heavy tread of the Horse-Rhinoceros upon my right. Then suddenly, through a polygon of green, in the half darkness under the luxuriant growth, I saw the creature we were hunting. I halted. He was crouched together into the smallest possible compass, his luminous green eyes turned over his shoulder regarding me.

It may seem a strange contradiction in me—I cannot explain the fact—but now, seeing the creature there in a perfectly animal attitude, with the light gleaming in its eyes, and its imperfectly human face distorted with terror, I realised again the fact of its humanity. In another moment other of its pursuers would see it, and it would be overpowered and captured, to experience once more the horrible tortures of the enclosure. Abruptly I slipped out my revolver, aimed between its terror-struck eyes and fired.

As I did so the Hyæna-Swine saw the thing, and flung itself upon it with an eager cry, thrusting thirsty teeth into its neck. All about me the green masses of the thicket were swaying and cracking as the Beast People came rushing together. One face and then another appeared.

'Don't kill it, Prendick,' cried Moreau. 'Don't kill it!' And I saw him stooping as he pushed through the under fronds of the big ferns.

In another moment he had beaten off the Hyæna-Swine

with the handle of his whip, and he and Montgomery were keeping away the excited carnivorous Beast People, and particularly M'ling, from the still quivering body. The Hairy Grey Thing came sniffing at the corpse under my arm. The other animals, in their animal ardour, jostled me to get a nearer view.

'Confound you, Prendick!' said Moreau. 'I wanted him.'

'I'm sorry,' said I, though I was not. 'It was the impulse of the moment.' I felt sick with exertion and excitement. Turning, I pushed my way out of the crowding Beast People and went on alone up the slope towards the higher part of the headland. Under the shouted instructions of Moreau, I heard the three white-swathed Bull Men begin dragging the victim down towards the water.

It was easy now for me to be alone. The Beast People manifested a quite human curiosity about the dead body, and followed it in a thick knot, sniffing and growling at it, as the Bull Men dragged it down the beach. I went to the headland, and watched the Bull Men, black against the evening sky, as they carried the weighted dead body out to sea, and, like a wave across my mind, came the realisation of the unspeakable aimlessness of things upon the island. Upon the beach, among the rocks beneath me, were the Ape Man, the Hyæna-Swine, and several other of the Beast People, standing about Montgomery and Moreau. They were all intensely excited, and all overflowing with noisy expressions of their loyalty to the Law. Yet I felt an absolute assurance in my own mind that the Hyæna-Swine was implicated in the rabbit-killing. A strange persuasion came upon me that, save for the grossness of the line, the grotesqueness of the forms, I had here before me the whole balance of human life in miniature, the whole interplay of instinct, reason, and fate in its simplest form. The Leopard Man had happened to go under. That was all the difference.

Poor brutes! I began to see the viler aspect of Moreau's cruelty. I had not thought before of the pain and trouble that came to these poor victims after they had passed from Moreau's hands. I had shivered only at the days of actual torment in the enclosure. But now that seemed to be the lesser part. Before they had been beasts, their instincts fitly adapted to their surroundings, and happy as living things may be. Now they stumbled in the shackles of humanity, lived in a fear that never died, fretted by a law they could not understand; their mock-human existence began in an agony, was one long internal struggle, one long dread of Moreau— and for what? It was the wantonness that stirred me.

Had Moreau had any intelligible object I could have sympathised at least a little with him. I am not so squeamish about pain as that. I could have forgiven him a little even had his motive been hate. But he was so irresponsible, so utterly careless. His curiosity, his mad, aimless investigations, drove him on, and the things were thrown out to live a year or so, to struggle and blunder and suffer; at last to die painfully. They were wretched in themselves, the old animal hate moved them to trouble one another, the Law held them back from a brief hot struggle and a decisive end to their natural animosities.

In those days my fear of the Beast People went the way of my personal fear of Moreau. I fell indeed into the morbid state, deep and enduring, alien to fear, which has left permanent scars upon my mind. I must confess I lost faith in the sanity of the world when I saw it suffering the painful disorder of this island. A blind fate, a vast pitiless mechanism, seemed to cut and shape the fabric of existence, and I, Moreau by his passion for research, Montgomery by his passion for drink, the Beast People, with their instincts and mental restrictions, were torn and crushed, ruthlessly, inevitably, amid the infinite complexity of its incessant wheels. But this condition did not come all at once. . . . I think indeed that I anticipate a little in speaking of it now.

XVII

A CATASTROPHE

SCARCELY six weeks passed before I had lost every feeling but dislike and abhorrence for these infamous experiments of Moreau's. My one idea was to get away from these horrible caricatures of my Maker's image, back to the sweet and wholesome intercourse of men. My fellow-creatures, from whom I was thus separated, began to assume idyllic virtue and beauty in my memory. My first friendship with Montgomery did not increase. His long separation from humanity, his secret drunkenness, his evident sympathy with the Beast People, tainted him to me. Several times I let him go alone among them. I avoided intercourse with them in every possible way. I spent an increasing proportion of my time upon the beach, looking for some liberating sail that never appeared, until one day there fell upon us an appalling disaster, that put an altogether different aspect upon my strange surroundings.

It was about seven or eight weeks after my landing—rather more, I think, though I had not troubled to keep account of the time—when this catastrophe occurred. It happened in the early morning—I should think about six. I had risen and breakfasted early, having been aroused by the noise of three Beast Men carrying wood into the enclosure.

After breakfast I went to the open gateway of the enclosure and stood there smoking a cigarette and enjoying the freshness of the early morning. Moreau presently came round the corner of the enclosure and greeted me. He passed by me, and I heard him behind me unlock and enter his laboratory. So indurated was I at that time to the abomination of the place, that I heard without a touch of emotion the puma victim begin another day of torture. It met its persecutor with a shriek almost exactly like that of an angry virago.

186

Then something happened. I do not know what it was exactly to this day. I heard a sharp cry behind me, a fall, and turning, saw an awful face rushing upon me, not human, not animal, but hellish, brown, seamed with red branching scars, red drops starting out upon it, and the lidless eyes ablaze. I flung up my arm to defend myself from the blow that flung me headlong with a broken forearm, and the great monster, swathed in lint and with red-stained bandages fluttering about it, leaped over me and passed. I rolled over and over down the beach, tried to sit up, and collapsed upon my broken arm. Then Moreau appeared, his massive white face all the more terrible for the blood that trickled from his forehead. He carried a revolver in one hand. He scarcely glanced at me, but rushed off at once in pursuit of the puma.

I tried the other arm and sat up. The muffled figure in front ran in great striding leaps along the beach, and Moreau followed her. She turned her head and saw him, then, doubling abruptly, made for the bushes. She gained upon him at every stride. I saw her plunge into them, and Moreau, running slantingly to intercept her, fired and missed as she disappeared. Then he, too, vanished in the green confusion.

I stared after them, and then the pain in my arm flamed up, and with a groan I staggered to my feet. Montgomery appeared in the doorway dressed, and with his revolver in his hand.

'Great God, Prendick!' he said, not noticing that I was hurt. 'That brute's loose! Tore the fetter out of the wall. Have you seen them?' Then sharply, seeing I gripped my arm: 'What's the matter?'

'I was standing in the doorway,' said I.

He came forward and took my arm. 'Blood on the sleeve,' said he, and rolled back the flannel. He pocketed the weapon, felt my arm about painfully, and led me inside. 'Your arm is broken,' he said; and then: 'Tell me exactly how it happened—what happened.'

I told him what I had seen, told him in broken sentences,

with gasps of pain between them, and very dexterously and swiftly he bound my arm meanwhile. He slung it from my shoulder, stood back, and looked at me. 'You'll do,' he said. 'And now?' He thought. Then he went out and locked the gates of the enclosure. He was absent some time.

I was chiefly concerned about my arm. The incident seemed merely one more of many horrible things. I sat down in the deck chair and, I must admit, swore heartily at the island. The first dull feeling of injury in my arm had already given way to a burning pain when Montgomery reappeared.

His face was rather pale, and he showed more of his lower gums than ever. 'I can neither see nor hear anything of him,' he said. 'I've been thinking he may want my help.' He stared at me with his expressionless eyes. 'That was a strong brute,' he said. 'It simply wrenched its fetter out of the wall.'

He went to the window, then to the door, and there turned to me. 'I shall go after him,' he said. 'There's another revolver I can leave with you. It's just possible you may need it.'

He obtained the weapon and put it ready to my hand on the table, then went out, leaving a restless contagion in the air. I did not sit long after he left. I took the revolver in hand and went to the doorway.

The morning was as still as death. Not a whisper of wind stirred, the sea was like polished glass, the sky empty, the beach desolate. This stillness of things oppressed me.

I tried to whistle, and the tune died away. I swore again—the second time that morning. Then I went to the corner of the enclosure and stared inland at the green bush that had swallowed up Moreau and Montgomery. When would they return? And how?

Then far away up the beach a little grey Beast Man appeared, ran down to the water's edge, and began splashing about. I strolled back to the doorway, then to the corner again, and so began pacing to and fro like a sentinel upon duty. Once I was arrested by the distant voice of Montgomery bawling, 'Coo-ee . . . Mor-eau!' My arm became less painful, but very hot. I got feverish and thirsty. My shadow grew shorter. I watched the distant figure until it went away again. Would Moreau and Montgomery never return? Three sea-birds began fighting for some stranded treasure.

Then from far away behind the enclosure I heard a pistol-shot. A long silence, and then came another. Then a yelling cry nearer, and another dismal gap of silence. My imagination set to work to torment me. Then suddenly a shot close by.

I went to the corner, startled, and saw Montgomery, his face scarlet, his hair disordered, and the knee of his trousers torn. His face expressed profound consternation. Behind him slouched the Beast Man M'ling, and round M'ling's jaws were some ominous brown stains.

'Has he come?' he said.

'Moreau?' said I. 'No.'

'My God!' The man was panting, almost sobbing for breath. 'Go back in,' he said, taking my arm. 'They're mad. They're all rushing about mad. What can have happened? I don't know. I'll tell you when my breath comes. Where's some brandy?'

He limped before me into the room and sat down in the deck chair. M'ling flung himself down just outside the door-way, and began panting like a dog. I got Montgomery some brandy and water. He sat staring blankly in front of him, recovering his breath. After some minutes he began to tell me what had happened.

He had followed their track for some way. It was plain enough at first on account of the crushed and broken bushes, white rags torn from the puma's bandages, and occasional smears of blood on the leaves of the shrubs and undergrowth. He lost the track, however, on the stony ground beyond the stream where I had seen the Beast Man drinking, and went wandering aimlessly westward shouting Moreau's name. Then M'ling had come to him carrying a light hatchet. M'ling had seen nothing of the puma affair, had been felling wood and heard him calling. They went on shouting together. Two Beast

Men came crouching and peering at them through the undergrowth, with gestures and a furtive carriage that alarmed Montgomery by their strangeness. He hailed them, and they fled guiltily. He stopped shouting after that, and after wandering some time further in an undecided way, determined to visit the huts.

He found the ravine deserted.

Growing more alarmed every minute, he began to retrace his steps. Then it was he encountered the two Swine Men I had seen dancing on the night of my arrival; blood-stained they were about the mouth, and intensely excited. They came crashing through the ferns, and stopped with fierce faces when they saw him. He cracked his whip in some trepidation, and forthwith they rushed at him. Never before had a Beast Man dared to do that. One he shot through the head, M'ling flung himself upon the other, and the two rolled grappling. M'ling got his brute under and with his teeth in its throat, and Montgomery shot that, too, as it struggled in M'ling's grip. He had some difficulty in inducing M'ling to come on with him.

Thence they had hurried back to me. On the way M'ling had suddenly rushed into a thicket and driven out an undersized Ocelot Man, also blood-stained, and lame through a wound in the foot. This brute had run a little way and then turned savagely at bay, and Montgomery—with a certain wantonness, I thought—had shot him.

'What does it all mean?' said I.

He shook his head and turned once more to the brandy.

XVIII

THE FINDING OF MOREAU

WHEN I saw Montgomery swallow a third dose of brandy I took it upon myself to interfere. He was already more than half fuddled. I told him that some serious thing must have happened to Moreau by this time, or he would have returned, and that it behoved us to ascertain what that catastrophe was. Montgomery raised some feeble objections, and at last agreed. We had some food, and then all three of us started.

It is possibly due to the tension of my mind at the time, but even now that start into the hot stillness of the tropical afternoon is a singularly vivid impression. M'ling went first, his shoulders hunched, his strange black head moving with quick starts as he peered first on this side of the way and then on that. He was unarmed. His axe he had dropped when he encountered the Swine Men. Teeth were *his* weapons when it came to fighting. Montgomery followed with stumbling footsteps, his hands in his pockets, his face downcast; he was in a state of muddled sullenness with me on account of the brandy. My left arm was in a sling—it was lucky it was my left—and I carried my revolver in my right.

We took a narrow path through the wild luxuriance of the island, going northwestward. And presently M'ling stopped and became rigid with watchfulness. Montgomery almost staggered into him, and then stopped too. Then, listening intently, we heard, coming through the trees, the sound of voices and footsteps approaching us.

'He is dead,' said a deep vibrating voice.

'He is not dead, he is not dead,' jabbered another.

'We saw, we saw,' said several voices.

'*Hul*-lo!' suddenly shouted Montgomery. 'Hullo there!'

'Confound you!' said I, and gripped my pistol.

There was a silence, then a crashing among the interlacing vegetation, first here, then there, and then half a dozen faces appeared, strange faces, lit by a strange light. M'ling made a growling noise in his throat. I recognised the Ape Man— I had, indeed, already identified his voice—and two of the white-swathed brown-featured creatures I had seen in Montgomery's boat. With them were the two dappled brutes, and that grey, horrible, crooked creature who said the Law, with grey hair streaming down its cheeks, heavy grey eyebrows, and grey locks pouring off from a central parting upon its sloping forehead, a heavy faceless thing, with strange red eyes, looking at us curiously from amidst the green.

For a space no one spoke. Then Montgomery hiccoughed, 'Who . . . said he was dead?'

The Ape Man looked guiltily at the Hairy Grey Thing. 'He is dead,' said this monster. 'They saw.'

There was nothing threatening about this detachment at any rate. They seemed awe-stricken and puzzled. 'Where is he?' said Montgomery.

'Beyond,' and the grey creature pointed.

'Is there a Law now?' asked the Ape Man. 'Is it still to be this and that? Is he dead indeed?' 'Is there a Law?' repeated the man in white. 'Is there a Law, thou Other with the whip? He is dead,' said the Hairy Grey Thing. And they all stood watching us.

'Prendick,' said Montgomery, turning his dull eyes to me. 'He's dead—evidently.'

I had been standing behind him during this colloquy. I began to see how things lay with them. I suddenly stepped in front of him and lifted up my voice: 'Children of the Law,' I said, 'he is *not* dead.'

M'ling turned his sharp eyes on me. 'He has changed his shape—he has changed his body,' I went on. 'For a time you will not see him. He is . . . there'—I pointed upward—'where he can watch you. You cannot see him. But he can see you. Fear the Law.'

I looked at them squarely. They flinched. 'He is great, he is good,' said the Ape Man, peering fearfully upward among the dense trees.

'And the other Thing?' I demanded.

'The Thing that bled and ran screaming and sobbing—that is dead, too,' said the Grey Thing, still regarding me.

'That's well,' grunted Montgomery.

'The Other with the whip,' began the Grey Thing.

'Well?' said I.

'Said he was dead.'

But Montgomery was still sober enough to understand my motive in denying Moreau's death. 'He is not dead,' he said slowly. 'Not dead at all. No more dead than me.'

'Some,' said I, 'have broken the Law. They will die. Some have died. Show us now where his old body lies. The body he cast away because he had no more need of it.'

'It is this way, Man who walked in the Sea,' said the Grey Thing.

And with these six creatures guiding us, we went through the tumult of ferns and creepers and tree stems towards the north-west. Then came a yelling, a crashing among the branches, and a little pink homunculus rushed by us shrieking. Immediately after appeared a feral monster in headlong pursuit, blood-bedabbled, who was amongst us almost before he could stop his career. The Grey Thing leaped aside; M'ling with a snarl flew at it, and was struck aside; Montgomery fired and missed, bowed his head, threw up his arm, and turned to run. I fired, and the thing still came on; fired again point-blank into its ugly face. I saw its features vanish in a flash. Its face was driven in. Yet it passed me, gripped Montgomery, and holding him, fell headlong beside him, and pulled him sprawling upon itself—in its death-agony.

I found myself alone with M'ling, the dead brute, and the prostrate man. Montgomery raised himself slowly and stared in a muddled way at the shattered Beast Man beside him. It more than half sobered him. He scrambled to his feet. Then I saw the Grey Thing returning cautiously through the trees.

'See,' said I, pointing to the dead brute. 'Is the Law not alive? This came of breaking the Law.'

He peered at the body. 'He sends the Fire that kills,' said he in his deep voice, repeating part of the ritual.

The others gathered round and stared for a space.

At last we drew near the westward extremity of the island. We came upon the gnawed and mutilated body of the puma, its shoulder-bone smashed by a bullet, and perhaps twenty yards further found at last what we sought. He lay face down-ward in a trampled space in a cane-brake. One hand was almost severed at the wrist, and his silvery hair was dabbled in blood. His head had been battered in by the fetters of the puma. The broken canes beneath him were smeared with blood. His revolver we could not find. Montgomery turned him over.

*

Resting at intervals, and with the help of the seven Beast People—for he was a heavy man—we carried him back to the enclosure. The night was darkling. Twice we heard un-seen creatures howling and shrieking past our little band, and once the little pink sloth creature appeared and stared at us, and vanished again. But we were not attacked again. At the gates of the enclosure our company of Beast People left us—M'ling going with the rest. We locked ourselves in, and then took Moreau's mangled body into the yard, and laid it upon a pile of brushwood.

Then we went into the laboratory and put an end to all we found living there.

XIX

MONTGOMERY'S 'BANK HOLIDAY'

WHEN this was accomplished, and we had washed and eaten, Montgomery and I went into my little room and seriously discussed our position for the first time. It was then near midnight. He was almost sober, but greatly disturbed in his mind. He had been strangely under the influence of Moreau's personality. I do not think it had ever occurred to him that Moreau could die. This disaster was the sudden collapse of the habits that had become part of his nature in the ten or more monotonous years he had spent on the island. He talked vaguely, answered my questions crookedly, wandered into general questions.

'This silly ass of a world,' he said. 'What a muddle it all is! I haven't had any life. I wonder when it's going to begin. Sixteen years being bullied by nurses and schoolmasters at their own sweet will, five in London grinding hard at medicine—bad food, shabby lodgings, shabby clothes, shabby vice—a blunder—*I* didn't know any better—and hustled off to this beastly island. Ten years here! What's it all for, Prendick? Are we bubbles blown by a baby?'

It was hard to deal with such ravings. 'The thing we have to think of now,' said I, 'is how to get away from this island.'

'What's the good of getting away? I'm an outcast. Where am *I* to join on? It's all very well for *you*, Prendick. Poor old Moreau! We can't leave him here to have his bones picked. As it is. . . . And besides, what will become of the decent part of the Beast Folk?'

'Well,' said I. 'That will do to-morrow. I've been thinking we might make the brushwood into a pyre and burn his body—and those other things. . . . Then what will happen with the Beast Folk?'

'*I* don't know. I suppose those that were made of beasts of prey will make silly asses of themselves sooner or later. We can't massacre the lot, can we? I suppose that's what *your* humanity would suggest? . . . But they'll change. They are sure to change.'

He talked thus inconclusively until at last I felt my temper going. 'Damnation!' he exclaimed, at some petulance of mine. 'Can't you see I'm in a worse hole than you are?' And he got up and went for the brandy. 'Drink,' he said, returning. 'You logic-chopping, chalky-faced saint of an atheist, drink.'

'Not I,' said I, and sat grimly watching his face under the yellow paraffin flare as he drank himself into a garrulous misery. I have a memory of infinite tedium. He wandered into a maudlin defence of the Beast People and of M'ling. M'ling, he said, was the only thing that had ever really cared for him. And suddenly an idea came to him.

'I'm damned!' said he, staggering to his feet, and clutching the brandy bottle. By some flash of intuition I knew what it was he intended. 'You don't give drink to that beast!' I said, rising and facing him.

'Beast!' said he. 'You're the beast. He takes his liquor like a Christian. Come out of the way, Prendick.'

'For God's sake,' said I.

'*Get* . . . out of the way,' he roared, and suddenly whipped out his revolver.

'Very well,' said I, and stood aside, half minded to fall upon him as he put his hand upon the latch, but deterred by the thought of my useless arm. 'You've made a beast of yourself. To the beasts you may go.'

He flung the doorway open and stood, half facing me, between the yellow lamplight and the pallid glare of the moon; his eye-sockets were blotches of black under his stubbly eyebrows. 'You're a solemn prig, Prendick, a silly ass! You're always fearing and fancying. We're on the edge of things. I'm bound to cut my throat to-morrow. I'm going to have a damned good bank holiday to-night.'

He turned and went out into the moonlight. 'M'ling,' he cried; 'M'ling, old friend!'

Three dim creatures in the silvery light came along the edge of the wan beach, one a white-wrapped creature, the other two blotches of blackness following it. They halted, staring. Then I saw M'ling's hunched shoulders as he came round the corner of the house.

'Drink,' cried Montgomery; 'drink, ye brutes! Drink, and be men. Dammy, I'm the cleverest. Moreau forgot this. This is the last touch. Drink, I tell you.' And waving the bottle in his hand, he started off at a kind of quick trot to the westward, M'ling ranging himself between him and the three dim creatures who followed.

I went to the doorway. They were already indistinct in the

mist of the moonlight before Montgomery halted. I saw him administer a dose of the raw brandy to M'ling, and saw the five figures melt into one vague patch. 'Sing,' I heard Montgomery shout; 'sing all together, "Confound old Prendick," . . . That's right. Now, again: "Confound old Prendick."'

The black group broke up into five separate figures and wound slowly away from me along the band of shining beach. Each went howling at his own sweet will, yelping insult at me, or giving whatever other vent this new inspiration of brandy demanded.

Presently I heard Montgomery's remote voice shouting, 'Right turn!' and they passed with their shouts and howls into the blackness of the landward trees. Slowly, very slowly, they receded into silence.

The peaceful splendour of the night healed again. The moon was now past the meridian and travelling down the west. It was at its full, and very bright, riding through the empty blue sky. The shadow of the wall lay, a yard wide and of inky blackness, at my feet. The eastward sea was a featureless grey, dark and mysterious, and between the sea and the shadow the grey sands (of volcanic glass and crystals) flashed and shone like a beach of diamonds. Behind me the paraffin lamp flared hot and ruddy.

Then I shut the door, locked it, and went into the enclosure where Moreau lay beside his latest victims—the staghounds and the llama, and some other wretched brutes—his massive face, calm even after his terrible death, and with the hard eyes open, staring at the dead white moon above. I sat down upon the edge of the sink, and, with my eyes upon that ghastly pile of silvery light and ominous shadows, began to turn over plans in my mind.

In the morning I would gather some provisions in the dingey, and after setting fire to the pyre before me, push out into the desolation of the high sea once more. I felt that for Montgomery there was no help; that he was in truth half akin to these Beast Folk, unfitted for human kindred. I do not know how long I sat there scheming. It must have been an hour or so. Then my planning was interrupted by the return of Montgomery to my neighbourhood. I heard a yelling from many throats, a tumult of exultant cries, passing down towards the beach, whooping and howling and excited shrieks, that seemed to come to a stop near the water's edge. The riot rose and fell; I heard heavy blows and the splintering smash of wood, but it did not trouble me then. A discordant chanting began.

My thoughts went back to my means of escape. I got up, brought the lamp, and went into a shed to look at some kegs I had seen there. Then I became interested in the contents of some biscuit tins, and opened one. I saw something out of the tail of my eye, a red flicker, and turned sharply.

Behind me lay the yard, vividly black and white in the moonlight, and the pile of wood and faggots on which Moreau and his mutilated victims lay, one on another. They seemed to be gripping one another in one last revengeful grapple. His wounds gaped black as night, and the blood that had dripped lay in black patches upon the sand. Then I saw, without understanding, the cause of the phantom, a ruddy glow that came and danced and went upon the wall opposite. I misinterpreted this, fancied it was a reflection of my flickering lamp, and turned again to the stores in the shed. I went on rummaging among them as well as a one-armed man could, finding this convenient thing and that, and putting them aside for to-morrow's launch. My movements were slow, and the time passed quickly. Presently the daylight crept upon me.

The chanting died down, gave place to a clamour, then began again, and suddenly broke into a tumult. I heard cries of 'More, more!' a sound like quarrelling, and a sudden wild shriek. The quality of the sounds changed so greatly that it arrested my attention. I went out into the yard and listened. Then, cutting like a knife across the confusion, came the crack of a revolver.

I rushed at once through my room to the little doorway. As I did so I heard some of the packing-cases behind me go sliding down and smash together, with a clatter of glass on the floor of the shed. But I did not heed these. I flung the door open and looked out.

Up the beach by the boat-house a bonfire was burning, raining up sparks into the indistinctness of the dawn. Around this struggled a mass of black figures. I heard Montgomery call my name. I began to run at once towards this fire, revolver in hand. I saw the pink tongue of Montgomery's pistol lick out once, close to the ground. He was down. I shouted with all my strength and fired into the air.

I heard some one cry 'The Master!' The knotted black struggle broke into scattering units, the fire leaped and sank down. The crowd of Beast People fled in sudden panic before me up the beach. In my excitement I fired at their retreating backs as they disappeared among the bushes. Then I turned to the black heaps upon the ground.

Montgomery lay on his back with the hairy grey Beast Man sprawling across his body. The brute was dead, but still gripping Montgomery's throat with its curving claws. Near by lay M'ling on his face, and quite still, his neck bitten open, and the upper part of the smashed brandy bottle in his hand. Two other figures lay near the fire, the one motionless, the other groaning fitfully, every now and then raising its head slowly, then dropping it again.

I caught hold of the Grey Man and pulled him off Montgomery's body; his claws drew down the torn coat reluctantly as I dragged him away.

Montgomery was dark in the face and scarcely breathing. I splashed sea-water on his face, and pillowed his head on my rolled-up coat. M'ling was dead. The wounded creature by the fire—it was a Wolf Brute with a bearded grey face—lay, I found, with the fore part of its body upon the still glowing timber. The wretched thing was injured so dreadfully that in mercy I blew its brains out at once. The other brute was one of the Bull Men swathed in white. He, too, was dead.

The rest of the Beast People had vanished from the beach. I went to Montgomery again and knelt beside him, cursing my ignorance of medicine.

The fire beside me had sunk down, and only charred beams of timber glowing at the central ends, and mixed with a grey ash of brushwood, remained. I wondered casually where Montgomery had got his wood. Then I saw that the dawn was upon us. The sky had grown brighter, the setting moon was growing pale and opaque in the luminous blue of the day. The sky to the eastward was rimmed with red.

Then I heard a thud and a hissing behind me, and, looking round, sprang to my feet with a cry of horror. Against the warm dawn great tumultuous masses of black smoke were boiling up out of the enclosure, and through their stormy darkness shot flickering threads of blood-red flame. Then the thatched roof caught. I saw the curving charge of the flames across the sloping straw. A spurt of fire jetted from the window of my room.

I knew at once what had happened. I remembered the crash I had heard. When I had rushed out to Montgomery's assistance I had overturned the lamp.

The hopelessness of saving any of the contents of the enclosure stared me in the face. My mind came back to my plan of flight, and turning swiftly I looked to see where the two boats lay upon the beach. They were gone! Two axes lay upon the sands beside me, chips and splinters were scattered broadcast, and the ashes of the bonfire were blackening and smoking under the dawn. He had burned the boats to revenge himself upon me and prevent our return to mankind.

A sudden convulsion of rage shook me. I was almost moved to batter his foolish head in as he lay there helpless at my feet. Then suddenly his hand moved, so feebly, so pitifully, that my wrath vanished. He groaned and opened his eyes for a minute.

I knelt down beside him and raised his head. He opened his eyes again, staring silently at the dawn, and then they met mine. The lids fell. 'Sorry,' he said presently, with an effort. He seemed trying to think. 'The last,' he murmured, 'the last of this silly universe. What a mess——'

I listened. His head fell helplessly to one side. I thought some drink might revive him, but there was neither drink nor vessel in which to bring drink at hand. He seemed suddenly heavier. My heart went cold.

I bent down to his face, put my hand through the rent in his blouse. He was dead; and even as he died a line of white heat, the limb of the sun, rose eastward beyond the projection of the bay, splashing its radiance across the sky and turning the dark sea into a weltering tumult of dazzling light. It fell like a glory upon his death-shrunken face.

I let his head fall gently upon the rough pillow I had made for him, and stood up. Before me was the glittering desolation of the sea, the awful solitude upon which I had already suffered so much; behind me the island, hushed under the dawn, its Beast People silent and unseen. The enclosure with all its provisions and ammunition burned noisily with sudden gusts of flame, a fitful crackling, and now and then a crash. The heavy smoke drove up the beach away from me, rolling low over the distant tree tops towards the huts in the ravine. Beside me were the charred vestiges of the boats and these five dead bodies.

Then out of the bushes came three Beast People, with hunched shoulders, protruding heads, misshapen hands awkwardly held, and inquisitive unfriendly eyes, and advanced towards me with hesitating gestures.

XX

ALONE WITH THE BEAST FOLK

I FACED these people, facing my fate in them single-handed—now literally single-handed, for I had a broken arm. In my pocket was a revolver with two empty chambers. Among the chips scattered about the beach lay the two axes that had been used to chop up the boats. The tide was creeping in behind me.

There was nothing for it but courage. I looked squarely into the faces of the advancing monsters. They avoided my eyes, and their quivering nostrils investigated the bodies that lay beyond me on the beach. I took half a dozen steps, picked up the blood-stained whip that lay beneath the body of the Wolf Man, and cracked it.

They stopped and stared at me. 'Salute,' said I. 'Bow down!'

They hesitated. One bent his knees. I repeated my command, with my heart in my mouth, and advanced upon them. One knelt, then the other two.

I turned and walked towards the dead bodies, keeping my face towards the three kneeling Beast Men, very much as an actor passing up the stage faces his audience.

'They broke the Law,' said I, putting my foot on the Sayer of the Law. 'They have been slain. Even the Sayer of the Law. Even the Other with the whip. Great is the Law! Come and see.'

'None escape,' said one of them, advancing and peering.

'None escape,' said I. 'Therefore hear and do as I command.' They stood up, looking questioningly at one another.

'Stand there,' said I.

I picked up the hatchets and swung them by their heads from the sling of my arm, turned Montgomery over, picked up his revolver, still loaded in two chambers, and bending down to rummage, found half a dozen cartridges in his pocket.

'Take him,' said I, standing up again and pointing with the whip; 'take him and carry him out, and cast him into the sea.'

They came forward, evidently still afraid of Montgomery but still more afraid of my cracking red whip-lash, and after some fumbling and hesitation, some whip-cracking and shouting, lifted him gingerly, carried him down to the beach, and went splashing into the dazzling welter of the sea. 'On,' said I, 'on—carry him far.'

They went in up to their armpits and stood regarding me. 'Let go,' said I, and the body of Montgomery vanished with a splash. Something seemed to tighten across my chest. 'Good!' said I, with a break in my voice, and they came back, hurrying and fearful, to the margin of the water, leaving long wakes of black in the silver. At the water's edge they stopped, turning and glaring into the sea as though they presently expected Montgomery to arise thencefrom and exact vengeance.

'Now these,' said I, pointing to the other bodies.

They took care not to approach the place where they had thrown Montgomery into the water, but instead carried the four dead Beast People slantingly along the beach for perhaps a hundred yards before they waded out and cast them away.

As I watched them disposing of the mangled remains of M'ling I heard a light footfall behind me, and turning quickly saw the big Hyæna-Swine perhaps a dozen yards away. His head was bent down, his bright eyes were fixed upon me, his stumpy hands clenched and held close by his side. He stopped in this crouching attitude when I turned, his eyes a little averted.

For a moment we stood eye to eye. I dropped the whip and snatched at the pistol in my pocket. For I meant to kill this brute—the most formidable of any left now upon the island—at the first excuse. It may seem treacherous, but so I was resolved. I was far more afraid of him than of any other two of the Beast Folk. His continued life was, I knew, a threat against mine.

I was perhaps a dozen seconds collecting myself. Then I cried, 'Salute! Bow down!'

His teeth flashed upon me in a snarl. 'Who are *you*, that I should. . . .'

Perhaps a little too spasmodically, I drew my revolver, aimed, and quickly fired. I heard him yelp, saw him run sideways and turn, knew I had missed, and clicked back the cock with my thumb for the next shot. But he was already running headlong, jumping from side to side, and I dared not risk another miss. Every now and then he looked back at me over his shoulder. He went slanting along the beach, and vanished beneath the driving masses of dense smoke that were still pouring out from the burning enclosure. For some time I stood staring after him. I turned to my three obedient Beast Folk again, and signalled them to drop the body they still carried. Then I went back to the place by the fire where the bodies had fallen, and kicked the sand until all the brown blood-stains were absorbed and hidden.

I dismissed my three serfs with a wave of the hand, and went up the beach into the thickets. I carried my pistol in my hand, my whip thrust, with the hatchets, in the sling of my arm. I was anxious to be alone, to think out the position in which I was now placed.

A dreadful thing, that I was only beginning to realise, was that over all this island there was now no safe place where I could be alone, and secure to rest or sleep. I had recovered strength amazingly since my landing, but I was still inclined to be nervous and to break down under any great stress. I felt I ought to cross the island and establish myself with the Beast People, making myself secure in their confidence. And my heart failed me. I went back to the beach and, turning eastward past the burning enclosure, made for a point where a shallow spit of coral sand ran out towards the reef. Here I could sit down and think, my back to the sea and my face against any surprise. And there I sat, chin on knees, the sun beating down upon my head and a growing dread in my mind, plotting how I could live on against the hour of my rescue (if ever rescue came). I tried to review the whole situation as calmly as I could, but it was impossible to clear the thing of emotion.

I began turning over in my mind the reason of Montgomery's despair. 'They will change,' he said. 'They are sure to change.' And Moreau—what was it that Moreau had said? 'The stubborn beast flesh grows day by day back again. . . .' Then I came round to the Hyæna-Swine. I felt assured that if I did not kill that brute he would kill me. . . . The Sayer of the Law was dead—worse luck! . . . They knew now that we of the Whips could be killed, even as they themselves were killed. . . .

Were they peering at me already out of the green masses of ferns and palms over yonder—watching until I came within their spring? Were they plotting against me? What was the Hyæna-Swine telling them? My imagination was running away with me into a morass of unsubstantial fears.

My thoughts were disturbed by a crying of sea-birds, hurrying towards some black object that had been stranded by the waves on the beach near the enclosure. I knew what that object was, but I had not the heart to go back and drive them off. I began walking along the beach in the opposite direction, designing to come round the eastward corner of the island, and so approach the ravine of the huts, without traversing the possible ambuscades of the thickets.

Perhaps half a mile along the beach I became aware of one of my three Beast Folk advancing out of the landward bushes towards me. I was now so nervous with my own imaginings that I immediately drew my revolver. Even the propitiatory gestures of the creature failed to disarm me.

He hesitated as he approached. 'Go away,' cried I. There was something very suggestive of a dog in the cringing attitude of the creature. It retreated a little way, very like a dog being sent home, and stopped, looking at me imploringly with canine brown eyes. 'Go away,' said I. 'Do not come near me.'

'May I not come near you?' it said.

'No. Go away,' I insisted, and snapped my whip. Then, putting my whip in my teeth, I stooped for a stone, and with that threat drove the creature away.

So, in solitude, I came round by the ravine of the Beast People, and, hiding among the weeds and reeds that separated this crevice from the sea, I watched such of them as appeared, trying to judge from their gestures and appearance how the death of Moreau and Montgomery and the destruction of the House of Pain had affected them. I know now the folly of my cowardice. Had I kept my courage up to the level of the dawn, had I not allowed it to ebb away in solitary thought, I might have grasped the vacant sceptre of Moreau, and ruled over the Beast People. As it was, I lost the opportunity, and sank to the position of a mere leader among my fellows.

Towards noon certain of them came and squatted basking in the hot sand. The imperious voices of hunger and thirst prevailed over my dread. I came out of the bushes, and, revolver in hand, walked down towards these seated figures. One, a Wolf Woman, turned her head and stared at me, and then the others. None attempted to rise or salute me. I felt too faint and weary to insist against so many, and I let the moment pass.

'I want food,' said I, almost apologetically, and drawing near.

'There is food in the huts,' said an Ox-Boar Man drowsily, and looking away from me.

I passed them, and went down into the shadow and odours of the almost deserted ravine. In an empty hut I feasted on some specked and half-decayed fruit, and then, after I had propped some branches and sticks about the opening, and placed myself with my face towards it, and my hand upon my revolver, the exhaustion of the last thirty hours claimed its own, and I let myself fall into a light slumber, trusting that the flimsy barricade I had erected would cause sufficient noise in its removal to save me from surprise.

XXI

THE REVERSION OF THE BEAST FOLK

IN this way I became one among the Beast People in the Island of Doctor Moreau. When I awoke it was dark about me. My arm ached in its bandages. I sat up, wondering at first where I might be. I heard coarse voices talking outside. Then I saw that my barricade was gone, and that the opening of the hut stood clear. My revolver was still in my hand.

I heard something breathing, saw something crouched together close beside me. I held my breath, trying to see what it was. It began to move slowly, interminably. Then something soft and warm and moist passed across my hand.

All my muscles contracted. I snatched my hand away. A cry of alarm began, and was stifled in my throat. Then I just realised what had happened sufficiently to stay my fingers on the revolver.

'Who is that?' I said in a hoarse whisper, the revolver still pointed.

'I, Master.'

'Who are you?'

'They say there is no Master now. But I know, I know. I carried the bodies into the sea, O Walker in the Sea, the bodies of those you slew. I am your slave, Master.'

'Are you the one I met on the beach?' I asked.

'The same, Master.'

The thing was evidently faithful enough, for it might have fallen upon me as I slept. 'It is well,' I said, extending my hand for another licking kiss. I began to realise what its presence meant, and the tide of my courage flowed. 'Where are the others?' I asked.

'They are mad. They are fools,' said the Dog Man. 'Even now they talk together beyond there. They say, "The Master is dead; the Other with the Whip is dead. That Other who walked in the Sea is—as we are. We have no Master, no Whips, no House of Pain any more. There is an end. We love the Law, and will keep it; but there is no pain, no Master, no Whips for ever again." So they say. But I know, Master, I know.'

I felt in the darkness and patted the Dog Man's head. 'It is well,' I said again.

'Presently you will slay them all,' said the Dog Man.

'Presently,' I answered, 'I will slay them all—after certain days and certain things have come to pass. Every one of them save those you spare, every one of them shall be slain.'

'What the Master wishes to kill the Master kills,' said the Dog Man with a certain satisfaction in his voice.

'And that their sins may grow,' I said; 'let them live in their folly until their time is ripe. Let them not know that I am the Master.'

'The Master's will is sweet,' said the Dog Man, with the ready tact of his canine blood.

'But one has sinned,' said I. 'Him I will kill, whenever I may meet him. When I say to you, *"That is he,"* see that you fall upon him. And now I will go to the men and women who are assembled together.'

For a moment the opening of the hut was blackened by the exit of the Dog Man. Then I followed and stood up, almost in the exact spot where I had been when I had heard Moreau and his staghound pursuing me. But now it was night, and all the miasmatic ravine about me was black, and beyond, instead of a green sunlit slope, I saw a red fire before which hunched grotesque figures moved to and fro. Further were the thick trees, a bank of black fringed above with the black lace of the upper branches. The moon was just riding up on the edge of the ravine, and like a bar across its face drove the spire of vapour that was for ever streaming from the fumaroles of the island.

'Walk by me,' said I, nerving myself, and side by side we walked down the narrow way, taking little heed of the dim things that peered at us out of the huts.

None about the fire attempted to salute me. Most of them disregarded me—ostentatiously. I looked round for the Hyæna-Swine, but he was not there. Altogether, perhaps, twenty of the Beast Folk squatted, staring into the fire or talking to one another.

'He is dead, he is dead, the Master is dead,' said the voice of the Ape Man to the right of me. 'The House of Pain— there *is* no House of Pain.'

'He is not dead,' said I, in a loud voice. 'Even now he watches us.'

This startled them. Twenty pairs of eyes regarded me.

'The House of Pain is gone,' said I. 'It will come again. The Master you cannot see. Yet even now he listens above you.'

'True, true!' said the Dog Man.

They were staggered at my assurance. An animal may be ferocious and cunning enough, but it takes a real man to tell a lie. 'The Man with the Bound Arm speaks a strange thing,' said one of the Beast Folk.

'I tell you it is so,' I said. 'The Master and the House of Pain will come again. Woe be to him who breaks the Law!'

They looked curiously at one another. With an affectation of indifference I began to chop idly at the ground in front of me with my hatchet. They looked, I noticed, at the deep cuts I made in the turf.

Then the Satyr raised a doubt; I answered him, and then one of the dappled things objected, and an animated discussion sprang up round the fire. Every moment I began to feel more convinced of my present security. I talked now without the catching in my breath, due to the intensity of my excitement, that had troubled me at first. In the course of about an hour I had really convinced several of the Beast Folk of the truth of my assertions, and talked most of the others into a dubious state. I kept a sharp eye for my enemy the Hyæna-Swine, but he never appeared. Every now and then a suspicious movement would startle me, but my confidence grew rapidly. Then as the moon crept down from the zenith, one by one the listeners began to yawn (showing the oddest teeth in the light of the sinking fire), and first one, and then another, retired towards the dens in the ravine. And I, dreading the silence and darkness, went with them, knowing I was safer with several of them than with one alone.

In this manner began the longer part of my sojourn upon this Island of Doctor Moreau. But from that night until the end came there was but one thing happened to tell, save a series of innumerable small unpleasant details and the fretting of an incessant uneasiness. So that I prefer to make no chronicle for that gap of time, to tell only one cardinal incident of the ten months I spent as an intimate of these half-humanised brutes. There is much that sticks in my memory that I could write, things that I would cheerfully give my right hand to forget. But they do not help the telling of the story. In the retrospect it is strange to remember how soon I fell in with these monsters' ways and gained my confidence again. I had my quarrels, of course, and could show some teeth marks still, but they soon gained a wholesome respect for my trick of throwing stones and the bite of my hatchet. And my St Bernard Dog Man's loyalty was of infinite service to me. I found their simple scale of honour was based mainly on the capacity for inflicting trenchant wounds. Indeed I may say—without vanity, I hope—that I held something like a pre-eminence among them. One or two whom in various disputes I had scarred rather badly, bore me a grudge; but it vented itself, chiefly behind my back and at a safe distance from my missiles, in grimaces.

The Hyæna-Swine avoided me, and I was always on the alert for him. My inseparable Dog Man hated and dreaded him intensely. I really believe that was at the root of the brute's attachment to me. It was soon evident to me that the former monster had tasted blood and gone the way of the Leopard Man. He formed a lair somewhere in the forest and became solitary. Once I tried to induce the Beast Folk to hunt him, but I lacked the authority to make them co-operate for one end. Again and again I tried to approach his den and come upon him unawares, but always he was too acute for me, and saw or winded me and got away. He made every forest pathway dangerous to me and my allies with his lurking ambuscades. The Dog Man scarcely dared to leave my side.

In the first month or so the Beast Folk, compared with their latter condition, were human enough; and for one or two besides my canine friend I even conceived a friendly tolerance. The little pink sloth creature displayed an odd affection for me, and took to following me about. The Ape Man bored me however. He assumed, on the strength of his five digits, that he was my equal, and was for ever jabbering at me, jabbering the most arrant nonsense. One thing about him entertained me a little: he had a fantastic trick of coining new words. He had an idea, I believe, that to gabble about names that meant nothing was the proper use of speech. He called it 'big thinks,' to distinguish it from 'little thinks'—the sane everyday interests of life. If ever I made a remark he did not understand, he would praise it very much, ask me to say it again, learn it by heart, and go off repeating it, with a word wrong here or there, to all the milder of the Beast People. He thought nothing of what was plain and compre-hensible. I invented some very curious 'big thinks' for his especial use. I think now that he was the silliest creature I ever met; he had developed in the most wonderful way the distinctive silliness of man without losing one jot of the natural folly of a monkey.

This, I say, was in the earlier weeks of my solitude among these brutes. During that time they respected the usage established by the Law, and behaved with general decorum. Once I found another rabbit torn to pieces—by the Hyæna-Swine, I am assured—but that was all. It was about May when I first distinctly perceived a growing difference in their speech and carriage, a growing coarseness of articulation, a growing disinclination to talk. My Ape Man's jabber multiplied in volume, but grew less and less comprehensible, more and more simian. Some of the others seemed altogether slipping their hold upon speech, though they still understood what I said to them at that time. Can you imagine language, once clear-cut and exact, softening and guttering, losing shape and import, becoming mere lumps of sound again? And they walked erect with an increasing difficulty. Though they evidently felt ashamed of themselves, every now and then I would come upon one or other running on toes and finger-tips, and quite unable to recover the vertical attitude. They held things more clumsily; drinking by suction, feeding by gnawing, grew commoner every day. I realised more keenly than ever what Moreau had told me about the 'stubborn beast flesh.' They were reverting, and reverting very rapidly.

Some of them—the pioneers, I noticed with some surprise, were all females—began to disregard the injunction of decency—deliberately for the most part. Others even attempted public outrages upon the institution of monogamy. The tradition of the Law was clearly losing its force. I cannot pursue this disagreeable subject. My Dog Man imperceptibly slipped back to the dog again; day by day he became dumb, quadrupedal, hairy. I scarcely noticed the transition from the companion on my right hand to the lurching dog at my side. As the carelessness and disorganisation increased from day to day, the lane of dwelling-places, at no time very sweet, became so loathsome that I left it, and going across the island made myself a hovel of boughs amid the black ruins of Moreau's enclosure. Some memory of pain, I found, still made that place the safest from the Beast Folk.

It would be impossible to detail every step of the lapsing of these monsters: to tell how, day by day, the human semblance left them; how they gave up bandagings and wrappings, abandoned at last every stitch of clothing; how the hair began to spread over the exposed limbs; how their foreheads fell away and their faces projected; how the quasi-human intimacy I had permitted myself with some of them in the first month of my loneliness became a horror to recall.

The change was slow and inevitable. For them and for me it came without any definite shock. I still went among them in safety, because no jolt in the downward glide had released the increasing charge of explosive animalism that ousted the human day by day. But I began to fear that soon now that shock must come. My St Bernard Brute followed me to the enclosure, and his vigilance enabled me to sleep at times in something like peace. The little pink sloth thing became shy and left me, to crawl back to its natural life once more among the tree branches. We were in just the state of equilibrium that would remain in one of those 'Happy Family' cages that animal-tamers exhibit, if the tamer were to leave it for ever.

Of course these creatures did not decline into such beasts as the reader has seen in zoological gardens—into ordinary bears, wolves, tigers, oxen, swine, and apes. There was still something strange about each; in each Moreau had blended this animal with that; one perhaps was ursine chiefly, another feline chiefly, another bovine chiefly, but each was tainted with other creatures—a kind of generalised animalism appeared through the specific dispositions. And the dwindling shreds of their humanity still startled me every now and then, a momentary recrudescence of speech perhaps, an unexpected dexterity of the forefeet, a pitiful attempt to walk erect.

I, too, must have undergone strange changes. My clothes hung about me as yellow rags, through whose rents glowed the tanned skin. My hair grew long, and became matted together. I am told that even now my eyes have a strange brightness, a swift alertness of movement.

At first I spent the daylight hours on the southward beach watching for a ship, hoping and praying for a ship. I counted on the *Ipecacuanha* returning as the year wore on, but she never came. Five times I saw sails, and thrice smoke, but nothing ever touched the island. I always had a bonfire ready, but no doubt the volcanic reputation of the island was taken to account for that.

It was only about September or October that I began to think of making a raft. By that time my arm had healed, and both my hands were at my service again. At first I found my helplessness appalling. I had never done any carpentry or suchlike work in my life, and I spent day after day in experimental chopping and binding among the trees. I had no ropes, and could hit on nothing wherewith to make ropes; none of the abundant creepers seemed limber or strong enough, and with all my litter of scientific education I could not devise any way of making them so. I spent more than a fortnight grubbing among the black ruins of the enclosure and on the beach where the boats had been burned, looking for nails and other stray pieces of metal that might prove of service. Now and then some Beast creature would watch me, and go leaping off when I called to it. There came a season of thunderstorms and heavy rain that greatly retarded my work, but at last the raft was completed. I was delighted with it. But with a certain lack of practical sense that has always been my bane I had made it a mile or more from the sea, and before I had dragged it down to the beach the thing had fallen to pieces. Perhaps it is as well I was saved from launching it. But at the time my misery at my failure was so acute, that for some days I simply moped on the beach and stared at the water and thought of death.

But I did not mean to die, and an incident occurred that warned me unmistakably of the folly of letting the days pass so—for each fresh day was fraught with increasing danger from the Beast Monsters. I was lying in the shade of the enclosure wall staring out to sea, when I was startled by something cold touching the skin of my heel, and starting round found the little pink sloth creature blinking into my face. He had long since lost speech and active movement, and the lank hair of the little brute grew thicker every day, and his stumpy claws more askew. He made a moaning noise when he saw he had attracted my attention, went a little way towards the bushes, and looked back at me.

At first I did not understand, but presently it occurred to me that he wished me to follow him, and this I did at last, slowly—for the day was hot. When he reached the trees he clambered into them, for he could travel better among their swinging creepers than on the ground.

And suddenly in a trampled space I came upon a ghastly group. My St Bernard creature lay on the ground dead, and near his body crouched the Hyæna-Swine, gripping the quivering flesh with misshapen claws, gnawing at it and snarling with delight. As I approached the monster lifted its glaring eyes to mine, its lips went trembling back from its red-stained teeth, and it growled menacingly. It was not afraid and not ashamed; the last vestige of the human taint had vanished. I advanced a step further, stopped, pulled out my revolver. At last I had him face to face.

The brute made no sign of retreat. But its ears went back, its hair bristled, and its body crouched together. I aimed between the eyes and fired. As I did so the thing rose straight at me in a leap, and I was knocked over like a ninepin. It clutched at me with its crippled hand, and struck me in the face. Its spring carried it over me. I fell under the hind part of its body, but luckily I had hit as I meant, and it had died even as it leapt. I crawled out from under its unclean weight and stood up trembling, staring at its quivering body. That danger at least was over. But this, I knew, was only the first of the series of relapses that must come.

I burned both the bodies on a pyre of brushwood. Now, indeed, I saw clearly that unless I left the island my death was only a question of time. The Beasts by that time had, with one or two exceptions, left the ravine, and made themselves lairs according to their tastes among the thickets of the island. Few prowled by day; most of them slept, and the island might have seemed deserted to a newcomer; but at night the air was hideous with their calls and howling. I had half a mind to make a massacre of them—to build traps or fight them with my knife. Had I possessed sufficient cartridges, I should not have hesitated to begin the killing. There could now be scarcely a score left of the dangerous carnivores; the braver of these were already dead. After the death of this poor dog of mine, my last friend, I too adopted to some extent the practice of slumbering in the daytime, in order to be on my guard at night. I rebuilt my den in the walls of the enclosure with such a narrow opening that anything attempting to enter must necessarily make a considerable noise. The creatures had lost the art of fire, too, and recovered their fear of it. I turned once more, almost passionately now, to hammering together stakes and branches to form a raft for my escape.

I found a thousand difficulties. I am an extremely unhandy man—my schooling was over before the days of Slöjd*—but most of the requirements of a raft I met at last in some clumsy circuitous way or other, and this time I took care of the strength. The only insurmountable obstacle was that I had no vessel to contain the water I should need if I floated forth upon these untravelled seas. I would have even tried pottery, but the island contained no clay. I used to go moping about the island, trying with all my might to solve this one last difficulty. Sometimes I would give way to wild outbursts of rage, and hack and splinter some unlucky tree in my intolerable vexation. But I could think of nothing.

And then came a day, a wonderful day, that I spent in ecstasy. I saw a sail to the south-west, a small sail like that of a little schooner, and forthwith I lit a great pile of brushwood and stood by it in the heat of it and the heat of the midday sun, watching. All day I watched that sail, eating or drinking nothing, so that my head reeled; and the Beasts came and glared at me, and seemed to wonder, and went away. The boat was still distant when night came and swallowed it up, and all night I toiled to keep my blaze bright and high, and the eyes of the Beasts shone out of the darkness, marvelling. In the dawn it was nearer, and I saw it was the dirty lug sail of a small boat. My eyes were weary with watching, and I peered and could not believe them. Two men were in the boat, sitting low down, one by the bows and the other at the rudder. But the boat sailed strangely. The head was not kept to the wind; it yawed and fell away.

As the day grew brighter I began waving the last rag of my jacket to them; but they did not notice me, and sat still, facing one another. I went to the lowest point of the low headland and gesticulated and shouted. There was no response, and the boat kept on her aimless course, making slowly, very slowly, for the bay. Suddenly a great white bird flew up out of the boat, and neither of the men stirred. It circled round, and then came sweeping overhead with its strong wings outspread.

Then I stopped shouting, and sat down on the headland and rested my chin on my hands and stared. Slowly, slowly, the boat drove past towards the west. I would have swum out to it, but something, a cold vague fear, kept me back. In the afternoon the tide stranded it, and left it a hundred yards or so to the westward of the ruins of the enclosure.

The men in it were dead, had been dead so long that they fell to pieces when I tilted the boat on its side and dragged them out. One had a shock of red hair like the captain of the *Ipecacuanha*, and a dirty white cap lay in the bottom of the boat. As I stood beside the boat, three of the Beasts came slinking out of the bushes and sniffing towards me. One of my spasms of disgust came upon me. I thrust the little boat down the beach and clambered on board her. Two of the brutes were Wolf Beasts, and came forward with quivering nostrils and glittering eyes; the third was the horrible non-descript of bear and bull.

When I saw them approaching those wretched remains, heard them snarling at one another, and caught the gleam of their teeth, a frantic horror succeeded my repulsion. I turned my back upon them, struck the lug, and began paddling out to sea. I could not bring myself to look behind me.

But I lay between the reef and the island that night, and the next morning went round to the stream and filled the empty keg aboard with water. Then, with such patience as I could command, I collected a quantity of fruit, and waylaid and killed two rabbits with my last three cartridges. While I was doing this I left the boat moored to an inward projection of the reef, for fear of the Beast Monsters.

XXII

THE MAN ALONE

IN the evening I started and drove out to sea before a gentle wind from the south-west, slowly and steadily; and the island grew smaller and smaller, and the lank spire of smoke dwindled to a finer and finer line against the hot sunset. The ocean rose up around me, hiding that low dark patch from my eyes. The daylight, the trailing glory of the sun, went streaming out of the sky, was drawn aside like some luminous curtain, and at last I looked into that blue gulf of immensity that the sunshine hides, and saw the floating hosts of the stars. The sea was silent, the sky was silent; I was alone with the night and silence.

So I drifted for three days, eating and drinking sparingly, and meditating upon all that had happened to me, nor desiring very greatly to see men again. One unclean rag was about me, my hair a black tangle. No doubt my discoverers thought me a madman. It is strange, but I felt no desire to return to mankind. I was only glad to be quit of the foulness of the Beast Monsters. And on the third day I was picked up by a brig from Apia* to San Francisco. Neither the captain nor the mate would believe my story, judging that solitude and danger had made me mad. And fearing their opinion might be that of others, I refrained from telling my adventures further, and professed to recall nothing that had happened to me between the loss of the *Lady Vain* and the time when I was picked up again—the space of a year.

I had to act with the utmost circumspection to save myself from the suspicion of insanity. My memory of the Law, of the two dead sailors, of the ambuscades of the darkness, of the body in the cane-brake, haunted me. And unnatural as it seems, with my return to mankind came, instead of that confidence and sympathy I had expected, a strange enhancement of the uncertainty and dread I had experienced during my stay upon the island. No one would believe me, I was almost as queer to men as I had been to the Beast People. I may have caught something of the natural wildness of my companions.

They say that terror is a disease, and anyhow I can witness that for several years now, a restless fear has dwelt in my mind, such a restless fear as a half-tamed lion cub may feel. My trouble took the strangest form. I could not persuade myself that the men and women I met were not also another, still passably human, Beast People, animals half-wrought into the outward image of human souls; and that they would presently begin to revert, to show first this bestial mark and then that. But I have confided my case to a strangely able man, a man who had known Moreau and seemed half to credit my story, a mental specialist—and he has helped me mightily.

Though I do not expect that the terror of that island will ever altogether leave me, at most times it lies far in the back of my mind, a mere distant cloud, a memory and a faint distrust; but there are times when the little cloud spreads until it obscures the whole sky. Then I look about me at my fellow men. And I go in fear. I see faces keen and bright, others dull or dangerous, others unsteady, insincere; none that have the calm authority of a reasonable soul. I feel as though the animal was surging up through them; that presently the degradation of the Islanders will be played over again on a larger scale. I know this is an illusion, that these seeming men and women about me are indeed men and women, men and women for ever, perfectly reasonable creatures full of human desires and tender solicitude, emancipated from instinct and the slaves of no fantastic Law—beings altogether different from the Beast Folk. Yet I shrink from them, from their curious glances, their inquiries and assistance, and long to be away from them and alone.

For that reason I live near the broad free downland, and can escape thither when this shadow is over my soul; and very sweet is the empty downland then, under the windswept sky. When I lived in London the horror was well-nigh insupportable. I could not get away from men; their voices came through windows, locked doors were flimsy safeguards. I would go out into the streets to fight with my delusion, and prowling women would mew after me, furtive craving men glance jealously at me, weary pale workers go coughing by me with tired eyes and eager paces like wounded deer dripping blood, old people, bent and dull, pass murmuring to themselves and all unheeding a ragged tail of gibing children. Then I would turn aside into some chapel, and even there, such was my disturbance, it seemed that the preacher gibbered Big Thinks even as the Ape Man had done; or into some library, and there the intent faces over the books seemed but patient creatures waiting for prey. Particularly nauseous were the blank expressionless faces of people in trains and omnibuses; they seemed no more my fellow-creatures than dead bodies would be, so that I did not dare to travel unless I was assured of being alone. And even it seemed that I, too, was not a reasonable creature, but only an animal tormented with some strange disorder in its brain, that sent it to wander alone like a sheep stricken with the gid.*

But this is a mood that comes to me now—I thank God—more rarely. I have withdrawn myself from the confusion of cities and multitudes, and spend my days surrounded by wise books, bright windows in this life of ours lit by the shining souls of men. I see few strangers, and have but a small household. My days I devote to reading and to experiments in chemistry, and I spend many of the clear nights in the study of astronomy. There is, though I do not know how there is or why there is, a sense of infinite peace and protection in the glittering hosts of heaven. There it must be, I think, in the vast and eternal laws of matter, and not in the daily cares and sins and troubles of men, that whatever is more than animal within us must find its solace and its hope. I hope, or I could not live. And so, in hope and solitude, my story ends.

APPENDIX

The Introduction to the first edition of
The Island of Doctor Moreau

ON February the 1st, 1887, the *Lady Vain* was lost by collision with a derelict when about the latitude 1° s. and longitude 107° w.

On January the 5th, 1888—that is, eleven months and four days after—my uncle, Edward Prendick, a private gentleman, who certainly went aboard the *Lady Vain* at Callao, and who had been considered drowned, was picked up in latitude 5° 3′ s. and longitude 101° w. in a small open boat, of which the name was illegible, but which is supposed to have belonged to the missing schooner *Ipecacuanha*. He gave such a strange account of himself that he was supposed demented. Subsequently, he alleged that his mind was a blank from the moment of his escape from the *Lady Vain*. His case was discussed among psychologists at the time as a curious instance of the lapse of memory consequent upon physical and mental stress. The following narrative was found among his papers by the undersigned, his nephew and heir, but unaccompanied by any definite request for publication.

The only island known to exist in the region in which my uncle was picked up is Noble's Isle, a small volcanic islet, and uninhabited. It was visited in 1891 by H.M.S. *Scorpion*. A party of sailors then landed, but found nothing living thereon except certain curious white moths, some hogs and rabbits, and some rather peculiar rats. No specimen was secured of these. So that this narrative is without confirmation in its most essential particular. With that understood, there seems no harm in putting this strange story before the public, in accordance, as I believe, with my uncle's intentions. There is at least this much in its behalf: my uncle passed out of human knowledge about latitude 5° s. and longitude 105° w., and reappeared in the same part of the ocean after a space of eleven months. In some way he must have lived during the interval. And it seems that a schooner called the *Ipecacuanha*, with a drunken captain, John Davis, did start from Arica with a puma and certain other animals aboard in January 1887, that the vessel was well known at several ports in the South Pacific, and that it finally disappeared from those seas (with a considerable amount of copra aboard), sailing to its unknown fate from Banya in December 1887, a date that tallies entirely with my uncle's story.

CHARLES EDWARD PRENDICK

EXPLANATORY NOTES

5 *Professor Simon Newcomb . . . a month or so ago*: Newcomb (1835–1909) spoke of four-dimensional geometry in his Presidential Address to the New York Mathematical Society in 1893; see also *Nature* for 1 February 1894. Speculation about four-dimensional geometry had begun with the work of Moebius seventy years earlier.

7 *plough you for the Little-go*: 'fail you in the Preliminary Examination' (at Oxford and Cambridge Universities).

12 *Linnæan*: a learned society in London, founded in 1788.

13 *Richmond*: a residential suburb, surrounded by parkland, on the River Thames about 9 miles south-west of central London.

15 *doing the Amateur Cadger*: posing as a beggar.

   Does our friend . . . Nebuchadnezzar phases?: the Editor is asking if the Time Traveller works as a street- or crossing-sweeper (which might explain his dishevelled appearance), or if he has been imitating Nebuchadnezzar, who lost his kingdom and went to live among the beasts of the field (see Daniel 4: 31–3).

16 *little Rosebery*: a racehorse owned by the Earl of Rosebery, British prime minister in 1894–5. The Editor is hoping for a racing tip.

   peptone: protein.

   shilling a line . . . verbatim note: a generous offer, since the proverbial free-lance journalist worked for a penny a line. A shilling was worth twelve pence.

   Hettie Potter: unidentified; possibly a contemporary actress or spiritualist medium.

26 *suggestions of old Phœnician decorations*: a rather elusive phrase, since ancient Phœnician art displays a mixture of Egyptian, Aegean, and Asiatic influences. Wells may have in mind the stylized palm-leaf design associated with Phœnician representations of the winged sphinx. Another common motif, the lotus leaf, would be appropriate to the Eloi.

27 *inextinguishable laughter*: this phrase echoes Homer's description of the feast of the gods in the *Iliad* (i. 599): 'And then inextinguishable laughter arose among the immortal gods' (Buckley's translation, London, 1861).

34 *the full moon . . . gibbous*: the moon enters its gibbous or 'humped' phase when it is between half and full. Either the moon in this passage is slightly less than full, or its shape has changed with the passage of time. Later, as he moves further into the future, the Time Traveller will report that 'All trace of the moon had vanished' (p. 81).

45 *a queer notion of Grant Allen's*: Allen, the novelist, essayist, and social radical (1848–99), was a friend of Wells. The story alluded to here has been identified as 'Pallinghurst Barrow' (1892).

46 *the younger Darwin . . . fall back one by one into the parent body*: Professor (later Sir) George Howard Darwin, FRS (1845–1912), was the son of Charles Darwin and a distinguished astronomer. Darwin argued that the distance between the moon and the earth was affected by 'tidal friction' which tended to check the speed of the earth's rotation. The moon had originally broken away from the earth; once it had reached a maximum distance, it would begin to draw nearer again. Darwin at first believed that tidal friction would account for the evolution of the whole solar system, though he later abandoned this view.

47 *Lemur*: this word means both a family of prosimian mammals (belonging therefore to the most primitive suborder of primates), and a ghost.

50 *I had no convenient cicerone in the pattern of the Utopian books*: most nineteenth-century literary utopias take the form of a travelogue in which the visitor is shown around the good society by its proud inhabitants. A cicerone is a tourist guide.

55 *halitus*: literally, a vapour or exhalation.

Kodak: the portable Kodak camera was first marketed in 1890.

58 *Carlovingian kings*: the ninth-century successors to the Frankish kingdom founded by Charlemagne. Edward Gibbon wrote of them in *The Decline and Fall of the Roman Empire* that, 'the ridiculous epithets of the *bald*, the *stammerer*, the *fat* and the *simple* distinguished the tame and uniform features of a crowd of kings alike deserving of oblivion'.

61 *the great precessional cycle . . . Only forty times*: the precessional cycle is the rotation of the pole of the equator round the pole of the ecliptic. Wells in *The Outline of History* (1920) describes this as a 'slow wabble' of the pole of the earth, like that of a spinning top. The complete cycle, formerly known as the 'Great Year', takes about 25,800 calendar years. During the Time Traveller's journey to 802,701 it should only have occurred thirty-one times.

Explanatory Notes

63 *Carlyle-like scorn . . . aristocracy in decay*: in book 3, ch. 8 of *Past and Present* (1843), Thomas Carlyle predicts the imminent demise of the 'Idle Aristocracy, the Owners of the Soil of England'.

64 *Megatherium*: an extinct giant ground sloth from South America, estimated to have weighed over a ton.

65 *some latter-day South Kensington*: the reference is to the South Kensington Museum, which in the nineteenth century was the generic name for the museums of arts and sciences clustered together at the south end of Exhibition Road in London. Today they form four separate institutions, the Geological Museum, the Natural History Museum, the Science Museum, and the Victoria and Albert Museum.

68 *The Land of the Leal*: a Scots ballad.

69 *Belemnite*: an extinct cephalopod or mollusc.

steatite monster from South America: an idol carved from soapstone, a soft, greyish rock.

73 *shone like carbuncles*: a carbuncle is a red precious stone.

81 *the work of the tidal drag was done*: another reference to G. H. Darwin's theory of 'tidal friction' (see note to p. 46 above). Wells assumes that tidal friction affects the whole solar system, so that the length of the terrestrial day will steadily increase.

86 *Pall Mall Gazette*: a London evening paper to which Wells was a frequent contributor in the years 1893–5.

88 *The gynæceum's odd*: the gynæceum is the female reproductive organ of a flower.

91 *plesiosaurus-haunted Oolitic coral reef*: the phrase evokes a scene from the Jurassic Age. Plesiosaurs are extinct marine reptiles with small heads and long necks; Oolitic is a sedimentary rock.

97 *dingey*: a small boat attached to a larger boat or ship; now usually spelt 'dinghy'.

Callao: the principal port of Peru.

Medusa case: the French frigate *Medusa* ran aground off the coast of North Africa in July 1816. Of more than 100 passengers who took to sea on a hastily built raft, only fifteen survived. Théodore Géricault's famous painting of the castaways was unveiled at the Paris Salon three years later. For a modern account, see Julian Barnes, *A History of the World in 10½ Chapters* (1989).

gig: dinghy or ship's boat.

97 *a small breaker of water*: a small keg. The word appears as 'beaker' in some editions, but a beaker of water between three men could not have lasted four days.

99 *thwarts*: the benches or seats of a rowing-boat.

100 *queer marks on the gunwale*: 'spots of blood' in the first edition. The gunwale is the upper edge of the side of a boat (formerly used to support guns).

Arica: a port in northern Chile.

101 *Ipecacuanha . . . certainly acts according*: the root of this Brazilian plant was used to induce vomiting—hence Montgomery's allusion to seasickness.

radula of the snail: the movable toothed structure in the mouth of a snail or mollusc.

102 *Caplatzi . . . what a shop that was!*: Caplatzi's sold scientific apparatus in Chenies Street, close to Gower Street which is the site of University College, London (where Montgomery studied medicine).

scuttle: a small circular opening in the side of a ship.

duck things: sailors' clothes made of rough linen or cotton.

103 *companion*: a ladder giving access from deck to deck.

the combing of the hatchway: the combing (also spelt 'coaming') is the raised border around an opening in a ship's deck, which prevents water from spilling into the hold.

104 *spankers*: fore-and-aft sails attached to the rear mast of a small ship.

taffrail: the stern-rail of a ship.

106 *hazed*: harassed or bullied.

107 *the law and the prophets*: referring to the Mosaic Law and the prophetic books of the Old Testament. The source of the phrase is Matthew 7: 12.

111 *whole bilin' of 'em*: the whole boiling, or the whole lot of them.

113 *standing lugs*: four-cornered 'lugsails' spread or hoisted.

115 *fastened my painter to the tiller*: fastened my tow-rope to the bar attached to the rudder.

piggin: a small, usually wooden, pail.

118 *Royal College of Science . . . under Huxley*: the Normal School where Wells studied under Huxley was renamed the Royal College of Science in 1891, so that Prendick's reference to it involves a slight

anachronism here. As a research student under Huxley, Prendick has studied biology to a higher level than Wells had done.

123 *silly season*: the period of the summer parliamentary recess, when there is a shortage of political news to fill the newspapers with.

124 *halitus*: see note to p. 55 above.

127 *crib of Horace*: a translation, usually for the benefit of schoolboys. Prendick has already remarked that he can only read Latin and Greek with difficulty.

128 *trailing epiphyte*: a creeper, or plant that normally relies on another plant for support.

138 *bogle*: a phantom or creature of one's own imagining.

141 *Comus rout*: Prendick thinks of the Beast Folk as sailors transformed into animals by Comus, the son of Circe, as in John Milton's masque of 1634. Wells is almost certainly alluding to Sir Edwin Landseer's painting *The Rout of Comus* (1843), which shows Milton's enchanter surrounded by writhing animal-headed monsters. 'Rout' in this sense means retinue or rabble.

145 *blackish scoriæ*: volcanic outcrops of aerated rock.

152 *like the haha of an English park*: a haha is a sunken wall or ditch marking the boundary between a formal garden and open parkland. It is concealed so as to allow an uninterrupted view from the house.

156 *Hi non sunt homines, sunt animalia qui nos habemus . . . vivisected*: schoolboy Latin for 'These are not men, they are animals which we have vivisected.'

159 *Hunter's cockspur . . . flourished on the bull's neck*: a—possibly apocryphal—reference to a pioneering experiment by the Scottish biologist and surgeon John Hunter (1728–93). In book 4, ch. 2 of *The Science of Life* (1930) Wells and his collaborators mention Hunter's experiments with a cock's spur, but they do not suggest that he or anyone else has succeeded in grafting it on to a wholly different species.

Algerian Zouaves: French light infantry recruited from the Kabyle tribes of North Africa.

160 *'L'Homme qui Rit'*: published in 1869, Victor Hugo's historical novel set in seventeenth-century England begins with an account of the fairground practices to which Moreau is alluding. The fact that the novel introduces two 'Beast Folk'—the quack doctor, Ursus, and his trained wolf Homo—may also have interested Wells.

163 *Mahomet's houri in the dark*: a reference to the descriptions of Paradise in the Koran. The houris, black-eyed virgins, are the reward of every true (male) believer.

Kanakas: Pacific islanders (from the Hawaiian for human being).

170 *fumaroles*: blow-holes or vents in the ground, a sign of volcanic activity.

There was no evidence of the inheritance of the acquired . . . characteristics: biologists up to the present have continued to look for such evidence, which was central to the evolutionary theory of the French naturalist Jean Baptiste Lamarck (1744–1829). Before the rise of modern genetics, Lamarck's beliefs attracted widespread support as an alternative to the Darwinian theory. Through Prendick, Wells is making his Darwinian affiliations clear in this passage.

171 *prognathous*: having a projecting jaw.

172 *fusees*: long-headed matches.

174 *a gleam of classical memory . . . his nether extremities Satanic*: the classical satyr was usually a man with goat's ears, horns, and a tail. 'Ovine' in this passage means sheeplike.

175 *Ollendorfian beggar!*: Heinrich Ollendorf (1803–65) was a German educator and author of foreign-language grammars. Montgomery is making fun of the Satyr Man's stilted English.

216 *Slöjd*: the teaching of woodwork in schools. 'Slöjd' is Swedish for handicrafts.

218 *Apia*: the capital of Western Samoa.

220 *gid*: a disease of sheep and goats, characterized by unsteady gait and loss of balance.

THE WORLD'S CLASSICS

A Select List

HANS ANDERSEN: Fairy Tales
Translated by L. W. Kingsland
Introduction by Naomi Lewis
Illustrated by Vilhelm Pedersen and Lorenz Frølich

ARTHUR J. ARBERRY (Transl.): The Koran

LUDOVICO ARIOSTO: Orlando Furioso
Translated by Guido Waldman

ARISTOTLE: The Nicomachean Ethics
Translated by David Ross

JANE AUSTEN: Emma
Edited by James Kinsley and David Lodge

Northanger Abbey, Lady Susan, The Watsons,
and Sanditon
Edited by John Davie

Persuasion
Edited by John Davie

WILLIAM BECKFORD: Vathek
Edited by Roger Lonsdale

KEITH BOSLEY (Transl.): The Kalevala

CHARLOTTE BRONTË: Jane Eyre
Edited by Margaret Smith

JOHN BUNYAN: The Pilgrim's Progress
Edited by N. H. Keeble

FRANCES HODGSON BURNETT: The Secret Garden
Edited by Dennis Butts

FANNY BURNEY: Cecilia
or Memoirs of an Heiress
Edited by Peter Sabor and Margaret Anne Doody

THOMAS CARLYLE: The French Revolution
Edited by K. J. Fielding and David Sorensen

LEWIS CARROLL: Alice's Adventures in Wonderland
and Through the Looking Glass
Edited by Roger Lancelyn Green
Illustrated by John Tenniel

MIGUEL DE CERVANTES: Don Quixote
Translated by Charles Jarvis
Edited by E. C. Riley

GEOFFREY CHAUCER: The Canterbury Tales
Translated by David Wright

ANTON CHEKHOV: The Russian Master and Other Stories
Translated by Ronald Hingley

JOHN CLELAND:
Memoirs of a Woman of Pleasure (Fanny Hill)
Edited by Peter Sabor

WILKIE COLLINS: Armadale
Edited by Catherine Peters

JOSEPH CONRAD: Chance
Edited by Martin Ray

Victory
Edited by John Batchelor
Introduction by Tony Tanner

NORMAN DAVIS (Ed.): The Paston Letters

CHARLES DICKENS: Christmas Books
Edited by Ruth Glancy

Sikes and Nancy and Other Public Readings
Edited by Philip Collins

FEDOR DOSTOEVSKY: Crime and Punishment
Translated by Jessie Coulson
Introduction by John Jones

ARTHUR CONAN DOYLE:
Sherlock Holmes: Selected Stories
Introduction by S. C. Roberts

ALEXANDRE DUMAS *père*:
The Three Musketeers
Edited by David Coward

ALEXANDRE DUMAS *fils*:
La Dame aux Camélias
Translated by David Coward

MARIA EDGEWORTH: Castle Rackrent
Edited by George Watson

GEORGE ELIOT:
Felix Holt, The Radical
Edited by Fred C. Thompson

Middlemarch
Edited by David Carroll

Scenes of Clerical Life
Edited by Thomas A. Noble

Selected Critical Writings
Edited by Rosemary Ashton

GUSTAVE FLAUBERT: Madame Bovary
Translated by Gerard Hopkins
Introduction by Terence Cave

BENJAMIN FRANKLIN: Autobiography and other Writings
Edited by Ormond Seavey

ELIZABETH GASKELL: Cousin Phillis and Other Tales
Edited by Angus Easson

My Lady Ludlow and Other Stories
Edited by Edgar Wright

J. W. VON GOETHE: Faust, Part One
Translated by David Luke

OLIVER GOLDSMITH: The Vicar of Wakefield
Edited by Arthur Friedman

THOMAS HARDY: A Pair of Blue Eyes
Edited by Alan Manford

HESIOD: Theogony *and* Works and Days
Translated by M. L. West

E. T. A. HOFFMANN: The Golden Pot and Other Tales
Translated and Edited by Ritchie Robertson

HOMER: The Iliad
Translated by Robert Fitzgerald
Introduction by G. S. Kirk

THOMAS HUGHES: Tom Brown's Schooldays
Edited by Andrew Sanders

HENRIK IBSEN: An Enemy of the People, The Wild Duck,
Rosmersholm
Edited and Translated by James McFarlane

HENRY JAMES: The Ambassadors
Edited by Christopher Butler

M. R. JAMES: Casting the Runes and Other Ghost Stories
Edited by Michael Cox

JOCELIN OF BRAKELOND:
Chronicle of the Abbey of Bury St. Edmunds
Translated by Diana Greenway and Jane Sayers

GWYN JONES (Transl.):
Eirik the Red and Other Icelandic Sagas

BEN JONSON: Five Plays
Edited by G. A. Wilkes

MADAME DE LAFAYETTE: The Princesse de Clèves
Translated and Edited by Terence Cave

WILLIAM LANGLAND: Piers Plowman
Translated and Edited by A. V. C. Schmidt

J. SHERIDAN LE FANU: Uncle Silas
Edited by W. J. McCormack

MIKHAIL LERMONTOV: A Hero of our Time
Translated by Vladimar Nabokov with Dmitri Nabokov

MATTHEW LEWIS: The Monk
Edited by Howard Anderson

MARCUS AURELIUS: The Meditations of Marcus Aurelius
Translated by A. S. L. Farquharson
Edited by R. B. Rutherford

KATHERINE MANSFIELD: Selected Stories
Edited by D. M. Davin

CHARLES MATURIN: Melmoth the Wanderer
Edited by Douglas Grant
Introduction by Chris Baldick

HERMAN MELVILLE: The Confidence-Man
Edited by Tony Tanner

Moby Dick
Edited by Tony Tanner

PROSPER MÉRIMÉE: Carmen and Other Stories
Translated by Nicholas Jotcham

MICHELANGELO: Life, Letters, and Poetry
Translated by George Bull with Peter Porter

MOLIÈRE: Don Juan and Other Plays
Translated by George Graveley and Ian Maclean

E. NESBIT: The Railway Children
Edited by Dennis Butts

EDGAR ALLAN POE: Selected Tales
Edited by Julian Symons

JEAN RACINE: Britannicus, Phaedra, Athaliah
Translated by C. H. Sisson

ANN RADCLIFFE: The Italian
Edited by Frederick Garber

THE MARQUIS DE SADE:
The Misfortune of Virtue and Other Early Tales
Translated and Edited by David Coward

SIR WALTER SCOTT: The Heart of Midlothian
Edited by Claire Lamont

ANNA SEWELL: Black Beauty
Edited by Peter Hollindale

TOBI... ...ry Clinker
Edited by Lewis M. K...
Revised by Paul-Gabriel Boucé

ROBERT LOUIS STEVENSON:
Treasure Island
Edited by Emma Letley

ANTHONY TROLLOPE: The American Senator
Edited by John Halperin

GIORGIO VASARI: The Lives of the Artists
Translated and Edited by Julia Conaway Bondanella and Peter Bondanella

VIRGINIA WOOLF: Orlando
Edited by Rachel Bowlby

ÉMILE ZOLA: Nana
Translated and Edited by Douglas Parmée

A complete list of Oxford Paperbacks, including The World's Classics,
OPUS, Past Masters, Oxford Authors, Oxford Shakespeare, and Oxford
Paperback Reference, is available in the UK from the Arts and Reference
Publicity Department (BH), Oxford University Press, Walton Street,
Oxford OX2 6DP.

In the USA, complete lists are available from the Paperbacks Marketing
Manager, Oxford University Press, 200 Madison Avenue, New York,
NY 10016.

Oxford Paperbacks are available from all good bookshops. In case of
difficulty, customers in the UK can order direct from Oxford University
Press Bookshop, Freepost, 116 High Street, Oxford, OX1 4BR, enclosing full
payment. Please add 10 per cent of published price for postage and
packing.